DAUGHTER OF THE SUN

DAUGHTER OF THE SUN

A MOTHMAR NOVEL
BOOK ONE

AMANDA AULER

SPIRELIGHT
PRESS

964 High House Rd #3042

Cary, NC 27513

For permissions contact: amanda@authoramandaauler.com

www.authoramandaauler.com

Cover by Fantastical Ink
Character Illustrations by Nemaiza Rhayne
Map Illustrated by Rebecca Paavo
Scene Illustrations by Kateryna Vitkovska
Chapter Illustrations by Sarah Cools
Edited by Eva Campney
Type set in Garamond EB

ISBN:

979-8-9865922-6-8 (paperback)
979-8-9865922-2-0 (hardback)
979-8-9865922-0-6 (ebook)

10 9 8 7 6 5 4 3

Library of Congress Control Number: 2022914706
Printed in United States of America

10 days or 10 years, my love

GLOSSARY

Austur – The easternmost village

Darlöh – A state of unnatural sleep

Dauda – A Mothmarian ceremony to honor the dead

Eldfall – The tallest mountain bordering the eastern side of the valley

Eldur – Someone with Heitt skilled enough to wield flame

Fera – The Gift, given by the Stars, that allows the Gifted to tether to an inanimate object

Häfa/Häfan – A Mothmari curse

Heitt – The Gift, given by the Sun, that allows the Gifted to warm and heal

Hekla – A volcano, also a Mothmari curse

Hytast – The meeting hall

Lóthkol – The advanced school that focuses on Gifts

Mothmar – A country

Rána – Someone born without a Gift

Sháskol – The primer school where students fulfill, at least, their first six years of schooling

Sodur – The southernmost village, Pallah's home

Taka Reu – Worship of The Mother, the Dark Gifts and those who practice them

Tala – The Gift, given by the Moon, that allows the Gifted to tether to an animal

Vestur – The westernmost village, Solyana's home

GIFTS

Acute Fera – The ability to manipulate only one specific type of object

Acute Tala – The ability to manipulate only one specific type of animal

Bein Fera – The ability to manipulate bone

Blou Fera – The ability to manipulate blood

Broad Fera – The ability to manipulate inanimate objects

Broad Tala – The ability to manipulate all animals

Gler Fera – The ability to manipulate glass

Lakimi Fera – The ability to manipulate muscles

Malmur Fera – The ability to manipulate metal

Predatory Tala – The Gifted's aptitude is a predatory creature

Prey Tala – The Gifted's aptitude is a prey creature

Stein Fera – The ability to manipulate stone

Vatin Fera – The ability to manipulate water

Vior Fera – The ability to manipulate wood

Falki Tala – The ability to manipulate falcons

Fiskur Tala – The ability to manipulate fish

Fugali Tala – The ability to manipulate birds

Heri Tala – The ability to manipulate hares

Ulfur Tala – The ability to manipulate wolves

MOTHMAR
Jonas
MOUNT HEKLA
ELDFALL
HASTA
ELD PLATEAU
HASTA PASS
THE PINES
VATINO SEA
HYTAST
LOTHKOL
SHASKOL
OUR HOME
SPRETTA RIVER
VESTUR
TEMPLE CELESTIAL
AUSTUR
KANA FOREST
SODUR
WHITE WOOD
SHADOW WOOD
BELTA RIVER
LEIF'S CABIN
ANA
SKRIM

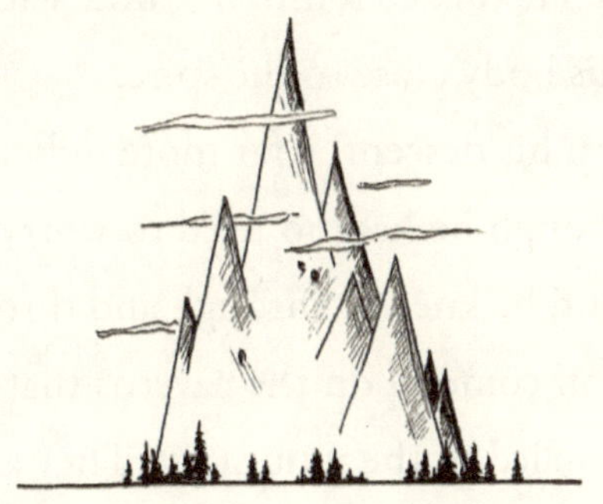

THE SLEEPING BOY

THE MOUNTAIN WAS IMPASSABLE and dangerous.

But not to Gunnar.

He scaled the winding spires of rock, climbing high into the clouds. The thinning air left his lungs aching, but he pressed on.

A few pebbles skittered to his left, and he peered around the tufts of moss to find a wooly goat and her kid making their way down the mountain. The sound of their hooves echoed across the valley that lay below, green, lush, and full of retreating light. Perhaps his sudden arrival had spooked them. Or perhaps it was simply time to turn in; it was nearly dusk after all.

Gunnar had not noticed how late it had become.

Or how far he had climbed.

His shaking fingers, frozen as they were, scoured the inside of a nest tucked in the side of the rock, his hand closing around his quarry. He pulled the feather free; it was larger and more beautiful than he had anticipated. He had only ever seen it on the backs of the great birds from a distance—but now he could add this one to his collection. He tucked it into his tunic with one hand, the other keeping his body close to the spire.

Then he began his descent, a far more difficult task than its counterpart. Though he had no need to worry, the mountain was his home, and he knew it through and through.

He would soon come upon the caverns that held the Seers, the men who dwelled in the mountain. They all had someone much like Gunnar, though he had never met them. They would be rising now from slumber, preparing for their watch. Unlike Gunnar, they were obedient, and they were rested.

The tonal melody of his people, their voices their only instrument, reached his ears, and he knew he was close. It mingled with the sounds of retreating goats and Gunnar's own panting breaths. Seers were not permitted to use their voices for simple speech, but they were allowed songs, so they chose to use them beautifully. Though he heard a litany of melodies, Gunnar knew the cadence of his own. The low hum led him to his home beneath the rock. He swung down and ran along the length of the cavern he shared with Osvald.

He entered the low-lit cave, a fire already steady in the center. That was supposed to be Gunnar's job, tending the fire. Tomorrow he would find some thistleleaf for Osvald's back, an appropriate apology if crushed and developed into a paste. Gunnar had often watched the old man apply it liberally after laborious attempts to extricate himself from his cot.

Osvald turned to his scribe, his tune pausing for a moment. The old man cleared his throat, his lips pulled tight in disappointment. Gunnar hung his head. He would do better tomorrow.

His Seer had the kettle at a boil over the fire. Gunnar scrunched his nose. He hated tea, but he knew Osvald expected him to drink every drop if he was to stay up for his watch. Gunnar grabbed a cloth, pulled the cast-iron kettle off the fire, and poured himself a cup. It sloshed a bit and spattered the stones below. Gunnar grumbled quietly to himself and placed the kettle to the side. Lifting the steaming mug, he made his way to his own bed beside that of his Seer.

He set his mug down—it was far too hot—and let out a yawn. He glanced quickly at his Seer. If Osvald caught him yawning, he would make him fetch the switch, and Gunnar didn't like to be switched. As a scribe, it was his job to stay awake while his Seer slept, for prophecies only came while the Mother of the Night ruled the sky.

Gunnar had snuck away in the morning hours while Osvald was meditating and enjoyed some time catching creatures. He loved collecting them, momentary though it was. It wasn't the first time Gunnar had committed this infraction; he had done it many times before, simply wasting away his day doing nothing more than enjoying the sun. Exhausted, he stifled another yawn between clamped lips.

Osvald, ignoring his scribe's exhaustion, laid down flat on his back, his hands folded together and resting peacefully on his chest.

Gunnar didn't know how his Seer slept so rigidly. Gunnar had tried sleeping like him, but he always woke on his stomach, blanket askew. He waited until Osvald's breaths pulled deep and slow, then turned to his mat. He pulled the feather out from his tunic, placing it on a small stone shelf near his bed, already littered with other unique finds. He admired them for a moment before grabbing his scroll and charcoal.

He unfurled the bit of wrapped parchment. Wrong one. This was his own scroll. He *must* be tired if he got those confused. Lifting his wayward blanket from the cavern floor, he found the scroll meant for prophecies. It was much different from the previous, which was worn and filled from so much use. The Prophecy Scroll was clean, fresh, and smelled of cedar.

Before placing his scroll back on the shelf, he looked at the start of it. It had been five years since he arrived at the ripe age of eight. He had written on his first night, his letters still wobbly and grammar still a bit backward. His parents had pushed him hard, knowing he wouldn't receive schooling later *if* he was cho-sen. Whenever a Seer was called into a life of isolation, he would choose a scribe. Always between the ages of eight and ten, the child would be brilliant, impressionable, and willing to grow, though Seers were never permitted to actually talk to them. Gunnar felt the painful truth of it as Osvald had spoken but one word to his scribe in the past five years.

"Come."

Torn between the pleasure of being chosen and the horror of leaving his parents, Gunnar left with Osvald that early morning. He wouldn't be allowed to return to his small village, his parents, or his baby brother, who kept the entire household awake in the night with his petulant crying. Though he had been annoyed at the time, Gunnar would give anything now just to see him again. Reading his words, his throat tightened and he struggled to swallow. He had written of his parents, of his father squeezing him and telling him to be brave, of his mother trying to hide her tears and failing, her kisses smothering his face.

Gunnar's head bobbed and he snapped to attention. He could not fall asleep. If Osvald prophesied and no one was there to write it down, his past five years would all be for nothing. He would have to remain a scribe, his task unfinished. He thought it funny this was the method of doing things, taking such young children to record such weighty truths. His parents had explained it had to do with their ability to be unbiased. But he wasn't even sure what the word "unbiased" meant.

He rolled his charcoal pencil in his hand; he was a competent writer now. Osvald sometimes wrote down notes here or there, though Gunnar didn't think he was supposed to. The Seer had caught him reading one once, but the older man didn't seem to be bothered by it and just kept on singing.

Ten years was the average prophecy rate, though he was hoping for less. After the Seer prophesied, the scribe retired as a simple priest, attending the village church, a freedom he couldn't fathom.

Though, more than that, his brother was at least five years old now. He had wanted a brother ever since he could remember, and then, right when he got one...they carted him off to the mountain. He couldn't wait to go back, if only to show him how to catch creatures or to climb the trees that surrounded his village. This was the only thought motivating Gunnar to stay awake. Could tonight be the night? A thrill of excitement ran through him at the thought of returning home. However, prophecy was the Gift of a Seer, and when a Gift leaves the soul, the soul leaves with it. Gunnar shuddered; he had never seen a dead body before.

He thought about a blue-tailed lizard he caught once. It was when he first arrived, when he couldn't quite sleep through the days as he needed to. He had kept the lizard in a crude cage near his bed, catching crickets and other smaller creatures to feed it. But the lizard wasn't meant to be in a cage. He had woken that next day, a stench reaching his nose, his lizard, curled up and dead. Gunnar had cried; Osvald had only sang his ritualistic chant and patted Gunnar on the head.

He was thinking of this act of affection, and it made him think of his mother, someone he hadn't seen in half a decade. He thought of a hug and reached around his own arms and squeezed.

Is that how it was done? He laid down in his own warm embrace. Closing his eyes, he reassured himself; he would think of his mother only a few minutes, that's all. Squeezing one last time, he promptly fell asleep.

Osvald was singing, but it didn't have the melody he usually preferred.

Gunnar was dreaming of his parents, but their faces were unclear.

Osvald's voice ebbed and flowed, yet it still felt so unlike a song.

Gunnar's parents came into focus, and he startled. They both had Osvald's face.

Osvald?

"...trapped, many will die at their hand, though unknown—"

Osvald! Gunnar sat upright, hands flying to the scroll and charcoal sitting between his legs. Hot tears sprung to his eyes. He had only been asleep for a few minutes, or was it longer? Angry with himself, he tried to recall Osvald's words.

He began to write. What, he didn't really know, but he wrote with hope and a prayer it would be enough. If he was a good scribe, he would go back down the mountain and let the village priest know of his failure. Then he would be reassigned to a new Seer until that one prophesied. But how long would that take? How old would his brother be by the time he left? Osvald was prophesying right now! No, he realized, if he was a good scribe, he wouldn't have fallen asleep at all. Gunnar wondered if any other scribes had made the same mistake and had simply guessed. Surely, he wasn't the only one. Osvald was still speaking, sitting up in bed, his arms raised to the cavern ceiling.

"But when all hope seems lost, and the world knows nothing but white, there will come one who will bring green. One who must follow the path of the sky. One who is all light to stand to the one who is all dark, of which there will be two. One who possesses the three as one, who will save us all through—"

Gunnar's charcoal pencil flung from his fingers and it clattered to the cavern floor. He scrambled to retrieve it and, in his haste, the scroll fell to the ground, too. Something made a cracking sound, stone on stone. Picking the pencil back up, Gunnar turned back around for the scroll, only to find it deepening in color, sopping wet. His once full mug of tea was now lying, broken and seeping into the sacred text.

"No!" he whimpered as he lifted the scroll and gave it a few quick shakes before pressing it flat against a dry part of the floor, examining the damage. The entire scroll was soggy; words were smeared across the page.

What had he done?

Osvald, unaware of his scribe's panic, finished his droning. "You will know this one by the mark, known by the one who brings the white." His voice rang in the quiet cave with a note of finality before falling silent. Then he careened backward into a crumpled heap, the air leaving in a *whoosh* from his lungs.

Gunnar, eyes wide as the moon, scribbled like a madman. He marked the details he remembered, and fibbed a bit where he didn't, trying to keep it as cohesive as possible. He had always had a sharp memory and knew he was hitting all the important bits...or at least he thought he was. He kept his eyes on his scroll, desperately not wanting to see Osvald in his new state of being. Or not being.

Gunnar took a deep breath, steadied his hand, and began rushing about the room. He grabbed his pack and stuffed it with his small pile of things, a wineskin, and the scroll. He needed to make it to the village by morning; the prophecy needed to be delivered. Pausing, he allowed himself a small smile at the thought of seeing his parents and his not-so-baby brother.

Steeling himself, he looked over his shoulder at Osvald. The man's mouth and eyes were open; something about that seemed wrong, irreverent. Gunnar knelt beside him and gently coaxed his eyes and mouth closed. Osvald didn't quite stink as his lizard had.

Time was wasting. He stood and unfurled the scroll for one last look.

One line was bothering him more than the others, but what could he do? How could he better it? He stamped his foot in frustration, reacting like the child he was. Then there was the trouble with the timeline. He hadn't caught *when* this prophecy would come to pass, which was an integral part of all other prophecies. He tapped his pencil on the scroll a few times before an idea formed. He would simply make it far enough out that he would be too old to question. No, even farther. Far enough that he would be dead! Perfect.

He scribbled out some more words, examined it again, and nodded before rolling it back up and sliding it inside his tunic. It would work. It had to.

Gunnar shot out of the cavern faster than any lizard he had chased, more deftly than any bird winding its way through the spires, and straight into the light of the full moon. The night was blue-hued and silent, the mountain crowned with fog. The wooly goat and her kid were curled beneath a shelter in the cliff face, their ears twitching in dreamy sleep, hooves still in breathy slumber.

They would not miss him.

Gunnar, former scribe, ran down the mountainside with adept knowledge of its dangers but with no fear. The wind howled past his ears, feet pounded in leather slippers, a grin lit his face. He was done with this mountain. He was going home.

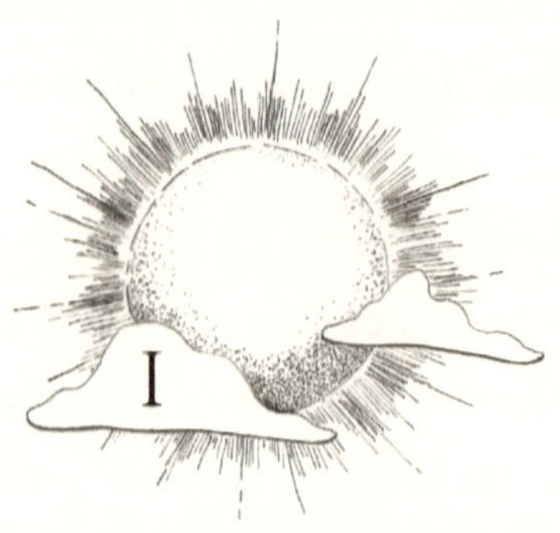

Honey Bread

Solyana

Temporal and fleeting were the tracks Solyana made through the deep snow as the wind whipped them away, filling the pockets with more powder until it was like she hadn't been there at all. She stopped and turned to see it for herself, her trail slowly melting back into the ever-changing landscape that was her country of Mothmar. She would affirm her place in this country at her Stada today, the day when all three villages of their valley would gather to see who was Gifted and who was not.

And Solyana was not.

The three villages that made up their valley spread over several miles, west to east: Vestur, then Sodur, and finally Austur. Solyana and her family lived in the first. Each, in turn, roused from sleep to greet the muted morning. Trudging forward, aching for warmth, she hoisted the dead hare off the ground, blood trailing behind.

She was careful this time not to get it on her parka, now that she was sewing most of her own clothes.

A plume of smoke signaled her family's modest hut. She pushed the seal-skin door to the side and stepped into the warmth, pulling off her outermost layer.

"Fridmey, you've been in there *forever*!" Rhuth stood atop her toes just outside the washroom. "Sol is back!" The small, dark-haired girl seemed to forget her prior urgency and scampered to Solyana's side.

"I'll be done faster if you would leave me alone!" Fridmey's muffled voice came from behind the thin leather door.

"Hang this over the basin, will you?" Solyana passed the hare over to her younger sister's eager hands.

"*Stars,* Sol." Rhuth examined the arrow's entry and exit wound. "You almost took its head right off." She pulled a stool over to the side of the counter and climbed onto it, securing the large legs of the rabbit over the basin. "It would be much cleaner if you would just let me go with you..." The wisp of a girl turned to Solyana; her chocolate brown eyes widened in such a display of overt manipulation, Solyana had to laugh.

"Nice try. I know you wish you could control me like you do the hares, but your Tala doesn't work on me, thankfully. I would be helpless." Solyana pulled her mukluks off one by one before walking to the counter and reaching up for Rhuth. "You know why I can't take you yet."

"I don't need your help if you don't need mine." Rhuth sniffed. "I'm not a baby." She jumped down with unexpected grace before looking back up at Solyana with a toothy grin. "Did you get this one at that spot, below Sodur?"

"Yeah, I did." Solyana nodded. "It's so tucked up into Shadow Wood, you would never know that an entire colony of rabbits lived there. Strange, but it was a great find, Little Fyug."

"Don't call me that!" Rhuth threw her hands up and stalked away, back to the eldest of the three sisters. "Are you done yet?"

Solyana grinned and turned down the small hallway to the room she shared with her sisters. She changed into a dry tunic and a pair of dry mukluks, then got to work on her hair. It was dark, much like Mama's; in fact, she and Rhuth resembled Mama the most with their dark wavy hair and pale skin. Fridmey got Papa's looks: all curly red hair and ruddy complexion, freckles covering them from head to foot.

As she braided, her mind wandered to her Stada. She would have to stand in front of the entirety of the three villages and reveal that she was, in fact, Rána. She wished there was a more private way of doing it. It wasn't as if anyone wanted to be Rána. She had always viewed her lack of Gift as something that simply hadn't had time to grow yet. But, now, on the day of the official ceremony to determine her Gift, she had to face the truth. The Celestials had chosen to leave her without.

She wasn't the only one. There had been an increase of those without Gifts. Year after year, more and more were born with no hint of the Celestial's favor. A few of them had even begun touting it as *better* than being Gifted. Solyana didn't understand that. It made her stomach hurt thinking about it.

"Good morning, Sol," Mama said from the stove as Solyana made her way back into the kitchen. "Great catch." She motioned to the hare, draining steadily.

"Thanks, Mama."

Rhuth sat at the table, a piece of toast in hand. She raised her eyebrows at Solyana, pleading.

"Mama, can Rhuth come out with me next time?" Solyana grinned, knowing the answer before it came.

Mama turned, extending a piece of toast to Solyana. "She just started at Sháskol, barely at the end of her first year." She smiled at her youngest daughter. "I know you want to go with your sisters, but let's stick to hunting with Papa for another few years, please."

Rhuth huffed and slumped back in her chair. A drip of melting butter fell to her tunic. Solyana leaned over and wiped it off. "Soon, Little Fyug."

"Mama, Sol keeps calling me a pig!" Rhuth whined.

"Excuse me?" Mama laughed.

"Rhuth, that's not what—"

"Yes, it is. Marin, from my class, told me so."

"Well, Marin does not have her facts straight. It means 'little bird.'"

"What?" Rhuth dropped her toast butter side down and began wringing her tunic. "Why that? Why do you call me that?"

"It's nothing bad!" Solyana sighed, Rhuth's hair was still unbraided. She stood and got to work, letting her own toast grow cold. "Come here. Look, no. Stop squirming and listen. When you were born, Mama convinced Frid and me to take on what she called 'Midnight Mother Duty.' We were tasked to respond to the squawks of a certain baby in the night." She worked the strands into something presentable. "As long as you weren't hungry, we soothed you to sleep."

"And somehow, you were *never* hungry," Fridmey said, finally exiting the washroom.

"I'm always hungry now!" Rhuth announced, stuffing the rest of her toast in her mouth. She hopped off her chair and away from Solyana, who had just managed to secure the end of Rhuth's braid. "More, Mama?"

"First, go." Mama pointed at the washroom, and Rhuth sped off, clutching at her tunic.

"I think it was your way of sleeping more." Fridmey nudged Mama with her elbow.

"I don't regret it. I was much better rested that third time around. I should have done it with Solyana, too. Then maybe you two would be as close as you are with your youngest sister."

Solyana and Fridmey locked eyes, and Fridmey gave a wicked grin. "Nah, she would still annoy me."

"*Me?* Annoy *you?*" Solyana rolled her eyes but grinned back at her.

"You all set for your Stada?" Mama sat across from her as Solyana bit into her toast. Although it was cooled, it still melted in her mouth. Her mother had slathered honey on top. Mama winked. "I save it for the most special of occasions. You only have your Stada once, my Light."

"Who still has bees?" Fridmey raised an eyebrow, peering at Solyana's slice.

"I think I'll keep my secrets," Mama quipped, biting into her own slice, burnt and crumbled.

"Where's Papa?" Solyana had wanted to talk to him before he left for the day.

"He had an early morning."

"He always has breakfast with us."

"One of the ice shanties isn't producing. He had to meet with some Fiskur 'Tala on site. He'll see if they can tether to any fish in the area."

"Another one?" Fridmey perked up. "That's the fourth one in this last moon cycle."

She was always inserting herself into village politics. It was no secret that she wanted the title of Chief. It wasn't her fault she wasn't born closest to the Blue Moon, as Rhuth was. But couldn't Fridmey just be satisfied she was strong in Stein Fera? Both Fridmey and Mama had aptitude for stone, but no matter how influential she became in Mothmar, or how skilled she became in Fera, she could never claim the seat as long as Rhuth was able.

"Yes, well..." Mama trailed off. "Your father is doing the best he can to reassure the people. Speaking of, we don't discuss any of this with others, you understand?"

The girls nodded in agreement.

"What can't we talk about?" Rhuth burst out of the washroom, her hair already mostly undone. "Tell me so I know what *not* to say."

"I think it's better you don't know at all." Solyana pointed out.

"Don't know what?" Rhuth wailed. "Wait, your Stada is today!" She clapped her hands together. "You don't want people to know you're Rána, right?"

Solyana tried and failed to stop herself from wincing.

"Most people already know that, dear." Mama leaned across the table and clasped Solyana's hand in her own. "And we love her all the same."

Mutinous tears welled up, but Solyana quickly squashed them down. She would *not* cry. "Besides," her mother continued, "almost half of our population is Rána now. They are just as much part of Mothmar as anyone else."

"Well, it begs the question why people continue to be born without Gifts. Perhaps some of us aren't pleasing the Celestials as we ought." Fridmey said, pointedly avoiding Solyana's eyes.

"Fridmey!" Mama gasped. "We will *not* have that talk in our home. It has nothing to do with the spiritual state of our people. They are born that way. It is simply a different way of being."

Solyana's stomach clenched. She had heard those types of rumors spread throughout Sháskol; her school was never an easy place for her. She fit in well with other Rána, but the more she found herself hanging out with them, the more bitterness grew in her heart toward her family and all those who had Gifts.

"Frid, Rhuth, will you give us a moment?" Mama asked.

Only when they were alone, did Solyana speak. "It's New Moon today, Mama." Her voice cracked, and it made her feel like the child she was. "There's no hope after today."

"Oh, my Light." Mama got up and moved around the table to hold Solyana close to her breast.

"I'm being ridiculous," Solyana said, tears finally falling and clinging to her mother's tunic. "So many people are born without Gifts. Why can't I just accept it and move on? Papa always tells me I'm fine the way I am, but I see how he looks at Frid and Rhuth. He loves them—"

Mama pulled away fiercely. "He does not love them more, Sol."

"Differently."

"No," her mother reprimanded. "He loves you all the same."

Solyana said nothing but peered up at her mother, trying to perceive the slightest untruth; however, all she found was sincerity. "Will he make it to my Stada?"

"He wouldn't miss it for the world." Mama brought her in for a hug, squeezing tight. "You will find your calling one day, Sol. Maybe not amidst Stada ceremonies and the new beginnings of today, but it will come. You will hear it here." She pressed one hand to Solyana's heart, and the other cupped her left cheek, her thumb softly wiping away the tears. "And you will know what you are to do. Let the Celestials guide you."

Solyana wiped her nose with her sleeve and stood. "Are you walking with us?"

"I'll start with you, but then I have to head over to Vatino Sea, just to be sure your father makes it on time." Mama pulled on her own mukluks. "Girls! Let's go!"

Rhuth came flying out of the hallway, Fridmey just behind her. "You're going to be the best Rána, Solyana! Hey, that rhymed! Rána, Solyana!" Rhuth giggled. "Don't worry. We'll cheer for you when it's your turn. I'll be so loud everyone will forget that you're Rána."

"Please don't." Solyana groaned and glanced at Fridmey. "Keep her leashed."

"I'm not the Tala here. I can't control animals," Fridmey quipped.

"Hey, I'm not an animal!" Rhuth giggled again before pulling on her knapsack and flinging herself out the door. Fridmey followed with a roll of her eyes, and Mama exited with a last look at Solyana who was taking one final look at her home.

She would be entering this home next as an established Rána. There would be no hope for a Gift after today; her life would be altered forever.

She took a breath, shouldered her bag, and stepped out into the cloudy morning. Rhuth plowed on ahead at high speed. Fridmey trailed just behind her with Mama, who linked arms with her oldest daughter. Perhaps they had sensed Solyana's need to walk alone. Her mother was good at that, intuiting things.

Wind danced back and forth across her path, whipping up flurries in her wake. Solyana breathed in the cool smell of pine. Fresh snow laced her eyelashes, and she held out a gloved hand. Was it supposed to snow today? She looked up at the rolling clouds, an ever-present blanket wrapping the sun. Of the three Celestial gods that reigned over them—Father of the Day, Mother of the Night, and Children of the Sky—the Father was most elusive. She thought about going back for her snowshoes, but the thought of dragging them around all day wasn't appealing.

Men, women, and children milled about, stoking fires, stretching meat to be cured, and readying clothes for washing. A few of them pulled sleds to the market while others turned to the woods and mountains to hunt. Up ahead, Rhuth became distracted by a sleigh of goods as it made its way to the courtyard. Solyana was glad she wasn't with her. She probably wouldn't be able to refuse if Rhuth asked for something. Solyana would give that girl the moon if she could.

A group of young Fera passed by, heading to White Wood, the woods of birch trees to the east that surrounded Vatino Sea. Baskets were strapped to their backs, their smiles wide, their laughter ringing across the grounds. A stab of something like longing sliced through Solyana, and she tore her eyes away. They surely had aptitude for plants, berries, or pinecones. Whatever it was, it bound them together. She imagined the friendship the group of them shared, the intimacy, and wished, if only for a moment, they would return with empty baskets. She shook her head at the jealous and illogical thought. They were finding food for all the villages, Solyana included.

Solyana crested the hill overlooking the courtyard, the market in full motion. Their valley might look like a frozen tundra, but there were copious amounts of vegetation, wildlife, and brilliant ingenuity within the wood and thatched roofs. Mothmarians were strong and hearty, filled with generational knowledge on the construction of greenhouses, bake ovens, dehydration chambers, canning, and apparently, someone still had a beehive. She would have to figure out who that was.

The Temple Celestial stood tall just north of the courtyard. A thick, stone building set with parapets and towers, as if it were the home of royalty. But the time of kings was over. With such a small number of people combined in the three villages, the title of

Chief was all they needed. Flags with the symbol of the Celestials lined the stone stairs that led to a set of large wooden doors. It was the oldest building of their valley, but Stein Fera, like Mama and Fridmey, kept it in good condition.

Solyana entered the courtyard, the bustle of noise meeting her ears in a clear cacophony. She smiled, breathing in something delicious. She looked to her right to find Thina's stall. The woman made the best tea. Solyana was trying to decide if she had time to stop for one when Thina's eyes met her own.

"Solyana!" the old woman called. "Is today the day?"

"Yes, Thina." She stepped up to the tea cart. "But I know I won't be admitted to Lóthkol."

"You know...*I* didn't go either." Thina smiled, and her eyes didn't leave Solyana's as she expertly folded a corn husk into a small cup. "Will it be lavender? Or perhaps..." She tapped a plump finger to her chin. "The foragers did bring me some saxifrage this morning. It's quite good."

"Saxifrage, please!" Solyana glanced up again at the Temple Celestial. It blocked her view of the schools Sháskol and Lóthkol. "I didn't know you were Rána." She tapped her fingers impatiently. She should have kept walking. She didn't even see her sisters now, and her mother must be at the sea already.

"Wouldn't have it any other way." Thina sprinkled saxifrage into the husk before pouring piping hot water over the top. "There's nothing natural about those Gifts. Maybe we're just getting back to how things were supposed to be." She handed the drink over. "Welcome to your *new* family, Solyana."

"Your eyes be upward." Solyana hesitantly raised the cup in thanks.

"And be filled with light," Thina responded with a wink. "If I may be so bold there, dear." Thina leaned conspiratorially on her cart, forcing Solyana to mirror her. "Those two years of focused learning those kids do at Lóthkol is all frills. What the people really need to learn is the stuff that keeps us alive: harvesting, foraging, canning, and the like. We need more gardeners, not wielders of stone. No offense to your family, of course." She released a girlish giggle. "All these folks with aptitudes for different materials and animals and such; sure, it's helpful, but at what cost? Their hands are soft, unburdened by the dirt and grit that we Rána experience every day. I know your father is Chief, and I would never say a bad word about Marus." The woman pressed a hand to her breast, aghast at the mere thought. "But I believe he needs to add a few Rána to his council. Someone to represent those who make up almost *half* the people now." Thina nodded, reassured of her own plan. "But of course, only say something if you feel so inclined."

Hearing Thina speak so openly about new reform, dangerously toeing the line of insubordination to her father's leadership, deepened Solyana's anxious ache in her gut. She reached into her knapsack for something to trade, but Thina shook her head with a smile. "It's on me, dear. Remember what I said?"

Solyana didn't want to be indebted to the woman but also didn't want to be late, so she continued on, sipping on her drink. It tasted sweet, and she hoped it would settle her churning stomach.

The deepening rift between Rána and Gifted had been an ongoing conversation in Solyana's home. Fridmey had strong opinions on the matter, but Solyana always felt awkward participating. Did they even want her opinion? What was her opinion? She hadn't been aware that kind of talk had leached that deeply into the minds of the people. Momentarily glancing back at Thina, Solyana caught the woman staring, a forced smile on her apple cheeks. Solyana turned away, uncomfortable.

Downing the last of her drink, she skirted the Temple's perimeter and was unsurprised to find Rhuth kneeling at the center of the Spretta River, her face pressed into the ice. A stone bridge stretched across a few paces east, but, of course, her younger sister had to go over the ice. The Spretta was wide and deep, and it flowed far west connecting Kana Ocean and Vatino Sea. Fridmey was on the other side of the Spretta, looking exasperated.

"Come on!" Fridmey yelled, beckoning with dramatic swings of her arm. "Sol, can you get her?"

Solyana altered her course from the bridge and stepped out onto the glassy surface. Her knees shook; she did not like the ice.

"Rhuth..." she mumbled as she shuffled across, careful not to look anywhere but her feet. "Come on, you're making me late."

"I just had to see something," Rhuth whispered.

Solyana finally made it to her younger sister and clung to her. "I will never get used to that." She squeezed her eyes shut. "Come on, Little Fyug, let's go."

Rhuth made no attempts to stand, but instead brushed away the culminating snow at her feet and peered through the ice again. "Sol..."

"Yes?" Solyana started shuffling slowly across the rest of the river, hoping that by the time she reached the other side, Rhuth would be well on her way.

"There are no fish."

"Because they're all at their Stadas today. At least they're not going to be late."

"But—"

"I'm leaving!" Fridmey announced and turned toward the triad of buildings on the hill just ahead of them. "Someone has to save us seats."

"Rhuth, did you hear that? You're not going to get a good seat if you sit here playing with the fish all morning."

"Solyana!"

Solyana turned, surprised to hear her full name from Rhuth, who usually preferred to call her by her nickname.

"There are *no* fish. There are always fish. But I can't tether to any...it's almost as if..."

Solyana blinked, confused, truly thinking about the problem for the first time. "The only time the fish leave is...when there's a blizzard coming."

Rhuth nodded and bit her lip as she looked up at the sky.

"There was a blizzard less than two weeks ago. It comes at the Full Moon, every Full Moon. You know this, Rhuth. There's another twelve days before the next one."

Rhuth nodded redirecting her gaze to the ice.

"Well, think about it. What could cause the fish to leave?"

"When something is brewing, the animals are always the first to know. But what could it be?"

"Maybe someone dispersed them with their Tala? Or maybe it's the same reason as the dried-up ice shanty on the Vatino." Solyana shrugged and held out her hand. "Walk with me? You know I don't do ice."

Rhuth grinned and slid toward her in a few messy strides across the river. Then they were hand in hand, walking across the Spretta and up to the large building at the center of the three on the hill, the Hytast.

"You know"—Solyana squeezed her sister's hand—"you have an amazing skill with Tala. I know I'm Rána, and I don't know much about it, but I do know Papa can only tether to one type of beast, and you can tether to almost anything."

"Well, that's because I have Broad Tala, and he has Acute Tala."

"See? You're so smart."

Rhuth giggled and broke away from her as they reached the triad of stone buildings. Lóthkol on the right, Hytast in the middle, and Sháskol on the left, the last being newly built in the last three decades to accommodate the Gifted as Lóthkol filled with Rána. They passed a large monument that stood in the center point of all three buildings, a stone obelisk that held an inscription of the Gifts and what they did on one face. On another, it held the symbols of the Gifts, each taking on a likeness of the Celestial from which it was conceived. Solyana glanced at Rhuth as she began repeating the words by heart, as she did most mornings since learning to read. Usually Solyana ignored it, but today, after that talk with Thina, she couldn't help but listen anew.

"The Gift of the Celestial Stars: The Children of the Sky.

Fera offers the ability to manipulate resources by order of aptitude.
Endowed with this Gift, the Gifted must serve, collect, and build for
the good of all.
The Gift of the Celestial Moon: Mother of the Night.
Tala offers the ability to whisper and persuade the animal kingdom
by order of aptitude. Endowed with this Gift, the Gifted must hunt,
protect, and garner trust for the good of all.
The Gift of the Celestial Sun: Father of the Day.
Heitt offers the ability to physically, emotionally, and mentally
warm and, in some cases, procure and wield fire itself. Those Gifted
with Heitt are under an even greater responsibility, as it is the most
self-sacrificial of all the Gifts.
All three can save or harm, create or destroy. We must honor the
Celestials by controlling, mastering, and wielding for the good of
all."

Solyana paused, her arm extended, hand grasping the metal handle of the wooden door that would open the meeting hall that was the Hytast. She thought she was resigned to her fate as Rána, but standing there, moments before her life would change in such a final direction, lingering hope remained. Not realistically—she had never shown signs, not once—but in her heart, she knew she would never be content being in the Rána "family," for it would forever separate her from her own.

"Can we go in?" Rhuth asked impatiently. Solyana opened the door, and Rhuth flitted inside, saying something about Ránas not being engraved into the monument and why was that?

Solyana looked up at the clouds once more, snow falling in earnest. "Please," she prayed, "if you have any affection toward me, change my fate." Then she stepped inside, the door clanging shut behind her.

THE HATCHET TREE

PALLAH

STEALING THE SCROLL HADN'T been difficult. The tattered ends fluttered softly, much like Pallah's own dusty blonde hair. Closing her eyes to the sun, she let the warmth and wind caress and awaken her senses. She inhaled and counted to ten slowly, then held it, long and to bursting. She finally let it back out again in a slow release that mimicked the wind.

Cold season was soon approaching and the Heitt acted as if each moment was their last full day with the sun. It made Pallah laugh. They were all so paranoid. Flitting from one sun-soaked spot to the next, basking lazily and calling it work.

She glanced down, ready now to open the scroll. Although all ancient texts on the Taka Reu were forbidden and locked away, this one was almost begging to be read. It drew attention to itself with its torn ends and water-spotted pallor. Not to mention the fact it had been placed on a high shelf as if students were incapable of moving a chair and reaching it, as she did. She had replaced it with a scroll from her own bag: homework, never to be graded.

It made her smile, the ease at which you could get away with things when you were plain and unpopular. It's the ordinary that get away with most anything, perhaps the only advantage of being plain, but a great one.

She rubbed the old parchment between her fingers. It was a crime, what she did. Any study or even talk of the Taka Reu was forbidden throughout all of Mothmar. But surely, they couldn't regulate an entire country.

You did well. It's about time you started heeding me.

Pallah squeezed her eyes shut, inhaled again, and counted to twenty this time. The voice had been back for a week now. She thought it had been gone for good since the last time. When it first came, she had screamed and cried and begged her parents for help. They told her to stop being dramatic, stop making things up, to calm down. They didn't believe her. In all honesty, Pallah didn't know what to believe herself. She took several deep breaths as she counted. Why wouldn't it just leave her alone? When she got to seventeen, hands gripped her arms from behind, coupled with a chuckle. Pallah jumped.

"Why?" she asked, though it was more of a statement.

"Do I need a reason?" Her brother sat beside her and bit into an apple. The crunch and slurp of his bite made her cringe. Pallah opened her eyes but didn't have to look at him to know his every mannerism and movement. They knew each other too well.

"Don't you have school?" She raised an eyebrow and fluidly tucked the scroll back into her knapsack, hoping he hadn't seen.

"Don't you?" They were practiced at this game, the give and the take. It was juvenile, yet Pallah couldn't be the first to give in. It would physically pain her. Plus, she couldn't very well confess to him the reason she was sitting out here during school hours, having just committed a crime.

"Early release day, Pal. It's such a warm day, they wanted to get all the Heitt in the sun," Ahren said, leaning back beside her.

"Ah..." Pallah whispered, squinting upward. "Of course. They do need to marinate, don't they?"

"Like a nice slab of elk." Ahren grinned, eyes squeezed tight against the afternoon light. He took one last bite of his fruit before tossing the core into a nearby bush. The corner of Pallah's mouth twitched upward. He was funny...sometimes.

At fourteen, Ahren was already the heartthrob of their village, Sodur. He and Vámae, Pallah's twin, were both beautiful people. The two of them caused heads to turn wherever they went, and the funny thing was, no one knew where they got it from. It was the stale joke that ran through the mouths of the town gossips like water through the Spretta River. Phyllir and Bogdur, their parents, wouldn't be recognized in a group of three people. They were that forgettable, and Pallah, well, she fit right in. All dirty blonde, stringy hair, muddled gray eyes, and low cheekbones, she took after her father. There was nothing that pronounced them unattractive, but instead something far worse: a plainness that caused the viewer to forget them the minute they were out of sight, or perhaps even while they were still in view. Though, as of late, Pallah had noticed that others had begun to view her with more wariness than apathy...and she didn't mind it. At least they *saw* her.

After sixteen years of being the twin sister to a dark-haired, blue-eyed beauty, she had learned to use her plainness to her advantage. She glanced toward her bag again, scroll tucked safely inside. Vámae couldn't have gotten away with that if she tried, not that she would.

Students milled about, retreating from the two stone buildings set atop the hill behind her, Lóthkol and the Hytast. Children grew up learning alongside their parents, doing chores, and experimenting with their Gifts: moving, whispering, and warming. By the time most of them began formal school at ten years of age, they were already proficient and studied in a more concentrated way, seeking the religion and theory behind each Gift, breaking down the methods and the means.

Pallah watched from the corner of her eye as a few students from her year were passing near where she sat with Ahren. They gave her furtive glances and whispers before scurrying by. She never broke eye contact and even smiled a bit as they went, just enough for them to see it didn't bother her.

"Why do you do that?" Ahren raised a dark eyebrow.

"Do what?"

"You antagonize. It almost feels like you don't want them to like you." Ahren—ever the optimist, the social butterfly—didn't know a thing about her world, a world that merely tolerated her.

"Oh, Brother..." She stood, gave a long stretch, her arms soaring high into the air, midriff catching the breeze before one of her hands rested on his head of thick hair. "You're so naïve, it's cute." He gave her a flat look. "They have preconceived notions that they won't like me, and they don't do anything to change it, so I don't either. I give them what they want. You see?"

"No." He smirked. "You're insane."

"You don't even know the half of it," she said, picking her knapsack off the grassy floor and swinging it over her back. "What are you doing with the rest of your day?" She began walking before he could answer; he would follow.

"Well"—he caught up to her—"a few of the guys are going into White Wood to practice. I thought I'd join them."

"Practice?" Pallah gave him a dull look. "You're the best in your class, Ahren. Those boys are doing what you did at five. You don't need them."

"There's always room for improvement."

"You know that's a lie."

Ahren quieted, but Pallah wasn't done. "You should be teaching them, you know. They should already have you employed in carpentry. I honestly don't know why you continue to bother with Lóthkol."

"Just because I'm talented at something doesn't mean I should make myself unteachable. I can always learn more."

"*Häfa*! You're better than all of them!"

"Pallah, calm down." He stopped walking, and Pallah realized she had begun breathing hard, her passion in the moment consuming her. The thought that Ahren was doing something useless infuriated her, but why? She took a deep breath and closed her eyes, counting to ten; that usually did the trick. Having to calm herself like this was a weakness she didn't like showing, but she trusted Ahren.

Careful there. The voice whispered in her mind as she finished her counting. She ignored it, hoping in denial it would disappear. But it had been a week now…and it hadn't.

"If I were you, I would focus more on your Tala than on my Fera." He poked her shoulder. The accustomed rage boiled beneath her skin. It was the very reason she couldn't let it go—he had the talent she lacked, and he *wasted* it.

"My Tala is fine," she lied.

Ahren was silent for a long time, and Pallah knew what he held in that silence. She willed him not to bring it up, but not even she could stop the inevitable.

"You never use it in front of anyone," he said meekly.

"Stop."

"I don't even know what your aptitude is."

"Ahren, leave it."

"Are you sure you don't have Fera? I could ditch the guys, and we could practice instead, if you like."

"Ahren!" Pallah sighed, tired of the old conversation.

He quieted. He was always sweet; she would give him that. He somehow got all the qualities her family lacked, and for that, she could only have the purest of love for her little brother.

Walking past the assorted homes of Sodur, Pallah spotted her family's towering chimney from a distance, a symbol of prosperity that shadowed their modest home. Comprised of birch and pine, it was nestled in the very back of the town. Although their home was nowhere near the largest in Sodur, it was the closest to perfection, built by Father's own hand. Their valley was a communal one, hospitality and openness key virtues of the people of Mothmar.

But Father's priorities were far more aligned with outward—rather than inward—excellence.

Ahren, accustomed to Pallah's over-long, dramatic pauses, stepped through the door, leaving her outside. She steadied herself, hardening more parts of her heart; her home was not a safe place.

Her Father's gravelly voice pressed through the wooden door. Pallah took a breath and entered. Ahren was sitting at the table in the center of the room, his eyes downcast, his shoulders hunched. Father's lean form was standing over him, one finger out, gesticulating in that way he did when his insecurities were eating at him.

Vámae, Pallah's twin sister, was sitting cross-legged on the living room floor, her long, dark hair falling in waves around her face. She had her chin on her fists and elbows on the floor, leaning over a scroll held open by two stones. A beam of light shone through the window and stretched across her back. Even with a half-day at Lóthkol, she still studied.

Watching Vámae read made Pallah think of the scroll in her bag once more. What had driven her to finally steal it? She had eyed it for weeks and had come up with a simple reason. She wanted to draw her own conclusions and stop accepting the word of everyone else in her life as truth. The Taka Reu was always touted as the epitome of evil, the destruction of all good. But was it *really*? Couldn't she be the one to make those conclusions? She wasn't going to keep the thing. Just read it before putting it back. No one would know.

Pallah glanced around for Mother, but she wasn't anywhere to be seen. She was probably outside, taking advantage of the sun. Even if she had been inside, she wouldn't have stopped her husband from his mindless verbal abuse. She was a timid woman, but her actions made her role clear: she was for Mothmar, and for the Celestials she served. Her attention, her life, her blood was not her own; her family received the shell that was left behind.

A difficult task though it was, Pallah tried to make herself small as she slid behind her father. It was her turn to make their midday meal and keeping busy was the best way to avoid detection. Pallah lacked in many areas of her life, but cooking wasn't one of them. Perhaps it was the only one at which she excelled. Her hands were deft at descaling the fish, removing the head and tail, before making quick and efficient cuts so that the single salmon would feed all five of them.

She coaxed the coals in the oven to life and brought a pot of water to boil over top one of the four spaces where heat released. As she worked, the conversation tapered away, but she hardly noticed; she was thinking on the scroll in her bag. When she turned, her siblings were gone, and her father sat at the table, one of his mukluks in one hand, a rag stained with oil in the other.

"Have you been oiling your mukluks regularly, Pallah?" Father's eyes never left his work, his stringy blonde hair swaying back and forth with the quick, circular movements of his hand.

"Yes, sir." Her lips formed the lie from muscle memory. Mukluks wouldn't be needed until winter. It was only now descending into fall.

"The state of one's possessions reflects the state of one's mind," he said with a tap to his temple. When she didn't respond, he glanced up at her quickly, his dark eyes betraying a more youthful man. "Dinner smells nice."

Pallah blinked. Her father wasn't one for compliments or anything other than commands, for that matter. "Thank you," she said in a half-whisper, turning back to the stove and stirring the pot of potatoes once before replacing the lid.

"Your mother will be home soon. Make sure it's ready right when she walks in. We don't want her drained."

That was more like it.

"Yes, sir."

After a few more minutes of silence peppered with the sounds of work, the door creaked open and quiet shuffling announced her family's arrival. Together, they sat down at the wooden table crafted by Father. It was a work of art and in impeccable shape at twenty years old. The chairs, too, came from his hand, and after every meal, each of the Bogson children knew to wipe down the chair they used, making sure to detail every engraved flower or leaf.

Pallah sat across from Mother and tried to catch her downcast eyes, but they remained on the meal, tentative and careful.

"How was your time in the sun today, Mother?" Vámae's airy voice broke the silence. All eyes swept from Vámae to their mother.

Mother lowered her fork and looked up at her family. Her thin hair was more gray than brown now, and her eyes were sunken and wrinkled around the edges. Mother was barely forty, but life as an Eldur was taxing, and being married to a man like Father, even more so. Perhaps she had been pretty once, though it had been stolen from her long ago.

"Beneficial," she said with a weak smile. "And yours?"

"Productive," Pallah's twin answered with a nod before returning to her meal.

Father nodded in approval as if they gave the right answers on a test, and Pallah sucked on her cheek, biting it softly. An old habit of hers, a small bite would keep her from speaking out when it would only make things worse. She was a prisoner here; they all were. Even using the wrong word in response could bring their father's wrath. She was thankful, however small the gratitude was, he never hit them. Father was too pious for that. He would never mark one of his own, not physically, anyway. But Pallah and the rest of her family had experienced enough of his rage to fear him properly.

"I will be working late tonight. I've been commissioned to begin a new altar for the Temple Celestial. Preparations begin this evening."

"Congratulations, Father." Vámae sounded genuine, and Pallah narrowed her eyes, trying to decipher if she was faking. "What an achievement to be recognized by Priest Skrifa himself."

"Indeed, husband. A testament to your skill." Mother's faint voice barely rose above their chewing.

Pallah's leg began its fervent bouncing. Should she congratulate him as well? Father didn't like noise. No, there was already too much talk. She stayed silent, deciding that the sound of wooden utensils scraping wooden plates was enough.

"What are you doing this evening, Ahren?" Father inquired.

Ahren's face fell a bit as he met Father's piercing gaze. "Helping you, Father." That's what his lecture must have been about when Pallah had walked in. Ahren would not be going to White Wood tonight.

"Indeed"—he turned to Vámae—"and you, Daughter?"

"I need to make preparations for the Feast of Haust in two days' time." Chief Olafur had asked Vámae to take the lead on the preparations for the festival welcoming autumn. It wasn't something that appealed to Pallah in the slightest, but Vámae was ecstatic to have been chosen.

"Good, good. And you?" Pallah looked up to find her father staring at her, and she swallowed what she had been chewing.

Oh dear, better answer carefully. The voice came to her mind unbidden, as always.

"I need to hunt," Pallah lied, blinking hard to rid herself of the cold chill the voice always left in her brain.

Weak answer...but it will do.

"Cellar's looking thin." She shoveled another bite into her mouth and began masticating as if to prove her point.

Father's eyes didn't leave her, his expression unreadable. Pallah's stomach clenched and she pushed her plate away. Pallah was the only Tala in her family, or at least she *thought* she was Tala; most Gifts were passed down generationally, but sometimes a Gift could simply appear. And though they needed to eat, her father seemed to look on her hunting as an inconvenience rather than a necessity.

They finished up, one by one, Father being last, as usual. Then they stood in unison and got to work on cleaning up. Dishes were washed, table and chairs wiped down, then oiled, and everything was meticulously put back into place.

Pallah finally escaped the stuffy hut and breathed in the late afternoon air with relief. She needed to get out of there and away from her family. It was unnatural, she knew, how they behaved. She pushed her family from her mind. There was only one place she could go where she felt comfortable opening the scroll, one place she would be entirely on her own.

She sped through Sodur, up over the hill and across the courtyard which was already filling up with decorations as people prepared for the Feast of Haust. She then headed east through rows of farmland, almost completely picked clean with the cold drawing near. Running through it, she headed straight for Vatino Sea. Her tunic and pants flapped against her skin; her knapsack hopped to the beat of her feet. She was free, at least for the evening.

Several Vior Fera, her father being one of them, designed the floating wooden bridge that spanned the dark waters. If Pallah was proud of her father in any area, it was this one; the bridge was a marvel. No matter how rocky the seas became, what animals decided to swim beneath, or if the cold froze the sea, the bridge remained. It didn't take long to cross at a run, and soon, Pallah was on the other side, making her way further east.

Torrah Falls roared in the distance to her right as she went in a serpentine up the northwest side of the mountain. Her leather slippers brought her soundlessly through the lush greenery until she came to a cleared space she had worked on for some time. It was quiet, the falls on the other side of the mountain. She pulled her hatchet out from where it was holstered on her hip, the handle designed carefully as a gift from Ahren four years before. It was about as long as her forearm, thick and sturdy. She ran her fingers over the intricate handle, the shapes of leaves, swirls of wind, and dashes of what resembled trees wrapped all around.

Pallah reared back, hatchet over her head, both hands gripping it tight before she let out a loud grunt and released it into the large oak tree ten paces in front of her. It struck with a crack that echoed into the woods. She grinned. It was nice to be home. She let her bag slide off her back as she approached the tree, placing one hand on the trunk and pulling the weapon out with the other. It loosened, and she stumbled back, bark flying off to the side. She ran her hand down the rough surface, her fingers finding the pocks and marks of many hours spent on the mountain. She would need a new tree soon; this one had served its purpose.

She walked back to her throwing point and eyed her pack. A few more throws, then she would open it. She had to relax first. She stood twenty paces back this time and held the hatchet by her hip at an angle. It spun with well-practiced accuracy, making three complete rotations before sinking deep into the wood, bark breaking off in messy resignation.

Finally, when she was stress-free and sweaty, she opened her leather bag and extricated the scroll. Taking a deep breath, she wiped her brow and unfurled it.

The Beginnings of the Taka Reu and its End

Archived by Priest Carval

Everything we have gleaned up until this point I have compiled here. This is not to be distributed or even read without the accountability of others. Taka Reu is a slithery beast and will be the demise of an entire culture if not kept under a careful eye. Reading this without proper allowance, sharing it, acting upon it, are all crimes punishable by the council.

It began with the mountain that was not a mountain—

A twig snapped.

Pallah whipped her head to the side.

No one came up this side of Eldfall. Perhaps it was an animal?

No, more twigs were breaking, leaves crunching. It was the sound of humans, careless and loud. She had been coming up here for years, and no one, not one person, had come up while she was there.

Feeling guilty, Pallah stuffed the scroll back into her bag and tore her hatchet from the tree before ducking behind it. She chanced a look over her shoulder. A group of six people—four men and two women—were making their way straight toward her. Her eyes grew wide, and she pressed herself closer still to the tree, sliding down to hide behind the bushes that lined the bottom.

She peered through the foliage and hoped they couldn't see her as well as she could see them. Then her eyes fell on her knapsack. She had tucked the scroll inside but failed to pick it up.

She cursed to herself. How could she have been so stupid?

Muffled conversation came with the late afternoon breeze, low tones, a girlish laugh. They moved past her bag. Maybe they didn't see it. She prayed it blended well enough with the dirt around, but no. The smaller of the women stopped short and reached down, picking it up. Pallah held her breath as the girl's eyes slid past Pallah's hiding place.

The girl had thick braided hair sectioned in three large portions on her head. Her eyes were bright, and she was pretty, really pretty. She looked only a bit older than Pallah herself. Grasping Pallah's knapsack, she held it up for the others to see.

"Whose could this be?" she asked, facing away from Pallah.

One of the boys answered her, but his voice was too low to hear.

The girl shouldered the bag, and the party made their way north of the clearing. Pallah waited until the crunch of footsteps could no longer be heard then scurried out from behind the tree.

"*Häfan* it all!" She threw her hatchet into the nearest tree. It gave an echoing *crack,* and she cursed again, glancing around.

She retrieved it; they weren't coming back, though this was problematic. She needed her bag. She would have to track them down and hope they didn't look inside. She had known what she was getting into when she stole that scroll, but she never imagined anyone else would have access to her bag. Though it was a crime, it didn't feel like one. But most crimes didn't if you weren't caught doing them.

Is it a crime? Pitiable. Was this voice just her basest thoughts manifesting? She looked down at her shaking hands. Was she going insane?

Pallah took a deep breath and stood tall. Control. She needed control. She would have to track them. She stretched her neck side to side, then began following the snapped twigs and turned leaves that the group had left behind. They obviously didn't know how to make their way around the woods without being seen. Although, she chided herself, neither did she, or her bag wouldn't have been taken.

After ten minutes of slow and careful tracking, she wondered if she had followed the wrong path. Perhaps an animal had just come through here and replicated the movements of the small group of people.

But without any other leads, she continued. A broken twig here, a group of leaves brushed aside there, and then she was forced into a hard right, straight into a rock wall that stretched as tall as the Pines north of the valley. She turned in a quick circle, eyes roving. They had been right here.

"Where did you go?" Her voice echoed away from her as if there was space beyond. Pallah moved aside vines that covered the rock's face and found it. There was a crack, jagged and long as it climbed up the wall. It was just large enough to admit a person. She ran her hand along the rough edges and heard what sounded like distant voices. Against her better judgment, she entered.

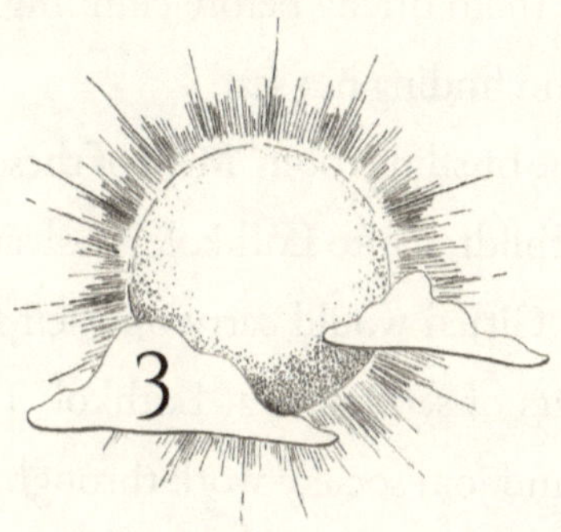

DIVINE INTERVENTION

SOLYANA

THE HYTAST WAS A building that had stood for centuries, periodically rebuilt piece by piece by Stein and Vior Fera, wielders of stone and wood. Just like everything in the valley, it was slowly disintegrating over time.

Where the other large buildings were multi-storied and filled with weaving corridors and hidden rooms, the Hytast stood in contrast as it held only a meeting space, long and wide and filled with rows of wooden chairs. These chairs were arched around the steps that led to the stage lined with a straight row of seats, just enough for the graduating class from Sháskol.

Festooning the perimeter, from window to window, were swaths of cloth so faded they no longer resembled distinguishable shades. Each held a stitched emblem representing the three Gifts, faded and lackluster. Mothmar had little use for such frivolities. Solyana passed a row of chairs. Her family sat together toward the center, and Rhuth had squeezed herself between Mama and Papa. Solyana waved at them briefly before climbing the steps with the rest of her class and finding her seat.

She surveyed the bustling room. Most of these families would be welcoming their children into Lóthkol, as Solyana's class held only seven Rána. The Gifted would carry on their family's Gifts into their last two years of schooling at Lóthkol. They would attend intensive classes and join society work through an apprenticeship supported by someone from one of the villages. For Rána, however-er, it simply meant plodding along through Sháskol another two years, coupled with an apprenticeship with another Rána.

Solyana wondered at the whole display. A Stada was a natural part of her world, but there was a time, she knew, when the word Rána didn't exist. When every single child was born with a Gift and, thus, holding a Stada to establish teenagers in the appropriate school, unnecessary.

Ms. Borta set down her chalk, dusted her hands, and walked to the front of the stage. The light from the slits of the windows all around the top of the room let in the sun at just the right angle, illuminating Ms. Borta's wiry gray hair and making her look angelic.

"Welcome! How are we today?" Ms. Borta taught the first and second-year students. The way she interacted with the crowd re-minded Solyana of time with her years ago. The crowd responded with claps and whistles. "Fantastic! Now, we are excited to bring to you this year's newest graduates. Our students have come prepared to either display their Gift, or not, and then let us all know what area of work they would like to be hired into."

Solyana blinked. She must have missed that from her last meeting about the Stada. How was she supposed to tell a crowd of people what she wanted to do when she didn't even know? Her mind raced as the crowd gave another round of applause. Mama had taught her to sew, and she was decent at it, but was it something she wanted to spend the rest of her life doing? She was skilled with her longbow, but compared to Tala, she was a novice.

Looking up, she spotted Rhuth, her legs bouncing off the end of her chair, staring at the ceiling. Solyana smiled. Maybe she could teach. She always liked that age, right when they began at Sháskol. But what did she have to offer?

"Don't worry, kids." Ms. Borta seemed to read Solyana's mind. "Whatever you announce to us here will not determine what you do. It just gives us a glimpse into your goals." The older woman motioned to a large chalkboard, twice her height. A small step stool sat next to it. "Then each student will come here and mark which classes they would like to attend. We'll take this information, along with their Gift, and come up with an apprenticeship that suits them."

A few cheers from those who lead the apprenticeships rang about the room. Ms. Borta laughed and clapped her hands. "Alright, let's get some representation and get our students excited." She peered out over the crowd. "Do we have anyone from the Greenhouses present?"

Three or four of the adults stood, a few waved to the students on the stage. "Ah, thank you!" She motioned for them to sit; her tiny frame birdlike in the light. "Anyone from our stock barns?" A few more stood, much more energetic than the last, whooping and cheering for their area of expertise. "Yes, yes, we know you lot." Ms. Borta chuckled and motioned them back down. "Lastly, anyone from our builders and engineers?"

"Yeah!" Fridmey clapped loudly, her red hair bouncing, and was joined by several more about the room. Fridmey was in her last few weeks of her apprenticeship and was recently asked to permanently join the team. "Stein Fera!" she cheered before settling back down in her chair. Solyana flushed red but chuckled at her sister.

Ms. Borta continued. "Finally, I just wanted to ask at least one of you to stand and explain what kind of work you do if you're Rána. We have quite a few this year. Anyone?" She scanned the room, and Solyana searched too, genuinely curious. A lanky man stood in the back and pulled his knit cap off his head, wringing it in his hands. "Ah, Svenick! Please, tell us a bit about what you do to keep our valley going."

"Well," Svenick hesitated. He looked very unsure of the number of eyes on him. Solyana glanced down the row at Mharna, Svenick's daughter. She was Rána, too, and looking like she wanted to be anywhere but there, her neck a fiery red. "I tend to the barns. I love animals, you see. I wanted to be around them and I've become quite good at cleaning." He stood tall, as if he had just decided to be proud of his work. "I've got a good relationship with them beasts. They're mighty sweet."

"As you are, Svenick." Ms. Borta scrunched her nose, and he sat, still wringing his cap. "Thank you all for your input. I'm sure you've given our students much to look forward to." The small woman turned to face them, her back to the audience. "Ready?" Her eyes twinkled.

"Sasha Abson," Ms. Borta projected as she sat next to the chalkboard.

The Stada had begun.

A round of exclamations, presumably Sasha's family, rang throughout the hall. Sasha, willowy and blonde, rose from her seat and stepped to the front of the stage. Her back was to the waiting class as she pulled an object out of her tunic and set it on the small table next to her.

"I would like to join the preservationists." Sasha raised a hand to the object on the table and stepped out of the way. Solyana could see it was a small glass jar. It lifted, wobbly at first, then drifted into the air, where it spun brilliantly in the sun.

The crowd erupted. There hadn't been a Gler Fera in at least two generations.

It was quite the start for a Stada. Solyana swallowed to rid her throat of the lump that had formed. What was a Rána compared to someone who could wield glass?

Sasha lowered her hand in tandem with the jar, wobbling only a little. She glided to the board where she marked her classes with precision, then sat.

"Excellent. Shall we proceed?" Ms. Borta continued to call out names in alphabetical order. Watching the students perform their Tala or Fera brought to mind Solyana's own memories of her sisters' acquisitions of Gifts.

Fridmey was nine when hers had appeared. They had been washing dishes in the kitchen when one of Fridmey's stone bowls began floating. Mama had been so happy. Solyana recalled feeling an immense jealousy.

Rhuth's Tala had come even earlier. When Rhuth was only eight months old, she had called Solyana's pet rabbit, Omi, back into their home after he had wandered off. It was one of the earliest fruition of Gifts recorded in their valley. Rhuth was slightly famous for it, of which she never forgot to remind her sisters.

Solyana had waited sixteen years for her moment, for that special feeling that the Gifted always described as a throb in the base of their skull, as a tether of connection to something that was part of them. But, nothing. No Gift had ever been recorded appearing after the age of sixteen. Her time was up.

"Solyana Marusda."

Solyana's head snapped up at the sound of her name. Ms. Borta motioned for her. "Please, come forward."

Solyana stood. This was it.

She made her way to the front. Most people knew she was Rána, but standing in front of so many without anything to place on the table beside her left her feeling hollow. She took a deep breath and took a moment to close her eyes. She thought of the prayer she whispered before entering the Hytast. Had the Celestials really chosen to keep her without?

Opening her eyes, she was surprised to see a few individuals standing about the cavernous room. Svenick was among them. Were they all Rána? Their eyes were set, chins held high. Finally, almost a belated gesture, her parents stood too, followed by an exuberant Rhuth and a reluctant Fridmey.

"Do you have a Gift to display today, Solyana?" Ms. Borta asked.

"No, ma'am."

"For each presumed Rána, we do admit one final test." Ms. Borta said, both to the room and to Solyana. "Close your eyes, dear."

Solyana complied.

"Now," Ms. Borta whispered to her, very close and coming just to Solyana's brow—she was a tiny thing. "Dig deep in yourself. Engage with the earth, the sky, the wood and stone around you. This Gift comes from the Children of the Sky. Anything?"

Solyana centered herself. Digging deep for a pull, a tug in a direction, any direction. But no, she felt nothing. "No, ma'am."

"Now, try with animals. This Gift, from the Mother of the Night. Real deep, now. Think of every animal you have ever had contact with, perhaps those you haven't. Hare, stag, wolf, seal, whale, or even polar bear."

Running through a list of animals she had seen or even simply heard of, the lump in her throat grew. Nothing was happening. She bit her lip and shook her head.

"Now, think of our Father of the Day, our great sun in the sky. Raise your arms to him."

Solyana did so, feeling foolish. There hadn't been a Heitt in centuries, why did they still test for it?

Waiting, her eyes closed. She set her mind on the sun.

Did something deep inside her tug? A warmth coming over her? She opened her eyes to see Ms. Borta's attention flick from Solyana's underarms back to her face. Dropping her arms, she held them tight against herself. She had sweat through her tunic. Her face grew hot.

"Alright then, sweetie, don't fret yourself." The teacher squeezed her shoulder and stepped back. "And your area of work?"

"I..." Solyana scanned the crowd, some looking almost relieved that she hadn't shown a Gift. She recognized a few of the people standing: a tailor, a stall cleaner, a midwife, someone in the back did inventory, another person to her far right prepared the ice shanties for fishing. None of it sounded appealing.

"I suppose I can do something with sewing...or hunting?"

"Oh, of course, dear." Ms. Borta said it in such a way, Solyana wished she had said she didn't know. "Go ahead and mark your classes."

Solyana could breathe again. The Stada was over. She stood, surrounded by her family as they comforted her. Those who stood when she and the other six Rána had approached the front, had each come by and made sure to congratulate her as well.

One woman, after gripping her forearm in customary Mothmarian greeting, bowed her head and whispered, "Welcome to your new family." Feeling supremely uncomfortable with the statement, she glanced up at her father. His face was flushed and her mother was gripping his hand.

When, finally, the Hytast emptied enough so they could talk privately, her father began without preamble.

"Are they forming some sort of coup I don't know about? Koláme, I'm telling you, we need to handle this before it gets out of hand."

"Marus, not here." Mama shushed him, but Papa's blue eyes were feverish.

"Sure, we have factions amongst ourselves in both Tala and Fera. It's healthy, creates a family-like atmosphere. But with Rána? It's more than togetherness. It's almost a..." He searched for a word.

"Uprising," Fridmey whispered, glancing around furtively.

"Oh, stop." Mama rolled her eyes.

"Exactly!" Papa snapped his fingers and pointed at his eldest, nodding. "There's an underlying animosity toward us Gifted that I can't ignore any longer."

"Us?" Solyana crossed her arms. Couldn't her family just be happy for her? She wasn't Gifted like they were, but she was still part of the family.

"You don't count, Sol." Her father's words came so fast, Solyana had to blink a few times to register them. "You come from *our* family. You'll get a better job than sewing, or whatever." He waved away the thought like it was a pesky creature.

"But in this case, blood doesn't matter, does it, Papa?" Solyana ground her teeth together, trying to keep from raising her voice. "Today sealed it. I'm *not* Gifted. I never will be."

"And that's fine, Sol." Mama put her arm around Solyana and squeezed. "You're an important part of this family."

"But not as important as Rhuth or Fridmey." The pressure of tears welled behind her eyes. She would not cry here. "No," she continued, wanting to stop the conversation before it got worse, "it doesn't matter. I'm Rána and I can't change that."

"The Celestials have a plan." Mama nodded, though it sounded like she was trying to reassure herself.

"Don't get caught up in their politics, Sol." Papa pressed. "You'll always have a place in this family."

"Yeah, making your clothes."

"Hey!" Mama furrowed her brow. "There's nothing wrong with that! I taught you everything I know."

"But it's *your* hobby. Something you do for fun. Do I want it to be my livelihood?" Solyana waved them away. "I need to get to class."

"Well, we're proud of you either way," Mama said with a final squeeze. It took everything inside of Solyana not to shake her off. "Keep shining, my Light."

Solyana entered Sháskol and opened the parchment on which her classes were listed. She had picked what interested her, though she knew most of it wouldn't necessarily help her apprenticeship, whatever it would be. Hunting sounded better than sewing, but she knew Tala would have first choice of that job.

Archery: Crafstmanship

Foraging

Dyeing and Tanning

Leather Curing

Plantlife in the Tundra

Heitt: A History

Solyana flipped it over and found the times and locations before hurrying off to the one for which she was already running late:

Heitt: a History. Curiosity had made her choose it; Heitt was something they knew so little about. Perhaps the class held insight as to why Heitt had all but disappeared.

Solyana made her way down the familiar halls of Sháskol, feeling a certain bitterness settle deep in her heart she wouldn't be entering the ancient halls of Lóthkol. She had walked through it once, with Fridmey. It wasn't much different from Sháskol—made of stone instead of wood—but it was for Gifted only, making her own schooling feel like less. Solyana wished they had simply kept all the students in one building. It did nothing but harvest animosity between the students.

The wooden floor creaked beneath her feet as she turned left down a hallway and found the door she was looking for. She closed her eyes, mourned her own dreams of being anything but Rána, then opened her eyes and pushed the door inward.

"Glad to have you join us." A voice came from just ahead and Solyana looked up to find herself face to face with Priestess Avi, her expression unreadable under her wrinkled skin. Solyana tried to hide her surprise. The priestess herself was teaching the class! Her only contact with the priestess was during their weekly worship at the Temple, and even then, it wasn't as if she came and talked with Solyana personally.

"As I just finished telling the class, you all know who I am, but I'll introduce myself anyway. I am Avi, and I am High Priestess of the Temple Celestial. I am Heitt; I heal and keep our valley warm on the nights that are coldest. I am an Eldur, which means I can wield fire. I am the last of our kind. Is there anything else our Solyana needs to know?" She addressed the rest of the class, who sat in silence; whether in awe or fear, Solyana couldn't tell. Priestess Avi *was* the very last Heitt, after all.

"Sorry, I'm a little late."

"Don't be sorry, just be on time. There's a seat open here." The old woman motioned, her hand outstretched from a flowing, cavernous sleeve, and Solyana only saw darkness past her bony wrist. Surely, she was but air underneath.

Simple pillows lined the floor, each claimed by a student. Solyana made her way to an empty cushion and focused her attention on the ethereal woman at the front.

"You have all been taught from a young age of the Seers and their scribes that lived atop high mountains of Mothmar, back when our land was lush and green, when we traveled from one coast to the next, monthly blizzards a work of fiction."

Solyana was drawn in by the melodic croon of the old woman's voice, a fireside story instead of a lecture. At a quick glance, the rest of the class was enraptured as well. Everyone from the three villages was expected to attend weekly teachings at the Temple Celestial with Priestess Avi, but never had Solyana listened to her in such close and intimate proximity.

"You were given an overview. Skim of the milk, if you will. I'm here to give you the milk. The meat. The entire elk. The pure, unadulterated version of the story, highlighting Heitt through the centuries. Throughout this course, we will explore a few separate theories, as this class always does, as to why Heitt is the first dead Gift."

The silence in the room changed, and Solyana knew every student was thinking one thing. No adult had ever admitted Heitt was dead. Dying perhaps, but never *dead*. And to also insinuate others were dying as well? Solyana's hands went clammy. Would she tell Papa about this? Could she? He would be livid.

"At the beginning of time, there was but one Gift, the Gift of Seeing. This gave those we called Seers the ability to articulate prophecies. These have been handed down throughout time; some have come to pass already, and some are yet to be fulfilled. All are valid and awaiting fruition."

Her eyes, concentrated on the place above her folded hands, flicked to Solyana's right. "Yes?"

A fair girl sitting beside Solyana lowered her hand and spoke clearly, "Are you telling us there are no contradictions or false prophecies?"

"Precisely."

"But my father says the system wasn't completely error free. The scribes were inconsistent, some prophecies ended slightly differently than they began—"

"How old is your father, girl?" the priestess asked, cutting her off, her voice still just as melodic but with more force.

The girl glanced at her fellow students. Solyana shifted her gaze away from her. The girl laughed softly. "Forty-five."

"So, while your father was still learning to use the washroom, I was already Speaker of the Skies, Priestess of the Temple Celestial, Eldur, and the only Heitt. So, I ask you, class"—she looked at them as a whole—"would we agree I have a bit more experience?"

The girl deflated, and tension blanketed the entire class.

"These Seers became a part of our ancestry, monks who worshiped the Celestials so wholly, their lives, down to their very senses, were dedicated to their singular job. Our people, though the records don't go so far back as to know how they came to intermingle with these Seers, realized the truth in the worship of the skies. They adopted it and gave the Seers wives, hoping to reproduce a line of Seers themselves. It worked, for a few decades, before the Gift of Seeing dropped away, and the three Gifts we know now—Heitt, Tala, and Fera—arrived. Where exactly did the other Gifts come from? Well, some believe it was a natural evolution of Gifts. Others believe it was when Hekla erupted, conceiving the three Gifts in its wake."

Priestess Avi's eyes shifted again to another hand in the room. Solyana looked over her shoulder at a dark-skinned boy who was lowering his hand.

"Priestess Avi, I was taught that the Gifts were always a part of us. They didn't come from evolution or an eruption, they came from the Celestials themselves, to aid and guide," his voice was not challenging, just curious.

"What is your name?" the priestess asked calmly.

"Bogdur, ma'am."

The old woman blinked. "Bogdur. How unfortunate." The students snickered, but Solyana thought she saw disgust cross over the teacher's face. "This second part of your education will test your resolve and stretch your minds, much unlike the first six years. You have been coddled, fed the easiest way possible to avoid the mess of thinking individually, but now? I want you to think with your own minds, claim your right to an opinion, and discover something that is out of the ordinary. These are theories, Bogdur. Theories."

"You are Priestess of the Temple Celestial." Bogdur turned to see if he had gained any support from the rest of the class. "You've never mentioned these teachings during worship. We are taught one thing at the Temple, and now you're saying something different?" The boy's eyebrows furrowed, and Solyana couldn't help but smile to herself. He was brave.

"I am Speaker of the Skies, am I not?"

Bogdur nodded.

"Trust me, there are things I cannot speak from the Temple steps that I *am* permitted to say in this classroom. Views I can give that are different. Not everything I say can be absolute truth, but you would be a fool not to explore the differing ideas." She addressed the rest of the class. "If anyone else is unwilling to lay aside preconceived notions about what they know and learn to interpret the scrolls for themselves, I suggest you leave and find a different class."

No one dared speak. Bogdur looked at his feet, crossed before him.

"No one? Alright then." The priestess laced her fingers together, hidden in her sleeves. "Let's explore the Hekla theory first. It's filled with molten ground and fire. Several ancient scrolls point to this mountain as the source of all Mothmar, how our country itself was formed, but many scholars interpret them differently. I'm curious what each of your parents believes on the subject. Ask them, will you? That will be your homework tonight."

Solyana raised her hand tentatively.

"Yes?"

"If you ask us to interpret it ourselves, will we get access to the texts? You say to question and believe a different narrative, but how can we know *you're* telling the truth?"

A gasp or two littered the room, and Solyana thought she saw Bogdur smile. Priestess Avi's face remained passive, though the corner of her mouth twitched upward.

"Astute question. The basement of the Temple Celestial holds the ancient archives dating all the way back to the Seers. I implore you, children, go and study, whenever you like. It is open to you. The more you fill your minds, the more we can discuss here. I would not like to lecture for long. I'd rather this be a discussion. Who knows, perhaps *I* will learn something new." Her eyes locked with Solyana's, and she couldn't help but feel a kindred connection with the old woman.

"Now, you're going to need some ancient Mothmari vocabulary..."

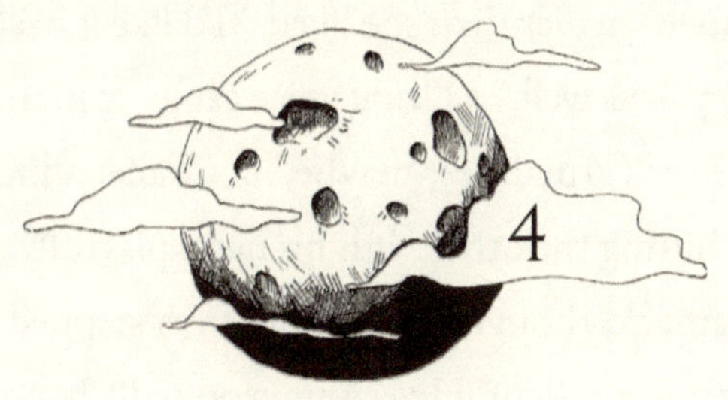

SISTERS

PALLAH

Unexplainable pressure compounded on Pallah as she entered the narrow crag in the rock. Not so much physical, although that was evident—her breath was siphoned like a wet rag over her face—but more so in her heart, in her soul. It was a strange pressing of the walls and the high ceiling that seemed to stretch upward to no end. Pallah's heart was in her throat as she weaseled her way through. The darkness was both physical and something deeper, foreboding. The cool, wet walls of the rock threatened to close in on her as her breathing became hurried.

Her feet scuttled like startled prey as she whipped through the narrow crag. Finally, she broke through into an open cavern where her momentum drove her to the damp ground, her eyes wide, trying to adjust to the darkness. Fortunately, there were some small flames alight. Unfortunately, the flames were held by those same six strangers.

Standing on aching knees from the abrupt landing, her hand brushed the hatchet attached to her hip. "My knapsack." Her voice came out much smaller than she liked. "I'd like it back."

"Hello to you as well," a lilting voice came from the left.

"Not one for formalities, maybe," a smaller silhouette spoke beside him, hitting the other with his hand playfully.

"*Your* knapsack, though?" A slender man stepped forward, his face coming into the light. He was unexpectedly handsome, much in the way a fox is, with a sly smile and eyes that glittered with mischief. He circled the bag once before picking it up. "Whose bag is this, guys?"

A few of them snickered, one spoke up, "Looks like it's yours, Vil."

"So...*my* knapsack," the man called Vil said, turning back to her. His smile was placating as he opened the bag. Casually, he pulled out a scarf, a canteen, and something wrapped in wax parchment that Pallah couldn't begin to guess how long it had been in there. Vil wrinkled his nose and tossed them one by one to the ground. Lastly, he revealed the scroll. "Homework?"

Pallah struggled to keep fear from crossing over her face.

"Yes." She loosened her grip from off her hatchet, hoping it wasn't too late to change her approach, something less threatening. "For Ms. Sherpa's class."

"Ms. Sherpa?" The pretty girl from before stepped into the light and stood next to Vil. "Let me see that." She unraveled the scroll, eyes scanning, brow furrowed.

Calm. She had to remain calm. The girl's eyes met Pallah's as she held the scroll open for Vil. Sweat rolled down Pallah's back.

"Just"—Vil snatched the scroll and rolled it into itself—"home-work." He smiled, though it didn't reach his eyes.

Pallah blinked. Who were these people?

"What's your name?" Vil asked, tossing the bag to her.

"Pallah," she answered too quickly, grabbing it before it fell to the floor.

"Pallah..." Vil mused. "Do you come up this mountain often?"

"Y-yeah." She clenched her hands shut, then open again, sweat beading her brow. "What are you guys doing here?"

The group chuckled as if she asked something silly, something obvious.

"Nothing to worry yourself over, Pallah," Vil said, his fox-eyes mischievous once more. "Wouldn't want you getting in trouble." Then his face lost all playfulness as he said, "Your eyes be down-ward."

Pallah's eyes grew wide, she recognized that phrase. The antithesis of Celestial worship, which encouraged its people to turn their eyes upward. 'Your eyes be downward' was a phrase reserved for those following the Taka Reu.

Once thought to be extinguished from all of Mothmar, the group of religious defectors known as the Taka Reu had sprouted again. Pallah knew little of them, as all talk of the Taka Reu was forbidden. But the sheer fact that they stood in opposition of the Temple Celestial, which Pallah's father held as truth, was enough to pique her interest. They deemed independence of religious thought the foundation of their practice; so different from the Temple which demanded unity of belief and was led by a single priest or priestess. Though if they did anything other than drink scub and pilfer scrolls, Pallah didn't know. Regardless, it had been her desire to seek other sources which challenged the status quo that had driven her to steal the scroll in the first place. Maybe it was time she crafted her own opinions on what she believed.

Pallah found her hand back on her hatchet. The shadows of each of the six people had extended to the cave wall behind them until they reached the cavern's ceiling like bats in slumber. Their faces flickered into view, but Pallah noticed nothing but the flames in their hands growing to double their previous size. They must have an Eldur among them. And how could she protect herself against someone who could wield flame? It seemed all too important to know how far she was from the exit. She took an involuntary step backward, reaching with the hand not on her hatchet, searching for the crack in the wall.

"You should leave," the man called Vil said flatly. "Stay off this mountain, girl. Go home."

Pallah needed no further encouragement. She ran, weaving her way back through the crack in the wall, the pack over her shoulder catching on grooves in the rock. The heavy press of foreboding only left her as she reached the wood once more, breathing in its crisp air.

The sun hung low, piercing the tree line. She shaded her eyes to find her path, then began an even-paced jog to the courtyard, all the while trying to shake the creeping darkness of the cave filled with ominous figures, deep in the mountain.

The teachings at the Temple had been focused on community and oneness in recent weeks, speaking against radical individuality as if it were a terrible sin. Her parents were faithful to the Temple

Celestial and had expected all three of the Bogson children to attend from a young age. But Pallah had long since stopped drinking it in. The Temple wasn't relevant. Individuality wasn't a bad thing. If they truly had a problem with groups of Taka Reu rising up or experimenting with Dark Gifts, they should use force, not useless words.

Vámae was the faithful one, going every week, agreeing blindly. Ahren hid his disdain for the Temple. Pallah knew from their many conversations he didn't care for the hypocrisy.

As she made her way through the darkening courtyard, her mind returned to the group again. Vil, who seemed to be the leader, and that woman with the braids, their faces burned into her memory. Were they truly Taka Reu? If they were, it would explain why they didn't react to the scroll. Could they tell from that one encounter she was searching? *Searching?* She didn't know what to call it. Perhaps that was why they let her go so easily. She rounded the bend and wove her way through Sodur. Her family's hut was in the last row before Shadow Wood and the steep incline that exited the valley.

The moon was high in the sky by the time she entered. Immediately she wished she had stayed out as her father's stony expression rose to meet her own.

"Pallah." He was holding her mukluks. The weather was still warm enough for her to get by with leather slippers. She hadn't seen those shoes for months. He must have dug through her things to find them. The idea enraged her. "These have not been oiled, as you so confidently assured me they were earlier today."

"Father, I—"

"You lied to me, yes?"

She stifled a snort of frustration and let her breath out slow, counting, always counting. "Yes."

He stared at her expectantly, scant eyebrows raised.

"Yes, *sir*," she repeated.

"And why did you lie to your father, Pallah?" His shift to third-person always made her shiver.

"I don't see why I need to oil them every week throughout the summer. I don't use them. I was planning on oiling them before the snows came."

"I didn't ask for excuses. I asked why you lied." His eyes widened almost innocently as he said it.

"Because I am disobedient and do not respect my father as I should," she mumbled, breaking eye contact to stare at the floor.

"Indeed, you don't," he spat. There was a moment of silence, and she knew he was regarding her, probably wondering where he got such an insolent daughter in the midst of his subservient brood. "You will find the seal oil on the table along with a rag. You will oil every piece of leather in this household; from every item of clothing, to every window covering, to every piece of furniture. And I still expect you to be in bed at a decent hour, so if you are unfinished tonight, you will rise early and finish tomorrow morning. Is that understood?"

Pallah locked eyes with him, ready to let herself rage, to let herself curse him and run from the house. She was so sick of his patronizing and humiliating methods of parenting. But as quickly as the urge overcame her, it disappeared.

"Yes, sir," she whispered again, reaching for the oil and cloth.

He smiled.

Pallah worked for hours before giving up and laying down on her mat. She held her hands above her, the lantern light showing the dark marks that covered her pale skin. The oil would take days to disappear, even with heavy scrubbing. She glanced over at her twin who was combing through her long dark hair, back erect, her posture causing Pallah to curate a mental image of a stick shoved up her sister's bottom. She chuckled.

"What?" Vámae asked, her eyes never leaving the mirror.

"I don't know how you sit like that," Pallah murmured, turning on her side, her hand propping up her head. She saw her twin's eyes crinkle in the mirror, a slight smile on her lips as she glanced at Pallah through the reflection.

"You know the village looks to us, Pal." Vámae continued with the whitewashed bone comb until her hair shone brighter than the lantern itself. "I have to keep myself above reproach."

"Oh, my! Where are they?" Pallah lifted her blanket and checked under her pillow before shielding her eyes and dramatically searching the room.

"You know what I mean. At least I don't throw my hatchet first and ask questions later."

"That was one time, and it was only a goat."

"Professor Fye's goat. He was furious."

"That thing needed to be eaten, anyway. If you let them get too old, the meat gets tough."

"I suppose you did learn to butcher an animal well after that one. Your hands were stained, just like they are now. Only red instead of brown."

Pallah's smile faded. "Why is he like this?"

Her sister stopped combing, eyes dropping to her lap. "You antagonize him, Pal, you know that? Why did you lie?"

Pallah rolled to her back, hands behind her head, the lantern flickering against the aged ceiling of their room. "It was just easier than telling him I hadn't gotten to it. How was I supposed to know he'd inspect them tonight?"

"Because he's Father. You should know that by now, *predict* it." Vámae's words were not unexpected, but the tone towed the line of insubordination, and it surprised Pallah.

"You know you're the only one he doesn't needle, right? Me, Mother, Ahren, he nitpicks everything we do, everything we say, or don't say...but you? Not," she leaned, "one," she took a steadying breath, "word." She kept her gray eyes locked on her sister's blue ones, awaiting a response.

"I'm obedient," Vámae replied sagely, and laugh burst out of Pallah so abrupt she started coughing. "What? I'm serious. I purposefully don't do anything wrong! You, on the other hand..." She drifted off as Pallah got a hold of her lungs.

"So, you never do anything wrong?" Pallah sat up, amused.

"Purposefully," Vámae amended, rolling her eyes.

"You never, not even once, have had an urge to defy Father, or anyone else?"

"Well, maybe when I was little or something, but not since I can remember. I've always tried to follow the rules."

"No wonder you're so boring." Pallah laid back down and covered herself with her fur blanket.

"I'm *not* boring!" Vámae argued, but Pallah was done. She didn't want their playful banter to dive headfirst into arguing. "I'm just...doing my duty."

Pallah thought about this duty. Vámae had a clear-cut path since she was one, when her Gift began manifesting itself. By the time she was four, she had grasped the concept of Heitt better than most ten-year-olds. She was already working alongside their mother to both bathe in the light in the warm season and warm the villages in the cold season. It was the task of every Heitt, of course. But in their case, they were given larger responsibilities than the others, their Heitt stronger, more enduring. She had even begun work as an Eldur this year, producing and wielding fire, surpassing their mother's skills.

Eyes closed, Pallah listened to Vámae move about the room, putting her things away in their appropriate places; her own shoes and clothes were piled in the corner. The lantern creaked and a soft puff of air doused the room in darkness. Vámae laid down next to Pallah, their mats separated by only a handspan.

Pallah glanced to her right, where her sister lay, outlined in moonlight, eyes trained on the ceiling. "What if you don't know your duty?" she asked, but in the silence that grew between them, she became unsure if she wanted to hear the answer.

Her twin shifted to her side, and then whispered, "You ask the Celestials to show you."

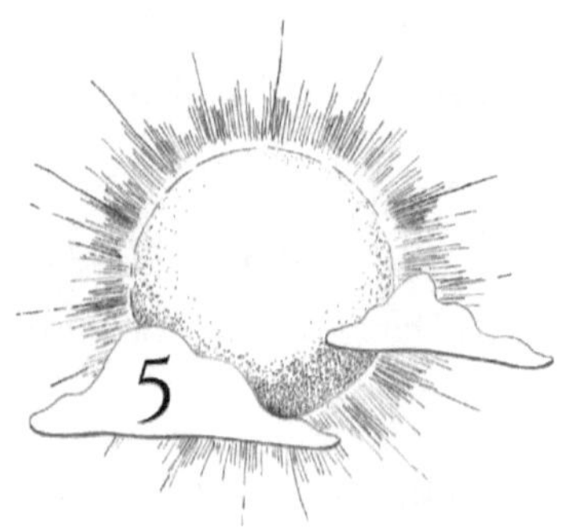

TOO SOON

SOLYANA

"**S**OLYANAAAAA!" A VOICE WOUND through the halls of Sháskol. Solyana turned to find Rhuth bounding toward her, bag flopping to the side, her hair a mess of tangles. The entirety of the two schools were breaking for the midday meal, the halls filled with the youth of their valley, eager and hungry.

"Hello, my little Fyug." Solyana grinned at her, happy for the company on the walk home.

"I know, I'm a squawking bird." Rhuth's lips twisted into a wry smile. "Is there another reason you call me that?"

"What do you mean?" Solyana laughed, slowing her steps.

"Papa thinks I have Broad Tala." Rhuth stopped in the narrow hall, a few parka-clad students piling up behind her. They scooted around the sisters with annoyed looks.

Solyana pulled her to the side. "Because you can tether to several different kinds of animals, as opposed to Acute Tala who can only tether to one, right?"

"Yes, you remember." Rhuth was fiddling with the fur lining on her parka. "But it has always felt...*different* with birds, like it's easier to talk to them."

"Well," Solyana began—she had no experience with Tala, but was touched Rhuth was confiding in her. "It's all birds? Or a certain type? Perhaps you're Fugali Tala. Have you talked with Papa?"

"No," Rhuth said quick and loud. "I know you don't really understand, but..." She gave Solyana a pitying shrug and Solyana fought the urge to end the conversation. "I hear them back, as if...*they* have a tether on *me*."

Solyana pulled Rhuth in for a hug, and she trembled slightly in her arms.

"Have you mentioned any of this to your teachers? Or even with Papa? I know I—"

Rhuth pulled abruptly away. "No! I don't want to tell anyone. I tried telling Papa, but he doesn't understand. And my teachers?" Rhuth rolled her eyes and marched past Solyana with the flow of students. "I shouldn't have told you, either."

"Wait, Rhuth." Solyana dropped her hands in exasperation. "Maybe...maybe you could show me what you mean?"

Rhuth turned on her heel, her face coming alight with a grin. "Yes! I'll show you! Then you'll see." She bolted around the corner at the end of the hall, leaving Solyana with no choice but to follow.

Her stomach grumbled and her parka grew hot, but she followed. She let her fingertips drag along the wooden walls as she went, feeling every familiar groove and crevice, a faint line where several children had grown up doing the very same thing. With only two years left, she already had a sort of nostalgia for the place. She sped up. Where was that girl going?

Solyana glimpsed her sister's green parka as it made its way around the bend ahead. "Where are we going, Rhuth?"

"Almost there!" Solyana followed the voice and ended up going through several vacant rooms until she found herself at the foot of a spiraling wooden staircase. How had she never seen it before? She tried to look up, but the stairs were so tightly wound, all she saw were wood planks. A squeak of hinges sounded from above. Solyana took the steps quickly as the ceiling came precariously close. Was that snow on the stairs? The steps led up through a wooden attic door, flung open, it revealed a circular room.

"*Stars to heaven...*what is this?" Solyana took the final steps until she was standing in the center of the drafty space. Snow dusted the floor. A gust of wind ruffled her hair through the slats of the naked windows that circled the room, a welcome reprieve. "Rhuth, where are..." But she didn't need to finish her sentence, her eyes growing wide as she realized they were not alone.

"Welcome to the falconry," Rhuth said breathlessly as she turned a slow circle, eyes full of wonder and pride. She pulled a well-worn glove, much too large for her skinny arm, past her elbow and held it up in the air expectantly. Although it was difficult to see in the farthest rafters, Solyana counted seventeen of the massive beasts, each one hooded, each one gripping a perch with deadly sharp talons.

A falcon from one of the higher beams took flight out of the shadows and dropped with a half-hearted screech onto Rhuth's shrouded arm. Rhuth smiled broadly at the dark bird, though Solyana could see through muted light its feathers held more color than met the eye.

"This is Halina." Rhuth gave the bird an affectionate scratch between thick neck feathers.

Solyana wanted to say something, anything, but her mouth was dry. They would get in trouble if anyone found them here, but more importantly, the falcons belonged to the only Falki Tala in Mothmar, and he was not a man to be trifled with.

"You ask why I can't tell Papa," Rhuth mused. "It's because he would find out about *this*. I've been coming up to visit Halina for weeks now, and if he found out, he would forbid it. But I'm ready. I know it. Want to see?" She looked at Solyana brightly, but all Solyana could see were the talons gripping her sister's arm.

"We need to leave, Rhuth." Solyana's voice shook. "This is beyond dangerous, and that's not even taking into consideration Asmund's reaction if he knew we were here."

Rhuth rolled her eyes. "I'm not scared of that blind old man."

"Your falcon is blind, too"—she motioned to its hood—"but that won't stop him from tearing prey, *or you*, to shreds."

"Her," Rhuth corrected, her hand hovering close to the bird's beak. "She told me her name is Halina."

"Rhuth." Solyana stared at her, choosing to ignore her sister's fantastical assumption that the bird spoke to her. "You and I both know those with Predatory Tala are required to have more classes, and more training before ever even tethering to their beast." She took a breath. "You are ten years old. You just started at Sháskol."

"Papa tells me all the time how talented I am."

"Then why not tell him about this?"

"I would get in trouble, like you said." Rhuth's chin lifted in defiance as she raised a hand, and with a jolt, Solyana realized too late what she was doing.

"Do not remove that hood!"

"It's fine. I've done it before!" Rhuth's defiant fingers grasped for the hood in a desperate attempt to prove herself. Solyana lunged to stop her, but the sudden movement frightened both the girl and bird. Rhuth's arm jerked upward, the hood coming partially undone. Halina flapped wildly, her wings beating both girls as they scrambled beneath her.

Her beak open in a silent scream, hood halfway off, the bird broke free of her perch, her wings beating the air, a whirlpool of snow cascading. But the bird miscalculated. With the hood blocking her view, she tore toward the open window, her talons flung out, too close to Rhuth, leaving a gash across her face. Solyana's stomach bottomed out as her sister crumpled to the ground with a scream. Feeling nothing but helpless terror, Solyana couldn't get her legs to work, her eyes roving from bird to sister and back again.

The massive beast continued her upward climb, and just before reaching the window, her hood snagged on a nail. Her roiling body struggled against it, knocking into other falcons, screeches erupting in chaotic dissonance. Finally, Halina broke free and shot out the window near the top of the turret, her hood left behind, a loud scream piercing the sky.

Although it had taken mere seconds for all of it to unfold, Solyana's frozen body finally broke free as she rushed to Rhuth's side. A river of blood poured from her brow to her chin. One of her eyes was completely hidden in the crimson flood, the other stared lazily upward. "Rhuth! No!" She frantically pulled off her scarf to staunch the bleeding. "Talk to me Rhuth. Can you hear me?"

"You...you scared her." Rhuth didn't acknowledge her injury. "I need to find her before..." She blinked, looking like she might pass out. "Before Asmund. She's all alone out there." Rhuth wiped at her eyes, lowered her hands in front of her face, and grew utterly still.

"I can't see," she said in a weak whisper as her body started shaking violently.

Solyana's mind was racing. It was her fault. It was all her fault. She had asked Rhuth to show her. She had spooked the bird. If Rhuth lost too much blood...no. She squeezed her eyes shut, if only to block everything out so her brain could work. One step at a time. "We need to get you to Healer Ashune. Come on."

"But I can't see!" Rhuth's voice was shrill and urgent and it threatened to stop Solyana in her tracks. No, she couldn't let it. Her sister needed her to take control. The bleeding had only gotten worse.

Scooping Rhuth up, Solyana stumbled clumsily through the square in the floor and down the stairs until she was threading the corridors of Sháskol. Where was everybody? The entire school was empty, and it only stoked her rising panic. She remembered the midday meal; everyone was home. Solyana's mukluks slipped on the wooden floor. She looked down. Nausea rolled through her as she realized it was her sister's blood beneath her feet.

"Stay with me, Rhuth!" Solyana wailed as Rhuth's one eye fluttered closed, her face a mess of red. "Oh, Celestials, *please.*" A sob rushed to the back of her throat, but she kept it at bay as she burst into the main hallway.

It, too, was empty. She was hoping a teacher or two had stayed behind, but no. As Rhuth grew heavier in her hands, she lifted her sister's body more securely in her arms and glanced down. Rhuth had slipped into unconsciousness.

Adrenaline pumping, she plotted the fastest route. The Healer's hut was in Austur, below the livestock barns. How long did Rhuth have before she bled out? Without any healing training, Solyana had no way to assess how bad it was.

Finally at the door, she fought to open it, as if the winds themselves had an agenda to keep her in the building. She struggled a moment more before it snapped open, launching them into the whirling snow.

And into darkness.

Solyana looked wildly around. What was happening? It couldn't be any later than early afternoon, yet everything was overcast in deep shadow. It had her questioning time itself. Had the dark months descended early? Was there a storm? The snow, which had been a soft drift just earlier that day, now lashed against her face in icy torrents. A snow storm? That was the only explanation.

Solyana kept Rhuth clutched tight to her in the limited light, their body heat providing some warmth against the cold seeking to burrow into her bones. Solyana trudged frantically forward, stumbling her way across the valley. She vaguely recognized ice beneath her feet, the Spretta River; she was going the right way, at least. She took it in twenty strides, sure on the ice for the first time, the blood warming her arms a reminder of time running out, driving her past her fear.

Something large loomed to her right. She squinted up at it. It was the Temple Celestial! Thank heavens, she was getting somewhere. She barreled on, wind and ice and snow pelting her face until it was numb. She hunched over her sister as best as she could, her steps growing slower. It was too much. No, she had to continue.

"Help!" She finally had the mind to call out. Perhaps someone was out in this torrent. But the wind laughed as it smothered her voice, pushing it back before it crossed the threshold of her lips.

A sound came to her then, from the left, like a scream. The livestock barns stuttered into view, the air itself undulating with snow, ice and debris. The sound was coming from there, an unnerving animal panic that tore through her, setting every nerve on end. What had gotten into the animals? Several creatures joined the cacophony of screams, and she remembered something Rhuth had said only that morning.

When something is brewing, the animals are always the first to know.

Her eyes grew wide. A loud pounding sounded, then another, and another, rhythmic and panicked. She gaped in horror. It was the pounding of animals flinging themselves in desperation against their stalls, their small homes filling with snow, so thick and fast, they were being buried alive. In their last moments, they were sounding the warning drum of something which was impossible.

The fish, the animals, the darkness, and the unending snow; this was no storm.

This was a—

"Blizzard." She felt her lips form the word, but the wind kept it from even her own ears.

It had come far too early and the scope of it too unnatural to be real.

Solyana, though she had never fully stopped, returned to her task with more vigor, running, panting, and careening wildly into the blizzard's unrelenting rush. No one stayed out in the blizzards, they were too dangerous. No, they were death itself. And only occurred once a month, on the Full Moon. But they were still days away from that. This was impossible.

She struggled with her sister's weight, cried out again and again, but her shouts were for no one but the snow. A gap in the storm revealed a glimpse of Austur, where Healer Ashune's hut resided. Then it was gone, veiled behind a sheet of white and cold. She slowed, realizing the enormity of her task, the impossibility of it.

She was going to die.

They were going to die.

Solyana gripped Rhuth in desperation, the only tangible living thing still allowing her to hope. She cocooned Rhuth close to herself, two sisters against the world. The Celestials could not take her.

No, they would not.

But the wind and the cold proved too much, and Solyana's world was pounding noise, deepening black, and soul-crushing fear.

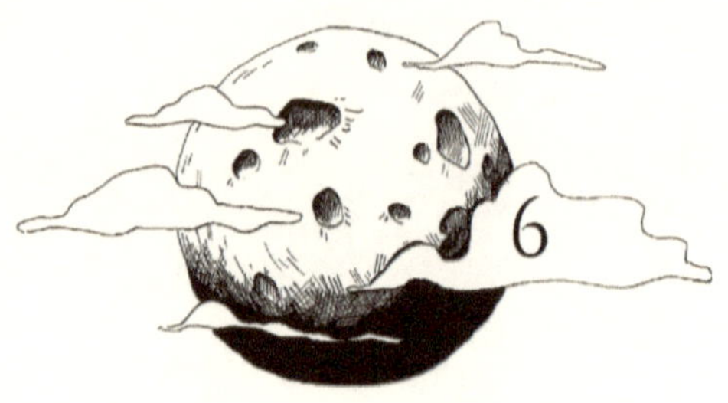

ONLY AN ANIMAL

PALLAH

PALLAH WOKE TO LIGHT streaming through her window. Vámae had long left to greet the sun, her mat empty and blanket folded neatly. It was a pleasant day, and when the sun was out, all Heitt made sure to store up as much energy from it as possible. Pallah peered out of her window to find people strewn all over the grass, looking like statues bathing in beams of light. Those with Heitt held that light deep within until they expelled it. A magic far beyond the depths of Pallah's understanding.

Gathering her things about the room, Pallah knew she wouldn't have time to finish the oiling, late as she was. She dressed and ran her fingers through her colorless, light hair, before snatching her knapsack from the floor. Searching inside, she remembered—only after finding it missing—the Taka Reu scroll was taken by the man called Vil. *Häfa*, she had been hoping to read more of it.

Attempting to avoid her father's detection, she crept into the kitchen only to find a piece of dry toast and a cold egg in the pan. Relieved, she scarfed it down, rinsed the dishes, and left.

She had a class on tanning first, one on knife throwing in the late morning, then her apprenticeship: tracking, for the afternoon. Perhaps she would go back to Eldfall today, find a new tree. Vil's warning drifted in the back of her mind, commanding her not to return.

Well, Vil didn't own the mountain.

The morning was spent salting various hides and scraping rotting flesh off new ones, then she practiced with her knives before lunch. It wasn't as satisfying as her hatchet, but it would do nicely in a pinch.

Finally, she sat next to Ahren at their favorite stone bench. Having forgotten her own meal, he had willingly given half of his to share. He spoke of his carpentry; he was working on something big that he wanted to keep as a surprise for her. It made her smile and she tried to get it out of him, but she didn't really want to know.

Parting ways, Pallah walked to the long open-sided barns that held her apprenticeship. She chose tracking because, as Ahren was quick to point out, she didn't really use her Tala. Choosing a specific animal-focused group would have been unwise. Not because she didn't want to use her Tala, but because she had never been able to truly feel Tala like others described. The ability to manipulate the emotions of another creature had never clicked. No secure hold or tether had ever fully realized to create a solid connection, no clear thread of communication she could pull taut or break. In tracking, however, she was given a free pass of sorts. They didn't actually do any animal manipulation, but focused on tracking and trapping.

The group of teens from Pallah's class stood in a cluster outside the door of the barn as Professor Sherpa slowly ambled over to them. Shaped like an apple with an ample chest, her slumped shoulders fell beneath the height of most of her students.

"Follow me." She waved a plump hand without giving them so much as a glance. The troupe of young people obeyed, the sounds of their leather slippers shuffling over the grass.

Pallah kept her eyes on her feet. They would probably have to pair off, and if she appeared unfriendly, hopefully, her partner wouldn't attempt conversation. The last thing she needed was someone's misplaced small talk slowing her down.

It wasn't that she didn't want friends. Quite the opposite, in fact. If she were honest with herself, she desperately desired the true community Priest Skrifa spoke of. But she knew, as it had happened too often to ignore, friendships required something in trade: a good time, popularity, or humor. Pallah possessed none of these.

"I thought I recognized you," a voice came softly from her left.

Pallah snapped her head to the side and found herself staring at the girl from the night before, her braids in three rows over her head, her eyes bright and playful.

"You!" Pallah whispered back, directing her gaze forward once more.

"Yes," the girl continued. "Me! I'm in your tracking class. Isn't that fun?" She clapped her hands together and scrunched her nose, her freckles bunching. A few of the other students turned toward them at the noise.

"I didn't expect you to attend Lóthkol."

"Oh? Why is that? Do I look too old?" The girl gave a pouty face.

"No, that's not what I—"

"Stop, I'm kidding. It's my last year. Did you think we *lived* on Eldfall? That's cute. No, Pallah, we just blend in well."

"What's your name?" Pallah's cheeks grew warm.

"Karav."

A cool breeze came across from the rippling Vatino Sea as they continued north into The Pines. The group talked amongst themselves as they passed the obelisk detailed with the Gifts, the Hytast, and Lóthkol, all teeming with the people of the valley, each going about their respective work. Once they were settled just outside the tree line, Professor Sherpa asked them to pair off and begin tracking. This time, she expected them to set traps near the creatures' homes. Before Pallah could object, the girl was taking her arm. "You're with me." She grinned. "You could learn a thing or two about blending, my dear."

"Blend?" Pallah pulled her arm away once they were out of view of the others and on a trail Pallah didn't recognize. "I blend. I do it well enough that people don't talk to me. It's how I like it."

"No, no. You don't blend. *That's* why people don't talk to you. If you were to ask any student in this apprenticeship who Pallah is, they would point to you in a heartbeat. But me? You obviously didn't recognize me in the cave, so I'm thinking you never noticed me before," she said. Her confidence was irritating.

"I don't really make it a point to get to know my peers."

"True enough." Karav was still grinning. Pallah's irritation slid toward disdain.

"What do you want from me?"

"Oh, nothing." Karav twirled once, then walked backward facing Pallah. "I think *you* want something from *me*."

Pallah didn't have time for these games and turned away from her, focusing on the trail. Soon enough, she spotted a snapped twig and a group of leaves pushed down. She began following it with purpose.

"There she goes again," Karav said, "always sulking."

Pallah swung around, her face directly above Karav; for once, she was grateful for her height. "*Häfan*, shut up! I'm fine with who I am."

The girl's eyes widened with joyous surprise. "Oh, she's got a mouth on her. Okay...*okay*! We don't mind."

"We?" Pallah raised an eyebrow.

"Our little group." Karav waved her hand dismissively. "Look, you're stubborn, but it's a weakness, not a strength. You should hang out with us sometime. We'd like to get to know you."

"Why would you want *me* in your group?" Pallah could sense her own hope rising, but quickly squashed it down. She didn't know these people. What could they want from her?

"We are quite particular about who we talk to, Pallah. Selective about who we choose to spend our time with. We want to make sure we have similar ideas. I'll admit, finding you yesterday was purely coincidental...but then we pulled that scroll out of your bag."

Pallah's chest tightened. Was Karav threatening her? "I'm not sure what—"

Karav's finger shot up to her lips in a shushing motion and stopped all movement. Pallah heard it then, too, the slight snuffling of a creature. The Pines were the tallest group of woods in the valley; the branches began far above their heads. They crept around the trunks unhindered by stiff needles. Crouching behind a low bush, they heard the thing rummaging on the other side. Peering over, they found a large wild boar, its nose and sharp, curving tusks passing over the ground in great sweeps of its head.

"Got you," Karav whispered and pulled a knife from her belt, at least the length of her palm, thick and made for butchering.

"We're just supposed to trap." Pallah regretted the words as they came out of her mouth. She sounded like Vámae, concerned with rules.

"We're going to have to work on that moral conscience of yours, Pal," Karav said with a grin, using the nickname without permission. She flipped the knife once in her hand, crouched low, and stared at the creature, her free hand pressed into the dirt. "Besides," she whispered, not taking her eyes from the animal, "this *is* a trap."

Eyes roving between beast and being, Pallah furrowed her brow. Was Karav tethered to it? She wasn't supposed to be, but between Karav's stoic face of concentration and the boar's steady walk toward them, Pallah was sure she was. Pallah had once attempted connection with the tame boar at the communal barns, maybe she would have more success with a wild one. But not this one. It was a rule between Tala never to tether to the same animal at the same time; too intimate for the people, too confusing for the animal.

The boar plodded toward them, its teeth much more frightening than the ones that grew on the boar they had back in town. She had never been so close to a large animal like this in the wild, and it scared her more than she cared to admit.

In a flash, Karav was jumping out of the brush, all tiny body and flying braids, shoving the knife directly underneath the beast's chin. Blood burst from the animal, its eyes widened and spun from fear to fury. It bucked and tried to tear away, but Karav held fast and laughed. She pulled the knife from its place and struck it again, directly behind the right shoulder. She twisted it with a grunt.

Pallah's mouth dropped open, her heart thudding hard against her chest. The boar wheezed and collapsed to the ground, twitching in its death throes.

When Karav pulled away, she was panting and wiping blood off her grinning face with her sleeve.

What do we think of her? Personally, I like her. Pallah shook her head. *You have it in you to be like that, too, Pallah.*

Pallah counted to ten.

The boar finally lay still, and the girls met each other's eyes. Karav smiled. "I recognize that look. Haven't you ever killed before?"

"Not like that." Pallah breathed.

"You get the next one, then." Karav wiped her blade over the animal's carcass, clearing most of the blood. "Oh dear..." She tipped her knife toward the animal's belly. "She's a mother...maybe only a few weeks post, if that."

A pang of guilt hit Pallah as she knelt next to the boar and examined its belly. "How can you tell?"

"Right here. See how she's swollen and stretched? She's ready to feed now. Squeeze one of them. You'll see I'm right."

Pallah pinched one of the boar's swollen nipples and squeezed. A stream of white sprayed in an arc, sprinkling Karav's shoes.

"You're in tracking class. It's good to know these types of things. Now, let's find the babes."

"Why?" The guilt deepened in her gut, would they kill the babies?

"To take them home for slaughter."

"I think Professor Sherpa is already going to be upset that we killed one animal." She really needed to stop sounding so much like her twin.

"We won't slaughter them *now...*" Karav sheathed her knife. "Obviously, we'll let them grow. We'll have them added to our stores." She moved forward, tracking the nest, the crunch of brown pine needles under her feet.

On the edge of Austur lived the animals they had been able to trap and keep for their resources. Most Tala, who didn't want to hunt and trap, ended up working there, tending to the animals, growing the farm, birthing babies. Only a few requested jobs in the slaughterhouse.

Each family from Vestur, Sodur, and Austur was given access to a portion of the barn and could store the animals they owned, but in agreement with the council, they also had to be willing to share with the community if the need arose. Pallah thought that part was ridiculous, but she supposed if she wanted to keep something for herself, she would just have to build her own barn near her hut. She briefly thought about bringing a baby boar home for herself, asking Ahren to construct some kind of house for it. Perhaps she could develop an aptitude for boar. Maybe then her father would be pleased. Maybe then he would see she was at least trying to find her aptitude. Maybe then she would finally know herself.

No, she chided. Aptitudes were recognized immediately, within the time it took to come in contact with the animal, sometimes even just thinking about them. It was like breathing, or so she had been told. She just hadn't found hers yet.

Karav was already slipping noiselessly into the wood. Pallah followed, even quieter. Before long, they began finding open plots of land, the ground disheveled and tree trunks scratched from their base up to the height of their knees.

"Do you see the signs?" Karav whispered, glancing at Pallah, who nodded. "There's a big group in these woods, twenty-five, maybe thirty-five with the babes. There's quite a few trees torn up here. The males mark their territory with their tusks."

"Maybe we should just turn back. I don't want to take the wrong baby."

"The wrong baby?" Karav gave her a look. "They're *animals*, Pallah. There's no wrong baby. They're all *meat*. We hunt, we survive, we do what's necessary." She laughed. "I didn't peg you to be such a softy."

"I'm not soft!" Pallah answered too quickly, only affirming Karav's accusations. "I just don't think we can take on an entire pack of boar."

"That's not what you're worried about," Karav said slyly, pulling back a group of tangled weeds. It revealed a litter of four grunting piglets, their tiny hooves clicking together as they scrambled to their feet. They looked terrified. But just as quickly, they calmed. Their bodies relaxed, and one by one, they trotted to Karav, as obedient as if she had raised them herself. "I think we found them." Karav hoisted one up and tossed it to Pallah without looking.

Pallah let out a gasp and hurried forward to snatch the placid beast. Karav laughed. "You really do care for the ugly things, don't you? Leif will like that. Let's bring them back."

They wound their way through the wood and back to Professor Sherpa who was picking at her nails. Her eyes searched them, narrowing as she landed on the piglets in their arms.

"Now...how did we acquire these young things?" Her hooded lids blinked slowly.

Karav spoke up, her voice rising to a pitch Pallah hadn't heard before. "We set up a weighted loop trap, and Pallah spooked them from behind, right Pal?"

"Y-yeah," Pallah stammered, unprepared for the lie. "It was pretty simple."

"Four young boar...was the mother not there? How did you find them?" Sherpa's strict gaze lingered on Pallah now, unblinking. "Using Tala is expressly forbidden in this class."

"Oh, of course, Professor," Karav spoke up, keeping her voice light and airy. "We worked as a team to trap them. The mother must be dead. Perhaps some other Tala got her this morning. You know, now that I say it, I do think I smelled something rotting up there. What happened, babies? Did your Mama not come home?" she addressed the two she held in her arms.

"And we located them through all the signs: tusk marks on the trees, rooting damage, and scat all around the area," Pallah interjected helpfully.

Sherpa waved a hand to quiet their chatter. "Get these to the farm. They'll be added to the lot. You may go."

They walked to the barns, boars still subdued and calm. Karav's Tala was one of the strongest Pallah had ever seen, four boar at once? Most Tala could handle one well, two when necessary. Three? Almost never.

They handed the piglets off to the handler, and Pallah knew the second Karav untethered herself from them. For when she did, they began to scream.

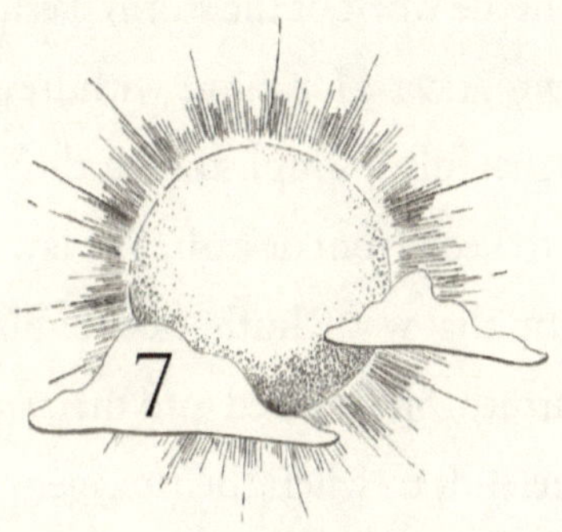

THE PROPHECY

SOLYANA

SOLYANA'S MOTHER WAS A seamstress, a skill passed down from mother to daughter. As a heritage that held both beauty and practicality, it was one of the only art forms Mothmarians encouraged. In fact, those two words described her mother in summary better than any others Solyana could conjure.

She, in contrast, felt much like a crumb, the leftovers of something once much more inviting and sustaining. Living in her mother's shadow, Solyana never allowed it to stop her from gleaning from her mother, seeking her approval, or reveling in her validation. Would Solyana ever receive her praise again? Embrace her again? See her again?

Solyana shifted, her arm was falling asleep. Bringing it back to her side, she brushed the crystalized blood from her sister's hair, frozen and matted as it was. Solyana thought she had been saving them when she had frantically dug a hole just big enough for the two of them curled up and pressed together. She thought she was keeping them from the worst of the storm. Perhaps she had simply prepared their own grave. Her mind withdrew, thoughts full of her mother, thoughts full of simple things, things from childhood. Anything, really, to keep from despair. She lay, too quietly, curled up around the form that was Rhuth, close enough to protect their last remaining warmth. She exhaled into their small space, pushing them closer to the end, to when their oxygen would deplete and their lungs would find nothing but stale air and death. Solyana raised her left arm slowly until her hand was pressed just beneath Rhuth's jaw, where her pulse would be...should be...wasn't.

Rage tore through her like a knife and she felt it all anew. Solyana tried to scream into the void but her throat was so dry it merely croaked. Why was this happening? How? Grief shoved the rage aside as she sobbed, tears hot against the ice of her cheeks. She had to stop; crying exhausted valuable energy. She sniffed and released a slow breath until her mind was like her fingers, numb in the hours since carving their dugout. She was barely able to move each individual finger on her hand, let alone feel a faint heartbeat. She hoped the fault was on her end.

Whether from the cold or Rhuth's bleeding, Solyana wasn't sure which would kill her sister first. If only she had been born Vatin Fera, aptitude for water, or better yet Broad Fera, aptitude for all inanimate things, she could have rescued them from their grave of ice. Tala would even be helpful; she could call her beast to dig them out, to signal someone, call for help. If Heitt wasn't a dying Gift, they wouldn't even be here. She would have simply kept the snow from piling around them, wrapped them in warmth; but here they were. Hours had passed with nothing but diminishing oxygen. She had buried them alive. She had tried to save them, but as always, she wasn't enough.

Adjusting her body again, Solyana scooted closer to Rhuth. She turned her mind to her father and his fireside tales, the one story their people clung to more than the others because it was more than a story; it was a prophecy.

She remembered being five, Rhuth, not yet born, and Fridmey, seven. They sat with at least ten other village children, Fridmey on Mama's lap and Solyana on the ground, just in front of Papa, not wanting to miss a single word.

"So!" Papa bellowed to the gathering of bundled children, squirming and piled in front of him. "We know the prophecies come from these old guys in the mountain. What were they called?"

"Seers!" a child called from the group.

"Right you are Christon, Seers." The fire popped, and Papa's face was cast into shadows, his voice lilting and melodic, enchanting the crowd. "What are some prophecies that have been fulfilled?" He opened his arms wide and scanned the crowd. "Anyone?"

An older girl with wispy dark hair spoke up from Solyana's left, "The Great Moose Cull."

"Yes, Avahna. Good one. The Seers prophesied we would see a large population of moose at the Blue Moon following the Eclipse. It fed our valley for two years."

Awe broke out from the children who, at this point of their lives, were starting to understand the difficulties of gathering and hunting daily. "Anyone else?"

"When the sea froze." One of the grandmothers had sat to listen. Solyana remembered peering over Mama's shoulder at the square-jawed old woman sitting with the children, her eyes sparkling in the firelight. "Well, it was long before your time, children...my time, even. But we have records."

"Indeed, we do, Grandmother Eronoh." Papa gave her a respectful partial bow. "So even prophecies that have come and gone before we were even alive hold weight. They tell us that the Seers and their scribes were a much-needed part of Mothmar history and culture, even today. Can you imagine the Vatino Sea being completely broken? Waves crashing and waters rippling?"

The kids giggled, and a few 'no's rang into the night.

"But we know these things were true, at some point. This world wasn't always one of ice...which brings us to one prophecy that has not come to be. One that doesn't have a specific lunar cycle or date. It remains a mystery, even these hundreds of years from the night it was foretold. It's the one that foretells our world transforming from white to *green*." The fire gave a loud *crack,* and a few children near the front jumped, but not Solyana.

"Anyone know the prophecy?"

The boy called Christon raised his hand, but Solyana's had been quicker, her tongue caught between her lips. Staring at her father with such admiration, she thought she would burst.

"Yes, Solyana." Papa's face softened.

Her tiny voice pierced the night. "*In centuries, the darkness will bring the world to a cusp of white, frigid and unending. But when all hope seems lost, and the world knows nothing but white, there will come one who will bring green. One who must follow the path of the sky. One who is all light to stand to the one who is all dark, of which there will be two. One who possesses the three as one, who will save us all through mastery of it. You will know this one by the mark, known by the one who brings the white."*

"Good job, my Light." Marus winked, and Solyana beamed. "This eternal winter won't last forever!" He spread his arms wide, drawing the audience back to himself. "Surely this is our year, my friends, the year the green will be brought back to Mothmar. Once, we lived in a world of seasons, of green grass and delicious fruits of the ground. It has been over three centuries since Mothmar has become a nation of cold and winter, but no longer! We will rise again in the warmth of the sun. By the Celestials, the chosen one will be known to us soon."

He paused dramatically, turning in a slow circle, taking in both young and old. "Your eyes be upward!"

"And be filled with light!" responded the people in unison.

Solyana came back to herself, to the cold coffin with Rhuth beneath the snow. Had she heard something? She could have sworn...

She shifted again and thought back to the prophecy. Her father was always so sure it would be soon, "The Great Thaw" or "The Green" or whatever he felt like calling it at the time. A traitorous anger rose into her throat. If that prophecy had just come true, she wouldn't be in this position. Rhuth would be alright. Her people wouldn't be ravaged by these storms.

Solyana took a breath and almost gagged. What was that smell? It had been floating around her senses, but now it seemed to intensify. She knew, with death, bodies ridded themselves of waste, but it was a different kind of smell, more rotten, less like bodily fluid. She couldn't shake the thought that it was coming from her.

"I guess," Solyana's voice was hardly there, "you answered my prayer." She chuckled, but it sounded more like a hiccup. "My fate has certainly changed." She took in a shallow breath, and the grief returned, rolling over Solyana as the truth of what was happening hit her again. "Save her. Just save Rhuth."

A tear fell down her face. When it reached her cheek, something about its touch burned like fire under her skin. Sleep was overtaking her; in spite of all she knew about freezing to death, she was ready to allow it.

A howl resounded, long and more importantly, close. She blinked. She *did* hear something. But her willpower had faded, the edges of her mind grown fuzzy toward sleep, or finally death, she wasn't sure which. She struggled to remember why it was so important to care.

Another howl, too close to be chance.

Her eyes shot open, the acrid smell pushing her into wakefulness. The packed snow was shifting about her, though not the precise movements of a Vatin Fera. No, it felt frantic, yet patterned...and she knew then that it was a wolf above her, digging her out.

She assumed the wolf was tethered to an Ulfur Tala. Solyana wanted to shout, to let them know where she was, but she had no voice left. She hardly had enough air for her next breath. Another worse thought struck her. What if it wasn't tethered to anyone? What if it was simply a predator looking for its next meal?

Snow dusted her face, which made her gasp in surprise. The animal had made faster progress than she thought possible. Whether the beast was tethered or not, her first danger became suffocation, as snow began falling in large chunks. Pain shot through every nerve as she rolled on top of Rhuth, keeping her body weight dispersed on shaking arms and legs. She pressed her forehead to Rhuth's and only an icy chill passed between them.

The snow rolled over them as the animal, still digging, was close enough now to hear. It was panting. She could hear the sweet inhale of breath that her own lungs were burning for now.

A muffled voice came through the snow. She couldn't hear a complete sentence but heard, "Good—still—up!" Solyana, having prepared herself to fight the thing with her bare hands, if need be, could hardly enjoy the relief of a human voice as the makeshift cave completely collapsed. Paws began digging into her back for a moment before they stopped. The wolf was standing atop her, whining and shifting from foot to foot.

"Vinur, off," the man's voice came again, close and warm. Arms encircled her waist and shoulders as she was lifted from snow. She opened her eyes, but everything remained dark and blurred. Her face burned with such ferocity she almost cried out, but it paled as she inhaled sweet air. She drank it in, life itself.

The stranger laid Solyana on the ground and wiped the snow from her eyes. The brush of his fingers made her inhale sharply from pain, her lungs gasping and sputtering like a landed fish. Why was her face hurting? Rhuth was the one with the cut, Solyana hadn't remembered doing anything during the panic.

"She-she-she—" Her tongue would not work, her lips were heavy, immobile. Solyana blinked rapidly, confusion pouring over her as her sight was slow to return. Was she looking at the sky? She was seeing oranges, pinks, and—yes, it must be dawn. Had she really been under the snow all night? She brought her hand up to her face, the burning sensation ceaseless. Her numb fingers felt nothing at first, but then a strange texture. When she pulled her hand away, sticky black strands came back with them. What *was* that?! She wiped her hand on her parka, desperate to get the unknown substance off.

The blurry form of a person loomed before her. She didn't recognize them, but was pretty sure it was a man, although his hair was almost as long as her own. Solyana's vision came back into clarity, and she tried again to speak.

"She-she's...still...there." She raised a slow-moving hand toward Rhuth, who was being pawed at by a...dog? She had sworn she had heard a wolf.

"Good boy, Vinur." The man helped the dog uncover Rhuth and pulled her onto a waiting sled before turning back to Solyana.

He was tall, almost her father's height. His hair was sleek and brushed the furs wrapping his shoulders. He wasn't wearing a parka. Those three things were all she could take in before her eyes fluttered closed once more. She just wanted sleep.

"Can you stand?" His voice came out clean and bright, so at odds with her heavy pull toward slumber. When she didn't answer, he picked her up and laid her on his sled, his scent of pine needles, damp cave, and smoke dispersing that rotten smell.

Solyana opened her eyes to see her sister, their faces so close she would barely have to move to touch noses, but she didn't; the fear of feeling nothing but ice terrified her.

"Is she alive?" Solyana whispered, but the man didn't answer as he climbed onto the skis of his sled and shouted a command. They lurched forward, and the rocking motion, coupled with the sounds of crunching snow, sent her straight to sleep.

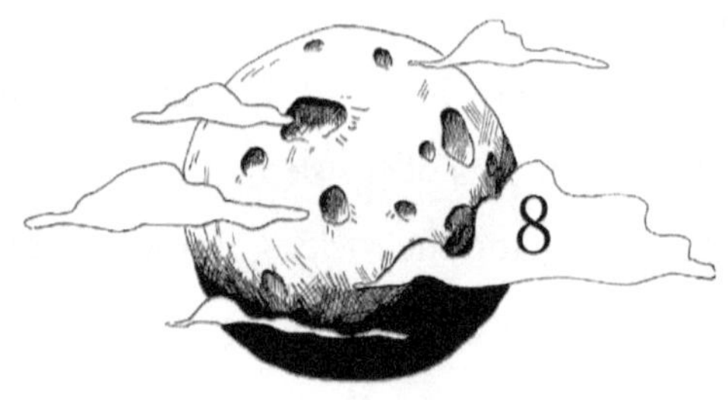

TAKA REU

PALLAH

PALLAH FOUND HERSELF FOLLOWING Karav into the woods for the second time that afternoon. Though this time into White Wood, the birch forest. Usually, she would need to go straight home for dinner, but with the Feast of Haust the following day, she knew Vámae wouldn't be there. Perhaps Mother, as well. And Ahren was probably still helping Father build the new altar. She wouldn't be missed, or at least that's what she hoped.

"So, you're saying your aptitude isn't even for boar?" Pallah asked. They had been discussing Gifts.

"Yeah, I'm pretty certain mine is something aquatic," Karav said with a shrug.

"Seriously?"

"It's hard to explain, like a really deep pull to the west and south. That's how I know there are bodies of water there without even going."

"Then you should go to Kana Ocean, or even Skrim Sea, and find out. I went with my family once—" She opened her mouth but stopped herself from saying she didn't tether to anything as she had hoped. Karav didn't need to know that.

"Did you go during whale season?"

Pallah shrugged. She didn't know much about whaling, although she should, as most Tala kept up to date on most animal migration and mating patterns. Her lack of actual experience kept her from learning more than she needed; she just didn't see the point.

The ground grew steeper making Pallah's lungs burn. She looked over her shoulder and through White Wood, at the water of the Vatino below. It was whipped up more than usual, the wind frothing the waves. She glanced out at her valley. The edge of Austur was visible from here, the eastern village, and just the tip of Sodur, her own village in the south. Crag and rock surrounded their valley on all sides, and just to the northeast was the towering mountain of Eldfall, where they were climbing now.

Pallah wouldn't call herself well-traveled by any means; her father had never seen the point of traveling farther from the Temple Celestial than needed. Mothmar was a large country, and routes through mountainous terrain were difficult to maintain. But she had been west through Kana Forest to Kana Ocean with her mother. Several Tala, she knew, traveled yearly to trade in whale, seal oil, and large ocean fish.

To the north, after the dense, needled floor of The Pines, mountain ranges jutted between a few small towns, until they finally gave way to Thonethren. The only city near them that was twice the size of their three villages combined. Her father had nothing good to say of Thonethren. He always said evil lurked there.

To the south, there was Shadow Wood which led to Skrim Sea; it teemed with tales of monsters dwelling in the deep. No one swam in Skrim. Getting there was less rocky, the terrain more marsh and bog, fat with perpetual rain. Pallah had never visited.

To the east of Eldfall, if you were able to make it over the Hasta mountains and through the pass, there was expansive land teeming with animals, valleys, rivers, and smaller bodies of water. More villages, other cities, and towns stretched across the way. With the Temple Celestial in their valley, most of the people from Pallah's village never found reason to go into eastern Mothmar. What other reason is there to travel than to please the Celestials? They did, however, occasionally receive news from people traveling on centennial holidays, or from a Leirman looking to sell his wares; they always had something fresh and exciting.

Steadily going up Eldfall, Pallah realized they were going a different direction than the cave entrance from where she had rescued her bag the day before. How had she gotten roped into this? She was naturally untrusting. If she was being honest, the only reason she was going was to cover her back. Those people knew she'd had an ancient scroll. They had something to hold over her now...the leverage rankled her.

"I thought your group met up that way?" She motioned her left hand toward her hatchet tree.

"That's our old place. Plus, you have to squeeze through that *häfan* hole in the wall." She shook her head, her braids dancing.

"Kristjan forgot something there, so we took the trip. You'll meet him and the rest soon, Pal."

Pallah blinked a few times. Her mother had called her Pal since she was young. She summoned the courage to correct Karav but decided against it. She grit her teeth and kept on walking.

After some time, they arrived at Torrah Falls, loud and roaring in their ears. Standing halfway up the waterfall, the water crashed boldly in front of them, daring them to approach.

Darmál cave, that lay behind the base of Torrah Falls, was well known among the students of the valley and undoubtedly their parents before them. It was a favorite for general debauchery; couples used its privacy; teens used it for scub and cliff diving. Pallah had gone once, but Ahren had been with her. A few years ago now, Ahren had been young and nosy. They had uncovered one set of kissing couples and stolen someone else's drink before Pallah decided it was time to go.

But they weren't at the base. Darmál was far below them. Midway up the falls and behind the crashing water, Karav led her to an almost imperceptible path that narrowed to a ledge. It wound its way just behind the pounding falls. How had she never seen it before? She glanced down, her heart racing and head dizzy, as she peered over into the salty sea far below.

Karav shouted something, but the volume of water before them stole her voice. Pallah shook her head and pointed to her ear, and Karav nodded and motioned to her feet, slipping off one leather shoe, then the next.

Pallah removed her shoes in kind and thought more about Karav's intentions. Perhaps they wanted her to attempt to use the

Taka Reu? She had never discovered her aptitude. Most children of their valley knew their aptitude by the time they were five; she was sixteen, and still had no clue. Her chest constricted at the thought. Maybe the Taka Reu was the answer...maybe this was what she was missing all along? Or maybe this was just a group of dropouts who drank scub and stole people's knapsacks.

Karav delicately crept onto the ledge and disappeared into the mist. Taking a deep breath, Pallah followed, trying carefully not to slip on the algae that grew at her feet. After a terrifying count of twenty, she stepped from the narrow ledge to the stony floor of a narrow cave that stretched deep, too far and dark to see.

With the falls behind them, Karav hooked her shoes to her belt, which had all sorts of different pockets, hooks, and loops filled with different things. Pallah was about to put her own shoes back on when something stopped her. The ground was warm. Uneven and rocky, but warm, most unlike the dank cool of the cave below the falls. Karav didn't seem to notice, her shoes swinging over the curve of her hips, making her way into the deepening dark.

Pallah slowed, running her hand along the cave's warm walls. Her fingers traced its grooves until they passed through something thick and soft, like grass. She pulled some away from the wall. It *was* grass. She furrowed her brow. Grass growing on the surface of a tunnel, through a mountain, in the *dark*? She explored back toward the entrance and found a patch of clover. She continued slowly toward Karav, far ahead now, until her hand brushed against something longer. She plucked it; a flower, though she couldn't tell what kind.

I like these people. The voice whispered, so unexpected she jumped and flattened herself to the wall. Was this how it was going to be now? The voice was speaking more than it ever had before. When it first came, it had been once a week. Now it seemed to be coming several times a day. But then again, it could still be her own mind, right? She shook her head, willing it to leave her.

A small flame burst to light as Karav struck some flint, the sparks catching a torch ensconced on the wall far ahead. Following the narrowing light, Pallah was hit by an unexpected breeze. She looked up to find a dark tunnel branching upward, the walls of it narrow enough to press her arms between one side and the other. She could probably shimmy upward. Harsh grooves lined the sides. The cool wind came again, blowing her hair off her shoulders.

Karav's voice echoed with sarcasm from up ahead. "Did you get lost?"

"No," Pallah said distractedly, as she moved away from the tunnel. She would ask about that later.

"Welcome to The Cove," Karav said, arms outstretched, "in all its glory."

"It's"—Pallah's eyes roved over the large cave, unable to hide the shock from her face—"amazing." It was nothing like the ominous cave she had squeezed her way into only the day before. The Cove was a work of art. Large braziers held glowing flames that extended high toward the tall ceiling above. Various pelts of large beasts lined the floor, dried so perfectly the hair of the animals provided a soft carpet. Pillows made of seal leather, by the looks of them, were clumped together in such an aesthetically pleasing way that

Pallah couldn't help but press a hand to each in turn. However, the truly captivating part was neither the pelts nor the pillows, but the meadow that blanketed the cave floor and walls. Lush grass, beautiful flowers, clover, and a few abnormally tiny trees decorated the cave wherever she turned, heavy with fruit.

"Kristjan does all the decorating," Karav said with a wave of her hand. "I think it's a bit much, but it keeps us comfortable."

"*Häfa*," Pallah cursed, still disbelieving. "How do...how does he do the grass? The flowers? How is this possible?"

Karav opened her mouth to answer, but the rest of the group arrived, their chatter, laughter, and clear camaraderie made Pallah smile by association. They seemed so different from before, when they had been all stoic glances and mocking looks in the shadows.

"Guys," Karav spoke above the clamor and motioned to Pallah. Their eyes turned at once in her direction, and the grin fell from Pallah's face. "Remember this one?"

There was silence. Were they waiting for her to say something?

"Hi, I'm Pall—" But at the same moment, one of the guys in the group spoke, and it created an awkward jumble causing a few of them to snicker. Pallah's face grew hot and she stared at the floor.

"Everyone, calm down." A man stepped forward with wheat-colored hair and kind sky-blue eyes. "Hi, Pallah." He stretched out his hand, interrupting her abashed downward stare.

They clasped forearms, and she locked eyes with the man she remembered as Vil. Perhaps a few years older than she, he was staring at her so intently, color rushed to her cheeks. "I'm Vilem, but everyone calls me Vil." His voice was kind, and his light hair softened his straight facial features, framing his temple.

"Hello," she said quietly, and before she knew it, the rest of the group was lining up behind him to introduce themselves.

"Leif," the next member said, stepping forward with a firm shake of her arm. His orange-red hair was braided in one large plait down his back. He was strong as an oak and towered over her, which didn't happen often, considering her own height was well above average.

"I'm Rolf, and this is my little brother, Kristjan." Rolf, reedy and small, gave her the customary arm shake and motioned to a boy twice his size, both in height and breadth. Kristjan gave a small wave. Everything about their size was in opposite, but their faces, identical.

"Nice to meet you." Pallah chuckled. Both were the color of light cedar, their hair a matching shade of dark brown. "Are you guys twins?"

"No, eighteen months apart. Rolf here just got the short end of the deal," Kristjan said with a crooked grin, his voice much higher-toned than his smaller, but older, brother's.

"It's getting old, Kristjan. Seriously, jokes can become stale."

"Thank you for having me," she said quickly, glancing from one to the next in succession until she landed on Karav. There was a lull, as if they were waiting on her to speak.

"Why am I here?"

No one answered, but Vil held up a finger in the air, twirled it once, and the group broke apart with purpose, each member adeptly completing a particular task. Karav began stoking a fire. Rolf and Kristjan were busy lighting candles, and Leif was jogging out toward the waterfall, tea kettle in hand.

Vil stepped around Pallah until their shoulders brushed. "May I call you Pal?" he asked, eyes trained on the group.

"Yes," she said, almost too quickly, glad he thought to ask. "Pal, Pallah, whatever you want." She clamped her lips shut.

He smirked. Their shoulders touched again, and shiver ran through Pallah's body. "Pal, the lot of us have been meeting up together a little under a year now. It was just me and Karav at first, Leif joined only a few days later, so I guess you could name the three of us the founders, or what have you. Rolf and Kristjan joined after four months, and Issha just started with us a month ago."

"Issha?" She hadn't met anyone by that name.

"She's standing watch at the falls." He motioned toward the mouth of the cave. Pallah thought she caught the silhouette of someone leaning against the wall. "I'm sure you'll meet her later." He glanced at her sideways. "And you, Pallah, you will join us tonight."

So, they wanted her in their group, but why? Pallah had never been picked for anything, unless it was her father doing the choosing. Experience taught her if they were choosing her specifically, it was for something they didn't want to do.

"Did I say something?" Vil turned to face her directly. He seemed to intuit her thoughts. "You're worried about our intentions, aren't you?" He placed his hands on her crossed arms, one above each elbow, and gave a reassuring squeeze. Pallah's knees felt like water, no one touched her, not like that. "It's hard finding people like us—wolves among sheep—without giving away who we are and sending the sheep bleating for the shepherd." A faraway look grew in Vil's eyes for a moment, then he was back. "You're a wolf, Pallah, unafraid to question the narrative, brave enough to seek truth when it's hidden deep in history." Pallah swallowed hard. He was referring to the scroll, she was sure of it. "We, too, ask why, instead of adhering to blind obedience. Pallah..." Vil spread his arms wide, releasing his hold on her. "We are the Taka Reu."

Pallah tore her eyes from him only to see each member, save Issha, sitting around the fire, steaming mugs in their hands. How had they done it all so quickly? They looked at her expectantly, and Pallah had a terrifying thrill it was one of those moments in life that changed the trajectory of everything. Tonight could change her world in the deepest, most abrupt way possible, and she couldn't wait.

Vil turned to his group where Karav held a mug out for him. He took it without thanks and held it high, a toast.

"We follow generational tradition no longer. Has it not proved wavering and ineffectual?" He paced around the room in a slow circle of his comrades. A soft myriad of assent rippled through them. "The Temple Celestial teaches the Celestial's power while ignoring the greatest source, resting just below their feet, hiding it from the rest of us. We demand access to the ancient scrolls of the Taka Reu; we demand equality in information; we demand our human right to choose."

Tension in the room steadily rose with every fevered breath Vil took. A strange mix of dread and inexplicable power filled Pallah.

"Preach!" Rolf thumped his palm against the grass-covered ground.

"Truth!" Karav pumped her fist, grinning wildly.

"Dastardly!" Leif bellowed.

"That's the crime, is it not? The proclamation of a thorough education at Lóthkol, when it's really the Temple Celestial's hand in everything. Chief Olafur and Priest Skrifa bedded together, indoctrinating the youth with handpicked, brainwashing tools. The Celestial Serviseers keeping a tight hold on all scrolls exiting and entering the Temple."

Vil's eyes no longer slid to each face, but instead, jerked back and forth in heightened excitement, his voice growing bolder. It echoed through the tunnel, reaching the silhouette of Issha still standing guard at the mouth. The zeal that emanated from this man was so fresh and new; Pallah had never come across anything like him. But that wasn't completely true. She lived with someone very much like this passionate man. Someone who stood like a rock on the extremes of his belief, who won obedience and submission through words and intimidation.

Physical pain twisted her insides as she thought of Vil being so like her father...but he wasn't, not truly. There was a core difference, a stark contrast she latched onto like a life preserver. Pallah, Ahren, Vámae, and although their mother never spoke out against him, her mother too—they hated him because he led by fear. But this man, Vilem? Pallah surveyed the smiling and engaged faces of the people around her. They *loved* him. They drank him in, deep and true.

"They have their hand in our education, in our families, at social gatherings. Our entire life is this dance to the celestial gods that we have no proof exist. We need those hidden scrolls...we need the information that could make us stronger, that could make us...exponentially more skilled in our craft." He bent down, a second mug appearing in his hand. He held it out for Pallah. "Someone in our midst has already proven useful, tactful, and resourceful enough to steal a very important piece of information."

Pallah realized with a jolt that he was talking about her. So, this was the true reason they brought her here. They thought her a competent thief when, in reality, it was opportunity and her need for chaos that had driven her to do it. They didn't want her for her, but for what she could do for them. If she was going to extricate herself, now was the time to do it. But they knew...they knew what was in that scroll. Though they had it now, it had been a crime to take it. Would they turn her in?

They want you. They need you. The voice was so soft, like an echo of her own thoughts.

"The plan, my friends, my family, is to take the scrolls for ourselves. A week from today, we raid the Temple Celestial! What say you?"

A chorus of cheers rang up, the cave amplifying the noise to make it seem like much more than their small band of six. Pallah stared at the mug in her hands, unsure when she had accepted it. Vil wrapped an arm around her, hand gripping her waist, as he cheered with the rest of them.

"To Pallah!" he proclaimed to the room.

"Pallah!" they cheered.

Then five mugs were drained at once. Pallah waited a moment, watching them tip the liquid down their throats. Things had escalated too quickly. Was she really going to join their group? And under the pretense of her capabilities of stealing scrolls? She had taken *one* scroll, and it was just happenstance. It wasn't planned. But they did seem to like her, even if they just wanted her help.

She thought of her time with Karav in tracking class, her maniacal laughter as she had killed the boar. Most would be terrified of her; her brother and sister would be. But Pallah felt a strange curiosity instead. She liked these people. Even if they were using her, she had never had anyone include her in anything before.

But how would she hide her relationship with them from her family? Sodur wasn't small, but it certainly wasn't large. She would be hard-pressed keeping anything a secret.

They want you. You. Not your twin.

Looking into the eyes of the hope-filled people all around her, she made her decision. Whatever intentions they had for her, she would comply. It would be worth it—it had to be. Then perhaps she would find the family who accepted her for what she was, not for what she wasn't.

Pallah drank the contents of her mug in three deep swallows.

She was unsurprised to find that it wasn't tea.

The scub went down easy, and it was well into the evening by the time it wore off. Pallah didn't regret a moment of it.

During that time, she had gotten to know the group in a much deeper way. The scub affected all of them; no one was exempt. Karav got incredibly flirtatious and grabby. Leif became emotional, spending the entire time sobbing about his grandmother and his pet rabbits; Rolf and Kristjan consoled him, impishly handing him a dirty sock instead of a handkerchief, and cackling behind their hands. Issha had remained at the mouth of the cave, ever vigilant. And Vil? He became absolutely hilarious, his former passion replaced with a constant stream of jokes and teasing. Pallah couldn't get enough of him.

Slowly, they all returned to themselves and cleaned up the area, doused the fire, and spread ash. Pallah looked around the place, a sudden longing to stay...perhaps she could find a place to sleep among the grass and fruit trees—but no. Her father would come looking. They couldn't have that.

"Don't forget the Feast of Haust is tomorrow. Let's use it as the distraction it is," Vil said as they all trickled down the cave's long entrance. "We'll meet at Eld Plateau, discuss plans."

There were a few mumbled assents and waves as everyone left, bleary-eyed and wobbly. Pallah wondered how they planned on scaling the narrow ledge. Images of them careening drunkenly over the side brought a dark chuckle to her lips.

"Will you come tomorrow?" Vil looked hopeful, and it pleased Pallah. "We can go any time after the feast begins."

The Feast of Haust was the annual festival that welcomed autumn. There were always tables filled with the best foods, games to play, music, and art exhibits to peruse. Pallah enjoyed going each year with Ahren and Vámae; she wasn't keen on missing it, though it would be different this year, with Vámae so heavily involved. Pallah missed her twin, if only a little. They had grown apart these last few months.

"I can meet whenever," she said, still unsure of what to do but not wanting Vil to think she cared about the feast.

"Great"—he smiled at her as they wound their way back down the cave—"we need to clarify our goals at that meeting. Access to the Taka Reu scrolls is imperative, and once we get strong enough in the Dark Gifts, we can begin to contradict Priest Skrifa openly. No one is going to take us seriously if we aren't competent in our craft. Then we can really start canvasing for others to join, pull some people away from that *häfan* temple of false gods."

Pallah had never heard someone talk so openly about the Celestials being false. Her father would keel over with rage. "So, you're going to teach me to use the Dark Gifts...instead of my Tala?"

"It's so much better, Pallah. You don't know the half of it. With the Celestials, the energy you're using for your Gift is traveling all the way from the sun, moon, and stars, right?"

"Yeah."

"Well, with the Taka Reu, it imbues us with energy straight from the Mother herself."

"The Mother?"

Vil stamped with his foot and grinned, signifying the ground beneath them. "She's right here. And she's ours for the taking."

Pallah rolled this over in her mind, a mix of anxiety and excitement making her stomach churn. It was dark in the cave's exit, all light extinguished before them. Vil's hand reached for her own.

"Stay with me"—he gave her hand a squeeze—"I'll lead us out." Pallah inhaled sharply. He was holding her hand. Was this normal for Vil? Did he hold Karav and Issha's hands, too? It was just because it was so dark. That was the only reason. But his hand was strong and warm and felt like freedom. She grinned wildly, uncaring as the darkness covered her face. They passed by a cold draft, and Pallah looked up at the tunnel, though she saw nothing but darkness.

"That was really cold." She laughed. "Any idea what's up there?"

"Up there?" He jerked his head toward the ceiling. "I'm not sure, probably just another entrance but up higher. Eldfall is filled with holes. It's a wonder it doesn't just collapse."

"Huh." They reached the end of the cavern. Releasing his hand reluctantly, they stood together on the ledge. Vil turned to her with a twisted grin before stretching out a hand to Torrah Falls, concentration set in his brow. The water came to a halt, the last of it trickling down and splashing into the sea below. Then he bowed slightly, motioning for her to walk ahead of him. She smiled. He must be Vatin Fera, and a strong one too. Or was he using the Taka Reu? There was so much to learn. She didn't know it was possible to stop the flow of the falls, but there they were. Dry. They hopped off the ledge, and the falls thundered again, as if nothing had stayed its flow.

They wound their way down the mountain, over the floating bridge, and into the courtyard. Quiet, Pallah was waiting for Vil to say goodnight and break away, but he didn't. She grinned to herself. The grounds were quiet, it was late, and the courtyard was filled with scaffolding, booths, and tables prepared for tomorrow. They passed through it slowly, Pallah letting herself drift to the memories of every Feast of Haust before.

"Did you find out everyone's Gifts tonight?" Vil's voice came through the darkness as he let his hand run across some wooden scaffolding. "I'm curious how open everyone got with you on some scub."

Pallah blushed hard at the mention of the plant. "Well...I learned Rolf and Kristjan are both Eldurs. My mom and sister are Heitt as well, but only my sister, Vámae, is an Eldur."

"Vámae is your sister?"

"My twin, actually," Pallah said, rolling her eyes.

"You're kidding." Vil turned to her, the full moon lighting his handsome face. "I've seen her. You two couldn't be more different."

Pallah's heart dropped to her stomach, and it took everything in her to keep jealousy from spreading to her face. He already knew Vámae? "Yeah...she's always been beautiful." She walked faster toward Sodur.

"No, Pallah." He jogged to catch up and grabbed her arm, turning her toward him. "I meant...you're cool and open to new things. Vámae seems pretty...devout."

"She's a pain in the ass." Pallah smirked.

Vil laughed, easing the tension. "Kristjan and Rolf have worked with her before. I've never actually met her."

Pallah nodded. "Yes, they told me they were Heitt. Makes sense." She began walking again.

"So, who else?"

"Well let's see...Leif is Tala, his aptitude is for hare." Pallah snickered. "Just very unexpected, that one. He's such a big guy, I just imagine him surrounded by tiny hopping rabbits." Vil grinned and nodded her on. "Karav thinks her Tala is something aquatic, though...the way she handled some boar in our trapping class...I would have bet my life on her aptitude being boar."

"She's the best Tala I know," Vil offered.

"I didn't meet Issha"—Pallah shrugged, then punched Vil lightly in the arm—"and you with the water trick up there?"

"Yeah, yeah, I'm Vatin Fera," he said nonchalantly. "Most experienced in liquid form. And yes...Issha. She's our newest recruit, aside from you." He smiled at her. "She hasn't told any of us what her Gift is. I'm starting to think it's something dangerous"—he wiggled his eyebrows and laughed—"all the better to keep her around, eh?"

Pallah laughed and quickly covered her mouth as her voice carried over the huts and cabins. Most of Sodur lay asleep.

"Pallah?" Ahren sat on the front stoop of their home but stood quickly as the two came into the moonlight. Pallah came to a dead stop. She hadn't realized how close they were. If her family saw her with Vil, her father would want a detailed report of who he was, his family, their status in the Temple Celestial. But it was Ahren...surely, he would keep her secret. He had kept so many before.

"Ahren." Pallah hurried to him and away from Vil, hoping he would get the hint and leave...he didn't.

"Who's this?" Ahren stood somehow taller than before as he took a step to come between Pallah and Vil.

"I'm Vil." Vilem reached out to clasp Ahren's arm, but it was left hanging in the air. "Ok"—he pulled it back—"I promise, I've returned her exactly as I found her." He smirked. Ahren stared stonily across at him.

"What village are you a part of?" he demanded.

"Ahren, stop, come on. Let's go inside." Pallah tugged on his arm and, for the first time, felt entirely too small next to her younger brother. He didn't budge.

"I get around." Vil still had that smirk on his face, and Pallah wished more than anything he would just turn around and leave. Her father could come out at any minute. Ahren stared at him with so much venom that Pallah swelled with a strange mix of pride and shame. "I'll see you tomorrow, Pal." Vil waved in her direction. "Nice to meet you, Aaron." Pallah couldn't tell if he purposefully pronounced his name wrong, or if it was an accident. Then he turned the way they had come and disappeared into the night.

Ahren turned on her the minute he was gone. "Pal? Tomorrow? I get around?" his eyes wild with accusation.

Pallah huffed. "He's just a friend. Come on, I'm tired." She tried pulling him into the house, but he stood, unmoving.

"Look, Pallah, I don't usually care what you do with your time; go up in the woods, attack helpless animals, whatever." She gave him a strange look. Did he really think she did that? "But this guy is bad news. I've seen him hanging around Darmál Cave. My friends tell me he and his gang meet somewhere up there, and they're a part of"—he lowered his voice to a whisper—"*The Taking.*"

The Taking was how most children referred to the Taka Reu in fireside stories, a less controversial way of stating that someone was a heretic. Pallah thought quickly, not wanting to lie, but also trying to come up with a plausible explanation that didn't give away her new friends. Could she tell Ahren the truth? She wasn't sure. As she and Vámae grew apart, she felt a small fissure dividing her and Ahren as well. Maybe it was best she revealed as little as possible.

"I don't know where you heard those rumors, but I met him through my tracking class. We just hung out while I practiced with my hatchet."

Ahren raised his eyebrows skeptically.

"By the Celestials, I promise," she said, holding a hand over her heart and then up to the sky. "We have to get up early for the festival. Can I sleep?"

Ahren gave a slow nod as they turned to the modest home together.

"Just friends, right?" he asked with a bit of his usual playfulness.

"Just friends." Pallah shoved him with a grin.

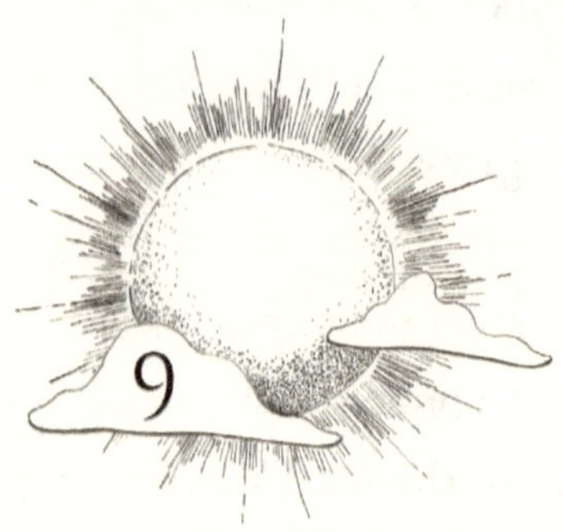

CRESCENT MOON

SOLYANA

THERE WAS A FIRE somewhere. Solyana could feel the warmth penetrate even her deepest chill. Dragging her eyes open, she didn't recognize where she was. A blanket was wrapped tightly around her, trapping her next to a stone hearth, her body thawing and coming back to life.

There was movement behind her, but she hadn't the strength to turn, solely content to sit and be thankful for the life she thought had been taken.

"It's time. It's finally time. I've waited so long. And finally. It is here," a woman's voice crooned, the sound of mortar and pestle coming together just behind where Solyana lay. She recognized the voice, but from where? It wasn't anyone in her family. "You, my dear, are my guarantor. I know, I know...but we all must make sacrifices, mustn't we? Ah, you're awake. Yes, you there, on the floor, Solyana of Vestur."

Solyana turned slowly to face the Priestess of the Temple Celestial, the pestle gripped in her knobby fingers. "Priestess Avi," Solyana whispered.

"Yes, yes. Welcome back. Sit up when you can, drink your tea."

There was a steaming mug keeping warm by the fire. She sat up cautiously, reached over, and winced at the pain in her aching hands.

"Just a bit of frostbite. Nothing to concern yourself over," the old woman reassured.

"Where is Rhuth? And what about my parents? Do they—"

"Hush, girl. She's here." The priestess motioned with the pestle before turning again. "But don't get up just yet. And stop with your questions." She paused, then softened. "Drink your tea, dear. I'll explain everything." The priestess raised her eyebrows. "Go on."

Solyana took a sip. It was saxifrage. Had the priestess known that was her favorite? It warmed her belly as the fire warmed her back.

"Yes, Rhuth is here. Yes, she is alive. No, she will not wake." The priestess spoke with such finality, all Solyana could do was hold her tea. Her eyes strained to make out her sister's features on the bed. Her mind felt sluggish, as if it was still thawing. "Your parents have been informed. They will be here in the morning. You were brought to the Temple Celestial. My quarters are here, and with my Heitt, it was your best chance of survival." Priestess Avi spoke as if checking things off a list, quick and precise. She paused to take a breath but Solyana interrupted her, remembering something important.

"Rhuth...her face. She was bleeding so much." She tried to stand, but her legs were too weak. She crumpled to the ground again, her tea splashing over onto the stone below. "It was my fault...I told her...I told her to..." And then there were tears streaming down her face. She had encouraged Rhuth to show the ability she had with birds. And if that wasn't enough, Solyana had been the one to lunge at the falcon, the reason for her sister's injury. She set her tea to the side and cried into her arm.

"Solyana."

She wiped her eyes and looked at the priestess.

"She's okay. Stay put, finish your tea. I will help you up soon. But first, let me answer a more pressing question." Solyana nodded and sniffed, wiping her nose on her sleeve. "Yes, it was a blizzard. No, it was not a normal one. Something is happening with the Celestials. I believe a prophecy is afoot. You, dear girl"—the old woman turned to her, and Solyana finally caught her in the full firelight—"you...my dear, dear girl. You are the answer." Priestess Avi's eyes were set in watery cups of skin, wrinkly and pulling to the ground, yet the way she spoke injected a vibrant youthfulness to her countenance. Her stark white hair fell like a wall of snow past her shoulders, unbraided but no less beautiful.

"Do you feel different? Power? Control? Anything?"

"What are you—"

The old woman waved a hand at her. "Oh, never mind, we'll get to that." She took the mixture from her bowl and scooped it into a chalice. Then she bustled near Solyana, pulled a kettle free from the flames, and poured water over the mixture. It bubbled and steam drifted lazily toward the ceiling. Priestess Avi blew on it twice before shuffling back to Rhuth's bedside.

Holding one hand over Rhuth's throat and the other tipping the chalice into her mouth, the woman began moving her hand rhythmically, just above Rhuth's skin. Rhuth swallowed the liquid, her face still hidden in shadow.

Solyana couldn't grasp what she was seeing. The Priestess was Heitt, which meant she had the ability to warm, and as an Eldur, she could wield fire. But what she was witnessing was the use of Lakimi Fera. Manipulation of the body that allowed one to control another person's muscles without ever touching them.

Two Gifts? Impossible.

"Yes, girl"—the old woman intuited Solyana's thoughts yet again—"two Gifts. You're not seeing things."

"I-I don't understand. How can you have two? No one has two."

"There is much you will need to understand in the coming days. Much you need to learn."

Solyana stared at this ancient woman, the spiritual guide for not only her, but her parents and grandparents before her. This woman was Speaker of the Skies, the one who communed with the Celestials, kept the prophecies, and sustained their villages on the coldest of nights. Yet, Solyana didn't truly *know* her; no one did, that was clear.

"You are aware of the Green Prophecy, yes?" The priestess moved away from the bedside and sat down on the floor next to Solyana, almost girlish as she crossed her aged legs beneath her billowing dress.

"Yes. Of course. Everyone is."

"Hmm...are they?" And then, as if summoned by inaudible command, a small boy cracked the door open just behind the Priestess.

"Priestess Avi?" The boy waited tentatively in the hall.

"Jonas, get me the Green Prophecy. And get me your book."

Before Solyana could get a good look at him, he was gone, scrambling to do what his mistress bid of him. After a short time, he was back and out of breath, his sandy hair sticking out to the sides. He came between them, lowered a few scrolls to the floor, and handed her a small book, the cover intricately painted.

The small boy turned to Solyana, his eyes wide, freckles making a gradient across his nose and cheeks. His eyes seemed to linger on her left cheek before he grinned at her. A few teeth were missing. It made Solyana think of Rhuth. She had seen this boy before, some type of scribe for the Priestess, a service boy.

"Now, shoo!" The Priestess flicked a wrinkled hand in Jonas's direction, and he scampered off. "Look." She unraveled a scroll, pointing at various weathered lines, most in ancient Mothmari. Solyana stared blankly at the old language. She couldn't read it. The priestess noticed and pulled it back to herself, peering down her nose at the parchment.

"*The mark is this: a crescent scar that mars the body, brought on by the Celestials themselves, given through trial. It will be reminiscent of the darkness that resides in the curse. It will ebb and flow like the tide. Unknown to most, it is an ebenezer to herald the time that will end the white and bring the green.*" Priestess Avi's gray eyes matched Solyana's own, so similar in color. "Do you see?"

"No. I don't know what's going on. Why are we even talking about this?" Solyana stood, but vertigo overtook her. Her fingers throbbed. She sat down, hard.

"Here, look." Priestess Avi read again. "*In centuries, the darkness will bring the world to a cusp of white, frigid and unending. But when all hope seems lost, and the world knows nothing but white, there will come one who will bring green. One who must follow the path of the sky. One who is all light to stand to the one who is all dark, of which there will be two. One who possesses the three as one, who will save us all through mastery of it. You will know this one by the mark, known by the one who brings the white.*"

"Yes, I know this. Forgive me, but we established that already. What does this have to do with me?" Solyana clenched her teeth, frustration coursing through her like a wave. The heat of it made its way to her head, where it burned her face like fire. Solyana pulled and released one long breath, trying to rid herself of the sensation.

The old woman stood, her eyes flashing quickly to Solyana's left cheek before crossing to a small table near the bed. She returned with a flowery hand mirror. "See for yourself."

Solyana reluctantly took the mirror, trying to control her anger, barely abstaining from throwing the mirror across the room. Then she smelled that acrid scent once more, of rotten flesh, rancid and sharp. She wrinkled her nose and, as she did, the left side of her face grew tight. She brought the mirror up and gasped; her left side, from eye to cheek, was a black and flaking piece of flesh.

And it was unmistakably in the shape of a crescent moon.

MONSTER

PALLAH

THE BOGSON SIBLINGS ROSE long before the sun, expectantly greeting the chilly morning. Vámae detailed exactly what she expected of Pallah and Ahren before bustling out the door, Ahren trailing behind. Pallah would complete her tasks before slipping away midday, present just long enough to make memories and be remembered.

She worked alone for the entire morning, but she didn't mind. It was true what they said about twins; Vámae knew Pallah all too well to put her with anyone but Ahren, and Ahren was needed elsewhere. So, alone she was, cooking over the stove in their house, preparing hundreds of fiflas, doughy morsels with fish in the middle. They were a yearly favorite, and Pallah took pride in the work.

Wiping her brow, she stood back from the stove and glanced through the window. Almost time. She placed the fiflas on a tray, taking care to present the perfect ones at the front. Dough caked her fingers and they smelled of fish, but she held the tray up proudly and pushed the door open with her shoulder.

She set the tray down on the long harvest table, teeming with color. Mounds of apples, loaves of herbed bread, and endless rows of colored corn surrounded her tasty contribution. She plucked a fifla off the tray and popped it into her mouth, letting herself enjoy it. It was perfect. Her fiflas drew attention every year, it was one area in which she truly shined.

"Pallah." Her father's voice was too close, and she whipped around, mouth still full of food. She chewed once and swallowed it, looking down at him; she always forgot how short he was. "Your sister has been working long nights and early mornings for weeks on this festival, and you're over here, eating before we've even blessed the food." He raised a scant eyebrow, but only his children and wife would know this to be an indication he was angry. The way he spoke, the slow way of it, might deceive the average villager into believing he was having a normal conversation. They would be very wrong. "She's also utilizing her Gift to please the Celestials and do her part in the community...but you...you are here...eating." He folded his hands in front of him, formal, still.

"I've been in the kitchen all morning, Father. I was testing one to make sure it was okay."

"Why wouldn't they be okay?"

"I just...I just wanted to make sure it was fully cooked."

"You made them, didn't you? Shouldn't you know if they are fully cooked?"

"Well, yes...but sometimes the oven—"

"No, no, no"—her father made a clicking sound with his tongue that made Pallah cringe—"we don't blame man-made objects for our failures. A weakness, Pallah." He squinted at her with his near-black eyes and gently prised the best-looking fifla off the tray. He pressed the tips of his over-long thumb nails into it and pulled it apart. He inhaled deeply as he waved the broken fifla in front of his face. "Underdone." He tossed it to the ground. "I would suggest you revisit your recipe."

A dark wave of malice roiled in Pallah, unlike anything she'd ever given credence to in the past. It burned from her stomach, filled her chest, and threatened to burst from her throat.

You could just do it. Go ahead. Curse him! Häfan Bogdur and his rules.

"And we will discuss where you were last night, *after* the festival. Do not leave these grounds." Father turned slowly and stepped on the broken fifla as he walked away, greeting someone with a wave.

Pallah was rooted to the spot, her eyes trained on the remains of the dough that lay pressed into the dirt. The voice had never been so vile before. It had never used that curse, had never told her to directly disobey her father. Aside from her parents, who had dismissed it, she had told only one other person about the voice. She wondered if she should talk to them again.

Priest Skrifa was blessing the feast. All around her, the villagers were bowing their heads and lifting their arms, but not Pallah.

Pallah counted to twenty.

When she reached her mark, music burst into the open air, and suddenly the town was alive. Like awakening from hibernation after a long winter, the Feast of Haust brought the Mothmarians to feasting, dancing, and gaiety. She looked up and found herself surrounded by people. She grit her teeth, her feet moving of their own will. She would find Ahren.

He would be working the game booths, as he did every year. Winding her way through stalls and revelry, she found him. He was handing a few crude hatchets to a young girl with two long braids down her back. She seemed to be more interested in talking with him than throwing the hatchets.

"*Stars to heaven!* I don't think I'm doing it right." The girl stood with one hip to the side, accentuating her slight form. "Can you show me again, Ahren?" The girl held limp hands up to him, and Ahren adjusted her grip with a shy smile.

"You've got it, Leirha. Just remember to follow through, and don't let go until you see it in your line of vision. I don't want any accidents at my booth." He winked at her, and she laughed the kind of laugh girls did whenever they were around Ahren.

"I don't know. I think Ahren could pull off the one-armed look. Make sure to aim for the left one. He's a righty," Pallah teased and the girl blushed.

"Pallah!" Ahren seemed to forget about Leirha, excitement in his eyes. "It's finished! Do you like it?"

"What?" Pallah glanced around.

"I told you I was working on something big." He stepped back, his arms spreading in a dramatic arch. "This is it!"

Pallah squinted as she stepped forward. The intricate leafy etching that made up her own hatchet was woven into the target. A matching set.

"Now, you don't have to hike all the way up Eldfall to do your throwing. You can do it here! Well, not here...after today, it will be set up behind our house." His dimples stood out as he grinned.

"Oh." Pallah sighed "Thanks, Ahren." She appreciated the gesture, but the whole point of throwing her hatchet was a way to channel her anger. She had recognized that long ago. She only continued to do it when she wasn't angry as an excuse to go somewhere, anywhere but her home. "It *is* beautiful," she amended as his face fell. "Really, it matches my hatchet. I like that."

"You *love* it!" Ahren corrected, narrowing his eyes and mock punching her in the arm. "Give it a try."

Pallah stepped up to the line carved into the dirt, effectively forcing a very put-out Leirha to stand to the side and hold up her remaining hatchet in offering.

"I have my own, thanks," Pallah said, pulling her weapon out of her side holster. The target was a large wooden structure with different shapes protruding off of the sides that looked much like different beasts: a mouse, a rabbit, a small wolf, and a bird. She reared back, but just before releasing her weapon, Ahren spoke up.

"That line is for beginners." She stumbled forward, her momentum putting her off balance. She rolled her eyes at him. He pointed to a second line drawn in the dirt ten paces behind her. "Try this one." Smirking, she stepped back to the designated spot, reared back, and struck the mouse directly in the head.

A few bystanders cheered. She grinned and went to retrieve her hatchet. When she looked up, Ahren was beaming at her. Pallah filled with immeasurable gratitude for him. Grateful for his constancy, when the rest of her life was anything but. She would speak with him about the voice, she decided. He was the only person she could talk to.

"Ahren, can we—"

"Pallah, there you are!" Vámae was suddenly beside them with an air of put-on authority.

"What's up, V? Want to try?" Ahren grinned at her, his dimples surely causing Leirha to swoon.

"No, of course I don't want to try. There is too much to do. Pallah, come here. I need your help." Her deep blue eyes hardly rolled over Ahren before locking on Pallah's gray ones.

Pallah said nothing. She secured her hatchet back onto her side, and followed Vámae out through the row of games, back to the harvest table.

"—all the way to the end, then up the side. Also, there's at least three decanters that need to be refilled, and we need a restock on your fiflas. Where did you put the rest of them?"

"The rest of them?" Pallah asked distractedly.

"Yes, I told you we needed at least two thousand this year since they were such a hit last year."

"Two thousand?!" Pallah barked out a laugh. "That would have taken me all day the last two days to even come near that number! I only made these this morning!"

"How many did you make?" Vámae looked close to panic.

"Around five hundred." Pallah shrugged. Her twin hadn't even thanked her for them. Did it really matter? There was so much food on the table that stretched the entirety of the court-yard; they would be fine. But Vámae would not be satisfied.

"What is *wrong* with you? I explained everything this morning. Do you know how hard I've been working on this?" Vámae spoke with the same sharp tension their father so aptly employed. Pallah's rage boiled hot beneath the surface. She kept it from appearing on her face.

Well, forget her, too. Häfan it all, right? She's just jealous.

"Well if it isn't the sisters, in the flesh." Vámae blinked rapidly and her chest continued heaving as they both turned to see two boys who, irrespective of their height difference, looked more like twins than Pallah and Vámae. They stared curiously, mouths full of food. Pallah's eyes grew wide.

"Excuse me?" Vámae pursed her lips and shook her head, inconvenienced. "Who are you?"

"She doesn't remember us, Roley," Kristjan attempted to whisper, his pitchy voice carrying.

"Just give her a second," Rolf snapped over his shoulder, then turned back with a placating smile. "It's me! Rolf!" He held his arms out as if waiting for an embrace.

Vámae looked him up and down with apparent disdain.

"Holy Hekla, you're right, Kristjan." Rolf crossed his arms and swallowed the last of his food. "We've only charged together *several* times...we even helped keep the entire Temple Celestial heated once last winter! Our Heitt, *together*"—he laced his fingers together and squeezed his eyes shut—"is magical."

"I'm sorry, I work with a lot of Heitt," Vámae attempted gracefully.

"Pallah remembers us, right? Did I dream that?" Kristjan crossed his tree branch-sized arms.

"I'm not sure now…" Rolf opened his eyes wider and stood on the tips of his toes, trying to get to Pallah's eye level. "Anything? Hello?"

"Yes." Pallah wished they would go away. "Of course I remember you two."

"How do you know two Heitt?" Vámae demanded. "You don't have friends."

"Ouch," Kristjan muttered.

"Yes, she does," Rolf defended her.

"No, I really don't." Pallah hoped the brothers would understand why she couldn't associate with them. "They're in my…um…class…"

Then a voice cut into their conversation that made Pallah think of grass-floored caves, the salt of the sea, and a steaming mug of scub. "I heard you made the fiflas. They're great! Could have done with a touch more in the oven, but other than that"—Vil held up the half-eaten pastry in his hand—"perfection!" He popped it into his mouth. "Oh, you must be Vámae!"

Pallah rubbed her temple. She needed to get out of this situation. Now.

"I am, and you are?" Vámae's tone had drastically changed. Pallah jerked her head back up, searching her twin's face.

"Vilem." He held out his arm for her to grasp in greeting. "But you can call me Vil." Pallah's eyes darted between the two of them as they shook, and a very light touch of pink dusted Vámae's cheeks as they broke apart.

Oh, the drama. She really is jealous of you.

Everything inside of Pallah darkened.

Vil stepped back and looked between the two of them.

"You two really are twins? You're not just like...messing with me?"

"Right?" Vámae snickered and flipped her shiny black hair over her shoulder. "It's crazy how different we look. No one ever believes we're even sisters."

In that moment, Pallah felt true hatred toward her twin. Vámae could literally have any man she wanted; all eligible bachelors of each of the three villages would willingly throw themselves at her feet. But nothing seemed to satisfy Vámae more than kicking Pallah when she was down.

"Thanks again for making these delicious little bundles, Pal. It was nice to meet you, Vámae," Vil said, holding up a second fifla and giving them both a wave before trotting off with Rolf and Kristjan. They were heading toward the mountain.

Pallah watched them go for only a moment before her eyes shot to Vámae, hoping she hadn't caught Vil's use of Pallah's nickname. But her sister was staring after Vil.

"Well..." Vámae finally let out a sigh and a dry laugh. "That was interesting. You know them, Pal?" her tone indicated she had forgotten all about their prior argument.

"Not really."

"He seems a bit old for Lóthkol," Vámae said dreamily.

Pallah shrugged and slowly began edging away from her sister.

"I've got to restock this over here," Pallah said, pointing in the general direction of the table.

"Oh yes, of course." Vámae grinned "Thanks for all your help today, Pal."

Pallah shook her head in disbelief as Vámae wandered away, seemingly floating on a cloud, her worries forgotten.

Afternoon dipped to evening, and Pallah still hadn't been able to sneak away. Between her father and Vámae, she hadn't had a moment alone to escape. But once the moon had replaced the sun, and all the young children were safe in bed, the festival livened as more music, drinks, and food were shared. It was finally her chance to slip away to Eld Plateau, if the group was still there. She desperately hoped they would wait for her. More accurately, she hoped *Vil* would wait for her.

Pallah threw on her cloak before scrounging up a few desserts, wrapping them in husk, and tossing them into her knapsack. Vámae and her father were nowhere in sight as the villagers laughed, danced, and told fireside stories. A set of large drums rang out from the center of the courtyard, and the rhythm set the beat of her feet as she ran off east into White Wood.

The tree cover shadowed the moonlight. Pallah rushed through regardless, vaulting limbs and rocks, tripping over roots, being loud and uncaring. No one would hear her anyway with the festival below. Finally, after making it over the Vatino, she was back on Eldfall for the third time in two days. She passed her old hatchet tree, then out to the ledge where there was a long, flat rock that jutted out the side and overlooked the courtyard.

Excited and uncharacteristically hopeful as she broke through the brush, Pallah's mind conjured images of what the night would be like. Could she count them as friends? Not yet. But the possibility was there. Without warning, a figure emerged from the darkness and, with only the sound of the wind leaving Pallah's lungs, she was flattened to the ground. A knee was pressing into her solar plexus, instantly making vomit rise in her throat. A hand splayed just above her face, dark as the night.

"Get off me!" Pallah threw her arms up, knocking the hand to the side. It came right back, steady.

"Stay down, snake." A woman's voice? From the weight and speed at which the figure had put her down, she had assumed it was a man.

"Issha?" Pallah wheezed. "Are you Issha?"

A bit of weight came off of Pallah's core, enough for her to roll out of her captor's hold. She stood, coughing, hand on her hatchet, annoyed—even in that moment—her first reaction had not been to grab her weapon and strike. "It's Pallah."

Issha stood, brushed her leather cuirass, and straightened her leather cuffs. "Ah," she said with a jerk of her shaved head. "Group's out there."

"*Häfa*, do you always jump unsuspecting people?"

"Only the ones that pose a threat to my tribe," the girl said stonily. She crossed her arms across her chest, full lips turned downward. "You should announce yourself next time. You were tramping through the woods like a drunk."

Pallah rolled her eyes and made to pass her, but Issha grabbed her arm. Their eyes met.

"I could've killed you," Issha hissed and shook her head, Pallah jerked her arm away, her cloak billowing behind her.

"With what?" Pallah motioned to Issha's outfit, but no weapon could be seen. "I'm the one with the weapon." She didn't like this one. By Issha's posture alone it was clear she thought herself better than Pallah. A protector, like her, but Issha actually seemed to handle what was thrown at her with confidence.

"Great deal that did for you," Issha said with no hint of humor. "Come." She turned and led Pallah to the group of dark silhouettes sitting together at the edge of Eld Plateau. A fire bloomed at their feet and Pallah heard Karav shriek in delight. Rolf or Kristjan, the resident Eldurs, must be wielding flame. Risky, they weren't supposed to do that for pleasure; it would be a waste of energy.

"Hi, Pallah!" Karav's head peeked over the group. "Issha take you out?"

Leif chuckled. "Issha can take me out any time."

"If Issha is taking anyone out, it's me," Rolf said arrogantly. "Tomorrow night? What do you say, Issy?"

"I say, if you call me that *häfan* nickname one more time, I'll throw you off the side of this cliff."

"Oooooh." Karav blew a stream of air on the floating flame and it licked at their leather shoes. "Burn, my friend."

"She's cold, man." Leif gave Rolf a conciliatory pat on the shoulder. "We'll get her to warm up, eventually." He nodded to the flame.

Rolf's face cracked a wicked smile. "Yeah, Issha...want me to warm you up? It can go one of two ways, my sweet, dark-skinned goddess." Using his Heitt, Rolf made the flame turn into an exact depiction of a heart, ventricles and all. It pulsed and expelled sparks in turn.

"And that's my cue," Issha said flatly, turning to leave. "You never know who else is lurking in these woods." Then, from over her shoulder, "Don't hurt yourselves."

"She cares—ah!" Rolf brushed at his arm as the sparks had jumped far enough to land on his tunic. "You've saved me, my love." Ignoring him, Issha disappeared behind the dark of the tree line.

Pallah marveled as the heart transformed back into a flame. She had never seen anyone use their Heitt like that. It was incredible. Was this what the Taka Reu could do?

"Ignore them, Pallah. Come have a seat," Vil spoke up. He sat closest to the edge of the plateau, one leg dangling precariously off the side, the steady wind rippling through his blonde hair, revealing his face touched with fire light.

Pallah dug in her bag, found the desserts, and passed them out as she went. An array of thanks chimed behind her as she sat beside him. She wanted to let her legs hang free below as well, but didn't want to look like she was imitating him. She settled for sitting cross-legged with her elbow on her knee, a closed fist propping her chin up to survey the festivities far beyond. She glanced at Vil, only to find him staring at her intently. He did not look away.

"What?" she asked, self-consciously bringing her other hand up to tuck a few stray hairs behind her ear.

"I didn't say anything," Vil said it with such softness that Pallah softened too. She had never been so aware of her every flaw beside anyone before. He was perfection. His full lips quirked into a half-smile.

"Why are you staring at me like that?"

"How can I not, Pallah of Sodur?"

Pallah inhaled sharply. "You don't know what you're saying."

"I do." Vil let his hand fall atop her own, and it sent a shock of sparks up her arm and into the depths of her. "You know...I realized you haven't told me *your* aptitude."

Pallah's mouth went dry, and she licked her lips. She had never told anyone that she didn't know what her aptitude was. Sure, Ahren suspected, her whole family probably did, but she had never explained it...never said it out loud to anyone.

"It's okay if you don't trust us yet"—he cleared his throat—"me yet. I get it." He released her hand but smiled warmly, the release not meant as a punishment.

"No, no. I do. But I..." Would they still allow her to be in their group if she didn't know? Would they laugh at her? Then she remembered Karav's words. She didn't know what hers was either, but she thought it was something aquatic. It gave her the courage to continue. "I don't know, Vil." She liked the way his name felt on her lips. "I know a lot of Tala can tether to multiple animals, others only to one. But I have never been able to attach. It's just never"—she locked eyes with him—"clicked."

Vil grasped her hand again and squeezed. "Well, this is just another reason bringing you into the fold was the right decision." He motioned to the scroll he had been reading. "This is the one we grabbed from your bag." He gave her a sheepish grin. "This is the kind of information we're missing, Pal." Vil's face was almost touching her own, his breath hot on her skin. "Look, knowing your aptitude isn't necessary with the Taka Reu. Because with the Reu"—his eyes locked with her own and Pallah held her breath—"everything is magnified." Then he began to read.

"With the Taka Reu comes worship of someone they call The Mother. From our research, we believe this is the earth, the ground beneath us. It coincides with the theory the eruption of Hekla brought forth the Dark Gifts, the ability to utilize the energy from deep within the rock.

Witnesses have claimed the Taka Reu's capabilities to be far more advanced than those using Gifts. I am hard-pressed to take this as fact. Why would the Celestials not allow us a way to contend against darkness? Perhaps they are simply strong in different ways. The energy coming from the Celestials is more enduring, the energy from the ground beneath us quick and fiery, much like the temperament of those who seem to be attracted to this darkness."

"Would you agree with that?" Vil asked her with a nudge to her shoulder. "Are we quick and fiery?"

Pallah giggled, girlish and free. "I mean, Karav is."

Their shoulders brushed, she let her legs dangle off the side of the plateau, and he continued.

"The evidence lies in the Era of Darkness, when so many cities throughout Mothmar were heavily laden with the Taka Reu. It didn't matter what someone was born with; Fera, Tala, or Heitt. The ability to do these things, while easier due to one's prior Gift, was not limited to it. Although we are still unsure how someone gains the ability to utilize Gifts unnatural to them through the Taka Reu, there is rumor, to gain these other Gifts, they must be taken from another. The Taking, in its truest form. I am reluctant to find answers to this; the information will bring more ruin than help."

Vil grew quiet, rubbing his hand on the back of his neck, reading the rest to himself. Pallah's mind chewed on the information. Did that mean she didn't need to know her aptitude? If she switched her source from the Celestials to the earth below—the Mother, as they called her—could she tether to an animal? She would officially be Tala. Her father would be proud of her, wouldn't he? If she finally used her Gift. But no...it wouldn't be using her Gift. It would be using the Dark Gifts...an important distinction. But would he be able to tell?

"I want to try it," Pallah whispered, but Vil was still engrossed in the scroll. She turned to see Rolf, hand outstretched, controlling his flame as it transformed into a bear. It battled Kristjan's flame, which he had morphed into a stag. Sparks flew as they clashed. It was unbelievably realistic. She had no idea Heitt could be used like that.

But no, she reminded herself. This wasn't Heitt. This was Taka Reu Heitt, a far more advanced Gift, a Dark Gift.

She wanted it; she needed it. How could she connect to The Mother?

"I'd like to try it, Vil," she repeated as she stretched her hands toward the rock beneath her. "Can I do it here?"

Vil snapped out of his studies and cocked an eyebrow at her. "It's difficult getting it the first few times. And...Pallah, you need to be sure. Absolutely sure. Most are hard-pressed to resume communing with the Celestials after connecting with The Mother. Maybe we need to take a trip to Hekla and go straight to the source. We've been wanting to go."

Overhearing them, Leif's square-jawed face lifted from the group, and he shouted, "A quest! To Hekla!"

The group of outcasts cheered and Karav started babbling excitedly, filling the cooling night with expectation. Pallah smiled as she imagined herself hiking into greater Mothmar, further from her valley than she'd ever been before. The thrill of joy quickly became tainted with the knowledge that she hadn't felt this way with her family in a long time. When? With Ahren, sure, maybe even with Vámae when they were young, but not with her parents, never with them. What had happened?

She had never told anyone about the way her father treated her or the apathetic way of her mother. Everything about her home life was stuffed deep inside her, tightly wrapped, never to see the light.

But as she watched Vil smile and laugh, she wondered for the first time if she *could* tell someone like him. He would understand, wouldn't he? Maybe he'd even save her from them, whisk her away. Their knees brushed as they both swung their legs over the side of the cliff. A chill crawled up her thigh. She tightened her cloak around herself against the cold. He looked back at her, his blue eyes striking, even at night.

"Vil—"

A scream pierced the night like an arrow whistling through the air, close and full of horror. The group halted, eyes and ears trained on the courtyard far beyond.

Like a colony of ants, the villagers split apart in all directions. More screams were bursting through the night, frantic and uncontrolled. Pallah stood, her cloak billowing as the wind caught it and attempted to pull her from the cliff face. Vil grabbed her and pulled her back. She hardly noticed as she searched the distant grounds for any clue as to what was happening. Her breathing became fevered as she glimpsed something inhuman darting through the scattering crowd.

"Karav, Issha, get down there—now!" Vil hissed. They obeyed him without question. Pallah had expected them to turn back toward the mountain, to make their precarious flight down. Instead, they hurried to the side of Eld Plateau where they extracted a few harnesses from the bushes. Issha threw one to Karav and slipped the other over her pants, tightening the cloth around her legs. Karav did the same before hurrying to the base of a tree. She grabbed a long rope secured there, looped it through the harness, and then leaned back, her face to the sky.

Issha followed close behind, and the two of them jumped back and away from the rock outcropping, into the open air. Then there was nothing but the hum of rope sliding through rope, rushing wind, and the screams of the courtyard below.

Pallah looked with wide eyes over the edge. She spotted only movement in the darkness as they made contact with the forest floor, detached themselves, and tore off to cross the Vatino. The only evidence of their flight being the trembling rope still hanging from the tree at the edge.

The screams continued on, prompting another look down into the valley told Pallah whatever was attacking was still at large. Even with their differences, Pallah's first certain thought was to get to her family. Ahren and Vámae were down there, in the thick of it. She needed to protect them.

She turned to Vil to ask him for a harness, but he was already standing behind her, harness in hand. "Step through," he requested as he knelt beside her. She steadied herself, one hand on his shoulder, and stepped into the harness. He slid it up her waist and cinched it, snug and stiff. His chest rose and fell and his breath was hot on her neck as he worked. Pallah's legs felt weak and it had nothing to do with the screaming below.

"Find your family, Pallah, and make sure they're okay," he said, bending down for the rope and threading it through the loop at her waist before placing it in her free hand.

"Do you have any idea what it is?" Her voice shook, wanting reassurances—*anything* from the man standing before her.

"If it's an animal, Karav can tether it. We'll make sure your family is safe, Pal. Don't do anything stupid. And don't let go." He squeezed each of her hands tighter around the ropes. The wind was pulling at her cloak once more as she leaned back over the edge. A thrill ran through to her toes and she cried out as she almost pulled Vil off the side. He gripped the tree with one hand and steadied her with the other, his eyes searching her own.

"You can do this. Hold tight." His hand moved from her arm to her face, holding her there, hesitating. Then, resolute and quick, he kissed her. "Don't die," he breathed, pressing his forehead into hers.

Pallah barely felt her body fall backward off the mountain. She was already floating. She maintained enough awareness to keep the rope taut and threaded through, the wind rushing past in a roar. Her heart pounded in her chest for one reason alone. Where had that kiss come from? She thought of his interaction with Vámae just a few hours earlier, and wondered if he would have done the same thing if she had been sitting with him on the mountain.

Men are nothing to you, Pallah. You need none of them. Trust only yourself.

She began a count to ten. The voice was the last thing she needed in her head just now. She thought of Vil's lips on her own as she reached the tops of the trees of White Wood. So warm and soft they were, like nothing she'd ever felt. Whatever was causing the chaos below was worth it, she decided. Because Vil kissed her. He *liked* her. More screams pierced the night, but she couldn't keep herself from smiling. Was she really such a monster? She pulled the rope free from the harness as her feet touched the earth below.

Yes, Pallah, you are.

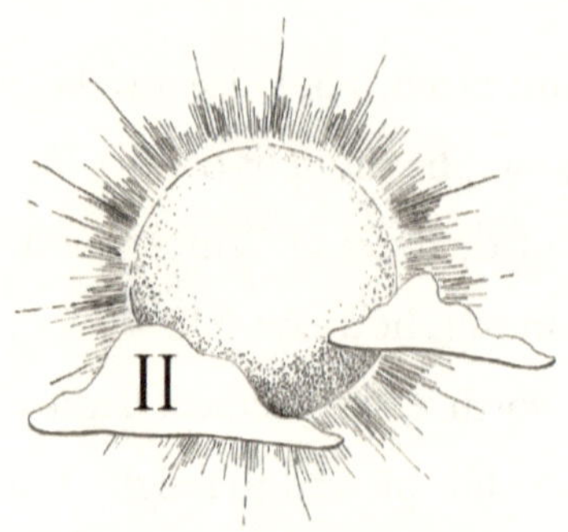

BROTHERS

SOLYANA

S OLYANA SCREAMED.

She was too attuned to what was happening around her, too awake. She pressed a shaking hand to the scar on her face, and when she pulled it away, strands of a sticky, inky substance clung to her skin and refused to let go.

The priestess, sitting patiently across from her, leaned forward, a fire blooming in her palm. She held it close to Solyana's face. Before she knew what was happening, the priestess's lips were pressing into Solyana's forehead and the burning hand to the crescent scar. The pain of searing flesh silenced Solyana's screaming as she thrashed against the old woman.

"Oh, hush"—Priestess Avi leaned back, winded—"look." She held the mirror up that Solyana had tossed to the side to show her face restored, the scar gone.

"Where is it? What *was* that?" Solyana's breaths came ragged. What in the *stars* was happening? She wiped her hands on the blanket, trying to rid herself of it.

"The prophecy said it would ebb and flow. I simply tucked it away for now. It will be back."

"Back? No. I don't know what that was...frostbite? What kind of frostbite leaves your face sticky?" Solyana was babbling and Priestess Avi cut in.

"It's not frostbite. I thought we went over this, girl. It's the crescent scar, the sign, the herald." The old woman sounded bored as if she had already explained enough and shouldn't have to repeat herself.

A laugh rolled up in Solyana like a pot at a boil, maniacal, uncontrollable. "No, no, no. That was frostbite. Thank you for healing me. Let's go, Rhuth."

The priestess stared hard at her, unmoving. "Sit down, Solyana."

Ignoring the old woman, Solyana's legs shook as she stood. She needed to get Rhuth and go home. She needed normalcy. She needed her parents.

"Solyana..." the priestess warned again, her voice softening as Solyana took a few shaky steps to the bed, the figure beneath the blankets laying absolutely still.

Clinging to the bed for support, Solyana made her way to the headboard, praying against all hope Priestess Avi had simply been mistaken and her sister was fine. Rhuth was only ten years old. Things like these didn't happen to little girls. They just *didn't*. Standing above her, Solyana's eyes rested on her baby sister's face for the first time.

Oh, *by the Celestials,* no...Rhuth. A choking gasp rose in her throat.

Rhuth's face was mangled, the right side of it deeply torn with a jagged cut from lip to hairline, straight through her eye. The eye, or what remained of it, was swollen shut, oozing a clear liquid over a landscape of purplish-blue. She had been stitched, but what a scar it would leave.

A sob released from Solyana, her own worries forgotten, her own facial malady a trifle against her sister's too-young face laid bare, destroyed.

"Rhuth...I'm so sorry," she choked. "I'm so, so sorry. This wasn't supposed to happen. You should have never been out there. We would have been home if I hadn't suggested you prove it to me. Why couldn't I have taken you at your word?" She took in a shaking breath and shouted in grief into Rhuth's hair. "I should have just believed you!"

"I did hear she is a talented Broad Tala," the priestess offered somewhere behind Solyana. "I'm sorry I never saw her in action."

Solyana glanced back at the old woman, appalled at her tactless words. She wasn't looking at her, but at Rhuth.

"Perhaps one day. When she wakes," Priestess Avi murmured. Was the old woman talking to her? As if in answer, the old woman's eyes snapped to Solyana. "You need sleep. Your family will be here early tomorrow. You must explain what happened; but I urge you not to mention anything of the prophecy quite yet. I have Jonas doing some more research and gathering more scrolls. We need to have a solid backing if I'm going to be sending out one of their daughters while another is lying close to death."

"Sending me out? Close to death?" Dizziness clutched Solyana as panic washed over her. "I can't leave the valley. No one leaves." She turned her back to Rhuth and crossed her arms, trying to keep herself from collapsing. "Why won't she wake?"

"She's in darlöh, girl. You know the term?"

Solyana squeezed her eyes shut and pressed her sore fists to her temple, her hair unbraided and falling around her face. Darlöh, a state in which the body is left in stasis, a waiting place, before death inevitably came. "And what of me?" She looked into the gray eyes of the priestess.

"You will need to go into greater Mothmar." The priestess took Solyana by the hand, leading her back to her mat by the fire. "It is foretold. You will seek out the blight that curses our lands and bring the green back to us. Oh, it has been far too long since we have seen grass, my dear. Far too long." The Priestess seemed barely able to contain her excitement. But could it be true? Could Solyana be the answer to the prophecy they had waited on for centuries? She was Rána...the interpretation of the prophecy was that the person to save them would have mastery of all three Gifts. She didn't even have one. It made her think of Priestess Avi's ability with two Gifts; maybe she did have the answers.

"Sleep now, Solyana." The woman helped her back onto the mat at the foot of her sister's bed. "I assume you would rather stay in here with your sister than have your own room?"

Feeling suddenly overwhelmed with exhaustion, Solyana nodded. "Yes, I'll stay here. Thank you, Priestess Avi."

"I am right down the hall if you need me."

Solyana hardly remembered laying down before her eyes closed in sleep, victim to dreams of ice and snow.

At some point in the night, Solyana climbed into bed with Rhuth, snuggling up with her as they had done too often at home. Mama always said she spoiled her younger sister, and it was true. Finally, when morning broke, Priestess Avi walked in, smiling warmly at them.

"How are you feeling?" Priestess Avi asked as she got to work with her mortar and pestle. "Face? Fingers?"

Solyana sat up and scooted herself closer to Rhuth. The bed wasn't large. "Better." She splayed her hands wide, the aching had almost completely receded. The purplish hue of her fingers now only looked a muted yellow. "A lot better."

"Well, it was a wise decision, him bringing you here. It saved your face, and your hands." Him? Solyana couldn't remember who brought her to the Temple Celestial. Jonas, the small servant boy from the night before, burst into the room with his ever-present grin.

"They're here." He wrung his tunic in his hands. "The Chief."

"Well, what are you doing up here? Go greet them properly."

Jonas took off in the direction he came, almost wiping out as he slipped in his socks.

"Remember what I said, dear. Not a word about this prophecy until we have it settled." The priestess's sparkling eyes held hers until Solyana nodded, unsure if she trusted the old woman or simply held a respectful reverence for her.

Within a few short minutes, Solyana found herself in the embrace of her family. They shared in their grief. Both for the trauma they experienced and for Rhuth's dismal state. Solyana explained everything: the falconry and beyond, reliving the blizzard, the frantic digging of their almost-tomb, the hours waiting alone. She said nothing of thinking Rhuth was dead. She didn't need to relive that.

They praised her ingenuity, though sorrow underscored every reaction as Mama clung to Rhuth's arm and Papa did nothing but nod, his eyes on his youngest daughter. Fridmey sat on a wooden stool in the corner, her head in her hands, her leg bouncing wildly.

"We've come every day since the storm, just waiting for you to wake. We are so thankful to the Celestials you're back with us, even three days later," Mama whispered.

"Oh." An emptiness filled Solyana. She had been robbed of the most precious thing, time. She hadn't known it had been more than a day.

"You were one of the lucky ones. It was quick thinking on Gamaliel's part, bringing you here," Papa said, squeezing her arm. "Several others were caught in the blizzard. Three others"—Papa took in a deep breath, steeling himself—"three others didn't make it."

The emptiness in Solyana deepened. Death was not new to them, but it was never welcome.

"We are honoring those we lost tonight, at the Dauda. Do you feel well enough to attend?" Mama asked tentatively.

"Koláme, don't pressure her. She just woke," Papa said.

"I"—Solyana hesitated as she looked at her sister's broken face—"I don't think I can leave her." She bit her lip to keep from crying again. She glanced at the window facing the courtyard below. "But I can watch out the window tonight."

"Anything you need to do, Middle One." Papa gave her a sad smile, and Solyana tried to return it. "Alright, well...Priestess Avi?"

The priestess stepped back into the room so quickly she must have been waiting just outside the door.

"We need to finish up preparations for tonight," Papa said, giving the priestess a bow.

"But of course, Chief Marus." She returned it.

"Papa?" Solyana asked. "Who is Gamaliel?"

"Ah." Papa looked suddenly uncomfortable as he scratched at his auburn beard. "The boy who pulled you from the snow."

"Can I meet him?"

Papa and Mama exchanged a glance Solyana couldn't quite decipher.

"He's indisposed," Papa's voice pitched, he cleared his throat.

"Indisposed?"

"We'll talk later." Papa kissed her on the head before turning back to the priestess, and the three of them walked out, leaving only the sisters together.

"That was weird," Fridmey spoke up. "Now, I want to know who this mysterious Gamaliel is."

A real smile touched Solyana's lips for the first time. "I only remember he was handsome."

"Oh, was he now? Now I *really* want to meet him!"

They grinned at each other in the silence, and Fridmey tucked a lock of her curly red hair behind her ear. "Look, Sol"—she took a breath—"I thought I was going to lose you both. I've been worried sick for three days."

"No, you weren't..." Solyana teased.

"Yeah. I really was." Fridmey pulled her in and hugged her hard. Tears sprung instantly to Solyana's eyes. "Just don't scare me like that again, okay?"

"Okay," she whispered into her sister's hair.

"Promise?"

Solyana thought of the priestess's words, of white turning to green, of a long journey away from their valley, of heralds and prophecies of old.

"Promise," Solyana mumbled, wishing she knew if it was true.

Solyana wiped at the window for the fourth time with the blanket she had wrapped around herself; the condensation distorted her view of the Dauda happening below. The large stone platform that lined the front of the Temple Celestial held Solyana's family, a place of honor for the Chief, and Priestess Avi stood with them. Stone steps descended into the courtyard where all three villages gathered, adults and children alike, separated from the front of the building by four iron pikes standing in a row, a flame at each tip.

Solyana knew, even when her mother had asked, she was too weak to go down, both physically and emotionally. How could she go back out into that forsaken land again? How could she live in this place that only tried to kill her and those she loved? And how could she face her people? They would have questions, and she had too many answers of which she was not yet permitted to speak.

She planned on walking back to her home in Vestur after the ceremony. There was no reason for her to remain with the priestess, now that she was conscious and healing on her own.

Muffled through the windowpane, she heard her people singing the song of death. She joined them reluctantly. When the song concluded, long and dreary as it was, Priestess Avi stepped forward.

The priestess handed her father a long iron rod with a bell-shaped piece on the end. Papa descended the steps and carefully lowered the iron bell over each flaming pike until they were nothing but a wisp of smoke. When he arrived at the fourth, he hesitated and glanced back at Priestess Avi.

The old woman glided forward, a long silver pole in her hand. She placed a hand on his arm, lowering his rod. Then she extended her hand toward the flame, and it smoothly came off the pike and came to greet her, alive in her hand. She began speaking, but Solyana couldn't hear through the foggy glass. She tightened the blanket around her shoulders, cranked the window open to listen, and let in the night's chill.

"One soul remains hanging in the balance." The priestess's voice rang out clear and bright. "We ask you, Mother of the Night, Father of the Day, Children of the Sky." She raised her hands heavenward, the flame still aglow in one palm. She released the silver pole which remained upright, balanced perfectly beside her. "Bring her back to us whole." Avi's robes shone bright in the moon's soft glow as she extended her hands from white, billowing sleeves. Then she turned, plucking her silver staff from its vertical position, and walked to Fridmey, who was holding a lantern. The Priestess placed the flame inside before carrying both objects back into the Temple Celestial, out of Solyana's view.

As one, Mama and Papa stepped forward, Fridmey at their side. "Your eyes be upward," they spoke strong and clear.

All the valley, some six hundred people, responded, "And be filled with light."

She started closing the window. The only sounds were the chatter of people dispersing, the weeping of mothers and the laughter of children, incapable of understanding the gravity of the ceremony. Then a voice stopped her, pitched lower than the others, directly beneath her window.

"Vinur, come here. What are you doing?"

Solyana recognized that voice and that name. But from where?

"Vinur! No!"

Solyana opened the window all the way and leaned out over the sill, her hair flying into the wind. The moon gave the man she was looking at a blue sheen, his hair so dark and long, and a staff was strapped across his back. He looked up. Solyana scrambled back, falling hard on the floor.

"Vinur!" his voice came again, muffled as it passed through stone. He was coming inside.

She crept past Rhuth's bed and out the door, entering a hallway that made her skid to a halt. The walls were expertly decorated with plants, rugs, colorful cloth and paintings on canvas. Unusual for one reason alone: her people focused on practicality. With life or death always hanging in the balance, art was seen as frivolous, borderline traitorous. Why waste your life doing something that couldn't keep someone from dying of hunger or cold?

Her eyes roved passed the woven rugs hanging over gaps in the walls; doorways or stairwells, she couldn't tell. Large paintings stretched taller than herself depicted a much different valley than the one she lived in now. A green one. She couldn't wrench her eyes away from them. Beautiful. So beautiful. Who would dare paint such things? And what kind of a woman was the priestess that she chose to embrace them?

The stairs were to her right, but opposite her, down the hallway, was another door, ornamented and large. Was that Priestess Avi's chambers? She had always seen the stairs leading up from the sanctuary of the Temple Celestial, but had never explored. She had never been invited to. Now, here she was at the top, feeling like an intruder.

"Vinur? Where did you go?" the voice echoed through the sanctuary below, reminding her why she was in the hallway.

Something cold and wet touched her leg.

"Oh!" A black and white dog was by her feet, his icey blue eyes peering up at her. "Hello there." She kneeled next to him and gave him a few scratches, which he leaned into, his tail wagging.

"Vinur?" The voice was at the bottom of the stairs. Solyana's eyes widened as she realized she was only in her short tunic and blanket.

"Um, I have your dog. But hold on!" She ran back into the room she was sharing with Rhuth, almost slipping around the door like Jonas had done earlier that day. She shoved her legs into woolen pants and fastened them under her tunic. Socks and mukluks came last.

When she finally entered the hallway once more, a man was standing there, eyes perusing the canvas paintings that lined the walls. The dog, Vinur, came bounding back to Solyana.

"Hello again," she crooned to him; she had always loved dogs.

"Yes, hi. I wasn't sure if you'd remember," the man spoke up, leveling his gaze at her.

Solyana blinked. "Remember?

"You said hello *again*. I thought you..." His eyes darted to the side, and he shrugged.

"I meant because your dog was just..." Solyana laughed awkwardly.

"Oh. Got it." The man puffed out his cheeks and crossed his arms. He wasn't wearing a parka but only a few choice furs. "Well, regardless, I would like to say hello *again,* and say it's great to see you up and well. I'm Gamaliel."

So, this was him. Solyana craned her neck to look into his eyes, far too aware of the color rising in her cheeks. His shoulders looked muscled beneath the furs, and the belt securing his staff hugged a waist that looked narrow enough she could wrap her arms around it. She looked up at his waiting smirk, his dark hair falling past his shoulders, his long face and skin the color of honey.

Solyana's eyes widened and she pressed a hand to her face, it was burning so much she thought the scar was back. It wasn't. "I'm sorry. I still don't have much of my memory from that day. You were the one who rescued me?"

"Well"—Gamaliel toed the floor—"Vinur found you first. But, yeah." He flipped some hair behind his shoulder. "Nice to see you on your own two feet."

"Right." Solyana kept her eyes on the dog. "Well, thank you, Vinur. You're a brave dog." She patted him once more.

"Wolf, actually," Gamaliel corrected, "though many have tried to tell him otherwise."

Vinur sniffed indignantly.

"So, he is your beast, then?" Solyana asked. A common question amongst her people for those Gifted with Tala.

"More like I am his," he said, patting his leg. Vinur jumped up, putting his paws on Gamliel's torso. "He's much better at social interaction than I am, anyway." He smiled again and Solyana's stomach flip-flopped.

"Well, I just wanted to thank you." Solyana forced herself to look into his eyes, somehow bright and dark all at once, flicking to her as she spoke. "For saving me and Rhuth."

"Of course."

"Gam!" A small figure came bustling up the stairs behind Gamaliel, arms full of various scrolls and parchment, his face hidden behind them. "Why are you here? You never come here."

"Vinur snuck inside; I had to get him."

Jonas peeked out from behind his scrolls.

"Hi, Ms. Solyana." The boy approached excitedly, his parchments fluttering as he spoke. "I know we didn't really meet earlier. I'm Jonas. That's J-O-N-A-S, but the J sounds like a Y." The words tumbled out of him in a rush. "I just wanted to say it's an honor to meet you." His eyes widened in wonder, and Solyana's discomfort grew as he repeatedly glanced at her cheek. Was her scar showing again? No, frostbite, it was just frostbite. Maybe all the scrolls and pieces of parchment Jonas was holding held the answers to her questions.

"Nice to meet you too, Jonas." She accentuated the Y sound at the front of his name and he grinned. Hoping to divert him, she asked, "You help Priestess Avi?"

"Oh yes, all the time!" He smiled his gap-toothed grin. "She has me grabbing all sorts of scrolls from the archives in the basement. She won't talk to me about it but"—he glanced around and then whispered—"I've been reading all the stuff she asks me to get for her, and I think I know what she's doing. Ms. Solyana, are you really who she thinks you are?" Gamaliel furrowed his brow and stared at her too. She felt herself going red again.

"Just Solyana. And...no. I mean, I don't know. I'm not entirely sure." She clasped her arms together, wanting to melt into the floor.

The idea that she was the fruition of an ancient prophecy had stayed in her mind like a horrible nightmare. There was no way it was true. What proof did she have other than Priestess Avi's word? She shook her head. She needed time.

Jonas and Gamaliel talked quietly between themselves, a familiarity between them. How had she never met them before? Their valley was by no means small, but the population itself wasn't large. At just over six hundred people, there was no way for anyone to fall through the cracks long enough to go entirely unnoticed.

"Where do you two live?"

"I live with Gam," Jonas said as if this explained things.

"And I live far enough from here that we need to get a move on, *now*," Gamaliel said, nudging Jonas with his foot and bringing his hair into a top knot. "You ready to go?"

"You're walking me home?" Jonas rolled his eyes. "I'm busy. I'll just come home later."

"Not with that random blizzard happening, you won't. I need to make sure you get home safely."

"I'm not a baby," Jonas unknowingly echoed Rhuth from only a few days before.

"I'm aware. But I still don't trust the weather. Come on, you can finish up tomorrow."

"Are you two brothers?" Solyana guessed.

They spoke at the same time.

"Yes!" said Jonas.

"No," said Gamaliel. "I'll give you ten minutes, then we're going." Gamaliel turned, ending the conversation. "Come on, Vinur." The wolf trotted next to him but came up short as Jonas sprinted off ahead, careening down the stairs, a flurry of parchments drifting lazily to the steps in his wake. "*Häfan* kid," Gamaliel mumbled, bending down to clear the stairs.

"Here." Solyana joined him.

"You heading out too?" he asked, looking at her mukluks.

"Yeah." She picked up the last few pieces of parchment. "I suppose I will. If I wait too much longer I'll be spending another night here."

"Where do you live? I can walk you home too, if you like." Solyana felt the blush creep up her neck once more and twisted her lips to keep from smiling.

"Sure. I just have to do one thing and I'll be ready to go."

Solyana trotted back up the stairs and ducked into Rhuth's room, kissing her forehead. "I'll be back tomorrow, Little Fyug." She grabbed her parka and trailed down the stairs after Gamaliel.

They crossed the stone-floored sanctuary together, and Solyana pulled on her parka. She waited for Gamaliel to do the same, but he seemed content in his low-cut tunic and few furs that lined his shoulders.

"Won't you be cold?"

"Will I be cold?" He scoffed. "Silly girl."

Solyana scowled at him.

"You're Marus's kid, right?" He turned his dark eyes to her as they stood in the foyer together, waiting on Jonas. "Jonas has been telling me about you."

Solyana had never heard of anyone calling her father by his first name without the label of 'Chief' in front of it. She was also slightly put-off that he called her 'kid.' How old was this guy?

"I mean, he's Chief. I don't think our life has the same level of privacy as everyone else." She crossed her arms. "What has Jonas been saying? How old are you, anyway?" She couldn't help herself.

"Nineteen," he admitted. "And just a few things about some prophecy..." He eyed her suspiciously. "Care to explain?"

"No," she answered truthfully. "Where did Jonas go?"

"Maybe he's already waiting outside."

Solyana hadn't remembered the doors opening but followed him as he walked out into the cold, dark night. And it *was* cold. Had she just gotten used to the warmth of the upper floor of the Temple Celestial, or was it something deeper?

"Well, whatever the prophecy suggests, Jonas is convinced." A blast of biting air blew through them as they descended the steps. "So, what's your Gift? Something really special, I assume."

"My Gift?" Solyana laughed, though it came out sounding bitter. "You're obviously not from Vestur, then." Her status was well-known in her own village. "Where *do* you live?"

"I believe you left my question unanswered." He pointed a finger at her and arched an eyebrow.

"You've asked enough, and I still know nothing about you."

"Fine." He cleared his throat. "I live across the Vatino."

"The Vatino Sea?"

"Is there another?"

Solyana blinked, her eyelashes already coated with snow she hadn't known was in the air. "Where?"

"At the base of Eldfall." He motioned in an easterly direction. "It's cozy," he added wryly. "Would expect it to be a bit too rough for someone like you, however."

"What's that supposed to mean?"

"Well, you know. Marus's daughter and all that."

"Chief Marus," Solyana corrected.

"Exactly, Princess. So, your Gift?"

"I'm Rána." She lifted her chin as she said it, attempting to be proud of something she was still coming to terms with herself. Besides, if she was Rána, then she wasn't the answer to whatever prophecy Priestess Avi claimed. Maybe accepting her position would encourage the Celestials to choose someone else, someone with actual ability.

"Oh." Gamaliel looked taken aback for the first time since she had met him. "That's...impossible."

"You're telling me." Solyana pulled her gloves on. Where was Jonas?

"No, really. That's impossible. You had a..." He made a sweeping gesture with two fingers toward her cheek, and she self-consciously lifted a hand to her face. Her skin was nothing but smooth.

"I had a what?" She dared him to speak of it, this thing she didn't want to believe herself.

"A mark," he blurted, unabashed. "There was a mark, wasn't there? Jonas has been chattering about it nonstop. Trust me, it's you...isn't it?"

A furious barking began, breaking the awkward silence and causing the two of them to look for Vinur. She hadn't even noticed he was gone. Gamaliel spun in a circle before jogging around to the back of the Temple Celestial, his bulk disappearing in the darkness.

Solyana followed, curious of Vinur but even more of the man. She caught up to him as he rounded the second corner, his stride longer than her own. The wind pushed them back in earnest, her hood falling off her head, her hair whirling in all directions.

Gamaliel turned to her, his eyes screwed up in the onslaught of wind and newly pounding ice. "Do you still hear him?"

Solyana glanced around, wary now as the darkness and wind culminated into something like déjà vu. "I thought I heard him barking from the east."

"Maybe you should go back into the Temple!" Gamaliel had to raise his voice above the thrall.

Solyana looked behind her through the moonlight to see a dark wall of clouds. "Gamaliel…" she mumbled through lips growing colder. She tore her eyes from the sky back to him.

His face hardened. "Stay with me." He grasped her gloved hand firmly and tugged her back around the front of the building. Solyana felt weak, memories coming unbidden as the wind and snow increased. This couldn't be another one. It was impossible.

But so had been the first.

She squinted through the onslaught of snow, keeping her guide's fur-covered shoulders in her sight. Before long, he stopped short. "What's—"

"Jonas!"

Solyana followed Gamaliel's gaze to find child-sized footprints exiting the temple. They were quickly being erased by the snow accumulating over the grounds. When had he left? Why? In search of them? They thought he had gone back to the archives, but they were wrong.

"It's another one, isn't it?" Solyana locked eyes with Gamaliel, her own fear mirrored in his face. "A blizzard?"

Without a word, Gamaliel released her hand and shot off into the night, determined to reach the small boy of the Temple Celestial before the cold did.

TAKE ONE, LEAVE ONE

PALLAH

THE SCREAMS ASCENDED FROM shocked terror to wails of grief, and Pallah feared what awaited her. Her mind worked efficiently, creating worst case scenarios as she tore through White Wood, harness tight around her waist. She hadn't taken the time to remove it. Finally exiting the tree line, she stopped, oriented herself, and bolted to the floating bridge over the Vatino Sea.

Pallah had never run across the bridge at that speed before and found it difficult, the black water rolling beneath. The wails rising and falling with the ceaseless waves, she dove headlong toward the very direction from which so many were fleeing. Finally, on level ground again, she was swept up in the fray.

People ran everywhere, many brandishing tools: pitchforks, hoes, or shovels. The better prepared gripped axes and swords, carried high and at the ready. Some people ran to their homes, slamming doors, eyes wide with unfathomable fear. Those with real weapons were shouting cries of revenge and jeers of war as they marched to the steps of the Temple Celestial. There Chief Olafur stood, like a beacon of hope amidst the barrage of confusion. The people flooded at his feet, raising their weapons, chanting something Pallah couldn't make out.

She scanned the roiling crowd for her father, sure he would be at the center of it all, perhaps inspecting the level of care the other villagers put into keeping their various tools up to snuff.

Massive braziers lined the steps to the temple and cast a stark light on the chief. The mass of bodies crammed in front of the stone steps were too packed together for her to recognize anyone. She stood in the courtyard, turning slowly, wondering which way Karav and Issha had gone. But they were second to Ahren and perhaps Vámae, too.

Pallah flipped the hood of her cloak over her dirty-blonde hair and slipped into the back of the group, keeping her head low. Someone was speaking, his voice projecting across the courtyard littered with festival ribbons, food, and overturned tables.

"Chief Olafur, we seek permission to destroy it before it comes back!" The man was in the center of the group, a flame held high, extending from his clenched fist. He was an Eldur.

"Tonight!" a woman's voice rang out, and the entire group shouted agreement.

"How many did we lose?" The chief's booming voice silenced all other noise as he spoke.

"Four, sir," the man in the middle spoke again, then he spat to the side. "Two were but babes." He raised his fist, and the flame from the top grew brighter. "We go now!" The group cheered so loudly it forced Pallah to cover her ears. What had attacked? Who *died*?

"I need all Broad Tala here now," Chief Olafur boomed to the crowd. A few hands raised, and the people parted for them to stand beside the chief. "An animal we have never tethered before could be even more aggressive after its hunt. Perhaps we need to follow it first and make sure we have the upper hand. The last thing we want is more death."

Pallah perked up. An animal that they hadn't tethered before? There was someone in each village for almost every animal. What animal could it be that they didn't have someone to cover it? She leaned forward in rapt attention, her urgency momentarily forgotten.

"Pallah!" Ahren's panicked voice came from behind her. She turned and embraced her brother, relief coursing through her as she clutched him tight.

"Ahren, what did this?" Pallah pulled away from him, seeking answers in his terrified face.

"I saw it, Pallah. It was terrible. I think something is wrong with it. It wasn't behaving like a normal predator."

"Saw what? What was it?" A plan fell into place as she became desperate for information. The group all around her was about to act. If Chief Olafur gave the word for them to hunt down the creature, she had no doubt they would find it and kill it outright. But what if it was just the animal she needed to meet? She needed to get to it before anyone else. She needed to leave now. "Ahren!" Pallah shook him violently by the shoulders.

Her little brother was trembling and limp in her arms, and he stared at her in desolate wonder. "You didn't see? Where were you?"

"Ahren! *Häfa* it all, tell me what it was!" Though she hadn't intended to shout at him, it seemed to loosen his tongue.

"I don't know, Pallah!" His voice cracked. "I've never seen anything like it. Some people said it was a big cat, like a snow leopard. Others said it was a mountain lion. But I saw it, full on." He shook harder in her arms. "It had...it had teeth like a boar...almost like...almost like...oh *stars,* it killed four people!" Sobs burst from him and pressure roared in Pallah's ears.

"The beast dies tonight!" The cry rose over the pounding in her ears, the villagers clattered their makeshift weapons in a cheer as they broke off in groups, searching for the beast.

Pallah released Ahren with a shove, the momentum driving him a few steps back. She stared at him a moment, her face becoming the mask she wore with everyone else but him. If she couldn't yet use the Taka Reu, this was her only chance of proving herself. "Don't wait up for me."

"What are you doing?" His tears stilled, his question soft and statement-like. He already knew. He knew her better than anyone.

"Go home, Ahren." Pallah touched a hand to her hatchet, then turned to disappear into the crowd.

"No one has aptitude for it, Pallah. We aren't even sure what it is!" he screamed at her over the shouts and cries.

"I said, go home!" Pallah shouted over her shoulder and set off back the way she came. Her mind already concluded what the animal was, though unready to admit it. They were mythical.

The monsters in fireside stories. Where would it hide? The barns? Somewhere quiet to eat? Had it simply mauled the villagers, or had it fed on them? Her stomach grew queasy, but she pushed it down. The beast was more important. She had to know.

Needing light, she grabbed a torch that jutted out from a doorway on her right. The pause calmed her mind. She cycled through possible hiding spots, but came up with nothing. She paced, theorizing, until her leather shoe struck a small boulder in the ground.

"*Häfa!*" She whirled on it and stopped in her tracks. Never had she been so thankful for Ms. Sherpa, teacher of her tracking class, as she recognized the soft impression of a paw, claws extending past the end of the imprint. She crouched down, bringing her torch close, and pressed it with chilled fingers. Something about the shape of the claws on the imprint reminded her...

Pallah closed her eyes and thought back to the warm cave, the grass on the walls, flower in her hand, a cool shaft of air blowing down from above. Her eyes flew open. The marks on the tunnel above her there. Those marks had been odd, like they hadn't been made by a tool...but by claws. Claw marks that led to, what had Vil said, unknown tunnels...or caves, or—

A den.

The moment she connected that space with the beast, something happened she had never experienced before. A tiny throb—almost like a headache but oddly pleasurable—began at the base of her skull, like a beacon, indicating something was there, and it was there *for her*.

It was enough to send her headlong in the direction of Eldfall once more, but this time going the back way that led halfway up

Torrah Falls. She wanted to pray, only for a moment, that the other groups would not find the animal, that she would be able to tether it first, to feel her Tala come to life for the first time. But then what would she do? Take home some hundred-pound cat and hope the village didn't arrest her for treason in owning the murderous beast?

Pallah pressed on, unwilling to think of a logical answer because, after all, what she was doing was incredibly illogical, even for her. Could she really be so cold-hearted that she wanted to save the life of the beast that killed four of her own? She expected the chastisement to slow her down, but her feet continued to carry her fast and quiet as she slipped through the woods, unhindered by man or conscience.

Fifteen minutes later, her fingers were brushing away a pile of leaves, revealing yet another print. She was at the base of Eldfall, feeling thankful that the path of broken branches, pressed leaves, and disturbed earth was obvious to her, and hopefully not to others.

After a precarious walk on the ledge behind the falls, and double and triple glances back to be sure she wasn't followed, Pallah stood at the mouth of the oddly warm cave, the depth of it seeming to go on far longer than she remembered. The light from the torch flickered in her shaking hand. Was she scared? No, she dismissed the thought. It was the anticipation, the idea that she could tether a beast...she was so close.

Pallah slipped her shoes back on, then glanced behind her. All she saw was rushing water from the falls, and she knew if a group of villagers approached, she wouldn't hear them over the water.

They would catch on; eventually, they would find this place, if not by tracking the same path she did, then tracking the path she inevitably left behind.

She just had to beat them to it.

Keeping one hand on the grassy wall, she crept down the tunnel. A cold burst of air caused her torch to waver, but then it was quickly gone. She backtracked and held her torch high. It flickered wildly as the cool air blew her hair back and off her neck.

She acted on pure instinct, guided only by the pulsing in her skull. She lobbed her torch up and over, realizing only after it left her grip what a foolhardy thing it was. The flame could come crashing down on her. But it didn't. Instead, it came to a clattering stop as it disappeared over a lip and onto a new level of cave, echoing far and long.

With the torch above, the light grew dim. Shoving her fears down, she placed a foot on either side of the narrow shaft, reaching up with both hands. She struggled to find any hand holds at first, but after slipping down once or twice, she finally found tiny crevices and jutted rock to cling to and moved slowly up the shaft.

Pallah was panting by the time she reached her burning torch at the top of the chute, hair sticking to her face, her hands sore and cramped. Hoisting herself up and over, she pushed the torch out of the way to make room for her lanky body. Breathing hard, she pressed her fingers against the cold stone beneath her. Deep cuts lined the rock. Instinct fell into line with evidence, and Pallah knew she was right. The cuts had to be claw marks left by the beast when it jumped to its home in the caves. She grabbed the torch and stood, hitting her head.

"*Häfa,*" she cursed quietly, wondering if she had picked up the habit from Vil and his group or perhaps from that voice in her head. She crouched before running at an awkward incline up the tunnel, her toes digging into the rock for traction. As she raced along the shallow cave, it occurred to her then she could be cornering the creature. If she didn't actually have aptitude for it, it would surely kill her as easily as it had struck down the people at the feast. She stopped then, the weight of the deaths coming to her in full force. Four of her own had died that very night, and here she was trying to find the creature, not to kill it, but to *greet* it.

Her own depravity made her feel ill. What had come over her? She knew she had been selfish, but could she really befriend this creature? Not befriend, she corrected herself. No, this creature would not be her friend. She would use it, like a tool. Somehow, thinking of the animal as a tool made her feel better. There was no way in Hekla she would miss out on an opportunity like this.

The cave seemed to stretch on forever, growing taller as she went so she didn't have to continue at a crouch. It kept growing until it stretched so far above, she couldn't see the ceiling. Vil was right. How did the mountain not collapse in on itself? Her torch fluttered. It would disappear completely soon. She knew the moment it went, she was a dead girl walking. The beast would have the upper hand in the dark. Well, if she was being honest, it had the upper hand in the light, too.

A bitter rush of air blew through her. She wrapped her cloak tighter around herself. She listened for movement, finally entering a small cave at the end of the tunnel. There was a small bed of rocks and a stalagmite or two on the floor. On the opposite wall, a crack spanned from the ground to far above her head, letting in a minuscule amount of moonlight. Snow trickled in, dusting the ground beneath her feet. She bent down to be sure of what she was seeing. It was only the beginning of autumn, but here was snow? Had she really traveled up high enough to warrant it?

Pallah turned in a slow circle, letting her eyes pick apart every stack of rocks, stalagmite, and pile of snow. The thing could be hiding in here with her, even in as small of a space as this.

But there was nothing.

Her torch only had minutes left and she was completely unsure of what to do next. That feeling of connection was still there. Was she connecting to traces of it? As if it had been here before, but wasn't here now?

A furious yowl came from the corner closest to where she had entered the cave.

She crouched immediately, ready to defend herself, one hand gripping her hatchet, the other holding the torch out straight. Nothing came at her. There were small shuffling sounds, a squeak, a hiss. She crept forward until her flame was directly over the offending noises.

Two pairs of eyes stared up at her, tiny beasts that they were.

Pallah had been right.

They were smilodon, sabertoothed tigers.

Stuff of legend. They weren't supposed to be real.

Yet here they were, living and breathing. And the moment Pallah's eyes locked with them, every part of her thrummed with energy. A jolt coursed through her, as if her tether needed to be attached, or it would surely burst from wanting.

So, she did.

Leaning on what she had been taught in her years at Lóthkol, she willed her tether to latch onto the smilodon on the right. Immediately, she understood. She understood when her classmates and teachers talked about the connection that was unlike anything else. The tethering that occurred, keeping them held fast, the power that surged through her as she instantaneously gained the ability to whisper and manipulate a creature of power—she was Tala, truly and finally.

"Come," she whispered.

The cub on the right, his fur white as snow and mottled with gray, stepped forward hesitantly, eyes full of innocent curiosity.

"Come to me," she amended, imagining the tiny creature sitting in front of her. To her elation, it obeyed, walking silently and sitting just in front of her. She switched to the other cub, his fur a soft gradient of brown and black. He hissed at her, batting a tiny, clawed paw in her direction.

"Come to me," she repeated, but the second one felt different, angry. She stared into its eyes, her torch quickly losing purpose. "Come, right here," she said, pointing to the space next to his sibling. The first one seemed to realize he was somewhere he didn't want to be and scuttled back into the darkness near his brother.

"No! Wait!" Pallah commanded, frustrated at the lack of light and lack of time. Her outburst startled them. They hissed and huddle together, fur raised in a ridge along their backs. The mother smilodon or the villagers would be joining them at any moment; she had to work quickly. Locking her eyes with the more compliant one again, she wordlessly commanded him to come. His eyes were a good indicator that her tether had latched, turning immediately from fear to compliance. Pallah couldn't help the smile that spread across her face.

She was Tala, and she had aptitude for smilodon. An animal that had not only never been tamed, but a creature no one even knew existed until tonight. And she, Pallah, was their master.

The thrill of knowing she was the only Smilodon Tala drove away every fear she'd ever had. Her power was unmatched. If the mother came back, she could simply step into her mind and will her to wait patiently. A mighty beast turned into a lamb.

She coaxed the white-furred cub on her lap, petting it softly and feeling the tether with her mind, exploring it. It was almost physical to her. She wasn't quite sure how others felt it, but she felt a tangible hold on hers, as if she could give the cub a leash and let it wander a bit. She decided to test it. So far, she had only used soft emotions like soothing and compliance. She stepped away from the cub and knelt to the ground again. But instead of releasing the tether, she simply changed the emotions to aggression, to attack.

His eyes changed first, from curiosity to pure fire, and before Pallah could react, the thing was bounding toward her, claws outstretched, tiny voice growling. Lacking experience and finesse, she wasn't quick enough to change the emotion of the tether but instead, released it, hoping it would stop the small cat.

It didn't.

He was on her arm in a flash, all teeth and claws and blood. Pallah flung her arm out in panic, the cub releasing with a gasp of air and spray of blood before smacking the cave wall with a grunt. It whimpered on the floor once before hissing and taking off toward his brother, huddled in the corner.

"*Häfa, häfa...*" Pallah dug around in her knapsack for something to wrap her arm. She found a wayward scarf and tore it in two with her teeth, cinching it tightly over her forearm.

"Come, now!" She said it with more bite than before, her tether connecting. But this time, there was a slight resistance, which she recognized as what she had felt with his brother. So, this was what resistance was, she thought. It was talked about in her classes, the animal's ability to sense it was being manipulated and its mind working to fight back. Guilt stabbed through her. Resistance only presented itself when an animal associated harmful memories with the Tala user.

Just last year, she read a few different scrolls for her classes on the opposing views of animal manipulation. The passive view declared that compliant and passive manipulation was the preferred way, rearing more favorable results. The author had a family of hares living all about her home, her aptitude for them. They were drawn to her tempered spirit and genuine love. Thinking about it now, Pallah thought of Leif. He had Heri Tala, too. In the scroll, the hares would willingly approach her to be used for dinner every evening. They continued to come back, even though one of them disappeared each night, for the simple affection the Heri Tala showed them.

Aggression was the opposing view. According to the Tala author, if authority was established early, the beast came faster, ran harder, or even committed self-harm. It was proven to be more effective at first; however, if the same animal was manipulated over and over, this view always cultivated more resistance than the other. The example used to showcase the aggression tactic had aptitude for killer whales. He lived near the coast and could draw his tethered beast to himself in a matter of minutes or hours, no matter how far it had swum away. His biography ended with the man and his whale both dead. The whale died by the spear the man shoved into him; the man died in the whale's mouth, bitten up to his waist.

Looking at the small cubs, noticing their soft fur and round eyes, her mindset shifted. She didn't want to end up like the man eaten by his own tethered beast.

But look at their teeth, prepared to strike you down at any moment. Yet, you have control over them. Complete control. Such power you wield.

The voice was clearer here, in this mountain. Was this her true mind? It *would* feel powerful to control them when no one else could.

Her arm was throbbing, soaked through with blood. But even with the pain, she hadn't lost her tether, her true accomplishment this night, overwriting any discomfort. A gust of frozen air blew in from the crag at the far wall and her torch flickered and died.

"*Häfa,*" she cursed as the darkness penetrated deeper than the cold. But how could Pallah leave the cubs behind to be killed? The angry townsfolk were surely coming up the mountain now. Two thoughts formed quickly as she stood still in the dark.

The first, just like the boar Karav killed in the wood, the mother smilodon's teats would be swollen and ready to nurse. If the mob found her first, they would know of her litter. Second, she couldn't take both cubs, or they would know someone was protecting them. They wouldn't stop hunting until the entire family of smilodon was dead. Leaving both meant death for all. Taking both meant suspended death for the cubs, but taking one meant death for the mother, death for one cub, and safety for the last. Or perhaps...the mother would come back in time to save the other cub. This was her only comfort.

Regardless, Pallah had one option. Shouldering her knapsack on her bad arm, she reached down to pick up the cub with the other, the softness of him making her feel soft inside, too. She heard the other cub, the brown one, whine softly. As if he knew his brother was leaving, as if he knew tragedy would befall him.

"I'm sorry," she whispered. She wanted to send her tether to him, to comfort him, but she knew any hold lost on the one in her arms would send him reeling again.

Pallah ran off down the long hallway, one arm clutched to her side, one arm around the smilodon cub, and one tether connected and thrumming with life.

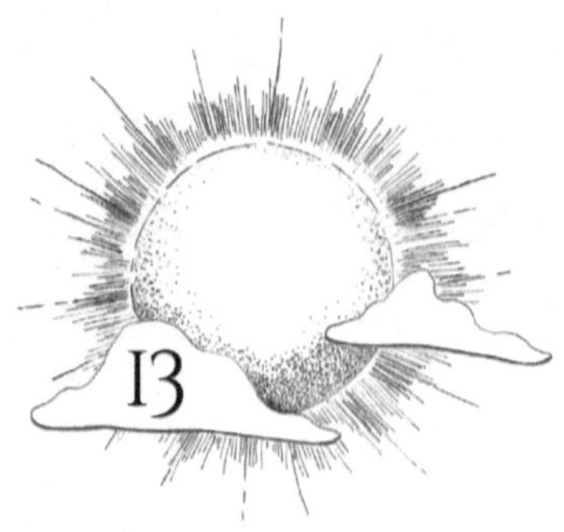

THE BURNING BOY

SOLYANA

S AFETY JUST A FEW steps behind her, Solyana knew she should retreat into the Temple. But what of Jonas? Gamaliel? She was the only one who knew where they were. The only one who had survived a storm like this before, and could possibly survive again. Bells clanged above and behind her. The priestess knew about the storm, and she was warning the people. But it meant nothing for the two out there now. If they died, she would never forgive herself.

She started forward, one foot in front of the other, making quick work in the wind. The part of her mind seeking reason screamed at her to turn around, to take shelter. Looking back at the Temple Celestial, she saw nothing but a sheet of endless winter storm. Was it behind her? How could she be sure? Was she even going in the right direction?

Something deep and resounding inside her drew her back out into the storm. She allowed it to pull her until she was forced to stop running, unsure of her location. Was that barking? A howl? Attempting to distinguish between the howls of wind, the pounding of blood in her ears, and anything else was impossible. Regardless, she followed it. Maybe it was Vinur, maybe it was death calling to her; there was no telling.

A dark mass broke through the endless white as Vinur ran headlong into her, the warmth of his body a welcome reprieve at her legs. He howled incessantly. Praise for that. He was circling her legs, herding her forward, and before she knew it, the ground changed beneath her, hardening from snow to ice. Solyana stopped in place. Had she really run all the way to the Vatino? Vinur clamped down on a piece of her parka, tugging her along. He must be leading her to them, Gamaliel and Jonas.

A glow emanated a distance ahead. Had the moon peeked through and shone on the glassy sea beneath? No, it was flickering and too bright to be a reflection.

Stumbling toward the light, the whiteout forced her steps to slow. Solyana tripped over two figures bundled together in the snow. Gamaliel was sprawled on the ice, Jonas beside him, curled up and unmoving. Solyana knelt next to them and shook Gamaliel hard.

"Gamaliel! Wake up!" He probably couldn't even hear her through the storm. "Gamaliel!" she screamed louder. Vinur was circling, barking and whining. "Vinur, help me," she told the wolf, unsure why she was speaking to him like he could understand her, but he was smarter than she gave him credit for. Vinur lowered his muzzle, wrapped his maw around Gamaliel's sleeve and began pulling him in quick jerks.

"Ah!" Gamaliel shot up, striking out and catching Vinur's nose with the back of his hand. "Oh, Vinur, sorry!" Vinur turned to Jonas, nudging him with his muzzle.

"Oh, thank the Celestials." But before Solyana could feel relief, a crack sounded deep beneath her. Her eyes widened and her knees began shaking. "We need to get off the ice!"

Gamaliel nodded, feeling the back of his head; he must have fallen and hit his head. He went to Jonas, shook him once, and when he didn't wake, lifted him onto his shoulders.

"Follow me!" he shouted over the thrall.

Then the glow appeared once more. It was on Jonas's hands, first flickering and then bright. Solyana's chest constricted as she recognized exactly what it was: fire. It emanated from the young scribe's hands...was he burning?

No, she amended. He was Heitt. Impossible. But he must be. Her feet pounded over the ice-laden sea, her eyes on the pair ahead. She almost missed the second *crack* beneath her, closer this time. She slowed and looked down. It came again, an echoing snap that rocked the ice on which she stood, dropping her enough to make her heart swoop. She shifted to keep her balance. The clouds above cleared for an infinitesimal second to reveal the moon, shining bright on the torrential storm raining down on them and their valley.

This was no blizzard.

Slackened with terror, Solyana stared with her mouth agape. What was she seeing? This was some kind of spiral of death for which she had no name; she could only imagine the destruction it would cause. Snow whipped so fast around and around, the cone picked up pieces of the courtyard: one of the pikes, a wooden bench. She watched in disbelief as the moon's last light showed the spiraling storm's movement, making its way into Austur, leaving a path of destruction in its wake as it trudged directly toward Solyana.

She felt more than saw when it hit the sea on which she stood. Leaving the shore, it rolled over the ice like it was nothing but dry parchment, shattering it, and launching pieces out of the sea. Hard ice became glaciers at jagged proportions as the cyclone made its steady way toward them. The moon disappeared in roiling clouds and darkness encapsulated the valley.

Solyana's feet began to chill, water soaking into her mukluks; she imagined being taken under. No—no! Her breathing, already ragged from her flight across the sea, began hitching even more.

"Gamaliel!" she shrieked into the night, but he did not turn, only the sounds of shattering ice answered her. "Celestials, guide me!" In almost instantaneous answer to her prayer, a bounce of flame flared in the distance, and she shot in that direction. Fear fueled her flight, her only goal outrunning the cracking and breaking of ice beneath her feet.

Each step was perilous as she weaved her way across the sea over the patches of sinking ice. Solyana's mukluks were sodden now, water sloshing and spraying up toward her face. The flicker of Jonas's hands was the only thing visible, and Solyana followed them like her life depended on it.

She launched around a massive break in the ice as Gamaliel crossed to sure ground. Jonas's hands were shooting a steady stream of flame and then abruptly winked out. Solyana had only been a few paces from land, but with the flame gone, her hope smashed to pieces. She halted, only for her right leg to plunge entirely into the water. The cold forced the breath out of her lungs, her mouth gaping in the bitter wind. Her body started shaking as she tried to find purchase, clawing at the ice. But her desperate movements only widened the break, threatening to swallow her whole.

"Gamaliel!" she screamed, arms flailing to hold on to something. She could see nothing but snow-battered dark and feel nothing but cold.

"I can't get to you!" he shouted over the noise. "The ice is breaking too fast—" She thought she heard him say something else, but the wind stole his voice.

Solyana creeped forward, gripping the ice through soaking gloves and kicking to extricate herself out of the hole. But the kick broke the ice into nothing, and her left leg joined her right. The cold was malicious, piercing bone and marrow. Her breathing shuddered in shallow bursts, but she had no power to slow it.

The storm was not far behind her. The sea whipped up waves as if to drown her was its sole purpose. She felt around with frozen hands for a stable piece of ice, anything to crawl on top of; hypothermia could set in within ten minutes, shorter in the worst of conditions. How long had she been submerged? Too long. She needed to get her body horizontal. She clawed her gloves off, kicking as hard as she could to keep her torso above the black water.

Her hope faltered as Solyana was forced to confront the real possibility, she would die here, and her parents would have two daughters to mourn. She flung her arms out in one last attempt at safety and felt the sharp edge of ice beneath her hand. Her heart in her throat, and though she was too cold to feel them move, she continued to pump her legs. Her upper body needed to get on the ice as quickly as possible. Using the last of her strength, she was able to pull the rest of her body onto the slab of bobbing ice.

Spluttering and coughing, her feet finally released by the sea, she began to take assessment of her body. She was surely hypothermic by now. She pressed the side of her head firmly against the ice, shaking and numb. She rolled onto her back, taking a slow moment to see the clouds parting. Something dark flew between them and started to dive. She blinked a few times, trying to focus her eyes. It was large and shooting like an arrow. It let out a screech that pierced even the loudest gale.

"Halina," she mouthed. Who would hear her anyway? The falcon steadied itself and dropped with surprising force in front of her. One of the curved talons snapped off with impact.

Wiping fruitlessly at her eyes, Solyana was unable to understand why Halina was there, or how? But any thoughts she had began to quiet; the water that soaked her clothes and skin began to freeze, her internal temperature started to fall, her eyes grew too heavy and her breath pulled too slow. Halina screeched again, then took flight once more, causing a small wave to pulse beneath her small boat of ice in a different tempo than the storm.

Solyana, eyes closed, thought of Rhuth, feeling an odd sense of being watched over. As if the falcon had come to welcome her to the other side. She waited for the cyclone to suck her into its wake. And then it began; her icy vessel sweeping backward, toward the storm that was waiting to consume her. Solyana gripped the ice, accepting her fate. But then it stopped going backward and changed direction. It propelled her forward, as if she was riding a wave.

Having prepared herself for a quick and cold death, Solyana's eyes flew open at the unexpected push toward land. The wave that carried her was too fast and too smooth to be natural. She braced herself for impact all the same.

The clouds broke once more, revealing the dorsal fin of some aquatic creature just beside her makeshift raft of ice, pushing it, carrying her swiftly across the raging water. Then, with a splash of dark tail against darker waters, it released the ice and broke away, leaving her to crash into land, the ice shattering around her.

The strangeness of events dissolved as Solyana crawled up onto the shore. Had she ever been so tired? So cold? She rolled on her side in time to see the cyclone over the center of Vatino Sea, its pure power whipping ice and creatures alike. It was no respecter of persons.

A hand grabbed her upper arm and dragged her over the snow. Gamaliel pulled her backward, but he only made it a few paces before bending down and picking her up.

Solyana turned to him, desperate for warmth. Held in his arms, she focused on breathing, emitting effort to note her surroundings only in fragments.

A dank cave with dripping walls.

A quiet void to what was happening outside.

A fire, inviting and warm, bloomed in the center.

A small, bundled figure lay beside it.

Then Gamaliel was stripping her out of her soaking parka and tunic, mukluks, and socks. She kept her eyes open, staring into the fire, as the young man she hardly knew removed ice-caked pieces of clothing from her shivering body. He wrapped her in a fur blanket and sat her in front of the fire, next to the small boy on the ground. He rubbed her arms with purpose, but when he stopped to feel her skin, his face fell. And soon enough, he, too, was stripped down to his underclothes and was wrapping her in his arms, his whole body enveloping her like a mother would hold a frightened child. He carried her to a soft bed and laid down beside her.

Solyana didn't know how long they stayed there. The fire crackling, Gamaliel breathing in rhythmic time, centering her. The wind outside surely breaking even the mountain above them. She didn't have to think on it long though, for in moments, she succumbed to sleep.

The reminiscent softness of skin on bare skin, the smell of musk and oil, the tickle of hair on the back of her neck. All of it seemed so real. Yet, when the tendrils of wakefulness pried her mind open, she still felt first for a body she thought was lying beside her, but wasn't. She nodded off once more without opening her eyes, convinced it had all been a dream.

Something savory was being roasted over a fire, but she still didn't want to leave the sweet embrace of sleep. Images from the night before flashed before her and her body ached in affirmation. She tried willing herself back to sleep, but the memory of being trapped on the ice and plunged waist-deep into freezing water shocked her out of slumber. She thought of Jonas, flame coming from his hands, but no, that couldn't be right. There had been so much happening, she couldn't be sure of what she saw. And Halina...why was she flitting around in the recesses of Solyana's mind? There was a vague memory of a broken talon, a dorsal fin.

"Eat, Jonas." Gamaliel's voice came softly from somewhere behind her. She opened her eyes to see a wall of stone, rough and uncut, so unlike the Temple Celestial. Ah, that's right, because she was in a cave.

"I'm not hungry," Jonas said. Solyana was glad to hear his voice.

"Eat," Gamaliel repeated. "Put those scrolls down. You're not going to find any answers in there, not for her, anyway." Solyana's throat felt suddenly very dry. "She's not the one."

"She has the mark. The Celestials made it clear," Jonas whispered.

"You saw it yourself?"

"Well, no." She heard a rustle of parchment. "But you saw it, you told me."

"I don't know what I saw." Gamaliel sighed. "Besides, she's Rána. It's impossible."

Silence hung for a moment.

"Maybe she's not," Jonas whispered.

"She had her Stada," Gamaliel mumbled.

Pressure built behind Solyana's eyes. She thought about her Stada. Before that day, she still had possibility. But once Ms. Borta had proclaimed her Rána, all the 'not yet's had turned into 'never.' With no Gift, Solyana was forever doomed to be the one that got rescued, the one that needed saving. Never the one to save.

There was a shuffling of feet and Solyana heard a knee pop beside her. She turned.

"You're alive," Gamaliel said plainly. He held out a plate, steam rising off the top. "And to keep you that way, you need to eat." Solyana sat up, keeping the blanket wrapped around her shoulders. It smelled wonderful. "Look…" He hesitated. "The bells sounded before the bulk of the storm hit the town and it was well into the night. Most everyone was already in their homes; your family should be safe."

Images of the massive cyclone over her town came to the forefront of her mind: the wind, the terror, the unknowing. It was a mistake to think of it. Her eyes stung, and she burrowed her face into the blanket. What time was it? How long had she been here? Her body ached for sun, and her soul ached for sky. Gamaliel seemed certain everything was fine, but he had been running headlong to his cave. Had he seen that massive cyclone over the sea that she had? Had her family survived the night? More than that, what if the entire valley was simply obliterated? A few warning bells couldn't save a people doomed to be buried.

She sniffed and released her blanket, reaching for the plate. How did Gamaliel look so flawless after such a horrible night? No shadows under his eyes, his hair looking neatly kempt. She shook her head, she probably looked like a half-drowned rat; she certainly felt like one. Why was he smirking? He averted his gaze. His face reddened and flushed. Then the cool of the cave tickled her bare skin, and her eyes widened.

Solyana let out a squeal and quickly pulled the covers back around her, moving much slower than she hoped, her body sore and, to her absolute shame, almost completely naked. She had no idea when she had stripped to her underclothes, but the look on Gamaliel's face led her to believe this wasn't the first time he had seen her like this.

With his eyes on the cave wall and that smirk on his face, he extended an armful of clothes in her direction. "They'll be dry by now. They've been by the fire."

Solyana snatched them from him. "Did you do this?" she grumbled, and he graciously put his back to her.

"Um, yes. And you're welcome...if I hadn't, you would be dead."

Solyana began the laborious task of standing on legs that trembled like water and bones that cracked like the chill of the sea. Slowly, she pulled on pants, tunic, and thick socks.

"Do you remember *anything* from last night?" he asked, still facing away from her.

Solyana cleared her throat, and he turned back to her, his eyes losing their playfulness. Looking at him now, she recalled in spurts the rush to remove her freezing clothes that were encouraging hypothermia. His warm chest pressed up against her back, breathing slow and soft against the nape of her neck as he rubbed the life back into her arms with his hands.

"I remember the blizzard," she said vaguely.

"I do, too," Jonas piped in, suddenly at Gamaliel's elbow.

"*Häfa,*" he spat out, startled.

"What?" Jonas glanced between them, oblivious to any tension.

Gamaliel rolled his eyes and gave Solyana a look she couldn't decipher before walking back to the fire. Jonas grabbed her hand.

"Ms. Solyana! Do you like our home? This is my bed." Jonas dragged her over to another area of the cave. The walls were stuck with different parchments and canvas, drawings and paintings, the types of trappings that made it a home. "We don't often have guests!" Jonas was chipper, his excitement infectious. He reminded her so much of Rhuth. "I'm so glad you're okay. I have been waiting to talk to you. You slept such a long time. Did Gam keep you warm? He's never slept next to *me* before, but you looked comfortable. Maybe he'll let me in his bed tonight."

Solyana's cheeks grew hot as he dragged her over to the fire. She didn't dare look at Gamaliel. "It's just, um, Solyana," she corrected him. "And your friend saved my life. I am thankful." She snuck a look at Gamaliel who sat on the other side of the fire, absently stroking Vinur beside him. She turned back to Jonas, annoyed Gamaliel's face was no longer red as hers surely was. "So, this is your cave?"

"If one can possess a cave...yes, it's mine," Gamaliel said, not unkindly.

"Why are you way out here?" Solyana couldn't imagine having to cross over the icy sea every day.

"That's a story for another time," Gamaliel said dismissively, rising to his feet. "I'm going to pack up. We should get you home."

Solyana furrowed her brow, and she caught a glimpse of Jonas's hands as he rifled through his bag.

"Oh *stars,* I almost forgot. Are your hands okay?"

Jonas turned to her, eyes questioning and bright.

"Last night, it looked like your hands were—"

"Vinur got to your gloves again!" Gamaliel interrupted loudly, and Vinur's head popped up at his name. "They were torn to shreds. I'll start on some new ones for you."

"Vinur!" Jonas whined. The wolf looked personally offended, glancing between Gamaliel and Jonas. "Stop eating my gloves!" he reprimanded and sighed heavily. "That's the fourth pair in the last few months."

"Yeah...it's a good thing he's cute, right?" Gamaliel crooned, stooping down to scratch Vinur's chin. Vinur, unamused, repositioned himself closer to the fire.

"Why doesn't he ever get to *your* gloves?" Jonas questioned.

"Why don't you ever put *yours* where they belong?" Gamaliel shot back playfully.

Solyana glanced between them. Hadn't she seen the boy shooting flames from his hands? Perhaps she had imagined it. But, no, there had to have been something to light her way as she ran after Gamaliel. She *remembered* a light.

Gamaliel locked eyes with Solyana and gave an imperceptible shake of his head before turning to a rough-hewn table at the back of the cave. Solyana made a mental note to ask him about it later. She ate her food with a smile, for now, content to be in this home with this stranger. How quickly she had grown comfortable with him, bonded in trauma as they were.

"Miss"—Jonas cleared his throat—"I mean, Solyana, may I ask you a question?"

"Sure," she said with her mouth full. Gamaliel had found a rabbit. It was delicious. Jonas extricated a long scroll from a leather tube and unfurled it across the floor. Solyana stopped eating, her stomach twisting at the topic she knew was coming.

"Do you remember what Priestess Avi talked to you about when you woke the other day? Your scar, the prophecy, the resolution to it?" The small boy spoke so affluently for his young age Solyana couldn't help the smile that pricked her lips.

"Yes, and honestly, I'm not sure—"

"Well, you can be!" Jonas interrupted her excitedly. "May I?" He held a small hand to her face, and Solyana jerked back reflexively.

"Give the girl a minute, Jonas," Gamaliel said, his back to them, throwing things into a knapsack.

"No, it's...okay." Solyana cleared her throat. "I want to know. I want to know if this is my duty, what I'm supposed to do with my life. Maybe...maybe whatever I'm supposed to do can save Rhuth." She leaned into Jonas's hand.

Jonas pulled a scroll up next to him with one hand, the other pressed to her left cheek. Then he read out loud, "*Syna oku merki.*" The moment the words left his tongue, the left side of Solyana's face came alive with fire, and she gasped in pain. She wanted nothing more than to scramble away from him, but something held her fast, transfixed.

Gamaliel was up, hand on his staff, his gaze boring into her. "*Häfa to heaven,*" he said reverently.

Jonas's green eyes moved from her cheek to her gray eyes, and he gave her another grin. "*Syna oku merki,*" he repeated, his enthusiasm mounting. "Show us the sign," he translated. "It says here these words would only work on the *true* mark."

She saw herself in Jonas's eyes, like a mirror, the fire flickering in his left eye, and in his right, the shape of a dark crescent moon was seared into her flesh.

TWO BROKEN TETHERS

PALLAH

TETHERING A BEAST WAS far more exhilarating than she could have ever imagined. It wasn't just whispering or manipulation, it was a relationship. A concept no lecture or scroll could ever teach. Pallah tugged gently at the tether in her mind and felt the tension that lay there, expectant. The cub was asleep in her lap, breathing in a quick rhythm. It purred and gave a shuddering yawn. Pallah held him tighter to her, his soft, warm fur tickling her skin.

She was sitting squat against a tree in the White Wood, just beyond Torrah Falls. The wind almost warm after feeling the biting cold of the snowy cave above. The moon, hidden by cloud, had dipped the night into the kind of dark that penetrated bones. If her new beast had been any other color but a mottled white, he would have been invisible.

Pallah made no attempt to wipe the tears that fell down her face as torch after torch made its way into the cavern behind the falls. They had checked Darmál first, of course, and then they discovered The Cove. She prayed to the Celestials, which she hadn't done in years, they wouldn't look up, wouldn't notice the cool breeze that wafted in from far above. But no, they would find it. Someone would surely see.

She couldn't save both of them, she knew. They would have killed the mother by now, wherever she had been hiding, and they would know she had been nursing cubs. Pallah had done the only thing that guaranteed the survival of at least one. Then a thought hit her like a bolt of lightning. With the tiny cub asleep in her arms, perhaps he wouldn't notice her release him and tether his brother. Maybe she could get the other cub to flee.

Classwork came rushing back to her then, information on tethering to a beast without sight of one. How it took training, skill, and prowess, the difficulty only increasing with the distance. But it *was* possible.

She slowly untethered the one in her arms, the release causing him to snuffle and turn in his sleep. She held her breath and waited. The cub continued his snoring. Pallah gathered her tether and pushed it out to the other cub in one stroke. Vertigo slammed into her and she stumbled from her crouched position, sitting hard on the forest floor, cradling the cub in her injured arm. Inhaling sharply at the pain of it, she looked down. He hadn't woken. *Holy Hekla,* she was being careless. The tether felt like it was flapping in an unrelenting wind, searching and searching but coming up empty. Releasing it and rocking back on her heels, she let her head fall back against the tree, the tears coming again. No, she had to reach him. She knew where he was; she knew how to find him. Closing her eyes, she pictured the mouth of the cave, its grassy walls and flowery entrance, then the shaft that led up above the rest, the long tunnel that led to the den.

Her tether shot straight, a mark in its sights. It passed different beasts, those of the Tala that marched to the cave, but she ignored them all. Bursting into the cave above, her tether entwined with the cub on the other end. It was a weak bind, but it was there, keeping her attuned to his emotions. As fast and calmly as she could, she tried to rouse him. Nothing happened. She knew in an instant, like a reflex long in hibernation now rising to the surface, her tether wasn't sure. Trying to strengthen it, she only managed to slip off and back on again several times. Without technical study, without practice, she was left scrambling, doing nothing but touching his emotions, feeling his warmth, his innocent ignorance.

The cub on the other end of her tether woke suddenly, though not of Pallah's doing. His warm slumber turned into fear and rage all at once. Her tears stopped and her blood ran cold. No, this wasn't happening. She was tethered to his emotions and unable to do anything about his fate. Rage boiled up in the beast, and she knew he was fighting. She encouraged him, but he would feel none of her emotions. He would never know that Pallah was there. He would die alone.

His rage heightened, and just before her tether snapped, she felt terror, raw terror that made her choke on the bile that rose in her throat. Then it was done. The tether snapped, for there was nothing left to attach it to. She leaned to the side and expelled her stomach. The cub in her lap stirred. She latched back onto him, as easy and as natural as raising an arm or blinking. He settled back into slumber, unaware of his brother's demise.

She heard muted cheers from Torrah Falls. How dare they be happy? She remembered then the people slain by the cub's mother. She had probably been trying to find food for her own children. Could she be blamed? She was doing what every mother was driven to do: survive and protect.

Pallah got to her feet and slipped away from the scene. If she wasn't in her room by morning, the consequences would be quick and heavy-handed. As she made her way over the grounds to Sodur, she was relieved to find her path clear of people. The whole city was waiting quietly for news of the slain beast or sleeping, if possible. She closed the door silently behind her as she entered her home, dark and hollow. Creeping into her room, she took care not to use her injured arm. She would have to clean it in the morning. Her exhaustion was all-encompassing; tethering cost her more than she thought it would. The smilodon was tucked under her good arm. She would wake before first light and find a more secure place to hide him, but for now, she needed sleep, and she couldn't risk leaving him somewhere while the Tala were still hunting.

It was so dark she couldn't tell if the two room she shared with Vámae was empty or not. She quietly grabbed one of her baskets of clothes, dumped out what was inside, and replaced it with the cub. Her tether would stay while she slept, right? She secured the top with a lid, just in case. Then she slipped into her cot, keeping her rage at bay at the injustice that had occurred to the cub on the mountain. Killing something because one feared it was not a righteous action; it was cowardly. The basket was next to her cot, her tether remaining fixed. Pallah vowed to herself she would keep this one safe, this one would have no reason to fear the more dangerous beasts, the beasts that walked on two legs instead of four.

Pallah knew something was wrong before she opened her eyes. She had dreamt in emotions instead of sight, a never-ending dark spiral of unresolved desire. She wanted to wake, but her body was too tired to do anything about it. Sight came then, bright and unrelenting. She was still dreaming, right? Yet, somehow, the sun was still coming through. The sun, one of the Celestials, Father of—

Pallah bolted upright, her eyes flying open and her hands reaching for the basket. Her stomach dropped; the lid was askew. The smilodon cub was gone.

"*Häfa!*" she hissed, louder than she wanted, and she glanced over to her sister's cot. Vámae was gone, too. Scrambling out of bed, tossing the fur blanket aside, she searched everywhere. Then she squeezed her eyes shut; she would use her tether.

Picturing the cub in her mind, his saberteeth and white-gray mottled fur, she tried to locate him. But unlike the night before, when she knew exactly where the other cub was in his cave, she had no idea where her cub had gone. The vertigo came back again as she attempted a latch, her tether reaching wildly. She stopped before she fell, frustrated.

Her pants felt too tight, and looking down, she realized she still had the harness on from her precarious trip down the mountain. She was able to wiggle out of it with help from only one hand, the other was hot and pulsing with pain. She shoved the harness under her blanket as she heard footsteps approach.

"Pallah." Vámae walked in, her eyes tired and her hair messier than Pallah had seen it in some time. "Father is waiting for you in the kitchen."

Pallah stopped scanning the room for signs of the cub and knew then her father had the smilodon. And if that was true, it was all over. She scanned Vámae's face for any hint of the conversation to come but saw nothing. She threw on a fresh tunic, hiding her injured arm as best she could. It looked even worse than it felt, which should have concerned her more than it did, but there was no time to worry for herself.

Father was standing over the kitchen table, one arm supporting his weight while the other maneuvered a cloth over the surface with meticulous precision. His need for order and beauty drove her mad, as if he was trying to make up for his plainness. He said nothing, of course, forcing Pallah to break the silence.

"Father," she prompted, her eyes searching and coming up short for the animal. "You wanted to see me?"

"Are you aware of all that happened last night, Pallah?" Her name was spat from his lips, a dribble of saliva making its way to the table, quickly overtaken by two revolutions of the cloth.

"There was an attack," she spoke plainly. "Four people were killed."

For some moments, the only sound was the stroke of cloth against the wood grain, the table creaking under increased pressure as her father leaned into it. Pallah stiffened. "Four," he said with a pause. "Four people." The table groaned. "Now, tell me, what attacked?"

Pallah's heart dropped. Had they caught the mother smilodon? Did they know the responsibility lay with a beast of legend—only now proven real? She kicked herself for not going straight to the Temple Celestial the night before. She should have found out all the details before falling asleep. "I don't know. I came back here to sleep before—"

"Stop lying!" he hissed, and in the same breath, one table leg cracked, but not beneath his weight, as he was a lean man. He was using his Fera. Pallah's good hand flew to her face, covering her open mouth. "You were not home last night, girl. You were nowhere to be found, not at the Temple Celestial, not anywhere. In fact, some said you were seen making your way across the Vatino." The loose skin of his sunken jowls trembled, his breathing came fast. "I remember strictly forbidding you from leaving the grounds last night. What were you doing?"

Well, he's in quite a state, isn't he? Häfa to you too, Bogdur. The voice in her head chimed in. Pallah shook her head, trying to dissipate it.

"I...I..." She needed a partial truth, something that gave credence to her crossing into White Wood. *Häfa* it all, who had seen her?

She knew what she needed to say, but it pained her to be so transparent. Father would only use it against her.

"I—I—don't you lie to me!" Father mimicked and jabbed a finger in her direction.

"I needed to know for myself, if it was my aptitude!" Pallah said in a rush. She couldn't recall the last time she had been this honest with her father. He stared at her, face blank, maybe even speechless for once. She pushed forward, "I've never done it, Father. I've never tethered a beast, but I know it's there, somewhere beneath the surface...I...I can feel it."

Her father shook his head, the air around him transforming from hostile to something less explosive but no less dangerous. "You thought your aptitude might be for...a smilodon?"

Pallah blinked and looked up at him, knowing she should feel shame, but didn't. "Smilodon? Those aren't real." She hoped she sounded convincing, but she couldn't stop her eyes from scanning for the cub.

He licked his lips and looked her up and down as if he was seeing her for the first time. "Smilodons were thought to be legend, but last night proved their existence...why would you think it was your aptitude?"

"I didn't know what it was before I started looking," she admitted the partial truth, fearing she would give herself away with any other answer.

He narrowed his eyes at her and whispered, "Hmm...impossible." Pallah didn't think it was for her, his eyes were untrained, looking past her shoulder. Then he seemed to come back to himself and searched her face. She furrowed her brow. He shook his head, then squatted down to examine the break in the table. "You bring shame on my family."

My family.

A fresh wave of rejection pierced through any calluses she'd come to develop.

She began to cry, and she hated herself for it. "I'm sorry."

Father's thin lips pulled back into a sneer as he looked at her up and down. "You're incapable at your own Gift, so naturally, you wanted to bond with a creature that murdered your people?" he asked, though she knew it wasn't a question. Pallah's hands were shaking. "You disgust me. Get out of my house."

The door swung hard, hitting the frame as she exited. The chill morning air was still except for a few decaying leaves skittering over the ground around her feet. She paced, attempting and failing, to calm herself. At least he didn't have the cub. It was her one and only consolation.

A tug stopped her cold, deep in her skull, directing her back to her home. Was it her tether? She was still so new at this, but no, there it was again. She followed its lead, stumbling over the browning grass until she saw her mother in the middle of their yard.

Dressed in the meshy tunic many Heitt wore to allow the sun more access to the body, her mother lay flat on her back in the frigid morning air. Most other Heitt exchanged the mesh tunic for warmer ones after the Feast of Haust, or they sat in the greenhouses to commune with the sun. Mother was shivering. It was probably on Father's orders. He made her do things like this, always aiming for perfection, to stay out all day when other Heitt were satisfied after an hour or two. She scanned her mother's body. It was frail and bony beneath her tunic, her face gaunt. When had she grown so old?

Then she saw him, the tiny fluff of fur curled up against her mother, and Pallah's breath caught in her throat. She tip-toed to her side and scooped up the cat while securing the tether that had begun to find him on its own. She sent calm to him and sleep. He remained snoring. Pallah looked down to see her mother's open eyes staring up at her. She froze, her fate suddenly hanging on her mother's response; it would be expected of Mother to go to Chief Olafur, have the cub killed, and Pallah publicly disciplined. But while Mother had never been overtly caring, she also had never been cruel.

Mother closed her eyes again and smiled, a rare look that appeared disjointed on her face. "You found your aptitude," she whispered, so quietly Pallah had to squat close to hear. "It's different with predators, I'm told. You will never be the same. He is your life now." Her mother peeked to the side, her eyes catching on something. "He hurt you already."

Pallah, eyes wide, stared at her mother's serene face, seeing more than she ever had before. Would she truly defy all of Mothmar and keep Pallah's aptitude a secret?

"Here, let me help." Her mother sat up, though Pallah could see the effort it took. Taking her daughter's sleeve in her hands she gently rolled it back, revealing Pallah's arm, crusted with dried blood and hot with the beginnings of infection. Her mother let out a hiss but kept her gaze on the wound. She lifted a thin hand and pressed it down directly onto the affected area. Pallah winced.

"With prey animals, it's easier to see them as a means to an end. But him?" She let out a sigh, her face bright in the sun. "Protect him, child. Do not let him come to harm."

"Mother?" How did she know so much about Tala? She was too stunned to formulate specific questions.

Mother released Pallah's arm with hesitancy, worry flashing across her face before staring up at the unfolding clouds that hung, low and dark. Pallah hadn't noticed them until now. "You aren't at risk of infection any longer, but it would help to get some salve on this." She motioned to her arm, now only a slight red mark, then laid back down, flat on her back. She sighed. "I loved once. A Tala man." Her sunken eyes flickered to her daughter and back to the sky. "He loved his tethered beast more than he loved me; maybe that passion was what drew me to him...though it was what eventually undid him. I've always been drawn to purpose," she said the last bit to herself before sitting up on one elbow. "Bogdur must not hear a word."

"Of course, Mother," Pallah said quietly.

"You put him—and yourself—at risk, if you allow him to lose control like that," she repeated, motioning to Pallah's arm and then the cub. "If he dies or is harmed, you will feel it as if it's your own soul."

Pallah's throat tightened. She swallowed, remembering how the tiny cub in the cave felt when the hoard of villagers descended on him: unrelenting terror, pure agony. She would do anything to keep that from happening again.

"What happened? With you and the Tala man, I mean."

Her mother gave a low chuckle and settled back to the ground, her body still quavering. "What didn't happen? But his beast was killed. It's a terrible tale. Part of him...part of him died with it, I think," she was whispering again, as if drifting to sleep. "He always said that when the tether was strongest, you were at your most vulnerable; whatever that beast feels, you will, too. He was gone one day. But then...he tried..." She fell silent, long enough for Pallah to wonder if her mother had fallen asleep, but then she continued. "He attempted something risky. It left him broken. Sometimes I wonder what would have happened if I had just trusted him." She paused, her eyes shifting from Pallah to the sabertoothed cub. "I never thought you would be the one to get it."

"Wait, get what?" Pallah stared at her mother, willing her to say more, but she slipped back into whatever state Heitt went into when charging. Her mind was reeling. Her mother had loved before. *Actually loved*, not endured, as she did Pallah's father. This woman, who she had come to view as little more than a breathing object, a puppet animated by any will but her own, had once been so bold. The same woman now, the way her father spoke to her, treated her, manipulated her, her humanity had slipped away soon after Pallah was weaned. Perhaps even before; an infant's hunger comes from necessity, not want. Had she ever truly *wanted* her mother?

Pallah stared at the woman on the ground soaking up the sun, absorbed in her religion or her husband's instruction, risking bodily harm for the sake of a greater good. She shook in her light tunic. What had she meant when she said she didn't think Pallah would be the one to get it? Pallah had never blended with her family, never understood her place amongst them. Finding out what her mother meant would have to come later. For now, she needed to find a place to practice with her new little companion.

Pallah crossed back into the house, grateful her father had left and Vámae was busy at the stove. Slipping back into her room, Pallah found a smaller basket, lid and handles attached, and placed the cub inside. He looked so peaceful in his sleep. She rotated her shoulder and lifted her arm. The pain was gone. Though her mother had healed her many times before, it never ceased to amaze her.

"I was up all night, you know." Pallah jumped at the sound of Vámae's voice and her eyes went immediately to the basket sitting on her bed before meeting her sister's water-blue stare. Vámae looked guilty, an emotion Pallah didn't often see on her. "I...I saw it coming down the mountain, Pallah. Just a flash of brown, but I saw it. I was confused and thought it was just the firelight playing tricks with my eyes, and I...I didn't say anything."

"Anyone would have done—"

"No, Pallah. I am responsible for at least one of those lives last night. They didn't even find the beast until after it had taken down a...a second. It was so fast, so quiet." She was crying now, her chin set in a quiver that reflected the shake in her hands. "Two were kids."

Moving to her bed, Pallah picked up the basket, aware of the carnivorous beast that lay inside, and the destruction it was capable of. "Does anyone know why it came down the mountain? Was it sick?" Pallah thought it odd that the smilodon, who had cubs so far up the mountain, would risk leaving them for what looked like purposeless killing.

"When they finally got to the beast, they realized she'd recently had a cub. She must have been hunting for it. Perhaps it was just weaned." Pallah nodded her on; they had figured it out as she'd thought they would. "Though, it does seem odd…that it would come all the way down from where they said they found the den. It wasn't even trying to take anything back up to it. They found her behind the Temple Celestial, almost…waiting for them, four people mauled in her wake." Vámae shook her head, her dark hair falling delicately around her face.

Pallah, too, found it odd that the mother would hunt so far from her cubs. Nothing was known of smilodons, perhaps it was normal behavior. But then, wouldn't they have seen one before? This animal was a work of fiction until now…something must have driven it down, forced the cat from her home. For a surreal moment, Pallah wondered if someone had been guiding the smilodon using Tala. Could someone else have aptitude for smilodon as she did? Or perhaps someone with Broad Tala, the smilodon simply being one of many tethers? And if they did, who could that be? Who would have such dark intentions against the people of her valley?

Karav and Issha had gone down the mountain first. She hadn't seen them at all after their flight down the mountain. Karav was the most experienced Tala Pallah knew of, and Issha…what was Issha's Gift? An unsettling feeling came over her as she thought about their plan to steal scrolls from the basement archives of the Temple Celestial…were they that desperate? Anger boiled in the pit of her stomach, but she pushed it down. She didn't know for sure what had happened. She needed to find the group of Taka Reu, and soon.

"The Dauda is tomorrow, I think," Vámae broke through Pallah's thoughts. "For Petah, Faerja, Agatha, and Old Danil." Vámae's voice cracked, and she cupped her hands over her face.

Pallah nodded solemnly, though only because it was expected of her; she didn't really know any of those people. Her tether became agitated. The small cub was stirring from his slumber, and she was having to work hard to keep him subdued.

"Wait, how come you don't know all of this already? Where were you last night?" Vámae stood. "Everyone prayed together, waiting at the Temple to hear if they got the beast. Where were you?"

"I was here," Pallah said, trying to keep her story straight. "I mean, I left when I heard the commotion and found a group at the Temple Celestial about to hunt down the beast. I—" How much could she tell her twin? Lying outrightly wasn't an option, Vámae would know. "I still don't have an aptitude, you know? I kind of wanted to see if..." Pallah trailed off. Somehow, it was much harder to tell Vámae than it had been to tell her father.

"You wanted to tether it?" Vámae's expression dipped between horror and curiosity. "Did—did you?"

"I didn't see it. I came home, went to bed," Pallah concluded, then coughed to cover up the sound of the cub rolling around in the basket. She had to get out of there.

"You just came home and went to sleep." Vámae looked angry now, and Pallah, wanting to avoid an argument, made to exit. "Don't you walk away from me! I, like the rest of Sodur, Austur, and Vestur, haven't slept all night! Want to know why? Because all I could hear was the screams and sobs of dying children and broken mothers! You look"—she paused to assess her sister, her nostrils flaring—"rested!"

"I don't have to explain myself to you," Pallah snapped and started out the door. Vámae had to amplify everything. She was so dramatic. "You're just mad that the first Feast of Haust you were in charge of won't be remembered."

"Excuse me?" Vámae's eyes flashed. "How dare you!"

"Look, I'm just saying, I don't think I should feel guilty for sleeping when everyone else was frantically searching for a beast that was just trying to provide for her cubs."

"Cubs?" Vámae stopped moving toward her, her eyes round as twin moons. "There was only one in the cave. One cub, Pallah."

Realizing her error, Pallah bit her cheek. She would dig herself in a hole if she continued arguing. "Cubs, cub, whatever. I was asleep." She powered through the hallway, throwing her knapsack awkwardly on her back while holding the basket in her arms. Then she was through the kitchen, Vámae on her heels.

"The fact that you seem to be fine with the death of your own people but are concerned for the health of a mother smilodon and her cub, is utterly disgusting and almost, shall I say, traitorous."

"Shall you say," Pallah mocked Vámae, unable to keep the sarcasm from rearing up like a venomous snake. "Drop the act for once, you *häfan* fraud! You think you're so important."

"Just because I have honed my Gift doesn't mean you have the right to lash out to make up for your incompetence!" With the last two words, Vámae stepped in front of Pallah, toe to toe. Her words hit Pallah harder than expected.

Pallah fell quiet, but her mind didn't. It screamed at her twin, cursing the day she was born, cursing the tie of twinship their bond was founded on. It cursed everything, from her beautiful face so opposite Pallah's plain one, to her perfect posture and articulation making Pallah's simple demeanor and speech so much worse by comparison.

The basket moved again, more noticeably this time, and she hugged it tighter to her side, one arm on the handle, the other cocooning it close. Their eyes locked together, Vámae either unaware of the moving object or uncaring, and Pallah felt the tether of their relationship snap, their twinship left broken and waving in a bitter breeze. Without another word, Pallah turned on her heel and stormed out of the hut.

Thorned branches tugged at her hair as she headed straight into the woods, keeping care to stay hidden as she crisscrossed over root and brush. Rejection was a familiar feeling, though coming so forcefully from her sister and her father in one morning solidified one thing to her: they were not her family, not anymore. Her tether thrummed at the base of her skull, reminding her she wasn't entirely alone.

Why had she always been on the outside? Of her family? At school? With anyone she would have considered a friend? Why was it always so *häfan* hard for her when it seemed so easy for everyone else? And now she had a Tala aptitude for something she couldn't even share with anyone. She couldn't tell her father; he would never be pleased with her, not that it mattered now. Perhaps she could tell Ahren. He still loved her...didn't he? But thinking of him now only made everything hurt worse.

She arrived at her old place, where the tree was marked with countless notches of anger, loneliness, and wanting. Just beyond it, at the edge of the wood, Eld Plateau overlooked the valley below. On that cliff face sat a group that *had* accepted her. So unlike everyone else she knew. They didn't keep expectations for her, they simply wanted her around...didn't they? As they laughed and bantered, she dismissed the idea it had been they who controlled the sabertoothed cat. There was only one group of people in her life right now that would be excited with her, pleased with her, *impressed* with her. And it wasn't anyone back in Sodur.

The Taka Reu had their backs to her, except for Issha, who was standing guard. Pallah wondered how far off the girl had seen her approach. Issha's dark skin was muted in the overcast sky, causing her to blend in with the darkness that loomed heavy in the pre-storm weather. The whites of her eyes like pricks of light that shone their beams on the basket in Pallah's hands.

"Pallah," she said, her voice smooth and strong in a way that rendered volume unnecessary.

The group turned as one, and Pallah's heart twisted as Vil's face broke into a smile. It reached his eyes and made his feet jump up to greet her. Karav watched with wry amusement, her braids tangled and falling apart. She looked as if she'd been awake most of the night. The atmosphere was so different on this side of the mountain; welcoming, warm, and so opposite the bitterness of her home.

Scrolls were strewn about the cliff side, rocks holding them down as they rippled in the breeze. She blinked at the sight of them and something in her gut squeezed. Had they caused the entire thing last night just to raid the Temple Celestial? Karav was surely strong enough to tether a smilodon. She looked at Vil, his eyes bright and full of such genuine joy at her arrival. How could she believe this group to do anything that heinous?

"Hey, guys," she said. "Look what I have." She lifted the struggling cat from the basket, her hand clutching the fur on its neck. Its saberteeth on full display, it gave a tiny roar.

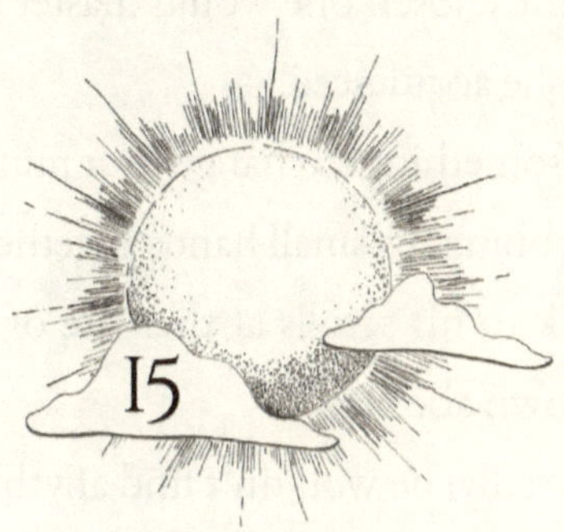

THE MENTOR

SOLYANA

"You believe me though, right?" Jonas asked Solyana for the seventh time as she lifted her hood around her sleep-tousled hair. She had to get back to Vestur and make sure her family was alright. Jonas would stay behind to research, just in case the weather worsened. Not his choice, of course, as he repeatedly asked to come along.

Solyana sighed and glanced at Gamaliel, but his face remained passive as ever as he and Vinur exited the cave. "Look, Jonas"—she turned to him—"I don't really want to believe. If this is true, what you say—"

"What *we* say." Jonas stood proudly. "Priestess Avi agrees."

"I know…" Solyana stepped backward to leave. "It's just a lot to take in. I mean, I'm Rána."

"Is that what's keeping you from believing? Even if this could save Rhuth?"

Solyana blinked. Was it? It was a definite wrench in the plan. The prophecy stated the chosen one would master all three Gifts. She had none. "Yes," she acquiesced.

"Then I'll find something to change your mind," Jonas said with renewed vigor, rubbing his small hands together. "Just you wait!" Then he was back to his scrolls at the base of the cave, blankets bunched and thrown about.

Solyana smiled sadly; he wouldn't find anything and she hadn't the heart to tell him. "Goodbye, Jonas. I'll see you later."

She stepped into the cold, the atmosphere immediately lifting from dank darkness to bright white, quiet with fallen snow. One would never know by looking a catastrophic event had happened the night before. But then she heard it, the biggest difference between the before and the after: the Vatino Sea. Having always been thick with ice, placid and silent but for the creaks and turns of the water below, the sea now lapped loudly at the shores, ice clinking together like shards of broken glass.

She trudged up the hill of piled snow that had gathered just outside of Gamaliel's cave to find him at the crest, his long hair pulled up high into a bun, his eyes trained on the windswept sea below. The prophecy explaining the Vatino's freezing had stood for centuries. The sea ice now broken, was its prophecy as well? Solyana thought about the hundreds of other prophecies, about their validity, about time. What else did the scrolls have to say about the state of the world? Of Mothmar? Of her? She would have to ask Jonas.

Vatino Sea was huge, its full length running from the very top to far past the bottom of their valley, funneling into Skrim Sea, deeply south below Shadow Wood. The wind tossed the waves and tips of dorsal fins could be seen skimming the surface. She couldn't help but feel hope amidst the desolation; perhaps it was just the appearance of melting as the sea lay in shambles. Her eyes could find and trace the Spretta River, jutting off from the very middle of the Vatino, feeding as far west as it would go until it fell into Kana Ocean.

Her people would take periodic trips to Kana, specifically those with Tala in oceanic creatures. Although the trips had slowed as of late—even before the last two sporadic blizzards—there were simply fewer and fewer born with any type of aquatic Tala, or even Tala at all. Her father, with his aptitude for leopard seals, was one of very few.

"We'll have to go around," Gamaliel said without preamble and pointed. "It looks like some Vatin Fera have begun clearing a path that way. We'll hike down through White Wood and continue north until we completely circumvent the sea. Then we can head west through The Pines and turn south back into town."

Solyana followed the point of his finger, her heart dropping as she realized just how far they had to go, now that they couldn't cross the sea. She was exhausted. "How long will it take?"

"Barring any major obstacles? At least until tonight. Although, if anything does happen, I would suggest we hole up somewhere."

"Where?" she asked doubtfully. There was nothing but open land, hills, and trees dotting the white landscape.

Gamaliel paused and gave a mirthless chuckle. "Yeah, we need to make it by tonight."

Gamaliel stopped to wait for Solyana to catch up for what seemed like the hundredth time.

"You need snow-shoes," he said with obvious frustration. Vinur sniffed the ground patiently.

"Well, I can't really do anything about that now." Solyana was just as irritated with herself, she didn't need Gamaliel making it worse.

"Right." He looked down at her then expertly shed his wooden shoes and tossed them at her feet. "Here."

"No, seriously, I'll be fine. I'll just"—but he had already turned away from her, making considerable distance in the snow with only his mukluks—"put these on," she finished, kneeling in the powdery snow to strap them to her feet. She stood and brushed her parka. It was still slightly damp from the night before, and a chill had already started to creep in.

Solyana followed behind and quietly marveled at Gamaliel's light footing; he barely left a footprint without snowshoes. How was that possible? There was already a running list of questions in her mind for Gamaliel, she added his delicate footing to the less-urgent side. He seemed content to walk in silence, Vinur leading the way. He was unlike any of her community back in Vestur, many of whom she had known since birth; they grew up like family down in the villages. But with Gamaliel, it was different. It was like meeting someone for the first time, without any knowledge of their background, family, or history.

"I can feel you staring at me, and yes, it's natural." He cast a glance over his shoulder.

"What?"

"The hair. It's not like a wig or anything."

She laughed and caught up to him. "How did you know I was looking at you?"

"I could feel your burning longing," he said dramatically.

She laughed again, "You wish! Do people think it's fake?"

He flipped a few strands around his face theatrically. "What, that my hair is a wig? You'd be surprised at what people can think."

Solyana welcomed the open conversation. They had a long walk, and she had a long list. "Why the lies?"

His eyes roved in her direction and he barked out a laugh. "That escalated quickly."

"I'm serious. Back there. You know, about Vinur chewing on Jonas's gloves."

He arched an eyebrow. "No lies. Vinur has a thing for them."

"Gamaliel, I..." She paused, remembering she, too, had lied, and told him she hadn't remembered anything from the night before. Images of his bare chest came to mind again, and her cheeks grew hot. "I do remember a bit about last night." She took a breath. "I remember seeing fire coming from...coming from Jonas. It's what kept me going in the right direction...out there." She surveyed the Vatino to her left, placid now, and unassuming. "I've never seen it without ice." Well, no one had. Maybe Priestess Avi...how old was that woman, anyway?

Gamaliel sighed and stopped walking. Solyana placed her hands on her knees and breathed deep, thankful for the break. The Vatino, released from ice, gave the air a new, salty smell. "If I tell you...you need to promise not to breathe a word to anyone."

"Of course."

"No," he said, his look hard and almost angry. "Really, promise me. There's a reason"—he looked down at his feet, hands on his narrow hips, and gave a mirthless laugh—"there's a reason there's only *one* left...if anyone finds out—"

"That he's Heitt?" she interrupted.

"Yes." Gamaliel's lips were set in a hard line. "Not a word."

Although she had guessed it, she was still shocked. She placed a hand on her heart and nodded.

"And"—he gave her one more look, as if it pained him to tell her more—"he doesn't know."

"What? How could he not know?"

"Well, it only happens during his...episodes."

"Episodes?"

"Since he was young. I didn't know him before his parents died, or the two years that followed, but he's lived with me...five years now."

Gamaliel continued his light walk on top of the freshly laid snow. "In stressful situations, when his emotions run too hot, or it can even come from a bad dream, his Heitt activates, and he never remembers. I can't tell you the number of new gloves I've made the kid. Worst of all, he thinks Vinur is a rampant glove-eater."

Vinur let out a soft noise that sounded very much like a *harumph.*

"I know…I should tell him. And I will…eventually." He glanced at her sheepishly. "I want him to be able to be a kid, to not think about this."

"But how can he be Heitt? There hasn't been a Heitt born in generations."

"I have no idea, Solyana. But I can tell you right now, I'm terrified to know what he'd be subjected to if people found out we have another Heitt. It's not safe for him."

Solyana smiled. It was sweet, the way he cared for him. "So, you're kind of his…dad."

"I'm not that old." Gamaliel rolled his eyes.

"How long has he been researching the Green Prophecy?"

"It started with his parents. They were obsessed with that prophecy. It's what got them killed."

"What? Why that one? How did they die?"

"Well, like anyone, they wished for a better future for their son. You know in the prophecy, where it talks about the path of the sky? The translation Jonas's parents sided with was the Norlos."

"The northern lights?" Solyana cut in. She had never seen them herself, their valley too low, and cloud cover too thick.

"Right." The snow crunched delicately beneath their feet, and other than their conversation, it was the only sound as they hiked farther north into the wood. "The kid saw it all. His parents were going on a trip to follow the lights and got a friend to stay with Jonas. He was only three or so, and he should've been asleep. But he crept out to follow his parents. They had made it up toward Eldfall, Jonas following all the way. When he crested the hill, he found his parents being attacked by some kind of sabertoothed cat.

He described it to me in more detail, but I'll spare you. I still have trouble sleeping after what he told me."

"Like a smilodon?" Solyana shuddered as they passed out of White Wood. She had never seen one before. They had once been believed to be something of myth. "I didn't think those things existed."

"Oh, they're definitely out here." He motioned haphazardly around. "They're an elusive animal. I still don't understand why it attacked them, almost like it was waiting for them. They aren't known to purposefully put themselves in the paths of humans."

Gamaliel stretched his neck from one side to the other. "Honestly, it's a miracle the thing left right afterward. Jonas was only three, he would have been easy prey."

"Why didn't I hear about this?" Solyana wondered aloud. "Papa must not have known about it."

"Oh, Marus knows. They all do." He motioned toward the villages, still far off. "Definitely not something they want to share with the people, though, especially since they didn't catch it."

Solyana fell silent, thinking. "You really should tell Jonas he is Heitt."

"I will"—Gamaliel sighed—"when the time is right."

"Why not now? He's going to find out, and he's probably going to hurt himself or someone else."

"Solyana." She turned to face him as the staff across his back brushed a bough laden with snow and it dusted his hair and shoulders. "I can't tell him. I have a theory, and until I know he'll be completely safe, I'm not going to put him any more at risk."

"You keep saying he won't be safe, but honestly, I think it's more dangerous to keep him from us. We need Heitt to survive the winters, and Priestess Avi is getting old." Solyana crossed her arms and tilted her head so her hood fell back. "Care to share this theory that's keeping a Heitt from all of us?"

"Calm down." He brushed his shoulders clean. "There's a reason more and more people are being born Rána. There's a reason there are no Heitt. I don't know what it is, I haven't worked it out. But when it comes to Heitt, which Jonas tells me used to be the most plentiful Gift, it doesn't make sense it would disappear entirely."

"What are you saying?"

"I think…" He sighed, untying his hair and shaking it loose. "I think someone is making sure there's no Heitt. I think someone is working with"—he stretched his arms out wide and motioned to the winter—"all of this."

Solyana rolled her eyes. "And I'm the one that needs to calm down? That's ridiculous."

He took smaller steps to be beside her. "Can you think of any other reason people are being born without Gifts? Why there are no Heitt anymore? Why would it just stop?" He was walking too close to her now, as if the energy he gave to the conversation could win his argument.

"I don't know," she said, exasperated. Gamaliel was a conspiracy theorist, great. He sounded like Fridmey.

"The colder it gets, the more we need Heitt, right? And now Tala and Fera are well on their way to disappearing, too." He held his arms wide, presenting his theory.

"You've been hanging out with Jonas too much." She grinned at him.

He didn't grin back.

"I don't know the answers. I'm just trusting the Celestials have a plan," she said primly.

He scoffed.

"Well, if you're so smart, then what are your thoughts on what Jonas says I am?"

Gamaliel let out a soft and low *hmm*. He pulled a canteen from the side of his bag and took a swig, keeping his pace, then passed it to her. She drank. "There's definitely something up with that face scar of yours. Glad to know I *did* see it, and I'm *not* crazy." He took the water back and popped the cork back in. "On the other hand, you're Rána." He shrugged and clipped the canteen back on the side of his knapsack. "It doesn't add up."

"No, it doesn't." Solyana nodded and was glad, even in its negative way, they had finally agreed on something. "Ok, change of subject, but how are you walking on snow like that?"

Gamaliel looked down as if surprised at his own footwork. "Practice." He did a little jig. "I'm actually surprised you don't know how."

"I've always used snowshoes."

He nodded and gave a little shrug. "I'll have to teach you some-time."

Her eyes remained on him, a slight smile on her lips. What were they? Something deeper than mere friendship had developed between them in such a short time. She was drawn to this hermit from the mountain, and she didn't want to admit to herself it might come from something more than friendship. Didn't her father mention knowing him? She remembered vaguely, the look that had passed between her parents when she had explained the night of the first blizzard.

She licked her cracked lips, trying to formulate the question. "How are you connected to all of this?"

He glanced at her. "Meaning?"

She cleared her dry throat. "I don't recall seeing you around, and I haven't heard anyone talk about you. We are a people few in number; how could I *not* know who you are?"

He slowed his pace to match hers, his feet sinking a bit further into the snow. Vinur came bounding toward Solyana and leaned against her side. Had Gamaliel used his Tala to get him to comfort her? The thought gripped her stomach. Was he manipulating the situation?

"We still aren't fully around the Vatino. It's going to be a while until we get back. I need you to trust me. I thought I had proved that by twice pulling you from the edge of death, but"—he stopped and turned to her with warm mirth—"I'll tell you my story, but please try to hold back your judgments. And remember I saved you, and fed you, and housed you." She let herself relax a bit. "Deal?"

She kept pace, Vinur by her side.

"I'm from Sodur." He spoke with authority, his voice matching their steps. "My mother died in childbirth, too much blood loss. My father couldn't come back from that. He passed me off to his sister, my aunt, though I found out later he told her he just needed a break. But really, he left on an expedition. And he never came back." He glanced her way, but his eyes saw past her. Solyana looked away, what could she say?

There was a time when the entire country of Mothmar was passable, unhindered by snow and cold. The Mothmarians of the valley never stopped believing there could be others out beyond the mountains or the sea, but for the last two centuries no other villages had been discovered. The old scrolls held stories of green and rolling hills, and of people who traveled them. Solyana had seen depictions of the green, but had no idea what it would feel like under her feet.

"My aunt was a saint for keeping me, but she never really had an affinity for children. There were too many things to do; she had a business to run. I ended up by myself a lot of the time. She didn't want me in Sháskol. She never told me why, but I always felt it had something to do with the fact she was Rána, and bitter about it. Anyway, she worked during the day, so I just ended up by myself for hours at a time. I started going out when I was about eight. I would just go into the woods and try to find animals to tether."

"Eight? That's incredibly dangerous."

He gave a humorless laugh. "Yeah, it really was. But I found and attempted a connection to a lot of different species. By the time I was ten, I was getting into all sorts of trouble."

"What kind of trouble?"

"Well...let's see. One time I sent a whole herd of elk—there must have been over two hundred of them—down through the courtyard. That had been an accident, for sure." He smiled at the memory. "Another time, I pitted two bears against each other."

"Grizzlies?" Solyana asked, aghast.

"Yeah." He rubbed his ungloved hand across the back of his neck. "That one was actually really bad. I got in a lot of trouble. I really had no idea what I was doing, was never trained in the way of the Celestials. I just had a general understanding and taught myself...then someone from Vestur took me under their wing. Taught me everything I know, of Tala and of survival, of living out here on my own." They continued to pick their way through the dense forest of The Pines. The sun, behind clouds, was creeping across the sky.

"Wait, what happened to your aunt? How did you end up out here?"

"Well, once my mentor stepped in, he encouraged me to skip Sháskol and go straight to Lóthkol. He always told me I was one of the most skilled Tala he had seen and that I could get in early. My aunt wasn't happy about it, but she couldn't really stop me, so I ended up in Lóthkol at ten."

Solyana looked at him, surprised. That was Rhuth's age. A light snow had begun to fall.

"I know, I know. I was too young." He sighed. "It was too soon for me. I had a few good years early on, but I was too cocky for my own good. By the time I was fourteen, I was into scub, and pranks, and all kinds of mess. The other kids didn't play nice either. It was just a bad combination of teen angst and unharnessed power. A group of kids, most of them dropouts, always wanted me to hang with them, and I did; I had no one else in school. They all hated me for my skill level, and I wasn't humble about it."

"Sounds awful."

"Yeah, it gets worse. They convinced me to go out to the tree line with them one day, and try to call as many wolves as I could."

"Why?"

He shrugged and gave an apathetic laugh. "They were stupid kids—I was a stupid kid. I was able to gather seven wolves before I lost control. I felt it slipping at three, but I kept on going. So stupid," he said with a shake of his head. "The wolves broke free and began fighting each other. I yelled for everyone else to run, but no one heard me. Most of them just kept cheering. They thought I was making them fight." He looked over at Solyana and grabbed his canteen off his bag again, taking a long draw. "You don't want to hear this next part."

She didn't need to, she remembered it. The memories flew back into her mind now, her earliest memories of death, grief, and pain. The wolf attack darkened the edges of her childhood. They had lost two of their own that day.

"You're remembering it now, aren't you?" he said, his dark eyes flicked over her face. "Yeah, you would remember." He took another gulp and wiped his mouth with the back of his hand. "That was me." He handed her the canteen. Solyana waved it away; she felt sick. "I was only fourteen. I couldn't control them. My tether was broken, and I didn't know what to do, so I ran. The wolves took down two of my friends, killed them outright, and injured so many more."

"So...you were banished," Solyana said as they continued on. "I remember the trial, vaguely."

"Been out here ever since," he said, opening his arms wide. "They let me come back for things; events, market days, but for the most part, I don't really feel welcome. Jonas keeps me company."

Vinur turned his head toward them, his tongue unfurling out the side of his mouth, almost grinning. "And you," he said, patting Vinur on the head.

"Your aunt, is she still here?"

"Yup, good ol' Aunt Thina."

"From Austur? She makes the best tea!"

"That's her." He pursed his lips. "Taught me everything she knows."

"I volunteer to be the judge of that." She smiled at him.

"Deal. Next time you recover from a blizzard in my cave, I'll make you tea." He grinned back.

They continued in companionable silence for the next few hours, Solyana's mind working over Gamaliel's past. She wondered who his mentor had been, but felt she had pressed him enough for the time being. They stopped for a lunch of jerky and stale bread at the tip of the Vatino. Solyana tried to convince him to make a fire, but he said they didn't have enough time. They walked on.

The sun was setting lower in the sky, the snow falling heavier throughout their walk, its appearance now a source of anxiety. Would this feeling of dread remain in her forever? Solyana only realized the drop in temperature when she heard the chattering of her own teeth. Gamaliel pulled his hood up, and donned his gloves.

They were finally weaving their way into The Pines after the long journey around the Vatino. Walking that far had left her weak, her body still recovering from the night before.

"How much longer?" she asked through blue lips.

"An hour, maybe two," Gamaliel mumbled.

Solyana stopped walking, defeat crashing down on her. Her body, exhausted from her fight the night before, wanted to collapse into the snow. No, she wanted to collapse into Gamaliel, as she had the night before. Thinking of it sparked a fire in her belly and she felt her cheeks grow warm.

He turned to her, probably thinking she was giving up. "Look, I didn't volunteer for this."

"Yes, you did," she began, thinking of how he had saved her twice. How could she ever repay him? "You pulled me from the first blizzard and guided me out of the second. I don't know what I would've done if you hadn't kept me warm last night, when we slept—" Solyana stopped herself before she said anything else that made her think of his bare chest pressed to her back. Her face flushed further.

His deep, brown eyes met her gray ones, and he took the few steps needed to close the distance between them. "You *do* remember."

"I do." Her stomach fluttered.

"Well…" He took a step toward her, causing a jolt of electricity to shoot from Solyana's belly to her lips. His gaze kept her frozen in place. She searched his face, unsure if she was misreading the moment. "Solyana…I…" His eyes, so deeply locked with her own, flitted away from her, his lips turning downward. "What's that?"

Solyana reluctantly turned to see a bird, growing larger by the second, heading straight for them. It passed overhead and she recognized it as it let out a long screech.

"Halina," she whispered, the spell broken.

"What?" He was staring at her lips. Her lips? Was he really? She pushed the thought away.

Solyana stepped back and held up her arm. The bird circled once before coming to land on her, the talons so sharp she felt the press of them through her parka, just thick enough to keep them from piercing skin. A thrill ran through her like a rush of wind, and she grinned. Had that just happened? This bird was her sister's tethered beast; just holding it made her feel close to Rhuth. Then she noticed one talon was missing.

"Didn't know you were a falconer." Gamaliel cocked an eyebrow, his eyes scanning the massive bird.

"I'm not. This is..." Solyana scratched the bird between neck feathers. "You rescued me," she said quietly.

Gamaliel exchanged a look with Vinur. "We established that already, but sure, I'm glad you remember. You're welcome."

Solyana rolled her eyes at him. "No, not you. She did. Halina."

"Ah." Gamaliel narrowed his eyes at her. "A bird rescued you." He looked at Vinur again who snuffled and shook his head. "I agree, boy. Suspicious."

Ignoring him she continued, "Last night, on the ice I only ended up on land because of her, and some kind of...orca, maybe? It pushed me to shore."

Gamaliel was looking at her with outright skepticism.

"I swear it!" Her nostrils flared as a theory fell into place. "I think...I think this is my sister." Before Gamaliel could laugh at her, Solyana found herself retelling the entire story. From her Stada, to

Rhuth's aptitude, to her sister's injury, and finally to when she was on the ice, Halina soaring through the torrent to reach her.

"So, your little sister, is somehow controlling this bird, while in darlöh?" Gamaliel carefully pieced it together. Halina was riding on his shoulder now, a taller and more comfortable perch, while the story passed the time.

"That's the only explanation I can think of. I need to get her to Rhuth. I need to test it."

They passed through the triad, the three buildings still standing, though damaged. The storm had pulled chunks of wood and stone from the schools and several of the narrow windows of the Hytast were smashed through. Spotting the rear of the Temple Celestial, Solyana noted the chunks of stone that had crumbled away, the building, so fortified and secure before, brought to its knees by the weather.

If the Temple was so damaged by the storm, how would her house have fared? She didn't want to think about it. She needed to reach her family.

Solyana glanced back at Gamaliel. He gave her an assuring smile, and his hope steadied her. Halina's head bobbed as he walked, she looked tired and Solyana wondered if it was the bird who was tired, or her sister.

"There's a window back here that's near the room you were in, I think. Let's get her up there," Gamaliel suggested.

"She'll fly away."

"If your theory is correct, Rhuth won't let her. Right?"

Solyana nodded slowly, hoping she wasn't wrong.

Gamaliel transferred Halina to his arm and then, finding the correct window on the back of the stone building, hoisted his arm into the air. Halina launched off of him and fluttered to the back window, where she patiently waited on the ledge.

Solyana and Gamaliel exchanged a glance, and Solyana smiled. Gamaliel returned it, and Solyana felt that tug in her belly again. This man did something to her that made her feel alive and brave and unsure all at once.

Rounding the Temple, the darkness Solyana had pushed away to the corners of her mind suddenly flooded in a crippling intensity. Dusk made everything look more destitute than it was, or perhaps, she thought, a more accurate portrayal. Huge stone tiles from the courtyard were missing. The few homes and huts, she could see in the distance, were smashed and broken. Upheaval and desolation were everywhere.

The large doors, scuffed and chipped from age and debris, loomed before them. Unsure of what they would find, Gamaliel reached for her hand, and she took it, finding comfort in his touch. She glanced at him, but his eyes remained on the doors. Would they find mangled bodies where their people used to be? Would it just be empty?

"Ready?" he asked.

"I think so," she whispered.

Gamaliel pushed open the door, leading her into a room smelling of roasting meat and smoke. Her eyes adjusted to the dimly lit sanctuary, four braziers burning in a large square about the room. The people of Vestur, Sodur, and Austur surrounded each one. Sounds of eating, talking, and the popping of the fire all came to a halt as a man, a girl, and a too-small wolf entered the building.

Recognition dawned on their faces. Whether of her or Gamaliel, she wasn't sure until someone near the front of the room stood.

"Solyana!" her father cried out and ran for her, his bulk parting the sea of people before him.

"Papa!" Solyana choked out and ran to meet him, releasing Gamaliel's hand with a tug. They collided, and she was enveloped in her father's familiar smell of wood smoke and seal oil. He pulled away from her just enough to look into her face, his tears pouring freely even as he cupped her face in his hands and wiped hers away.

"Middle One. I thought...I thought the worst. You're okay?" he asked, his giant, calloused hands starting to rub her skin raw.

"Yes." She smiled so hard she thought her face would break. "Yes, Papa, I'm fine. Gamaliel has been helping me." She turned back to see Gamaliel retreating awkwardly back out the door.

"Gamaliel." Papa wiped his eyes with one hand, his face resolute, and wrapped the other around Solyana's shoulders. "Are you staying long?"

Gamaliel stopped, his hand on the open door. "I have to get back to Jonas," he said meekly, without eye contact. Though they were close to the same height, he seemed so small compared to her father.

"We will send someone for him." Her father's deep bass reverberated next to her. "Besides, I believe I have found you with my daughter twice now, when I thought she was lost to me. Perhaps this can absolve your past." Gamaliel's face jerked up, though his back was still to them. "It was so long ago."

There was a tension in the air, so thick Solyana couldn't breathe. Gamaliel slowly turned to face her father. "Maybe...I'm satisfied with my current living situation." Solyana's eyes widened.

Unexpectedly, Papa chuckled. "*Perhaps* you need a mentor once more," he said, not unkindly.

"We tried that before." Gamaliel crossed his arms and leaned against the wall behind him. "It didn't really work the first time."

"Then maybe it's time you did the mentoring."

Gamaliel's passive eyes turned from the chief to Solyana, and the corner of his mouth twitched upward.

"Maybe it's time I did."

COLD SNAP

PALLAH

"That's a smilodon." Kristjan's high voice was the first to pierce the silence as he extended a meaty finger toward the cub that Pallah pulled close to her chest.

"No, it's a duck." Rolf rolled his eyes at his younger brother. "Of course it's a smilodon, Kris! Look at those chompers!" He swept his hand dramatically, highlighting the cub's massive incisors.

"I didn't think those were real," Leif said, eyeing it from a distance.

"I didn't either until I saw one last night," Karav agreed.

"It's kind of cute, though." Kristjan leaned down to pet the soft, mottled fur.

"Don't touch it," Karav reprimanded before Pallah was able, the warning on her own tongue. "It's not your tether." She placed her hand on Kristjan's, pushing it back down gently.

"Wait...Pallah, you have a tether on that thing?" Rolf spoke up, eyes bright, his face breaking into a smile. Pallah grinned wider and blushed, avoiding the group's collective gaze.

"Your tether," Vil whispered, his excitement lighting a flame in Pallah she was beginning to recognize as desire. "You found it." He stepped forward, locking eyes with her.

"Yes," was all she could say before the entire group erupted in cheers and laughter, clapping her on the back. Leif even gave her a hug. It was overwhelming and loud, and with all the emotions charging the air, her tether began to slip.

Kristjan let out a yelp of surprise as the beast wrenched itself confidently out of Pallah's grasp and came at him, claws extended. The tiny thing latched onto him for a moment before it dropped to the ground and tore off toward the cliffside.

"Move!" Pallah yelled, scrambling to get around the group. Where was he? He moved like lightning. The group parted and Pallah glimpsed a flash of white fur running, terrified and uncontrolled, toward the edge of the cliff. He was going to fall to his death, and then where would she be? They had killed his mother, his brother. This was her last chance. "No!" she screamed and flung her tether out with her mind just as the cub reached the cliff. Too late. His eyes shot wide in fear as he slipped off the side.

The tether pulled tight, on the verge of snapping, as if the Gift was a tangible thing, taut and reaching. She didn't have time to think, just react, and reaction, for Pallah, was never surrounded with love and calm; she had not grown in a home that warranted it. Anger and violence flooded out of her, demanding his return, forcing him to grip to the side of the cliff, compelling him to stay.

She leaned out over the edge, Vil right behind her, hands at the ready to help where needed. The cub screamed and clung to a ragged patch of grass at the base of a small mountain tree. Vil held her by the waist as she leaned out farther and plucked him up by the scruff of his neck. Pulling her back from the edge, Vil helped her up, and Pallah lifted the cat high in the air like a trophy.

The group cheered.

The cub wailed.

Pallah grinned so wide her cheeks ached.

They stayed on Eld Plateau for the rest of the day. Pallah tested her tether, Karav and Leif coached her and showed her the influences of negative and positive emotion on the animal. The group decided they would set up camp later at the old cave, only a few hundred paces from where they were now. The Cove was no longer safe, now that the villagers had undoubtedly discovered it.

"They'll probably make an announcement soon. No way they missed it." Rolf chewed on a piece of cara root and spat to the side. "Anyone leave anything incriminating in there?" He gave Kristjan's leg a thump with the back of his hand.

"What?" Kristjan shrunk.

"You insisted on making the place so *häfan* pretty. They'll be suspicious."

"Not of me." Kristjan tucked his thick legs up against his belly. "No one knows I'm good at that stuff."

"They will know there are Taka Reu, regardless. The grass, the trees," Issha spoke softly. "But they can't trace it back to us." When had she joined the circle? "I went straight there last night when I came off the mountain and grabbed anything that could link us to it. Just had a feeling we needed to clear out." Pallah wondered how the greenery reflected the Taka Reu, but kept quiet.

"Good thinking Issha." Vil mirrored her soft tone. "Thank you."

"We'll be fine as long as no one gives us away." Issha's eyes slid from each member until she landed on Pallah, where she stared pointedly.

"I haven't said a word!" Pallah said defensively. She was just beginning to feel like she belonged there, yet they didn't trust her? Maybe she needed to connect to The Mother for them to believe her loyalty.

"Yet." Issha poked at the fire with a stick.

Pallah looked hopefully at Vil, but he was staring at the scrolls near his feet. She needed to redirect the attention.

"So...the whole thing last night, that was all you guys, right?" Pallah leaned back, and every pair of eyes slowly swung to meet her own. "You got that smilodon to come down so you could sneak into the Temple Celestial." She tried to keep the shake from her voice. If they admitted to that, if they said yes...she would have to leave them, wouldn't she?

"Excuse me?" Leif threw his braid over his shoulder, his face growing a more intense shade of red than his hair. "You thought we...you think we killed..." One meaty hand came up to his shocked mouth, the other clenched in a fist.

Karav patted his shoulder, shock in her round eyes. "Of course we didn't, Pallah."

"But you and Issha went down the mountain so fast, I just thought maybe it was supposed to be a distraction that—"

"Is she so wrong for asking?" Vil stood suddenly, his hands carefully rolling a scroll back into itself. "It seems to me Pallah is not assuming the worst, but assuming we are serious. Serious enough to get the job done, no matter the cost." He walked between them slowly, tucking the scroll behind his back. "I am pleased to know she sees us as we expect to be seen, true to our cause, and perhaps a bit dangerous." He swiveled to Pallah, mischief on his face. "But no, Pal. We did not tether that cat out of the mountain. Though...Karav, you got a look at it, right?"

Karav tensed. "Maybe we should wait before—"

"Tell them!" Vil snapped in a sudden burst of authoritative energy; Pallah sat up straighter.

Karav narrowed her eyes at him and sighed. "I saw the cat before heading into the Temple Celestial. I attempted to tether her, draw her away, and found her mind...blocked."

"Blocked? This is the first I'm hearing of this," Leif said, sitting back so he could see Karav better. "She was resistant, then?" Pallah recalled her own experience with this, when she had mistakenly thrown her cub against the cave wall. He had been more difficult to connect with, if only for a time.

"No..." Karav splayed her fingers, explaining carefully. "It was different than that. Almost like there was a wall my tether couldn't find its way around. I've never felt anything like that before. It didn't feel...natural."

"Are you saying, you think whatever was blocking her mind was man-made?" Issha asked, eyebrows raised.

"All I'm saying is, someone or something pushed that beast down to the Feast of Haust and made sure no one could alter her course." Karav shrugged. "Maybe we'll find some answers in those scrolls."

"Not tonight, we won't." Vil tucked the scrolls in a leather knapsack. "Our first priority just became that." He pointed at the smilodon, happily chasing a grasshopper. "Where he sleeps, what he eats."

"Does he have a name?" Leif asked, a grin on his square jaw.

"A name? No." Pallah hadn't even thought of it.

"Leif, don't tell me you name every hare." Karav's eyes crinkled at the edges. "There are a million of them, and you eat them."

"Of course, I do! It's disrespectful to leave them without names. I need to name them, to properly thank them for their time."

"Don't you get attached?" Pallah asked.

"Yes"—he paused—"but I think it's healthy." The cub crouched, hips shaking as he pounced on the grasshopper. The group had formed a large circle around him and Pallah was able to keep her tether strong and secure. "How can you thank a creature for its service to you if you don't know its name?"

Karav let out what sounded like a scoff. "You're soft, Leif. If I named every animal I came across, I would run out of names. Besides, how am I supposed to kill them afterward?"

Pallah laughed with the rest, however, she agreed with Leif. How could she command this creature? How could she learn to wield it when she didn't know its name? She searched the tether then, her mind tugging on it, giving it up a bit, then pulling it again, this way and that. It made her think of the other one, the cub she left behind.

"Tinloh."

"Tinloh?" Karav asked curiously.

"Twin," Vil said, looking at the cub from the other side of the circle and then up at Pallah. She flushed.

"Yes."

"It's an old Mothmari term," Vil said to the others. "Pallah…" he trailed off, hesitant. "Why twin? What happened last night?"

Pallah coaxed Tinloh to herself, needing his comfort. He came to her and circled on her lap before laying down, munching happily on the grasshopper. She didn't think she was ready to talk about it. How could she? It was the single most terrifying and most vulnerable moment of her life. Everything in her was laid open and flayed as her connection to Tinloh's brother had screamed in red hot terror before snapping into nothingness. But as she looked at the faces around her, she was beginning to feel welcomed, valued, and known. She told the story in quick spurts, careful to keep her voice steady.

When she finished her tale, no one spoke until Leif furrowed his brow and cleared his throat. "You were still connected? You didn't let go?"

"I was trying to save him." Although she had recounted the entire story without crying, the tears threatened now. "But I could save one. I saved Tinloh." She caressed the cub's soft fur. "And I won't let anyone harm him."

"A memory then, nothing more. Best not let it leave this circle. No one needs to know there were two." Vil nodded and stood, the rest of the group followed. "Let's lie low until after the Dauda. Our town needs to heal. No one goes back to The Cove, understood? If they find us all together after this, it could be blamed on us."

The group gave nods and mumbles of assent. "As for the cub…" Vil tapped a finger on his chin, eyes darting to Leif, who was whispering something to Karav. She laughed. "Leif."

"Yeah, boss?"

"You still have that cage for the sick rabbits?"

"Yes…" Leif looked like he knew what was coming and didn't like it. "Why?"

"We'll keep Tinloh at your cabin, then." When Leif protested, Vil held up a hand and closed his eyes. "Please, Leif. There's nowhere else to put him. It's temporary."

"My hares will never trust me again!" He lifted his arms high. "Generations of built-up trust, gone, in a matter of a day!" He let his arms flop to his sides with a sigh.

"*Häfa,* Leif. They repopulate so fast, there will be plenty more before the first round grows cold," Karav poked him in the side playfully as they all began their way back down the mountain.

"Your heart is colder than ice, Rav," he said, but Pallah could tell he was fighting a smile as Karav wrapped her arms around his waist and pulled him close.

"Maybe." She shrugged, staring up at him, her eyelashes fluttering, her lips turned to a pout. "Warm it up, Leify."

Leif bent down as if to kiss her, but right as he was about to touch her lips, he pinched her and ran off ahead of the group, his bulk crashing through branches on the way.

Karav's shriek turned into a giggle as she chased after him. "Bastard!"

"I can warm you up, Karav!" Rolf called out, jogging to catch up.

"She'd have to stoop to kiss you, Rolf," Kristjan bellowed.

"I'm not ashamed to stand on a chair!" Rolf shouted over his shoulder. The brothers dove into the woods after them, leaving Vil and Pallah walking together, Issha following at a distance behind.

Pallah smiled and glanced at Vil. He was looking at her, eyes holding something she didn't have a name for but made her heart turn over with pleasure. She turned away from him and transferred Tinloh from her arms to her shoulder, his paws reaching close to her neck. She kept one hand on him for support. Had Vil really kissed her the night before? It had fallen to the back of her mind with everything else that had happened, but now they were together, she couldn't stop thinking about it.

"I didn't know Leif and Karav were a thing." She smirked, trying to keep her eyes on the trail and not the man beside her. "They're cute. Like if a rabbit and a bear were a thing."

"Perhaps a very vicious rabbit, and a very docile bear." He chuckled. "I wouldn't say they're together, though."

"No?"

"Karav is just like that...with everyone." With Vil? Pallah tried to hide her disappointment. "I think Leif actually does care for her, though," Vil mused. "Poor guy."

"So, you don't?"

"I don't, what?"

"Care for Karav...like that." Pallah felt childish, but it was strangely important to her to know for sure.

"Me and Karav?" Vil laughed, a loud staccato. "No *häfan* way." He smelled of coal and the musk of the woods. Something akin to butterflies burst in her stomach as their shoulders brushed. "Besides, I like blondes."

Pallah's face grew hot. Between Vil's comment and Tinloh, joyfully chewing on a strand of her hair, she felt herself growing soft. Toying with the tether, she attempted not to manipulate, but to simply feel his emotions. The little cub was joyful. She wondered how easy it would be to replace her own thoughts with his. There was a class on experiencing the tether in this way. She tried to remember how to do it; something with releasing part of her tether while maintaining a hold on the animal's emotions. Gradually her own stress and tension floated away, and she felt lighter. Tinloh was so carefree, so amiable and sweet. How could Chief Olafur have sentenced him and his family to death? He was just a creature, subject to nature's calls of hunger and protection, as they all were.

The urge to comfort him overwhelmed her, he had endured so much loss. Did he even know? Did he just think his family was missing? She pulled him off her shoulder and tried to nuzzle his fur, but immediately felt the tether go taut and strained. She had a moment of warning as a low growl rumbled through his chest, and she withdrew before Tinloh's saberteeth snapped at her nose. Surprised, Pallah dropped him, and he tumbled to the ground, eyes blazing and fur rigid down his back.

She didn't understand. The tether was still there, but he was reacting as if he was unattached. "Vil? What's happening?"

"Issha," Vil called quietly and she appeared out of nowhere.

"Don't move. He looks like he'll either attack or bolt," Issha said smoothly, then she whistled three lilting notes in the wooded silence. "Karav will come."

Pallah crouched next to the beast, working at her tether, attempting to adjust it, to persuade Tinloh, but he responded to nothing. Was he so resistant already?

Karav was red in the face as she jogged back to them, breathing hard. "What's happening?"

"I don't know. He won't respond to me." Pallah attempted to grab him forcefully, but he swiped with a clawed paw, growling.

"Did you let him tether you?" Karav asked in a hushed tone, crouching down.

"I don't know, did I?"

"Were you letting his tether lax in your mind?"

"I was trying to figure out what he was feeling. He was so happy," she said, her eyes wild.

Karav shook her head, keeping her gaze fixed on the cat. "You need to take back control. You've let him keep the tether without establishing yourself as alpha. He is a predatory creature. You need to keep a heavy hand."

Pallah thought of when Tinloh had begun to run off the cliff, and she had to throw everything at him. It worked, but she had felt guilty. "I don't really like doing—"

"If you want him to slay you in your sleep, you're well on your way," Karav said, her jovial nature gone.

Pallah let her eyes go back to the angry little beast in front of her, her eyebrows knit in concern. She attempted to convey to him the need to be partners, not to rule with a tyrannical hand, but to work together toward a common goal. To her relief, Tinloh calmed, his fur flattening once again into the smooth palette of snow white with gray rings. She gathered the tether in her mind, pulling it taut but not quite sending force. Instead, she persuaded him to walk to her. Scooping him into her arms, she glanced at Karav.

"See?" she said with a smile, scratching behind his soft, cotton ears. "He was just scared."

Karav let out a huff and stood. "You're what, seventeen?"

"Sixteen," Pallah mumbled. "What of it?"

"I've got two years on you," the smaller girl said. "I knew I had moderate strength with most predators since I was seven. I may not know my aptitude, but I think I know what I'm talking about." With finality, she flung her braids over her shoulder again and turned back to Vil, saying something to him in a hushed tone.

Pallah's cheeks burned, and her anger rose.

They won't respect you until you join them in their Dark Gifts. Then they'll see how strong you are.

She squeezed her hand into a fist and then looked up. Had Vil been staring at her the whole time? His face held something...was it pity? She forced her feet forward, angry at herself for trusting them so quickly.

They spread out and walked in pairs as they crossed the Vatino, then through the far west side of Austur, before looping south to the bottom of Sodur. No one spoke. Pallah kept the cat hidden at her side.

"Leif's cabin is just over this hill," Vil said, filling the empty space between them. Karav and Issha had gone further east before making their way down, trying to keep prying eyes off them all.

They exited the clearing, and the cabin came into view. Surrounded by a semi-circle of trees that almost closed it off from the rest of the village, Pallah wondered how Leif had managed to get such a private home.

There were rabbits everywhere, surrounding the house as if it was made of carrots. Different shapes, colors, and sizes, they bounded up and down, uncaring of the group walking toward them. Leif was among them, letting them come up onto his lap like children awaiting a story. The group reconvened among the flock of fluffy creatures, though Kristjan and Rolf seemed to have left for the evening.

The cabin was far enough back from Sodur, Pallah felt comfortable leaving Tinloh there. Though seeing the number of hares surrounding his home, she knew it would decrease substantially, even in a month's time.

As if reading her mind, Vil said, "Leif's familial home. His parents passed away when he was a kid, and then it was just him and his grandmother. She died last year, and now it's just Leif."

"How old is he?"

"Eighteen. I know." Vil grinned. "He can grow a better beard than me, and I'm a year older."

Pallah smiled back at him. "Does he have a tether on all of these at once?"

"He wishes," Karav said. "These rabbits have been bred into obedience. Plus, Leif and I have differing views, but it takes a softer hand when dealing with prey versus predators."

"Why is that?"

"Think of how you worked your tether with Tinloh on the plateau, and when you did it just now in the woods. The first time, you used force...out of fear. You struck out with violence, right?"

Pallah nodded, feeling ashamed.

"Don't worry, you needed to. I don't think he would still be here if you hadn't grabbed him like that with your tether. But the second, you convinced him with good feelings, right?"

"Yeah, and he calmed down," Pallah said with a lift of her chin.

"This time." Karav smiled placatingly. "Leif uses that tactic *always*. His great grandmother authored that scroll"—she snapped her fingers—"what was it called?"

"*The Theory of a Positive Tether,*" Vil said, leaning down to pet one of the hares. It stood on its hind legs, enjoying the attention.

"Ah, yes." Pallah was reminded of the scrolls she had referenced upon finding Tinloh's den. "So, all of Leif's ancestors were Heri Tala?"

"You know how strong those red-headed genes are. But they've found a hereditary connection for most Gifts." Karav continued, "These animals have evolved into domestic creatures. Leif barely needs to twinge his tether, and they pepper and salt themselves for dinner."

Pallah laughed.

"Hush, Rav. They'll hear you," Leif said, standing and opening the door a few paces ahead of them. Rabbits parted like petals scattering in spring as the three of them entered the small hut. It felt much larger on the inside than it had appeared on the outside. Pallah placed Tinloh on the floor and he began to investigate. Karav went on ahead to the farthest room where she rummaged around. Pallah sat down cross-legged on the floor.

"I think he's hungry."

"You must be too," Vil said, leaning against a support beam in the room. "Leif will make us all some rabbit stew."

"That would be..." Her smile faded as quickly as it had come. "But no, I have to get home."

"Are you sure you can't stay?" Vil asked.

The butterflies came back with a flutter through her stomach as she stared at her charge, sniffing at furniture around the room. "Not tonight. Maybe tomorrow." She didn't want to leave Tinloh, and if she was being honest with herself, she didn't want to leave Vil.

Karav returned with a small cage built from rough-hewed wood. "We'll have to keep him in here when we're not around. If anyone from the villages discovers he's here, Leif will be implicated, and the cub will be killed." Karav stared at Pallah as she set the cage in the middle of the room. "He cannot be free to roam when no one is around."

"Not to mention my rabbits," Leif said defensively.

"Well, I don't know if I can tether him from my house."

"Either way, don't try. If you establish connection only to let it slip, it could be disastrous," Karav said with finality. "I'll take it from here."

Like the mother of a newborn, Pallah painfully released control and allowed Karav to take hold. The speed and accuracy at which Karav was able to tether and hold him caused immediate doubt in Pallah. Karav led him directly into the cage with no trouble at all.

"You can tether him that easily?" Pallah sat back on her heels, disappointed. "He's *my* aptitude. You don't even know what yours is." She didn't hide the disdain in her voice. The one thing she finally learned to do with Tala and Karav could do it, too.

"You saw me with the boar, Pallah. They're not my aptitude, but I still have some sway over them."

"Some?" Tinloh was purring loudly, docile and calm. Pallah stood and motioned to the cage. "Why do I even need to be here?"

Karav rolled her eyes and Vil shot her a glare.

"Pallah, remember what we talked about last night?" He didn't wait for a response. "The Taka Reu brings a whole different source to our Gifts. It's undoubtedly more powerful." Vil sighed. "I know you don't understand yet, but you will. Know that your ability with Tinloh is incredible, considering you are still using *your* Tala." He handed her the scroll in his hands. "This belongs to you. Read it over; it explains things much better than I could."

Licking her dry lips, she took the scroll she had stolen from Lóthkol. Everything Vil had said was considered heresy, and Pallah knew if anyone outside their group heard it, he would be put on trial.

"Keep him safe," she said to Karav.

The older girl nodded.

Pallah exited the modest hut, the sea of rabbits parting beneath her feet as she strode across the grass. The cool air rustled through the trees, causing her to hug her arms tight to herself. It was growing colder much quicker than last year. Odd...it was barely autumn.

Her feet made quick work of the grounds as her long strides took her out of the dense tree line of Shadow Wood. Her knapsack was weighty with the forbidden scroll back inside; she would read it tonight.

Shadows covered the ground all around her family's hut like a silken blanket, signaling earlier evenings and longer, colder nights. She was exhausted from keeping a constant hold on Tinloh. Though it hurt her very soul to be unattached, she was grateful Karav took over, though she would never admit it.

Thinking longingly of her bed, she sighed, warm breath visible in the chill of the night. She stopped, lifted her hand in front of her face, and breathed against it. White puffs of condensation floated away. It wasn't just unusually cold; it was impossibly cold. Almost as if...as if—

"Mother!" a scream erupted from just ahead. Ahren's voice was high and broken. He sounded frantic. It had become so dark, Pallah couldn't see what was going on as she ran forward to find her brother, the silhouette of her home in view. Thunder rippled in the distance. What had happened? Was her mother still where she had been that morning? Surely her father hadn't left her to freeze, to be consumed by the very Celestials she served.

Pallah's eyes adjusted to see Ahren lifting a lifeless form into his arms, his face in anguish. She skid to a halt at the sight of her mother's pale face, and knew with surety her Heitt had snapped, her Gift collapsing in on itself. Siphoning so much from the Father of the Day, the body became incapable of storing any more heat. If the Heitt didn't expel some of it, they could freeze from the inside out. Pallah's rage burst up in her like an active volcano and she turned to search for her father. This was his fault; she would beat him; she would kill him.

The bastard. What will we do to him? the voice growled.

"Pallah, help me!" Pallah turned back to Ahren. He was struggling to carry Mother by himself. He was only fourteen; Pallah forgot that sometimes. She clenched her teeth and bit her cheek in the process; blood oozed into her mouth, but it calmed her, focused her. Her hatchet was in her hand. When had she pulled it out? Sliding it back into her holster, she ran to help her brother. Pallah hoisted her mother's limp form up on one side, arm and leg; Ahren had the other. Mother was unresponsive and freezing, and together, they carried her inside.

BRING HIM BACK

SOLYANA

SOLYANA BARELY HAD TIME to wrap her mind around the fact her own father had been Gamaliel's mentor all those years ago, when the atmosphere shifted dramatically. Fridmey had pulled Solyana to the side and explained to her what had happened when the blizzard hit. Though many were in their homes when it struck, almost the entirety of the three villages had made their way to the Temple Celestial now to take a census.

And there they had remained...arguing.

Solyana had never before experienced this kind of disarray in her people who were usually agreeable and cohesive. But the Rána of the villages had come together, making a strong case to move out of the valley and into deeper Mothmar, someplace safer, free from destructive storms.

The Gifted were on the opposing side, claiming it their birthright to be in the valley, claiming the power of the Celestials demanded they remain. The Temple Celestial was a holy building; long ago, when the world was green, people traveled annually to come to it. And now they would leave it? Because of a bit of suffering? No, the valley was their own.

Papa and Mama sat between the two groups, their faces haggard, eyes wary as they facilitated conversations turning progressively more combative. The room had naturally separated into the two factions. Solyana was quite unsure which side to sit on, so she sat in the back with Gamaliel, wishing desperately he would reach for her hand again.

"We've been over this," a man named Johssan, from the Rána side, spoke loud and clear. "The ice shanties were sparse before, and now, they're destroyed; the woods are dry of wildlife; the storms have stripped any bushes or roots we would forage. There is nothing left for us here."

"How would you know? You can't feel them," a woman with flowing red hair spoke from the Gifted side. Solyana thought her name was Cahris.

"Well then, tell me, what do you feel?" Johssan needled.

Cahris fell silent.

"We need to rebuild the greenhouses. This is just a season. We've had bad storms before," Korun, a Tala man with aptitude for elk, spoke up. "I'm still feeling twinges of connection. My tether is still active. We just need to give the animals time. They are rebuilding, just as we are."

"And how long will that take? How many of us will have to die before the wildlife rebuilds? We need to decide, sea or mountains?"

Johssan's voice was rising now, and Solyana eyed her father, who made to stand but was restrained by his wife's hand.

Solyana glanced at Gamaliel with worry. She wanted to slip away and get to Halina; they would have to go soon before it got much later, and Rhuth would be forced to send the bird away. *If* Solyana's theory was correct.

A slurry of voices rose, proclaiming support for either cave living or coastal dwelling, before it descended into chaotic argument.

Papa stood.

"If we *leave* here, we will all die." His deep voice reverberated in the large space and made the Gifted quiet, but not the Rána.

"If we *stay* here, we will all die!" Johssan fought back, and a clamor came from his side of the sanctuary. Solyana didn't like where this was heading. The arguments rose to a fevered pitch when one voice rose above the rest.

"I have a question for the priestess!" The room fell silent at the request. While village politicking was done in the presence of the priestess, her input was not usually sought; she was Speaker of the Skies, not speaker of the people.

Priestess Avi's gray eyes were alight as she followed the discussion, blinking at the call of her name. She was sitting in a corner at the front of the room, her silver-poled staff standing unnaturally vertical beside her. She nodded.

"If anyone knows a third option, it would be you. Right, Priestess Avi?" The man's name was Fennick, a Rána, a few years older than Fridmey.

The old woman cocked a wisp of an eyebrow.

"The priestess is the only one who has access to the ancient scrolls, is she not? The scrolls that hold the tales we hear around campfires, from our great uncles who want to give us a good scare before bed, or from our mothers who want to keep us from going too far into the wood." Everyone hung on Fennick's words, anticipation spread throughout the room. "This mystery resides in the past, and I think it's time we brought it back to the present."

Solyana glanced at the priestess whose mouth was held in a firm line.

Fennick continued, "If the Celestials aren't going to help us, we need to turn to something that will. I propose we employ the Taka Reu!"

An explosion of sound rocked the room; the villagers gasped in shock and descended into arguments once more.

"Silence!" Papa commanded. "Silence!" His voice echoed in the hall, and the entire room went flat. "Taka Reu? How quickly we turn from the Celestials when things become difficult." His face portrayed such disdain, Solyana cringed as if she had been the one to suggest it. "Apologize to Priestess Avi for your heresy." He looked Fennick up and down, his lips turned downward in disgust. "And sit down."

Fennick and Papa stared at each other. Solyana could feel the rage rolling off them. At long last, Fennick caved. "Forgive me, Priestess Avi." He sat down in a room of loaded silence.

The priestess stood; her stark white robes made brighter in the dimly lit room. "Your eyes be upward, Fennick," the woman crooned.

"And be filled with light." Fennick's voice was barely audible, his shame covering it almost completely.

"I have walked this earth for many years. I have seen many turn to the Taka Reu for answers, feeling the Celestials have failed them; a path that has always lead to destruction." The Eldur made her way to the center between the two groups.

A murmur of regret began passing through the crowd. A few fell to their knees in penance. The priestess held up her hand. They quieted once more.

"I am not judging your hearts; hearts are fickle, and that is not my place. But out of the need to shepherd you, I must know: who has entertained these thoughts? Who has considered, even for a moment, the Taka Reu?" She looked around, eyes open and bright. A prickle of energy spiked in the room and Solyana suddenly felt too warm. "Anyone?"

One by one, hands began rising all over the building. She began counting them quickly before they disappeared. There were more than fifty. Most were Rána, though a few were Gifted, as well. Perhaps those without Gifts from the heavens were more likely to entertain thoughts of other gods, ones that might offer them the abilities the Celestials seemed to withhold. She felt sick thinking about it. It was never something she would consider, never.

Priestess Avi scanned the crowd, her face sullen and drawn. Her wrinkles seemed even more pronounced, as if she had aged a few years in those few moments. "I see." She cleared her throat and then shifted her eyes directly to Solyana. "Fennick is not wrong. I *do* have a solution. And the Dark Gifts play a part in it. Sit down. All of you. I have a tale to tell."

The room shifted, but aside from the babble of children and the collective intake of breath, no one said a word. Dread seeped into the bottoms of Solyana's feet. She wasn't ready for this, not yet. They had barely discussed it. Jonas had only begun to make it more clear for her that morning. Could she really be the answer? And if the priestess announced it now, the people would have hope. And hope was dangerous, it propelled people.

"Long ago, when the world was green, a boy was trapped on a peak." Priestess Avi's voice lulled the crowd. So accustomed to fireside stories, they settled into their reception by rote memory. "For ages, this boy has used his Gift to tether to light itself, weaving the colors of the Norlos."

A murmur rippled through the crowd; they *did* know this story. Although the Norlos was too high to be seen from the valley itself, the more adventurous climbed Eldfall during the one month of the year the Norlos shone brightest. The iridescent colors streamed over their valley and into greater Mothmar, their end, presumably at this boy who tethered them.

"But!" Avi settled against her staff, a finger punctuating for effect. "Why was the boy atop this peak to begin with?" Brows furrowed and quizzical heads tilted amongst the crowd. "I am here to tell you! For in the reason, lies the answer to our great Green Prophecy!"

Again, the crowd tittered, a new tale! Even amidst turmoil and conflict, Mothmarians valued a good story.

"Every prophecy given by the Celestials above, has an opposing curse from the Dark Gifts below. When the Taka Reu was conceived, the discovery of curses came with it. The language of the ancients paired with specific actions, could strike down entire villages, flatten mountains, dry a sea, or"—she scanned over their faces, upturned and rapt—"keep someone in one place forever. This boy was victim of such a curse, one called Stasis, keeping him eternally trapped on the peak of the mountain; separated from both place and time, never to age or return home. He began experimenting, tethering to the skies themselves. This angered the Celestials, and the more he tethered, the more the Celestials withdrew their favor.

"Long ago, our land was lush and green, our rivers full, our forests ripe for picking, but this boy's blatant disregard—tethering to the skies themselves—brought the Celestials' wrath in the form of the cold. Freeing this boy will bring the fulfillment of the Green Prophecy! We will witness our beloved valley, our beloved Mothmar, go from this wretched cold to the warmth we lost. But...how do we do it?" She paused, turning to walk back to the stage, the entire room awaiting the conclusion. "Solyana Marusda, please join me here."

A collective gasp rang out as every single person turned to Solyana. She, however, only had eyes for her father, his brow furrowed, the creases of his forehead deep in question. She couldn't be this chosen one of the Green Prophecy; she was Rána. Mama seemed to understand quicker, her nostrils flaring, her eyes darting from Solyana to the priestess at the front of the room. Gamaliel nudged her knee, and she met his gaze.

"Go," he whispered.

Solyana stood and walked carefully to the front of the sanctuary to stand beside Priestess Avi. How did Solyana look to them? This disheveled girl without a Gift, perhaps they wouldn't believe the priestess. Perhaps they would all laugh and leave Solyana a caretaker for her sister until she woke. Or perhaps...they would throw her at the mercy of the storms, determined to find any relief, even if it came at her demise. She stood next to the old woman, clutching her upper arms tight to herself, unsure of what even she wanted.

"The Green Prophecy speaks of a path in the sky. I believe this to be the Norlos. We have found extensive evidence of the chosen one, the one with the mark, to be the one to break the curse. There are stories, scattered throughout the archives, of this peak: an oasis, a meadow of clover and flowers, untouched by the ice that has built up around us. This is the evidence of the boy, invisible to everyone but the chosen herself." The old woman lifted a billowing sleeve to direct attention to Solyana standing beside her. "She will free him."

"Solyana?" Papa's voice rang out, the start of an avalanche of words that began tumbling out of every mouth in the room.

"The prophecy states there will be a mark. I don't see one!"

"She needs three Gifts? Impossible. She doesn't even have one!"

"That prophecy is inconsistent! The timing is wrong!"

"She will die if she leaves!"

"What other option do we have?"

The priestess's staff made a resounding *whump, whump,* on the wooden stage beneath their feet, effectively quieting the group before them.

"We have one opportunity before we will have to wait another year for the Norlos to be bright enough again. In a week's time, the skies will be ready. The Gifted are not wrong; leaving this valley would surely crush us even faster than staying. But for how long? Can we last another year?" The old woman shook her head sagely. "I implore you, my people of the valley, if Solyana does not go now...we are out of time." With a flourish, Priestess Avi extended her palm toward Solyana, eyes still on the crowd, and Solyana's face began to burn.

She knew what was happening but still willed it to stop, not the scar. Not now. She squeezed her eyes shut and turned away from the people. She had wanted importance her whole life, something to define her other than her lack of Gift. But this? This was not what she had in mind when she had prayed to the Celestials outside of the Hytast only a week before. She reached up to feel her face, her head pounding. The crescent-shaped scab burned into her skin, callous and rigid. She wrinkled her nose and felt the patch hindering her, keeping her face tight. With each appearance, it had grown continually stiffer, as if it longed to remain for good. Solyana turned back slowly as gasps of shock rang out about the room.

"The mark!"

"It's true!"

"It's a crescent moon! Unmistakable!"

"The chosen one, here among us!"

All around the room villagers began to kneel in reverence to her, the one marked by the Celestials. She found her parents again. They were staring at her, but not with the admiration her people now displayed; the faces of her family held horror. Loneliness slithered down into her gut, enveloping her as her parents stared as if she were a stranger.

Suddenly Priestess Avi's hands were clasping her own, her long white hair framing her aged face as she stepped in front of Solyana, shielding her from the tumult. "The Celestials are making the way clear! This is the path you must go. Are you ready?" Solyana stared back at her, struck by the mottled gray eyes that held a youthfulness at odds with her aged face. Above the wrestling words that tumbled and fought against each other, Solyana heard a noise rise above the rest, a wail. She looked around the priestess to find her parents. They were together, holding each other. Mama sobbed into Papa's shoulder, her wails the cries of a mother who had lost one child and would soon lose a second. Papa's sky-blue eyes were staring into Solyana's, bereft.

Priestess Avi turned to address the crowd once more. "I know you have questions. She is Rána, yes. But where the Celestials have provided us guidance, we have the will to fulfill it. I believe she will be able to reverse the curse that has been on this land for far too many years. She must follow the Norlos to the peak and free this boy from the curse, bringing the Celestial's favor back upon us all."

"Priestess Avi." Papa extricated himself from his weeping wife, keeping a tight hold of her hand. "Perhaps if we all go. We can all make the journey and—"

"She has but thirty days Marus, too many would slow her down."

"Yes, but if we—if *I* went with her. Surely she needs protection! She's just a girl of sixteen. She's Rána, for *stars sake*! We—"

"Marus Gladson, son of Gladohn." Priestess Avi's voice rang with authority. "You will sit down and allow your people a vote. This is bigger than you or I, and you are needed here. These are your people, you will not abandon them." Papa remained standing, fire in his eyes.

"*Häfa* Avi, she is my daughter! With all due respect, you do *not* have a child."

The room was silent again but for the charged space between the chief and the priestess as they stared each other down like predators rallying to fight.

"No biological children, Marus, in that you are correct. But my job is to protect all of you, my children of our great country of Mothmar."

"It's not the same!" He shook his head vehemently. "No, out of the question. No!"

"What about my daughter, Marus?" Svenick stood, unshed tears shining in in his drooping eyes. He wrung the cap in his hands. "Mharna is dead. In the blizzard yesterday. Could your daughter have prevented this?" Solyana's mouth dropped open, and she covered it with a shaking hand. Had it only been a week before she and Mharna had shared their Stada on the stage of the Hytast?

"What about my son?" another strained voice called from the back.

"Are we not as valuable, Marus?" cried another.

"Please!" Mama stood now, grasping her husband's arm. "We cannot bring your children back. We grieve with you, but we don't want any more death! We will find another way. Perhaps we can move out of the valley, perhaps we can find a new—"

"And risk all of our lives in the process?" Fennick launched to his feet; arms spread wide. "What is one girl's life to so many?"

It happened too fast. Papa was on Fennick like a dog on discarded entrails, pounding down on him with large fists. Screams erupted through the crowd, and Solyana stumbled backward as a group of men rushed to pull Papa off the man. With much struggle, they pried them apart. Fennick's lip and nose were bleeding. He was tended to by Healer Ashune, who pressed her tunic to his face.

Papa, restrained by three men, jerked his arms, but was unable to extricate himself. "You've taken this too far, Avi!" he spat in Priestess Avi's direction. "This is fear-mongering at best, and you're willing to risk my daughter for a prophecy made centuries ago! You're *reaching!* You've lost your touch."

"You, Marus, are *not* the Speaker of the Skies. When they decide to commune with you, you let me know. Solyana is fulfilling her duty as Chief's daughter, and, more importantly, as a daughter of the Celestials." The old woman seemed winded, her shoulders sagging as she took a breath. "Marus, these events are unprecedented; the people of this valley, your people, need their leader. Our unity, and our strength, is bound in the balance of the prophetic"—she gestured at herself—"and the present"—she gestured to Marus and all eyes turned to him. "I am not cruel. I can understand the love between father and daughter. Solyana can make the decision. She may choose one or two to go with her." She turned to Solyana, her face taut. "What do you say, Solyana?"

Solyana felt like the floor was being removed from beneath her. Was it all really happening? Her mother was still crying, reaching out for her, tears splashing the stone. Her father, eyes pleading, arms still held secure by men, the men he had entrusted to keep their family safe. She knew if she stood with her parents, she would be ostracized, condemning her family with her. They may even be left in the valley as the rest of their people moved on into deeper Mothmar. She was searching for answers and found Fridmey standing next to Gamaliel, her bright red hair impossible to miss.

They locked eyes for a moment before Fridmey shook her head and made her way to Mama. She crouched down and held their mother on the floor. A stab went through Solyana's heart. She looked up again at Gamaliel. He was staring at her hard, resolution set in his brow. Though her ties to her family were strong, she could not help the deep thrum in her soul she only now allowed herself to recognize. Jonas was right, Priestess Avi was right. She would save her people. She would save Rhuth.

"Promise me," Solyana began, turning back to the priestess. "Promise me you will look after my family." The woman nodded, and Papa's face brightened with hope. Did he think she would choose him? But how could she? Her family needed him, Rhuth needed him, the people needed him. "This will bring back Rhuth?"

"I believe her future and the future of the entirety of Mothmar are directly linked, yes."

Solyana nodded, noting the priestess didn't fully answer the question. She turned back, standing with a confidence she didn't feel before her people.

"I just want Gamaliel, if he will do it," she stated. Gamaliel stood immediately.

"Solyana!" Papa bellowed and the men restraining him tensed, rightly afraid he would resort to violence once more. "No! Avi, she doesn't know what she's saying! She's a child!"

Whump whump. The priestess's staff came down once more. Papa went slack, the fight gone out of him. Solyana had to bite her lip to keep from crying as she saw his eyes glisten in the firelight.

"Will you accompany Solyana on her quest?" Priestess Avi inquired of Gamaliel. Solyana held her breath. What if he said no?

"Yes, Priestess Avi." His words sent relief through her chest so strongly it unbalanced her for a moment. Gamaliel made his way to the front and stood next to her, as strong as one of the stone pillars in the room.

Papa shook off the men that held him and crouched down to hold Mama and Fridmey instead. Solyana felt so distant from them in that moment, but she reassured herself that she was doing this *for* them, not *to* them.

"All in favor of Solyana Marusda leaving our valley to break the curse that has frozen our land...all in favor of her turning white to green, in accordance with the prophecy."

Hands all around the room raised to the ceiling. Every single hand but three. Mama, Papa, and Fridmey stared at her, hurt coursing so deep between them Solyana felt it strike her like a slap to her scarred face.

"And all against?"

Mama, Papa, and Fridmey all raised their hands high, proud, and defiant.

"Motion passed. They leave in one week," Priestess Avi said, matter of fact.

"I request to go as well," a clear, female voice rang out as a long-legged, willowy girl stepped out from the crowd. "You will need a Fera. I am at your service, Chief's daughter." She knelt and bowed her head slightly in front of her and the priestess.

"Lone Ashune." Priestess Avi's face held a genuine surprise as she looked down on the Healer's daughter. "Are you certain?"

"Yes, Priestess. Please accept my allegiance." The girl peered up at them. She looked about Gamaliel's age with cropped hair so blond it was almost white. Like her mother and sister, Lone's Gift was Bein Fera, the ability to manipulate bone. It could be useful on a trip like this. However, Lone's father was on the council, and he was staunchly prejudiced against Rána. She hoped Lone didn't hold the same views.

"I accept," Solyana said as she caught Lone and Gamaliel exchanging shy smiles. "Thank you." Solyana felt small beside the taller girl.

"Solyana Marusda, may the Celestials guide you and keep you. Bring back the green for us, dear girl. Banish this wretched winter and save your people. Your eyes be upward!" she said, lifting her staff high into the air.

"And be filled with light!" the people of Mothmar answered in unison, fists raised as one. Solyana felt her own hand lift upward. She turned to see Gamaliel's hand clasping both hers and Lone's, raising each girl's hand high with his own.

Solyana said nothing.

Hours later, when the braziers had silenced and the sanctuary had emptied, Solyana found herself sitting at a table made of aspen in the dank basement of the Temple Celestial. Priestess Avi had requested she stay the night to finalize plans while the rest of their valley found sleep, restless though it would be. The room was low-ceilinged and low-lit, a few scattered lanterns lining the walls. It was long and layered with wooden shelving, large barrels burst with ancient and modern texts. Hints of Jonas lay about the room: charcoal pencils, brightly colored and scattered, a pair of leather shoes, and a row of freshly made books. She realized, with pleasant surprise, she missed him.

Priestess Avi had led her down before checking on Rhuth. Solyana stood up and stretched, wishing she could go to bed. The priestess had made it clear, however, there were more details to talk through before that could happen.

Solyana's family had gone home. Minimal, soft words passed between them before setting out. What was there to say? Solyana had not chosen any of them to go with her. She had picked Gamaliel. Had it been a mistake? But how could she put them at risk? She cared for Gamaliel, yes, but who would mourn for him? He had no wife, no children. Then guilt twisted her stomach. He had Jonas, who had already lost his parents. Would he survive losing Gamaliel, too?

Squeezing her eyes shut, she pressed her forehead to the table. The responsibility of it all was too much. Less than a week ago, she had left her Stada being named Rána. She would have joined the ranks of other Rána, maybe set up a clothing booth in the courtyard during the market. And now? She was expected to journey off into the far reaches of Mothmar in search of some legend of the Norlos? Some boy on a distant mountain in need of saving? It seemed too farfetched, too unreal.

Sitting up, she spotted something glinting in the light near the door. She stood and crossed toward it to get a better view. Leaning against the door frame was the priestess's metal staff, left to wait for her as the woman checked on Rhuth. It was as tall as Solyana herself, made of pure metal, and etched with designs that swirled over the length of it. She picked it up with both hands, and the weight surprised her; it was unnaturally light. She turned it over, tracing her fingers over the designs. Some skilled Malmur Fera had taken his time with this. The priestess truly had an affinity for beautiful things. Did they still have anyone with aptitude for metals? It was an arduous process without the aptitude, the smithy near the greenhouses remained quiet for months at a time.

She tossed it from one hand to the other. Her father had trained her with a longbow, but she had always wanted to learn to use a staff. Gamaliel had one. Maybe he could teach her while they traveled. She tossed it back again, and when she grabbed it, something clicked deep inside the metal. Without warning, from each end of the staff, large sharp ends of axe heads shot out. She held tight but jumped away, looking like she was holding a poisonous creature.

"Exciting, isn't it?" A voice came from behind her.

Solyana let out an exclamation of surprise and turned, the staff still outstretched. The priestess had a sly grin on her face, and Solyana's face flushed.

"I'm so sorry, I just...I shouldn't have touched it."

"Oh, don't apologize." The old woman held her hand out for it and Solyana passed it over. Her eyes widened as the priestess twirled the staff back and forth in front of her body and then to the side, crouching slightly. With the staff held high, she punched with it, and with another fluid click, the axe heads collapsed back into the staff. Then she twirled it twice and set it down vertically, releasing it. It stood of its own accord.

Solyana couldn't help the grin that was plastered on her face. "I had no idea."

"No one does." The priestess smirked. Her face seemed younger. "I could keep up with the best of them, once upon a time."

"It's so intricate. Where did it come from?"

"My," she hesitated, "my father made it." Priestess Avi's smile disappeared as she said it. "He was a smithy."

"He was Malmur Fera?"

"No." Suddenly the old woman's tone was cold, and Solyana wondered if she had said something wrong. "I dug up an old text I'd like you to read. You have a lot of studying before setting off."

Solyana rubbed her eyes but sat back down at the table. The old woman pulled a scroll from her dress pocket. "Read it out loud, dear, if you wouldn't mind."

Solyana spread it over the table and began.

"Priest Torvin of the Temple Celestial,

This is an account of the battle of The Rebellion.

I have taken it upon myself to rectify the account of The Rebellion. Everyone seems apt to forget it ever happened, but if we erase history are we not bound to repeat it? Is this not proof? I have gathered what I can, but so much has been laid to waste. So much information destroyed because of the actions of so few. I will consider what I have gathered and try to present it, as promised. Though, I cannot vouch for the hands that will find it and invariably choose to skew history once again.

It started with a Temple Serviseer who had allied themselves with a leader of the Taka Reu. This was the first crack in the stronghold.

The Serviseer disappeared, along with her brother, both suspected to have joined the Taka Reu. It was these disappearances that incited the events leading to the battle of The Rebellion. The disappearances, spiking fear in the people, they began a search. What they found was not what they expected; it was what they most feared.

The group of Taka Reu had grown to a vast number, their skill grown to a dangerous level, enough to contend with the valley and those who followed the Celestials. They had obtained enough ancient texts to hone their crafts unchecked; their prowess and skills made clear by the abhorrent acts they were able to commit.

Whether they feared a first attack from those who found them, or from some other reason unknown to us, the Taka Reu broke from their hiding to confront the valley. This Rebellion, as it has been named, was quick and bloody. The villagers, taken unaware, were left strewn about the streets, chewed and discarded. It is unclear from the testimonies of those involved, who or what exactly could cause such carnage. A Tala and their beast led the charge, but was it a bear? A wolf? One account claims the animal had saber-like teeth, but all accounts are sure of one thing: they were singularly intent on destroying anyone who stood against the belief that the Taka Reu is the one true way.

There were three points of particular interest to the group, three places where the most desolation was found: the Temple, the infirmary, and the home of the family of the Serviseer. When the carnage subsided, all villagers were either fatally mutilated or brought under submission of the Taka Reu. The Serviseer that started it all, and the brother that was with her, both remained missing. But how could it be known? From the descriptions of the battle, there had been no way to identify the bodies.

There is one account that tells of the brother and the leader of the Taka Reu embracing by the sea, something quite like ash, dark and roiling, swirling up around them. Alas, this report is messy and lacks credibility.

Thus is the story of the Rebellion. May these heinous acts never be repeated."

Solyana set the parchment down, a heaviness in her heart, and looked at the priestess. The old woman was staring past her, so when she spoke, it felt as if she wasn't speaking to Solyana, but to the space beyond.

"All I have found points to this. This, being the reason for the cold, for the white. This embrace"—she pointed to the appropriate spot in the scroll—"the dark ash, the disappearance. I believe this is the curse being placed upon the boy, the same boy you are to find on the mountain." She turned abruptly to Solyana. "Your scar, it is truly the greatest clue we have of the Celestials' intentions. Although...it is not completely of them."

"Who else would it be from?" Solyana had been made to believe it was the Celestials' sign. It was the only reason she felt any semblance of calm about the darkening scab that ran over her left cheek.

"Well"—the priestess took a breath and leaned on her staff, her face drawn, weary once more—"it was sticky at first, yes?"

Solyana's memories of the first blizzard came back to her, the sticky feel on her fingers as she had pulled it away from her face, Rhuth dying beside her. "Yes," she mumbled. She brought her hand to her cheek, it was there, but rough and dry.

"I believe it's something called '*aska,*' a manifestation of the Taka Reu in physical form. A representation of the darkness that lies inside. It comes in different forms, a powdery ash, a sticky substance." Solyana's hands grew clammy thinking of it. "It is the shape of the Mother of the Night," the priestess amended, "but it has properties of Taka Reu that cannot be ignored. I believe this only furthers my theory: one curse of the Taka Reu, meeting one prophecy of the Celestials." The old woman stood straight and interlocked her fingers with a shake. "Two warring deities coming together to fix something neither is willing, or able, to fix themselves."

"Deity? Who is the deity of the Taka Reu?" Dread clawed at her as she talked about the Dark Gifts. Speaking of it was hardly accepted. Researching it was forbidden. Practicing it would surely mean death.

Priestess Avi grasped her staff and pointed with it to the stone below their feet. "Why, Mother Earth, of course."

Solyana looked at her feet. "So"—she rubbed her eyes again—"let's see if I'm getting this right. A boy—held by some kind of curse—is trapped on a mountain peak, causing this eternal winter. The Celestials *and* the Taka Reu are working in tandem, *through me*, to find this boy, break the curse, and return spring to our valley?"

"Indeed, dear girl." Priestess Avi nodded sagely.

"One question." Solyana held up a finger. "How will this save Rhuth?"

"You receiving that mark while protecting your sister, was no accident. I believe her fate is expressly tied to what's happening here." The priestess made a motion with her finger that mimicked the crescent on Solyana's face. "I've tried everything in my power to wake her. It's up to the Celestials now."

Solyana nodded, thinking of Rhuth. She would spend the night here with her again, and if Halina was still waiting, she could test her theory. "Secondly"—she raised her arms—"how will I acquire three Gifts? I don't even have one!" Her arms dropped to her sides.

"This is why I have brought you to the archives; I believe the answers lie here. I know you have not forgotten of my two Gifts." The priestess stared at Solyana, her gray eyes searching, almost fevered. "I must confess something to you now, dear girl. I ask you be of an understanding spirit and that you keep the information to yourself. It is for no other."

Solyana eyed her warily but nodded. The old woman leaned forward; palms pressed into the table.

"I use the Taka Reu to use multiple Gifts. Drawing from the earth, drawing from the Celestials above. I have found a way, in my years, to do both, in a balance of light and dark."

Solyana gasped, her hands flying to her mouth. Fear surged through her, and she struggled to remain still, fighting the impulse to put distance between them. She used the Taka Reu? For how long? How did the people not know?

Priestess Avi, uncaring of Solyana's distress, continued on. "If we find no way for you to acquire these Gifts before you leave, I will ask that you try the Taka Reu. It is part of this as much as the Celestials are; both are at work in your scar. Mother of the Night"—Priestess Avi brought one hand up—"and Mother Earth"—the other hand rose, and she brought them together—"working to the same end."

Solyana shook her head slowly, her eyes unmoving from the old woman's face. Was the priestess of the Temple Celestial truly asking her to utilize the Dark Gifts? After everything she said to Fennick's argument in the sanctuary above, mere hours before? She couldn't believe her ears.

"That's heresy." Solyana's voice sounded weak even to herself. "How could you use something that you, yourself, said would lead to destruction?" Was she accusing the Speaker of the Skies? So what if she was? What had she to lose? She was about to be sent away from the valley, away to her death.

"How can I not, when without it, this valley would have collapsed long ago." Priestess Avi stared off into the long room once more, her eyes unfocused. "Regardless of how it happens, you will reverse it, Solyana. You must. Now..." The old woman snapped her head, her eyes locking on Solyana's with intensity. "I need you, not only to find this boy, but to bring him back here."

"Bring him back?" Solyana laughed, though she found nothing funny. "And if he doesn't want to come with me?"

"He will, if you give him this."

The old woman produced a package from one of her sleeves, a parcel wrapped in loose leather hide. The item was large, about the size of Solyana's forearm.

"Take it, girl." Priestess Avi gave a shuddering breath of anticipation.

Upon holding it, Solyana knew instantly it held a weapon, its shape and weight felt through the soft leather. She carefully removed a hatchet and held it up to the light. It was ancient, something out of the histories, with its solid, timeless metal head and intricate flower and foliage etching wrapped around the wooden handle.

"He will come with you, Solyana. He will recognize the hatchet. For he made it."

HOLLOW HOME

PALLAH

"I'M GOING TO FIND Vámae," Ahren said in a rush as they finished stoking the fire and swaddling their mother in blankets. Pallah knew even while they did it, it would have little effect. They needed Heitt to bring her back from a snap. Pallah had heard of it happening, the air still crystallizing with her breath, but she never imagined it happening to her mother.

"Ahren!" Choking on grief, Pallah's voice was unrecognizable. Her brother stopped, his hand on the front door, his eyes blazing with fury. "He made her do this, didn't he?" She didn't have to specify who she was speaking of.

"Wait for me," Ahren said, cautionary. But the look in his eyes was anything but; he was equally as ready to confront their father as she was. "Just...wait." Then he was gone through the door, a flash of lightning and rolling thunder leading him away. The storm had arrived. Pallah was left alone with her mother, whose eyes hadn't opened once, whose lips were the color of a fresh bruise.

The silence at his departure wrapped her like a wet blanket, suffocating, making her paranoid. Her leg bounced uncontrollably as she stared down at the woman who had given birth to her, raised her. When had they last had a conversation that was more than commands or expected etiquette? When had they last talked away from the prying eyes of her father? Thinking of their conversation just that morning, Mother felt more human to her now than ever before. Pallah brushed the hair away from her mother's cold face. She had spoken of the man she'd loved, and had given advice on keeping Tinloh. It gave Pallah the push she needed to speak, even if her mother couldn't hear her.

"Mama." The word was foreign on her lips; when had she last called the woman before her anything but Mother? But feeling desolate and alone, she repeated it. "Mama." Pressure forced its way behind Pallah's eyes, she wiped at them before grasping at her mother's hand. It was so cold. "The things you told me this morning, I want to know what truly happened to him, to the man you loved. What was his tethered beast?" She took a shivering breath, anxious as her thoughts coalesced. Karav's talk on most Gifts being hereditary fresh in her mind. "Did you know him when you knew Father?"

Her mother lay still, unresponsive. Pallah pressed on. "What was your life like before all of this? Was it anything more than laying out, charging for others to use you?"

She let the question hang and threw another log onto the flames. It was warm on her back as she stared at the weathered face of the woman in front of her. "I think you were pretty," Pallah whispered to her, carefully tracing the lines on her mother's face with her fingertips. "Before all the days in the sun. Before..." Taking in her mother's looks without reserve for the first time, Pallah realized her face seemed morphed, as if it had been reshaped, changed into something different...and then she understood. It *was* different, shaped by her father's hand. "He hits you." How had she never seen it before? "Your nose didn't have this bump before." She traced the line of it, jutting out at an odd angle. "And this cheekbone." Her fingers fluttered over her mother's face.

"I have often hated you," Pallah confessed, her voice barely a tremble in her throat. "Hated you for allowing him to speak to us as he does, keeping us under lock and key, ordering us around as if he owned our very souls. I hated you for bowing to him, submitting to his backwards leadership. But...you fought him, didn't you?" She raised her mother's hand, examining her knuckles and found what she was looking for. They were scratched and scabbed. "You"—she choked out a sob that turned into a laugh—"you fought him." She let her head hang for a moment, overcome by the realization. Then she counted to ten, bringing herself to practiced discipline. "Why did you *marry* him? What did he have that was the least bit desirable?"

With his skinny, slight body, stringy hair, and drawn face, she couldn't imagine him as anything but weak; just clever enough to manipulate and subjugate his family. Shaking her head, she expelled thoughts of her father. Mama was important right now, they had so much to catch up on, didn't they?

"His name is Tinloh," Pallah mumbled. "My little smilodon. My sabertoothed tiger." Her heart swelled with affection. "He is perfect. My friends love him." She let her eyes search her mother's face, half expecting Mama's eyes to open. "Yeah, I think I have friends." Pallah smiled conspiratorially, as if her mother had leaned in, excited. "You know where I go to throw my hatchet? Well, I guess you don't know. But it's near their old hideout. They found me, and...Karav? She has the strongest Tala I've ever seen. It's amazing. Vil? He's a Vatin Fera, and Mama...he's beautiful. I think...I think I like him. And I think he may like me."

Pallah began unraveling the tale of the last few days. It came apart faster and faster, like a stone rolling down a mountain, picking up speed. She felt like a girl again; strange, she was only sixteen, but she had begun to feel much older. She left out any mention of scub and Taka Reu, but told Mama most of the rest. When Pallah approached the part where she had been only partially tethered to Tinloh's brother, the rhythm of her speech slowed to a crawl. She thought of the conversation with her mother that morning, that had haunted her throughout the day.

"I think I understand a little about a tether snapping. I have felt it. I didn't know until it happened, how awful it was for me to...for me to let go. The man you loved, what happened to him after—"

The door flew open, smacking the wall behind it. Pallah's head snapped up to see Vámae and Ahren crossing to her, both soaked through. Thunder roared, the sky broken open. So deep was Pallah in her one-sided conversation, she hadn't noticed.

Vámae was all precise movements from the moment she entered. Still dripping from rain, she dropped to her knees next to Mama and carefully twirled her long, dark hair into a wet knot at the nape of her neck, her cheekbones glistening in the firelight. Across from Pallah, Vámae rolled her sleeves up meticulously, rivulets of water making tracks down her forearms. Then she brought the heels of her hands up and across her eyebrows, clearing water down and off her face in one fluid motion.

The twins locked eyes, and Pallah's chest tightened. One twin, all dark hair, blue eyes, and striking beauty; the other, over-tall, colorless blonde hair, almost invisible eyebrows, plain. She had forgotten about the morning's argument until this very moment, guilt knotted her stomach and shame formed a lump in her throat. By the look in Vámae's eyes, she had not forgotten either, but with a slow blink of her dripping lashes, her back straightening to that perfect posture, and a terse nod, Pallah knew her sister was laying it aside for the greater good, as she had always done.

Vámae lifted her arms until one hand was hovering over her mother's heart and the other over her abdomen. Vámae closed her eyes and only then, when she had broken their gaze, could Pallah breathe again.

Heitt was not visible, of course, aside from the Eldurs' ability to wield fire. It was an invisible art, but that did nothing to dampen its power. Something in the room shifted.

Mama's chest now produced a steady beat. Her brow, which before had been creased in pain, lay relaxed and placid. Lightning flashed and thunder rumbled just outside of their small hut. Pallah curled up into herself, her back near the embers that burned low in the fireplace.

Will you kill him for this, Pallah? Do you have what it takes to protect your family?

The voice gave credence to her own feelings, warring deep inside. Now that her mother was healing, grief gave way to rage.

Ahren hadn't moved from the wooden bench in the corner, his eyes boring into the back of Vámae's head, gaze unseeing, knee bouncing wildly. They both did that when they were anxious, didn't they? Pallah had tried to make eye contact with him a few times but, unwilling to disrupt Vámae's concentration, remained silent.

Thirty minutes passed before a clap of thunder launched Pallah from her seat. Ahren, too, was up and running for the door. Turning, Pallah saw her father, a bag slung over his shoulder, all of him dripping, a scowl on his face as Ahren plowed straight into his chest, knocking him backward, the bag falling to the ground with a loud *thump*.

Lightning flashed again, illuminating a flurry of fists and feet. "Ahren!" Pallah scrambled toward them, jostling the cot holding her mother. Vámae's eyes flew open, but her hands remained steady, her eyes darting around wildly, until she found the altercation at the door.

"Stop him!" Vámae said through her teeth, and Pallah didn't know to which *him* she was referring.

Ahren, only fourteen but larger than Bogdur by height and breadth, was on top. His fists slammed into Father's face once, twice, three times; each blow hit its mark with such accuracy, Pallah found herself admiring it. The urge to join the frenzy ignited in her.

You can do it, the voice prodded and she welcomed it as it fed the fire that burned strong inside. *Kill the häfan wife beater.* Yes. But how? With her fists? Her hatchet?

"Pallah!" Vámae's voice, even in chaos, sounded more measured than Pallah's most level thought. "Stop *Ahren*." Pallah turned to look at her sister. Vámae's lips were quivering. "Don't...don't do this." Something in Vámae's eyes made Pallah think again; Vámae was terrified, but not of Bogdur.

She feared Pallah.

Her hand ached and she looked down to see her hatchet clutched hard in her grip. She hadn't even realized she'd grabbed it.

Do it, Pallah. Prove you are the protector your family has never had. Who is Bogdur, anyway? Your mother loved someone else once, and probably still does. Break him. Reach down. Gather your energy.

Her feet moved mindlessly toward the wet thumps that were her brother's fists against flesh. Pallah splayed her fingers wide and pressed them to the floor. She would do it now, use the Taka Reu. But right as she closed her eyes, she heard a crack almost indistinguishable from thunder. Her eyes flew open to see the kitchen table with a jagged break down the middle. Shards of wood burst from the finished top, shooting like arrows into the air. Then, before Pallah could react, the knives of wood shot into the side of Ahren's face, his shoulder, and ribs. He fell back, screaming, clutching at his face, legs kicking erratically.

Then the table shook mightily, half of it coming apart with an unnatural crunch. Father's fingers stretched toward it, his mangled face twisted with such malice, it transformed him more than his injuries. Realization at what he was doing hit Pallah and she screamed at the man about to crush his own son. She took aim at the table and threw her hatchet as it began its descent onto Ahren.

It made contact with a satisfying *whack* and was thrown off-kilter, slamming into the wall next to the boy. She ran to it, wrenched her hatchet out, wondering if she had picked the wrong mark. Father pulled himself to standing, a violent sneer showed white teeth amidst the bloody mess of his face. Pallah leapt on top of him, shoving him back with a leather-shod foot, her hatchet at his throat.

He breathed in deep, his nostrils flaring. Pallah decided if he so much as flinched, she would slice him open right then and there. Instead, he settled back onto the floor, a malicious smile playing on his lips, split and bleeding.

"What's your plan, Daughter?"

Pallah felt her body anew as the first wave of adrenaline began to wane. Sweat dripped down her arms as if she had just been out in the rain, her heart pounded hard against her ribs.

"You're too weak, *tik*," he sneered, his tongue relishing the derogatory term. Her stringy hair, so similar to his, stuck to her forehead as she struggled keeping her face clear of emotion. "You...won't...do it." He used each word to propel him more and more upright until his face was so close she could smell the iron in his blood.

"Pallah! Don't!" Vámae yelled from somewhere behind her. Ahren was crying to her right, his soft sobs betraying the boy he was. "He's your father."

"Father?" Her voice broke. "Not to me." In her lapse of control, Bogdur attempted escape, but she was faster. She brought the hatchet down hard, the blade pinning his pant leg to the floor, barely missing the leg itself.

"You've gotten good with that hatchet, *tik*," he said, his eyes descending into a darkness she had always guessed was there but had never truly seen. His repeated use of the derogatory term for women made the rage boil inside of her. "I suppose you needed something going for you, being Giftless." Pallah blinked. He truly believed she didn't have a Gift? He didn't know she was Tala. He didn't know of the beast that lay waiting. "Yes, I've known you were broken the moment I held you. Vámae always had talent. Ahren will get by, but you? You're nothing but a worthless piece of—"

Kill him.

She knew it wasn't her, although it seemed to be, and an unseen hand raised her hatchet back. Bogdur's pronouncement over her continued to spill out of his mouth, his eyes dancing as if he wanted her to do it, but believed she wouldn't.

She focused her energy on the ground beneath her, demanding it propel her forward. That pull at the base of her skull she associated with her Tala suddenly moved to her chest and centered her, grounded her.

The voice in her mind laughed. *Yes...yes!*

It felt different, malevolent, and...

Oh...*häfa.*

So very powerful.

"Pallah." A soft voice came from behind her, but too late. Her fury, and whatever was driving it, brought the hatchet down. In the moment it took to slam into her father's face, something snapped her hand back, so hard she thought her bones shattered. The hatchet was yanked from her grasp and all she managed to do was knock her father out cold, her hand curled into a fist at the side of his head.

Dumbfounded, she searched for her hatchet. Then she heard Ahren, breathing hard, his one eye open wide in fear, his other eye swollen shut, shards of wood still embedded in his skin. He held the hatchet high above his head, his arm trembling.

"WHY?" Pallah screamed, her emotions narrowed to a driving force of hatred. "You were about to kill him just before! Why stop me?" She stood fast, pushing herself off her father, her legs shaking.

"Pallah." The soft voice came again, but this time it captured her attention, pulling her out of whatever state had darkened the edges of her mind. She turned to see her mother sitting up, her face a ghostly white, her eyes sunk so deep into her brow, it made her look skeletal.

"Mama." Shame flooded her, and she wondered how much she had seen. Then, as fast as shame had come, pride replaced it. Pallah motioned to the man that used to be her father, refusing to look at him. "How long has he beat you?"

Her mother was staring past the scene, unfocused, empty.

"Father doesn't beat—" Vámae's quavering voice said in defense, but a look from Pallah silenced her.

"How long?" she asked slowly, her nostrils flaring.

Her mother's dark eyes found purchase on Pallah's own.

"You," she said the single word with such sorrow, it caused Pallah's heart to hitch. "Since *you*."

"Mama?" Her voice wavered, her eyes flicking to her twin and back again. Vámae's face was unreadable. Whatever twin relationship they had before finally dissolved.

"He will wake," Mother said, her eyes turning to the man on the floor, so small, so peaceful there, with his bleeding head and rapidly swelling eyes. "I will corroborate your story, so the three of you will be safe. Vámae?" She turned and Vámae grasped her mother's hand in her own. "Go fetch Chief Olafur. It is time for Bogdur to be turned over." Vámae started to leave, but her mother restrained her.

"Mother?"

"Say nothing on your way over." Mother's eyes were feverish now, almost in panic. "Say nothing to anyone."

"Yes, of course," Vámae said quickly, then paused. "What should I tell the chief?"

"Tell him," their mother spoke as one who had been waiting too long to finally say the words, "that Bogdur of Sodur has been found and stands accused of beating his wife and attempting to harm his children. That he's been subdued, and needs to be detained."

"Yes, Mother," Vámae whispered, and Mother released her hand. The door swung as Vámae ran into the rain with one last look at the still form on the floor.

"Ahren, go clean yourself up," Mother whispered, her frail body shaking as she attempted to get off her cot.

"Mama." Pallah stepped forward, holding out her hand. Her mother glanced at her, recognizing the endearment from a time long ago.

"There is a slight chance"—her mother steadied herself on Pallah's shoulder as Ahren left for the washroom—"they will not believe our story."

"Of course they will! We were all witnesses. They will." Mother was shaking her head.

"Hush, girl, listen to me."

"No, there is no way that man is going to continue under this roof. We will—"

"*Häfa!*" Pallah had never heard her mother curse before and it silenced her immediately. "Just...stop talking and listen, for once." They walked slowly as they made their way down the small hallway that lined the three bedrooms beyond, each covered with a leather flap that was a poor excuse for privacy.

"This isn't the first time this has happened. It did not end well before."

"What? With whom?"

"Pallah."

Pallah closed her lips firmly.

"There's no time to give details, but once, someone stood up to him, beat him senseless. I thought he was going to kill him; Bogdur doesn't fight back when he knows he will lose, because he knows he can talk his way out of anything if he's the victim. And he's *very good* at being the victim. I was there, with you and Vámae, Ahren but a babe, and when he was brought before the chief and council, Bogdur spun a tale so...believable, they took his lies as truth."

Pallah helped her up onto her bed, where she settled herself down on a flat and yellowed pillow. "What I'm saying is, if we feel it going poorly, if the council is disbelieving, you need to run."

"Run? Where?"

"You said you have friends now."

"You could hear me?"

Pallah's mother ignored her question. "Move in with one of them, or better yet...find Freya. But whatever you do, don't let Bogdur know where you are. He will come for you." Her eyes were haunting, and Pallah didn't have the strength to ask what would happen if her father did find her.

"Just me? I can't leave Vámae and Ahren...and you. Who is Freya?"

"I told you, Pallah, this began with you. It's always been different with you."

"Why just me?"

Her mother's eyes were drifting closed, and Pallah tried hard to stay in her line of sight. "You are proof of something he wants to forget. Freya will explain."

"*Who* is Freya?" Pallah chewed at her cheek, feeling frantic. Blood coated her hands from her father's wounds, the sight made her nauseous.

"My midwife." Her mother's eyes closed completely. "Like I said, it started with you."

"Mama!" Her panic must have shown through her tone because her mother gave a half-smile.

"I'm tired, not dead. Go back out to Ahren. Tell him nothing. He doesn't need to know. I'm proud of him, you know?" Her voice continued to dip into quiet. "He fought for me so well...good boy, that one. I'm so glad we tried for a boy..."

Her soft snores steadied Pallah. She stood, trying to make sense of the conversation, and ran into Ahren coming out of the washroom in the hall.

"Is he up?" he asked, hand over one eye. "How's Mother?"

"She's asleep." She blinked. "I don't know." She had all but forgotten Bogdur was still there, that she had not, in fact, succeeded in taking his life. Her hands were shaking. Had she really been prepared to do that? What had come over her?

You know what it was, the voice assured her.

Pallah counted to ten as the two of them returned to the scene to find the chief and Vámae walking through the door. Bogdur was as they had left him, his chest rising and falling with unjust ease.

The chief was strong for a man of sixty; his long beard was braided into three parts and wrapped skillfully to keep it off his thick neck. His meaty hands grasped a staff with a beautifully carved knob on the top, signifying his leadership in the village. He was dressed in a simple tunic and tailored pants which rested above his muscled calves. Beneath his eyes were caverns, harried and worn. Pallah wondered if Vámae had stayed quiet as their mother had asked, but judging by the chief's expression, she wasn't hopeful.

Behind him, the door opened to two council members Pallah recognized as Einar and Percival. Each of them was dressed in the long black robes of the council, robes they seemed to have thrown over their clothes on their way over; Einar's elbow was caught in the sleeve as if he had tried to pull it on with his arm bent.

They are fools, Pallah. You will need to run. Your friends wanted to go to Hekla, did they not? The voice was suggesting future plans for her now? Is this what she truly wanted to do? She could leave Vámae, maybe. But Ahren?

"Chief!" squealed Einar, pointing to the man on the ground that had started sputtering and coughing. Blood spurt out as Bogdur sat up, his hand on his head, his eyes swollen to slits.

The chief's large frame turned; his deeply hooded brow moved slowly over the scene.

"Bogdur, are you able to stand?"

Pallah's father emitted a short grunt before spitting to the side, something white clicking to the ground. "Chief"—his voice was thick—"there's no need for you to be here." He cleared another glob of blood from his mouth. "Just a domestic matter." He stood, though unsteadily.

Chief Olafur stared at him, unmoving. His eyes darted from Bogdur to the kids, to the table that lay broken, the room in obvious upheaval.

"Your eyes be upward, Chief," Bogdur said, one last attempt to rid himself of the authority.

"And be filled with light," Einar responded, finally getting his arm through the sleeve. "As he said, Chief, this is just a domestic matter." Bogdur was a loyal member of the village of Sodur and a constant presence at the Temple Celestial. As panic rose in her chest, Pallah began to understand what her mother had said. They *would* believe him over them.

"Chief Olafur." Pallah stepped forward, and all eyes in the room were suddenly directed at her, her father's, filled with so much hate, only made her stronger. "Please."

"Quiet, girl, you were not addressed," Percival interjected. Einar nodded in agreement. There was a beat that passed. Pallah didn't let her eyes leave the chief's.

"Please," she whispered again.

"Where is Phyllir?" Chief Olafur's rolling voice addressed her.

"She's asleep. In the bedroom."

"Is she well?"

"No. She still needs a Heitt Healer," Pallah said, her eyes going to her father who was seething beneath his stoic exterior. "She was commanded to stay out for her charge. I believe she snapped."

"She's fine," Bogdur said thickly over the council members as they mumbled about Pallah's admission. Snaps were rare.

"Einar, Percival, it looks as if Bogdur has sustained some minor injuries. Let's get him to a Healer."

Pallah almost crumpled to the floor in relief as the men escorted her father out of the room, placid on the outside but vehement beneath the surface. Vámae and Ahren made their way to Pallah's side, and the three of them stood together. Ahren, between the twins, reached down and grasped both of their hands. They stared blankly at the scene before them, their house in shambles, their life cracking at the seams.

The rise and fall of Ahren's breath calmed her own. His eyelid was punctured and swollen, crying blood. She squeezed his hand. Thick silence laced the room, uncharacteristic as it lacked Bogdur's barking commands or his expectant silence that hummed dangerously through their home.

Gone.

Empty.

The familiar hollowness inside of Pallah broadened, her family seemed to drift away, their home broken, the physical finally matching what had been happening internally for years.

"Kids." Chief Olafur turned to them. The three of them stood straighter. "I believe we have some things to discuss."

ONLY A LEGEND

SOLYANA

S OLYANA WOKE TO A tapping sound and found herself clutching the hatchet the priestess had given her only a few hours before. She was tucked up beside Rhuth, much like they would have been during a storm, before they had become the victims of one.

Rhuth had always snuck into Solyana's cot during the night if the winds had been too strong. Their fingers laced together, the younger falling peacefully back to sleep, snuggled up beside the older. But now, it seemed she would never wake, a reality Solyana couldn't accept. She would do what she must to bring the green back for Rhuth. Perhaps that was all she needed.

The tapping continued and Solyana swung her legs over the side of the bed, yawning. Dressed in a simple tunic, she felt a chill as she left the warm bed, her socked feet sliding over the wood floor. Halina, backlit by the moon, waited patiently on the windowsill, tapping to come in. Solyana had checked for her before bed, but she had been missing. Grateful she had returned, Solyana's pulse quickened at the thought of testing her theory. She cranked the window and the bird glided to the foot of Rhuth's bed before turning her yellow eyes on Solyana.

There was still a small fire glowing in the hearth, and, by its light, Solyana looked between the scarred face of her little sister and the massive bird at her feet.

"You're in darlöh, I know this. But I think you're, somehow…in here." Solyana motioned toward the bird before holding her arms tight to her sides. She took a breath. "I think you saved me, Little Fyug. I believe you are tethered to her."

The bird blinked her large yellow eyes in slow regard. Then with a silent open beak and a dip of her head, Solyana knew Rhuth was in there. A Tala connection, but something much deeper. Almost as if Rhuth was Halina, and Halina was Rhuth. Had this ever happened before? Rhuth was a strong Tala, but this kind of strange humanly connection was unheard of.

"Rhuth." Solyana's eyes filled with tears; she had her sister back. Not fully, not really, but she was alive. She was right here.

"How is this working? Are you okay? Why won't you wake?"

Halina's lids lowered slightly, and her feathers ruffled.

"Ah, yes sorry. You can't actually talk…" Solyana looked around the room for some way to communicate but came up short. "Does anyone else know?" Halina leaned down and nipped Solyana's hand who jerked it back to herself. "That's a 'no,' then?"

Halina's feathers ruffled then smoothed.

"And it's best we keep it that way?"

The bird preened herself.

The experiments Rhuth would be subjected to, Solyana could only imagine. She decided, for now, there was a reason Rhuth hadn't shown anyone but her. She would keep this secret for her.

Solyana stared at the creature, stoic and poised on her sister's prone form. "Are you"—she searched for the right words—"are you okay? Are you safe?"

Halina, quick and sure, nipped Solyana's hand once more before sitting back, her head swiveled back toward the door. Dread seeped into Solyana's belly, "I'm not sure how to wake you, Rhuth. Is it just because of your darlöh? Or—"

Halina made a soft *kak, kak, kak* sound, eyes flicking from the door to Rhuth.

"This is so frustrating. Look, Rhuth"—she stopped pacing and grabbed her sister's hand—"a lot has happened in the last week. I don't know how much you know, but I want you to hear it from me. I am going to be traveling out of the valley. Priestess Avi thinks...well, I think as well, I am the answer to this prophecy, the Green Prophecy. We believe we can, not only bring back the green, but save you in the process."

Halina suddenly spread her wings wide, her wingspan going much farther than Solyana had remembered. She stepped back from Rhuth's bed as the bird gave a guttural screech.

"Shh! Rhuth, I know it's a lot. I know I'm Ràna, but..." Solyana thought of the priestess's admission to using the Taka Reu. It had kept her awake a long time before she'd finally fallen asleep. She was unsure how to feel about it, but decided she was willing to open her mind to what was needed if it would save her people. "Priestess Avi has a way. We will figure it out."

The bird fluttered from the bed to the base of the door where she began pecking it.

"Rhuth!" Solyana shuffled across the room and opened it, brows furrowed as Halina continued on. Her wings were a flurry as she fluttered from one spot to the next, making her way down the hall.

"Rhuth, where are you going?" Solyana hurried along, looking around for Priestess Avi; the woman kept strange hours and it would be unsurprising to find her roaming the halls at night.

The bird came to a stop in front of the large door at the end of the hall, Solyana swallowed hard. She looked down at Halina.

"Here?"

Halina pecked at the door in answer.

Solyana knocked once. Hearing no response, she opened the door and peeked her head inside. Solyana's mouth fell open as she entered the priestess's room. The old woman, praise the Celestials, was nowhere to be seen. There was an ancient elegance to its decor; every piece of furniture was old but well-tended, their age unrecognizable but for the design and the quality of wood that gave it away.

The ceiling took her breath away. Small flames danced everywhere, like stars sprinkling the night sky. She wondered if they were always there, if the priestess was just so skilled, she didn't even have to think about the hundreds of tiny flames lying naked and dangerous in the space above.

The room smelled of musty leather and oil and was even more cluttered than the hallway leading to it: leafy plants, scrolls, and animals—dead animals, but animals all the same. Although she had never seen one before, she recognized a taxidermied smilodon in the corner of the room, its pose so passive and unsuspecting, Solyana would have thought it a friend. Its massive incisors reached from its snout to far beneath its chin. There were a few rabbits surrounding it, none of which were posed in any kind of action; she wondered why she'd bothered having them stuffed at all. Taxidermy was not a largely practiced art, reserved solely for more personal use, but Priestess Avi had never struck her as one who would keep her kills...especially something as mundane as rabbits.

Solyana turned quickly to a tearing sound, expecting the priestess to be in the room with her, but only found Halina, talons on a scroll, ripping it in half with her beak.

"No!" Solyana rushed over and grabbed Halina off the paper in a moment of bravery. Reminded again of the bird's weight, she grunted in surprise. Halina simply held the length of scroll high for Solyana to grab, then wriggled free of her grasp and flew in short spurts back to Rhuth's room.

Solyana took one last look at the room. Something felt amiss, but she heard the loud clang of a door being shut in the distance. She had to get out of there.

She was back in Rhuth's room in less than a minute, sweat dripping down the side of her face as she struggled to get Halina back out the window, the bird screaming protests. "Stop screeching! If Priestess Avi finds you in here, she'll ask questions!" She stuffed the bird out into the open air, hoping she wouldn't be spotted. The bird stayed just outside the window, still letting out frantic cries.

Solyana held up the piece of scroll the bird had stolen and waved it back and forth. "I have it. I will read it, okay?"

Halina blinked and took off, quickly becoming a dark speck in the sky. Solyana cranked the window shut and held up the scroll. She scanned the first couple of sentences.

...late again. Father is going to skin her alive, and honestly, I have no pity. She is choosing the wrong path; she's making her own future, and it is one far bleaker than anything I look forward to. Enough about her, though. I need to write out my ideas for the Feast of Haust. I was so pleased that Chief Olafur asked me to head it up...

She unfurled it a bit more and skipped ahead.

...and she's been missing for ages, but every time I ask V about her, he just says he was only ever interested in her because he thought I was out of his league. I suppose that makes sense. He's a powerful Vatin Fera, but I'm one of the most powerful Heitt now. We would make some beautiful children...powerful children. But I'm getting ahead of myself. Besides, I'm a Serviseer now. My life is for the Temple Celestial...well, at least until I turn 18. Then maybe—

Solyana's head snapped up at the sound of the stairs just beyond the door creaking. She stuffed the scroll into her parka that was laid over a chair and slid back under the covers alongside her sister, feigning sleep. Whatever Rhuth had stolen from the priestess's room must be important. She would have to keep it a secret.

The door creaked open and Solyana, whose body was facing the window, couldn't tell who it was until her voice broke the silence.

"Someone disturbed my quarters, girl." The priestess's voice was hushed, but no less strong. "Surely you haven't been able to..."

There was a beat. Was the priestess talking to Solyana or Rhuth? Solyana kept her breathing steady and slow.

There were sounds of tinkering in the corner, a concoction coming together. The old woman made her way back to the bedside, and an unseen hand guided her sister's body upward so she would drink. "I have met no other that could tether in this state." The priestess chuckled. "We're more alike than you think. You sleep now, girl."

Solyana didn't know how long she lay awake after they were left alone, thinking on the words of the priestess, wondering what exactly she meant.

A loud crack of wood on wood resounded through the chill as Solyana and Gamaliel sparred. When Papa had suggested Gamaliel start mentoring her, Solyana had pictured long evenings of study or in-depth chats by the fire. However, Gamaliel's idea of teaching her was a bit more exciting. Mock fights had become the norm over the last six days, and somehow, he was able to keep up a steady conversation while Solyana could barely respond through her labored breathing.

"Have Jonas and Lone found anything yet?" he asked, swinging his staff around to sweep her legs. She awkwardly jumped before bringing her own staff down to connect with his side. He was too quick for her and had already brought his staff back up to block it. They broke apart and circled each other slowly.

"Nothing on acquisition of Gifts. Papa isn't helping things, though. He's been so focused on the maps; he's got Jonas tied up in painting new ones for our trip."

"Don't we have enough maps already?"

"Jonas refuses to take anything from the archives. He doesn't want to lose anything out there. Plus, he says he's a better cartographer."

"He does have an uncanny ability to make maps of places he's never seen."

"Well, he reads a lot," Solyana pointed out. "He knows the ancient tongue. He's probably reading all about the—"

Gamaliel took two quick steps forward and then stopped. Solyana raised her staff and an eyebrow, her mouth falling open in a wide grin. "Stop trying to fake me out!" She laughed.

"Just keeping you on your toes." He smirked and then launched forward, his staff coming in a quick one-two-three strike. Solyana blocked the first two, but the third caught her between neck and shoulder.

"*Stars to heaven*, Gamaliel," Solyana hissed as she massaged the sore muscle.

"You'll get there, Princess." Gamaliel had taken to calling her this, knowing it riled her. He walked forward, hand outstretched for the staff. Solyana twirled it until it was horizontal and pulsed it quick into his stomach. He doubled over. "Not...fair..." he wheezed.

"You'll get there, Old Man." She grinned down at him.

"I'll take that." He straightened and took the staff from her. "You're going to hurt yourself." It was probably the last time they could practice in The Pines as they were due to leave in the morning. They began walking back to the Temple. "How are you feeling about possibly having to use the Taka Reu?"

Solyana shot him a look, the snow building up around her mukluks as they walked. "I told you not to talk about that. I wasn't supposed to tell anyone. And I'll say what I said before: I'll do what I need to do to save Rhuth. If that means gleaning energy from The Mother, so be it."

Gamaliel made a noise of disapproval. "That, coupled with what she said when she came in to check on Rhuth..." Solyana had told him about the strange one-sided conversation and was beginning to wish she hadn't. "I don't know, Solyana. I don't trust the woman."

Solyana stopped walking and turned to him. "Who am I supposed to trust, Gam? What other path is there? I would love to know." The fear that lived in her stomach since the vote cropped up again. "Should I just hole up in a cave somewhere and hope everything gets figured out for me?"

"Hey!" Gamaliel's eyes flashed. "Not fair. I was banished."

"How is this any different? At least they let you live in peace!" Solyana flung her hands out to the side, suddenly filled with emotion that was waiting to be released. "I don't have Gifts and I'm just being sent away. Am I just some sacrifice for the Celestials? Are they not pleased with us so much they've decided to kill us off one by one until...until..." Tears pressed the backs of her eyes so forcefully she had to stifle a cry, her hand covering her mouth, catching anything before it escaped.

Gamaliel was staring at her. When she gathered the courage to meet his gaze, she was not met with judgement, but compassion; Solyana's resolve began to crumble. Why must all of this hinge on her? She blinked rapidly, willing the tears away, wishing she was anywhere else, alone, so she could release them like a flood.

"Hey, it's going to be okay," he said gently, taking a step forward.

She shook her head, her hand still over her mouth. They had grown close over the last week, but she had kept her inward thoughts to herself. She was a symbol of hope now, she couldn't falter. Weakness wasn't allowed.

"Solyana..." With her name on his lips all resolve broke and she let the tears come. He dropped the staves and took her in his arms, hugging her tight and secure. Her sobs couldn't be stopped, and she was grateful for the release. His arms held her when she couldn't hold herself. She leaned into him, crying into his warm chest. One of his hands was at the small of her back, the other on the top of her head, gently brushing her hair back. He said nothing and she was grateful. When her tears finally subsided she sniffed, embarrassment whirling through her.

She wiped at his chest; the furs layered there grown darker now they were damp. "This is not what I was made for." She shook her head. "This was never supposed to be—"

"But it is." He gripped her arms just above the elbow. "The Celestials chose *you*, Solyana. And I'm glad they did."

She stared into his dark brown eyes and furrowed her brow. "Glad?"

"Well"—he released her arms and ran a hand down his face—"yeah, I mean...I would never have met you if this hadn't happened." He took a step toward her and took one of her hands in his own. Although they had just embraced, this touch was far more intimate. It couldn't be mistaken with anything platonic, something about it bordered desire as his eyes reached so deep into her own. Solyana's breath caught and a thrill of excitement ran through her belly. He leaned close to her face, his eyes studying hers. "Or if it did, we wouldn't be—"

"Gaaaaam!" Jonas's shrill voice came as an echo over the pine trees all around them.

"*Häfa.*" Gamaliel stood straight and released her hand. The moment broke, if it had been a moment at all.

"Gaaaaaaam!" His voice came again, and this time Solyana spotted Jonas's sandy-haired head bounding through the snow toward them, Vinur galloping beside him, tongue flapping in the wind. "There you two are!" the boy said, a grin spreading across his face.

"Impeccable timing, Jonas. What's going on?" Gamaliel said, his hand rubbing the back of his neck.

"I found it!" Jonas said as he stopped running. Vinur kept going until he was at Gamaliel's side.

"Found what?" Solyana heart quickened.

"How to get Gifts, of course!" Jonas motioned for them to follow as he took off, back in the direction of the Temple. "Follow me!"

Solyana and Gamaliel walked with purpose back to the Temple. On the way, they passed several people who were preparing goods for the trio's journey outward. Some greeted her, others kept their distance, eyeing them from behind their work; the valley at large still at odds with her role, she knew some blamed her, though she didn't understand it. But for every one that saw her as the cause, another saw her as the answer, and for that, she was grateful.

When she returned—*if* she returned—would things go back to normal? Would those she counted as friends and family still view her as the cause of the blizzards? Still see her as the reason their loved ones had perished? Would her father lose his position as chief, the people tying her fate with his authority? Would her family suffer for her sake? She tried to ignore the eyes following her as she jogged up the steps to the Temple Celestial. No, she decided then. Normalcy would be gone.

They passed through the sanctuary and descended the steps into the archives to find Lone leaning over Papa's shoulder, a slender finger pointing at the page. "Right here?" she asked.

"Yes, Hasta Pass. Entering it is tricky, getting through it, even trickier…" he grumbled as his meaty fingers traced over the parchment.

"Chief Marus!" Jonas squeaked, red in the face. Solyana and Gamaliel walked in behind him. "It hasn't dried yet!"

"Oh." The chief peered through his bushy eyebrows to spot the brown paint smudged on his finger. "So sorry, Jonas."

Jonas took a measured breath and gave an abashed smile. "I apologize, Chief Marus. I should not have yelled at you." He gave a dramatic bow of his head.

Papa let out a hearty laugh. "Don't worry, my boy. It's fine!" He laid the parchment back on the table and leaned back in his chair. "I'll leave it here to dry."

Jonas nodded and disappeared into the rows of shelving.

Solyana circled the table and sat beside Papa, thankful for his presence. He wrapped one arm around her, squeezing tight.

"I'm proud of you, Middle One. I know I haven't been great at making that clear, but I am. Truly. The Celestials will keep you safe," he said as if trying to reassure himself more than her.

She squeezed him back.

"If you've changed your mind..." he began.

"Papa"—Solyana pulled away from him and caught a glint of tears in his blue eyes—"please."

He had spent the week helping where he could, but Solyana knew her father would give his right arm to keep her in the valley, or for her to ask him to come along. But she couldn't, she wouldn't.

"Jonas, what did you find?" Solyana asked as the boy pulled a scroll from the table's end and brought it up to read.

"It's the only place I've found any reference to having more than one Gift. But it's in ancient Mothmari."

The group waited patiently.

"Basically, it's an account of someone who didn't think Gifts were natural. They wanted to be rid of their Blou Fera."

Lone's head snapped up, one eyebrow raised. "Blou Fera? Aptitude for blood?" The term reminded them of their darker history, a genocide against all those with bodily Gifts, considered too dangerous, too lethal.

Jonas nodded, his forehead creased, then continued. "So, they found someone willing to take it. It turns out, it has to be...gifted. A gifting, of a Gift." He looked around at the group innocently and it reminded Solyana of just how young he was. He turned back to the page, reading it word for word.

"Blood from the Gift must come to the one without, for the Gift is found in the blood. Establishing the connection together...and then apart." Trying to translate, he shook his head and kept reading, spreading the scroll a bit wider in front of them. Papa leaned in close, and Solyana rested her head on his shoulder, grateful for his closeness.

"Utilizing it together, combining it, spiritual and physical, with all trust." Jonas looked up and shrugged.

"What happens to the person who was born with the Gift? Can they get it back again if they change their mind?" Solyana asked and looked up to see Gamaliel staring at her. A blush creeped up her neck as she turned to Jonas.

"Legend has it, if you lose your Gift...you lose yourself." Papa's voice rumbled from Solyana's right. "At least that's what was believed back when Seers sang in our mountains."

Jonas nodded, pointing a finger at the chief. "I *have* heard that."

"Legend, yes. But is it truth?" Gamaliel cut in. "What does the scroll say? Did the Gifted die?"

"It doesn't say," Jonas said quietly.

Silence fell as all of them considered the same implication. Even if she could convince someone to give her their Gift, how could she do it knowing it would end in that person's death? How could they test something like that? It was too costly. She could not ask someone to make that kind of sacrifice.

"It's only a legend," Lone said with a shrug, her eyelids hung perpetually low; it made her look bored in spite of her hopefulness. "Maybe someone will be willing to offer theirs."

"Are you volunteering?" Gamaliel cocked an eyebrow at her and grinned.

"Well, no," she admitted.

Papa grunted and stood. "Keep searching, Jonas. There must be more accounts. We can't do anything with this information. It simply isn't enough to work with."

Jonas nodded, looking a bit defeated, but he rallied, shuffling around the room once more, his head in a scroll. The group dispersed, leaving Jonas in the archives. Papa and Lone disappeared out the door and into the afternoon light, discussing travel plans as they went. Solyana gathered her things to follow when Gamaliel spoke up, stopping her in the middle of the sanctuary.

"Thoughts on Lone?" he asked coyly.

The door shut and Solyana turned around. "What do you mean?" Alone in the sanctuary, their voices echoed through the expansive room.

"You've hardly spoken to her this last week. I was just wondering what you thought of her."

"I mean, she's fine." Honestly, Solyana felt a bit insecure around her. Lone was tall, confident, and unaffected, everything Solyana wasn't. "I haven't had much time to get to know her, with everything going on. What do *you* think of her?" Solyana's pulse quickened as Gamaliel stepped closer and she wondered if they would finish their earlier conversation before Jonas interrupted them.

"Oh, Lone's great. I mean, we used to be close, so...I'm glad she's coming. She's a really talented Bein Fera."

Solyana blinked. "You used to be close?"

"Well, yeah," Gamaliel tried to backtrack, and Solyana's excitement fizzled.

"Did you two used to…" Solyana guessed.

"Oh, I mean…yeah. A while back. I was allowed to come back for larger market days. We met at one of them. It's been a while though. It ended amicably. Anyway, she's a great person, you're a great person. I figured you two would hit it off."

Solyana held her smile painfully. She hoped Gamaliel couldn't see through the facade.

He narrowed his eyes at her.

"Could we finish that conversation we were having outside?" he asked, trying to amend the situation.

"I don't think there's anything more to discuss." Solyana knew she was being unfair, even as she said it, but she couldn't believe she was about to go on this journey with Gamaliel and his ex-girlfriend.

Jonas's small frame popped out of the archives and shuffled by, his arms full of scrolls as he made his way to the stairs.

Gamaliel ran his fingers through his hair, staring at the boy as he passed. "We're having a conversation, Jonas."

Jonas slowed down until he was almost crawling up the stairs.

Solyana glanced between them.

"Jonas!" Gamaliel cleared his throat.

Vinur's head peeked out of the doorway that led to the archives. He located Jonas and took off in his direction. The two of them scrambled up to the floor above.

Solyana shook her head, determinedly keeping her eyes on the door into which Jonas had disappeared. "Have you talked to him yet?"

"Jonas? About what?"

"'About what?' He's Heitt, Gamaliel! Or are you denying that, too?"

"Wait, too? Solyana, I'm confused."

Solyana rolled her eyes. "I just didn't know you two had dated."

"Me and Jonas?" Gamaliel chuckled.

"You and Lone!"

"I didn't deny we did."

"You weren't clear about it! It's been almost a week of us just talking about her. Only now it comes up?"

"Why does it matter?"

"It doesn't." Solyana pressed her fists to her temples, feeling flustered. "Look. You need to talk to Jonas before we go. He's going to get himself hurt."

Gamaliel looked at his feet and rubbed the back of his neck, his long hair falling in front of his face. "I'll talk to him, okay?"

"When?" Solyana demanded.

"Tonight! Sheesh." He shook his head. "Remind me not to get on your bad side."

Jonas was at the top of the stairs again, Vinur at his side.

"Jonas," said Gamaliel, and Solyana could hear the tension in his voice. How long had the boy been standing there? "What are you doing, buddy?"

"Uh, I've got to go," Jonas said weakly. Then, in a flurry of parchment and scrolls, he ran down the stairs, passed Solyana and Gamaliel, through the foyer, and straight out the temple doors.

"Jonas!" Solyana called to him, then turned to Gamaliel. "Do you think he heard us?"

Vinur trotted down the stairs and stood next to Gamaliel, his chin held high.

"You're with him all day, and now you choose to stay behind?" Gamaliel asked him with a groan. "Well, he either heard us, or he discovered some other grand revelation. Either way, we need to find him. Come on, boy." Gamaliel and his wolf exited the Temple.

Solyana was about to follow them when she heard voices above her. She went up the stairs. She would say goodbye to Rhuth tonight; they were to leave bright and early in the morning.

When she entered the room, she found Fridmey next to Rhuth, hands clasped together. Fridmey, usually stoic and void of much emotion, turned her tearful eyes on Solyana.

"I didn't know you were here." Solyana crossed to her.

"Well"—Fridmey huffed a laugh—"here we all are. The three Marusda sisters, one last time."

"Not the last time." Solyana glanced at Rhuth.

Fridmey nodded to herself and sniffed. She looked up at Solyana and pulled her close so she could hold Rhuth's hand in one and Solyana's in the other.

"I'm afraid for you, Sol."

"Afraid for me?" Solyana wanted to hear Fridmey say it. Her sister was particular with who she released her feelings to, and Solyana was looking for assurances.

"You're leaving to go out in this." Fridmey motioned toward the window and Mothmar beyond. "I just need you to come back, okay?"

"I will. I promise, I will." Solyana tugged her close for a hug. They stood there for a moment, breathing in each other's scents, all seal oil and smoke, home and childhood.

Fridmey pulled back, wiping her blue eyes. "Well, good. I'll let you say goodbye." She kissed Rhuth's forehead and exited the room.

Solyana looked down at her sister, so peaceful in her sleep. She thought of Halina and of her sister's abilities to control the animal. Solyana had lain awake a few of the nights, reading the torn piece of pilfered scroll. It held, what seemed to be, the personal account of the Serviseer mentioned in the scrolls Priestess Avi had presented to her. So far it hadn't revealed anything incredibly relevant, but maybe she was missing something.

"Hey there, Little Fyug." She gave Rhuth's hand a slight squeeze. "I'm leaving, and"—she took a shuddering breath, feeling far too hot in her parka—"I don't know when I'm coming back."

Rhuth's face remained passive, though Solyana could see her swollen eye had parted slightly of its own accord, oozing clear liquid.

"Your eye seems to be healing. You're going to have a pretty cool scar. Actually, both of us do...though I would take yours over mine any day." She bent down and pulled Rhuth's hand up to cup her scarred cheek. "It comes and goes, but it feels more and more like my skin every time it happens." She took a breath. "Don't give up, okay? Stay strong. I will save you from this. Just hang in there. Give me a month and I'll be back. I will save you Rhuth, I promise."

THE WOLF

PALLAH

THE CUP OF TEPID water in front of Pallah rippled in time with her knee that bounced beneath the rough-hewn table. They had brought her to a small room in the Temple, barely big enough for the table and the two chairs it held, there were no windows. Horizontal crooked planks paneled the room, a few of them met at disjointed angles. Ahren could have done a better job with the design; it was shoddy, careless. A single lantern burned at the end of the table in front of Pallah, its light constant and steady. The room smelled like sweat and blood. Her stomach twisted as she ran over the events of the night. The chief had brought her mother to the infirmary for healing. Bogdur was brought to the cells for questioning. Pallah and her siblings were separated throughout the Temple Celestial. Pallah supposed the chief wanted as truthful of a story as he could get; sequestering them was the best tactic for it.

She had counted to twenty, at least forty-five times. A small husk cup in front of her cast a shadow toward her. She reached for it and didn't realize her hand was shaking as much as her knee until she raised it to her lips. Too difficult to drink, she set it down and pressed her hands onto her thighs. Showing any type of weakness could lead to disbelief in her story, she knew, but her hands would not stop shaking.

"Stop!" she commanded them through gritted teeth as the wooden door in the corner swung open and Chief Olafur himself stepped into the room.

"Pallah Bogson," he said, his lilting voice deep and rolling.

She swallowed hard. Mothmarians determined last names by the father's first name. Unfortunate in her situation, she wondered if she could change it.

"I'm pleased to make your official acquaintance." He extended his hand and crossed to her, but she kept her hands pressed into her legs, making fleeting eye contact. If she shook his hand, he would know how nervous she was. He let out a long stream of air, lowered his hand, then sat in the chair opposite, the table separating them.

"I've seen your whole family grow up here in this valley. Some of our eldest family lines come from your father's side, some real skilled Fera there. Your mother, she's a dedicated Heitt. Your sister, Vámae, she's strong in Heitt, an Eldur, actually. She's always been around the Temple Celestial. She directed the Feast of Haust this year. And Ahren, he'll certainly be one of the top carpenters in the villages, if only to match your father's work, little though he makes..." Pallah looked up at that, and the chief grinned, his wiry braided beard hiding most of his teeth. "We probably get something from your father twice a year. Bogdur is a meticulous man."

Pallah huffed.

"An understatement, surely," Chief Olafur said. "But that's where I need your help, Pallah. Unlike your family, you keep your Gift close to your chest. And that's fine! You don't need to tell me. What I would like to know is the events of tonight and what led to them. If your father deserves to have justice meted against him, we need to know why. Understood?"

She leveled her gaze at him, his stark blue eyes so bright in his weathered face, his wiry hair and beard an indeterminate mix of gray and black, his skin taut and almost completely covered in the gray from his beard. But then his eyes wrinkled in the same fashion Pallah knew her mother's did when she was happy, rare though it was, the creases spreading from corner to temple. She found his lips amongst his beard, he was grinning.

"You're a watcher." He nodded.

"What? No...I—" she stammered, looking down at her hands.

"Not a bad thing!" he said, pulling a handkerchief out of his pocket and rubbing at his eyes in turn. "It means you have brains. I've just been trying to figure out if you're stupid."

"I'm not."

"No"—he sighed and relaxed further into his seat—"you're not. So, where do we start?"

Pallah took a breath, finally getting a hold of her shaking hands and legs, growing still for the first time in half an hour.

"My father beats my mother." It tumbled out of her, surprising even her in its boldness. She pressed on. "Although I just discovered that tonight. He also abuses me, though not in the same way. It's happened for as long as I can remember."

The chief's eyebrows knit together as he nodded her on.

"Sometimes my brother and sister, too. But mainly me." She shook her head, "That isn't as important though. The important part is Mother. I only realized tonight. Bogdur told her to stay outside all day. And she snapped, you know." Pallah's gray eyes flicked up to meet Olafur's blue ones. She thought she saw a bit of shock in them; snaps were rare. "That's how we found her, Ahren and I."

"Well, your mother still made the choice to remain outside, even if her husband told her to do it. What else makes you think there's abuse happening?" Although Pallah didn't think he was trying to be obtuse, his question made her pause and look over him once more. Is this what her mother was afraid of when she thought they wouldn't be believed? Had the chief already talked to her father? Had he already chosen a side?

"If my mother had felt comfortable going against the wishes of Bogdur, she would not have snapped. She knows what she's doing, she wouldn't have stayed."

The chief nodded her on and scratched at his beard.

"And I could tell, by her face. She doesn't look how she used to. And after everything that happened tonight, she admitted it to me."

Blinking, the chief sat up straighter. "She did? What did she say?"

The words came back to Pallah.

You. Since you.

"That it's been happening since I was born," Pallah summarized. "Almost seventeen years." The impact of her own statement hit her so forcefully, a lump formed in her throat. How had her mother taken it? How had she remained in that house? Pallah wanted to upend the table and smash the lantern against the wall.

She breathed and counted to ten.

"Well, tonight then. Why is Bogdur in the infirmary?" the chief prompted. "What happened there?"

"Ahren found Mother behind the house..." Pallah began to recount the tale of the evening, being careful to lay out the facts and not presume the thoughts of her siblings. Though it would have been easy to describe the hate in Ahren's eyes, she didn't want him getting in more trouble.

From Vámae's quick work in bringing Mother back, to Ahren's beating of her father; to her father's attempt on Ahren's life, the spears of wood in his shoulder, and the heavy piece of table thrown so close to her brother's writhing body.

"And I pushed him back down, I didn't want him coming after me, after Ahren, after my mother. I didn't feel safe." Her hands had begun their shaking once more, her voice rose as she felt her mind scream at her to stop, to self-preserve. She couldn't tell him how close she had been to killing him. Thinking back on it now, she couldn't believe she had been filled with enough hate to come that close herself. But hadn't she? Remembering the depth of dark that had rolled through her, the feeling of an unseen hand raising her own, the pull in her chest, much like the pull she usually felt at the base of her skull. Had it been the Taka Reu? Had she been using it?

"Then what happened, Pallah?" the chief prompted, his eyes kind.

"Ahren thought I was going to strike him with my hatchet. I wasn't," she lied. "I was just trying to scare him, keep him in one spot. But Ahren used his Fera to grab my hatchet, and I knocked Bogdur out."

"And what was the purpose of that?"

"I was neutralizing the threat," Pallah said slowly, eyes coming up to meet the chief.

"Mhmm," Chief Olafur mused, scratching at his beard again. "And all of this was...unexpected from Bogdur? I've never known him to be a violent man. Why would you think he would have come after you?"

"I just told you." Pallah's chest constricted. Here it was, the disbelief, the dismissal. "I had figured out he had abused my mother. He was getting what—" She barely stopped herself. She didn't think the chief would condone the sentiment, true as it was.

"And you were just trying to...scare him? With your hatchet to his throat?"

Pallah's face flushed, and, through gritted teeth, she said, "That's right."

Chief Olafur grunted, looking tired but determined, his eyes still sharp even at the late hour. "Pallah"—he rubbed his eyes again with the cloth—"this is quite the tale."

"It's the truth," she asserted, her mother's warning still echoing in the back of her mind.

"Well"—he smiled warmly at her, pocketed his handkerchief, pressed his hands into the table to help himself up, and stood—"I'm sure my men have your sister and brother's stories by now. We'll confer. I'm sure you're exhausted. Thank you for taking the time to do this properly."

The chief exited the room, and she laid her head on the table. The room, windowless as it was, was beginning to make her feel trapped and Pallah wondered how deep into the night they were. She hadn't had a moment to breathe since she had arrived home earlier that evening. What was that, two hours ago? Three? It struck her then that if something had happened with Tinloh, she wouldn't know. It's not like the small cat could connect to her tether of his own will, only she could do that. She shook her head of anxieties. He was probably fine. Leif and Karav would take good care of him.

Though, she *could* make sure. She closed her eyes and focused on that small cabin deep in the woods, surrounded by hordes of rabbits. The tether wavered for a moment, in search of the smilodon, but then, in an instant, she was attached. Warmth spread through her extremities, and she wondered why she hadn't thought to do this before. Her leg stopped its shaking. Tinloh was asleep, restless, but asleep. She couldn't tell if the connection was complete or not, could she just feel his emotions? Could he feel hers? Or could she command him, as she had done when she was physically near him? She was far north of the villages, and Leif's cabin was due south. They were a long way apart.

"Pallah Bogson?"

She jumped and her knee hit the table. The light flickered, and her tether hummed as Tinloh awoke.

"Sorry to frighten you." A small woman stood at the door, her face wrinkled and hook-nosed, her robes gray and lined with fringe. Pallah recognized her garb as one that committed their life to the Temple as a Serviseer. "As it is unfit for you and your siblings to return home at the moment, we are offering you beds, to rest for the night." The woman lifted a tightly fitted sleeve, a lantern held in her hand. "Follow me."

They walked in silence as they turned through endless corridors. She tried coaxing Tinloh back to sleep but he resisted her and began gnawing on his cage.

The small woman in front of her arrived at a door, knocked once, then opened it, revealing a tiny room complete with a cot in one corner and a small table in the other.

"Someone will be by to fetch you in the morning, washroom is right down the hall," she said with a wave of her hand. "Your eyes be upward." She turned and headed back down the hall, lantern in tow, unwilling to wait for the response Pallah wasn't going to give anyway.

As the light retreated, Pallah backed into her room, feeling colder and lonelier than she had in a long time. Closing the door with a soft click, she turned to her moonlit room, the storm long since subsided. The cot groaned once as she laid down, then steadied. Where was Ahren? Vámae? Were they still with Einar and Percival? She looked out the modest window above her, straight at the moon.

"Hi," she whispered through dried lips, her eyes steady on the Mother of the Night, a sliver of white in the sky. "We haven't spoken...in a while." Had she ever? But the ache for something deeper, something outside her problems and her worries, consumed her after experiencing the worst night of her life. It couldn't hurt to pray. "My friends think you're fake, a conjuring of hopes and wishes that people assign to a visible object to give them purpose."

The Mother of the Night said nothing.

"I don't know what I think of you. If I'm being completely honest, I've never had much of an opinion. But"—she took in a shuddering breath as an image of her younger brother carrying their mother's limp body flashed in her mind—"I want to believe in...something. Anything really. I'm not picky. I just want to know that I'm not...it's not...pointless. All of it. I'm not going to blame you for our wrongdoings. We are human. We make up our own minds. We hurt our own. But I could blame you for not interfering when we needed help."

You're right. She can't hear you.

"Get out of my head!" Pallah sat up. She had never addressed the voice she heard in her mind, not out loud. "Stop. Just stop speaking."

You don't mean that. Stop praying, Pallah. It does nothing.

"You do nothing." She pulled her knees to her chest and buried her face into them, shoving her fingers into her hair. "You're just in my head. You aren't real."

Oh, but I am. More real than you, Pallah. You are nothing.

Pallah sat upright, every muscle tense, poised to act.

You

She stood and gripped the nightstand.

Are

Her chest heaved.

Nothing!

She screamed, lifting the nightstand and slamming it down once, twice, three times. Spit dripped from her teeth as the scream transformed into a sob and she let go, finally, after far too long keeping it in. She collapsed back onto the bed and cried, for the loss of the family she had, and the family she never had; for what the Temple Celestial had done to her father—poisoning him, to think his wife had to come so near the grave to please the great beings of the sky; she cried for her isolation, never knowing her aptitude and struggling in Lóthkol; she cried for the face she was given, but more so for the one she wasn't given when she looked at her twin. She cried, for she felt so alone and always had. No one had brought her into their fold; no one reached out to that plain little blonde girl and asked her to play, no one. No one...until Vil, and his group.

Gasping for air, she brought in shaky mouthfuls that burned her lungs. At least, she knew, Bogdur would finally get what he deserved, or some portion of it. He wouldn't be able to control her anymore. Chief Olafur would see to it she was safe, that she would be protected. This thought brought her peace. She sniffed and wiped her dripping nose on her sleeve.

It occurred to her then her siblings could be close to her room and could have heard her. She wiped at her eyes, formulating a plan. Where were they?

Pallah exited and found the washroom first. She relieved herself and turned on the tap, grateful for running water; the Temple Celestial was the only building to have that luxury. She took a few moments to scrub her arms, hands, and feet in the sink until she couldn't smell herself any longer.

A low rumble of voices grabbed her attention as she left the cramped room. She froze, glancing around. Far at the end of the hallway, a soft glow spread under a door, beckoning her to come see. She padded softly down the corridor, a sense of apprehension rising in her as her brain began interpreting the rise and fall of sounds into words.

"...and Ahren didn't say anything about that kind of behavior to me, either. Well, he mentioned a few times his father was a very controlling and particular man, but nothing like what you're saying, Chief."

"Neither of your charges?" Pallah recognized Chief Olafur.

It was quiet. She pressed her back against the wall and peered into the room, the door slightly ajar. The council sat in a circle of chairs. The group of men deliberating the Bogson children's fate in the dead of night. Pallah spotted the chief, the top of his staff, struck through with quartz, glittered in the lantern light.

"So, Pallah claims there has been some type of...shall we call it, abuse?"

"I would call it that," the chief mused.

"She claims there was abuse since she was a child, and not only to her, but to her mother. Healer Rohdar has done a preliminary examination and has confirmed that Phyllir has suffered some major traumas and injuries, in the past and the present. My recommendation is to remove her from the living situation and get her in care as soon as possible. Her current injuries are unknown, but Rohdar isn't hopeful. In fact, she mentioned placing her in end of—"

"Let's discuss her later, Percival. We're all tired, and we need to make a decision on the children tonight."

Pallah blinked, too stunned to move. Were they thinking of placing her mother in end-of-life care? No, she had been fine. A lump formed in her throat.

"Right," the man called Percival said, his voice catching. He cleared it. "Vámae and Ahren both corroborate Pallah's story, at first..." He retold the events up until Vámae began healing their mother.

"Are we doing anything about this infraction? She is still underage," a tinny voice piped up.

"Overruled, her actions saved her mother's life," another said.

Percival grunted in agreement and continued on. Pallah listened intently, but when they arrived at the breaking of the table, her forehead began to break out in sweat.

"...throws her hatchet, she hits the piece of wood, it knocks it off balance, then she's on top of Bogdur, weapon in hand and at his throat," Percival recounted.

"Now, Pallah tells me she was simply trying to knock the piece of wood off balance so Bogdur would lose control of it. I think she was trying to keep her father from hurting her brother," the chief added.

"I doubt it. From what Vámae tells me, the girl was close to killing him, once she had the opportunity. She probably missed her mark and hit the table instead."

Pallah squeezed her eyes shut and cursed to herself.

The chief grunted, giving no indication whether he believed her or not.

"Vámae and Ahren both stated Pallah had lifted the hatchet like she was going to strike Bogdur with it, which is why Ahren, also Vior Fera, pulled the hatchet from her hand, and her fist came down on him instead. Does Pallah say the same?" Percival asked.

"She told me she was never going to strike him. She was just trying to scare him. But Ahren was afraid she would and took her hatchet," the chief answered.

There it was. She knew it was risky, but she was desperate for them to believe her. Blurring her intentions was the only way she thought they would have a chance. But now, she second-guessed herself. Maybe she should've told Chief Olafur the whole truth.

Silence was still stretching in the room beyond. Pallah's mind raced, trying to decide whether or not she should run or stay, find her brother and sister, or leave without saying a word. She turned quietly on the pads of her feet and began sneaking back down the hallway when she heard the man called Einar clear his throat.

"I suppose we can interview again, just to be sure. We still haven't heard Bogdur's side of the story. Meanwhile, I propose we place the children back in the custody of their father. We'll keep their mother under Rohdar's care, and all of this will be done with mandatory welfare checks, done by one of us here on the council, until we can either fully prove or deny the alleged abuse."

Pallah froze, her muscles tensed to bursting.

"I was going to propose my own," the chief said with a smile in his voice. "Of course, I didn't know we were just proposing whenever we felt like it." There were chuckles from members of the council.

"Chief Olafur, please forgive me." Einar's high-pitched voice quavered. "You don't usually propose. I apologize for my haste."

"I think..." He paused. Pallah stayed frozen in place. Would her story change his mind? Did he believe her? "I think there's something to what Pallah has said, and if I were in her shoes, I believe I, too, would attempt to put myself in the best light. She's a scared kid, let's not forget."

"Vámae seemed to be fully honest to me. They're the same age," Einar argued.

"Vámae doesn't claim her father is abusing her," the Chief pointed out.

Einar let out a chuff of air.

"As I was saying, she's young. She's scared. I would bet my right hand they all are. Let's put them into work placement; it will keep them under our watchful eye, and Bogdur will stand trial after a thorough investigation. Until then, he stays in the cells, though clemency can be granted if he repents of his failings. If Phyllir does not recover, however..." Pallah's heart contracted, and a ball formed in the pit of her stomach. "I think that would call for a more permanent solution for him." The meeting concluded with chairs scraping and joints popping. Pallah pressed herself against the wall, but mercifully no one exited the room.

"All in favor?"

A slurry of 'aye's peppered the air.

"Passed." The chief's staff thumped the ground, and it made her jump.

"Where will the children be placed?" Percival's voice broke in.

"Hmm." The chief didn't have to think long. "Send the boy to Yuri, they will treat him as their own. Keep the girls here, they will serve as Temple Celestial Serviseers until they can return home under better circumstances, or until they turn eighteen. Now, we have a Dauda tomorrow we need to focus on. Everyone, get some rest."

Pallah was already down the hall in the other direction, her soft leather shoes silent on the cold stone floor. Her heart pounded so hard it seemed to jostle the tether that delicately connected her and Tinloh. She vaguely felt him, anxious and clawing at something; she pushed it to the back of her mind, one thing at a time.

The hallway, with its carved stone walls, split in two. One led back to the main entrance where she had entered earlier that evening, and the other led upward in a spiraling staircase. There had been a time when she would have spared little thought for her siblings, but on a night like tonight, she felt united with them in a way she had never experienced before. United in hatred, united in tragedy, the emotions whirled in her, pushing her to seek connection, to be a family once more. She followed the stairs, taking them two at a time, until she came to a second hallway, this one a bit narrower and cozier than the last. Beautiful cloth lined the walls, and the lanterns were kept at a dim glow instead of extinguished like the hallway below.

There were five doors before the hallway stopped, the last door larger and more ornate than the rest. It was the priest's room, the others the quarters for the most elite of The Temple Celestial; her siblings must be there.

Checking the doors one by one, she found all to be locked. She was being reckless, and she knew it. But what else could she do? Finally reaching the last of the four in the hall before the priest's room, she knocked on it quietly and entered.

"Pallah!" Ahren sat on the bed, and Vámae was on a stool in the corner. So, they had already found each other...and hadn't bothered looking for her. Standing up, Ahren wrapped his arms around her, his chin nestled in the space between her neck and shoulder.

"Have you heard something? What's going on?" Vámae looked small and out of her element. "I found Ahren. We didn't know where you were." Pallah peeled away from her brother and recounted what she overheard.

"...and I think we should demand we stay at the house, together. If they decide to release Bogdur, there's someone Mother told us we could trust, but until that happens...I think we need to refuse placement." Pallah looked between them. Their eyes looked glazed over. Had they even been listening?

"What's happening to Mother?" Ahren's eyes were wide, innocent, exhausted.

"I'm not sure. They just mentioned she's with the Healer. She's not doing great." The moment she said it, she'd wished she hadn't as her brother's face fell. "But we don't know exactly," she amended.

"And what's so wrong with Ahren going to Yuri? With us being Serviseers?" Vámae asked, hugging her knees. "We would be safe."

Pallah bit the inside of her cheek. That was the core difference between her and her twin: Vámae valued safety over freedom, but

Pallah did not. She would never accept the oppressive rule of the Temple. Never.

"And...what about Father?" Ahren asked.

"Father?" Pallah scoffed. "Is he still 'Father' to you? You beat him to Hekla because of what he did to Mother. We can leave that *häfan* bastard to rot in his cell." The spite launched out of her with curses her siblings didn't usually witness.

"Pallah!" Vámae's head jerked upward, her blue eyes afire.

"What?" Pallah was hot with anger.

"You should not call Father that."

"Do you know what he told me, when I had my hatchet to his throat?"

"Stop, Pallah." Vámae was shaking her head and Ahren continued to stare, his mouth open.

"He called me a *tik*. A *tik*! And Giftless."

Vámae gasped and Ahren blinked, unmoving.

"So, yeah, I'm going to have to disagree. He's a *häfan* bastard, like I said."

"Father wouldn't say that," Vámae whined, standing.

"Vámae, I think maybe he—"

"Shut up, Ahren," Vámae snapped and stepped forward to stand toe to toe with Pallah. "And you. Stop! Just stop! You're constantly trying to tear down others because it makes you feel elevated. You bully people who don't share your apathy, and you think all of this makes you stronger? Maybe you are a *tik*. And as for being Giftless? I've never seen you practice Tala. I've never even seen signs of it. How do we know you are one? Just because you've told us?" She took a breath and Pallah tried to jump in, but words failed her.

"We're twins, Pallah. I know you. I know when you're hiding something. I don't know what you're up to with that group of people, but I don't want to be involved. You're making some stupid decisions and it's time you woke up." Vámae clapped her hands in time with the last two words, emphasizing them before allowing pity to seep into all her beautiful features.

"I get it"—Vámae wasn't done—"I would hate being the plain one, on all accounts. But we get what we get, and we shoulder whatever responsibility comes with it. You need to learn to stop antagonizing everyone and simply do as you're told. Besides, if I need to become a Serviseer for a time, so be it. I'll be safe, and I'll be closer to the Celestials than ever." Piety oozed from her.

"To Hekla with you," Pallah bit, tears streaming down her face. Her sister had always seemed like such a passive bystander. She couldn't imagine she would hit everything so accurately, and she hated her for it. "Let's go, Ahren." Pallah turned and gripped the doorknob but heard no movement behind her. "Ahren?" She turned to see her brother standing between them, looking utterly broken.

"You said they were placing me with Yuri? She's my favorite teacher. I'll be safe there."

"You too?" The last of her hope flooded out of her like an uncorked bottle, tipped and bled dry. "You too," she resigned, wiping her face with the back of her sleeve. They wouldn't come back to the house with her, and she wouldn't feel safe staying there alone. Would the chief even allow her to be there by herself?

"Pallah, please," Ahren attempted. "I don't agree with everything Vámae said. We want you here. We *need* you here."

"Ahren, stop. She's already made up her mind. Let her go," Vámae said coldly.

"Goodbye, Ahren." Pallah looked at him once more, her heart cementing a final wall.

"Pallah—"

But her brother's words were cut off as she slipped out the door and ran down the hall in one swift motion. Down the stairwell and into the second opening that led to through the sanctuary, she ran until she stood in the foyer of The Temple Celestial. It was all arching ceilings, stained glass, and a chandelier half the size of her family home that refracted every flickering flame that surrounded her, casting star-like light across the room. She stopped, breathing hard.

A mirror sat above an opulent table that stretched across one wall of the foyer, tall enough to catch the chandelier in all its glory. She couldn't take her eyes off the girl standing across from her: disheveled, dirty, eyes red and puffy, streaks spreading down and curving under her chin. Her hair was greasy and hanging in limp strands around her face, some parts of it muddied with blood or dirt. Her body was lanky and covered with a tunic, recently torn. She moved her hand to her waist and realized, with a lurch, her hatchet was not at her side.

The lights danced across her face, and she thought of her mother, her face always lifted to the sun, her frail body always accepting the beatings of both weather and spouse. She wondered about the man her mother used to love and, for a moment, was overcome with the need to find out who he was, what his Tala aptitude had been. Perhaps it was a creature much like hers, all-encompassing, legend, and dangerous. She wondered where he went, and how her mother ended up with someone like Bogdur.

Because a sheep behaves like a sheep. Not you, though, Pallah. You are a wolf, and a clever one. Be free. And it's time I introduced myself...I am Erval.

Thrilled at the freedom she could only begin to comprehend, she smiled at the girl in the mirror, but only managed to look menacing. She felt for her tether, but it had snapped at some point. And she couldn't bring herself to care. Was this her true self? Years of searching for her place in the world, to find it on the night her life exploded into a million pieces. But isn't that what she always wanted: to make her own decisions, to be independent, to be free?

"Nice to meet you, Erval," she answered the voice with acceptance, mildly relieved it wasn't her own mind, but someone—something—else. It cackled back at her in delight. Pallah turned from the mirror, crept out the Temple door, and fled into the night.

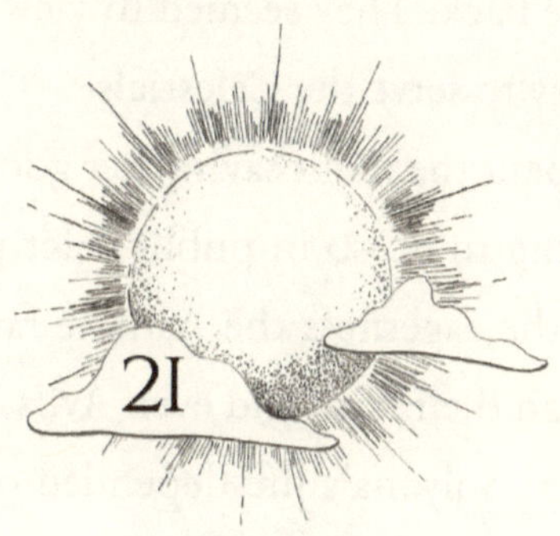

HEITT

SOLYANA

SOLYANA WALKED INTO THE throng of people gathered at the steps of the Temple Celestial. The market came to a standstill as everyone began imparting final gifts and goods to the trio leaving their valley.

Gamaliel was tending to the sled dogs, kneeling on the cold stone of the courtyard, recently cleared by Vatin Fera. He had assembled a group of twenty sled dogs and placed Vinur among them. They would take two sleds, Solyana riding with Gamaliel in one, Lone leading the other.

Lone was still rearranging a few items on her sled, having meticulously packed all medical supplies and weapons. Solyana was quickly learning the older girl was orderly in all areas of her life. The Ashune family gathered around Lone and embraced their eldest daughter. Their excitement was palpable, as if this was the best path they could have imagined for her. Each of her sisters squeezed her in turn, but Lone stood stoic as ever, giving them each a pat on the back. They seemed to view her volunteering as an opportunity to serve the Celestials.

Solyana had spent the night saying her goodbyes to her family to avoid having to do so in public. Her parents' attitudes failed to reflect the eagerness the Ashune family displayed; it made her question their faith and even Avi's confidence. What if she was wrong? Solyana's life depended on her interpretations. She had lain awake long into the night thinking on it, feeling a growing dread as she listened to her mother's quiet sewing in the next room. Mama had stayed up all night finishing their new parkas, pants, and gloves.

Solyana touched the left side of her face to find the scar. How fitting it was visible today. She smoothed her parka, unusual for one main reason: it was white. Solyana wasn't used to the brightness of it; she had always worn brown or green, but white? When she asked about it, her mother said it was perfect camouflage. She was Rána, after all, and if any creature attacked them, she would stand a better chance of hiding in the snow.

Gamaliel made his way to her, dressed more modestly than she had ever seen; none of his chest was visible. His forest-green garb was practical, crafted specifically for long hours of mushing. Heavy cord wrapped his thick fur-lined mukluks. Unlike the rest of his outfit, they were old, perhaps handed down from a late relative. Lone stood on the other side of him, her white-blonde hair spiked up, the tips of her ears and nose pink. Her parka and pants were cut to match her toned and muscled shape, dyed black, giving her a sleek look that made Solyana feel garish in her white and bulky gear.

"What's wrong?" Solyana asked, noting Gamaliel's expression. "You didn't find him?" Solyana had stayed with her family the night before; Gamaliel had searched for Jonas alone.

He shook his head, his hand rubbing his freshly-shaved chin. "I checked everywhere, but if I had gone to the cave, I wouldn't have been back in time to leave. We'll check there on the way out."

"He did hear us then." Solyana's shoulders fell. "I'm so sorry for bringing it up. That was my fault."

Gamaliel waved her off. "Where else could he be? I'm almost positive he just went back home. Let's move forward. We need to go. Got the maps?"

Solyana turned so he could see her knapsack. "Check. Longbow, too. Papa said I should take it."

"And I have your staff."

"We seem to think I'll be doing most of the fighting here." She smirked.

"I'd just like you to have a way of protecting yourself from wild animals." He gave a soft smile.

"I thought that was *your* job." She jabbed a finger into his chest, and he held up his hands in defense.

"Nah, you can protect yourself." He flicked his hair off his shoulder and swaggered away from her. She laughed.

The people all around them held a dichotomous buzz of excitement and fear. Her stomach in knots, Solyana seemed to waver between the two herself. Perhaps she was simply trying to convince herself her death was not inevitable once they left the valley. And the only way to do that was with a lightness that seemed unfitting.

Priestess Avi's stark white robes were pristine as ever as she walked to the center of the top of the steps to the Temple. Extending her metal staff, she beckoned the travelers to join her. Solyana turned to her family. Mama gave her hand a squeeze, but Papa avoided her eyes, as he had done all morning. She was sure he was crying. Solyana was the first up the stairs, Gamaliel and Lone made their way through the crowd.

"It's time, dear," the priestess said for Solyana's ears alone.

"So it is." She nodded. She had reservations about the woman now; too many comments whispered she didn't understand, too many things left unexplained, but what could she do? Her path was clear, Solyana had read the scrolls herself. She would go. She would save her people. She would save Rhuth, regardless of the priestess's own intentions.

"Solyana..." Priestess Avi lifted a wrinkled hand and traced the scar on Solyana's face. "A fitting name you have, girl, 'Daughter of the Sun.'"

Solyana nodded, she had known. But the name held new meaning to her now, new expectation.

"It is no coincidence your name heralds your journey. Our Celestials are good, dear. This prophecy is of them, to them, and through them. You were meant to go; you are meant to find the cause of these storms; you will fulfill this prophecy and save our people. The Celestials will protect you."

"But what if you have the wrong person...what if it's not me?" Solyana hadn't shared her fears so openly with her before, but felt she needed to, now or never. "I will let everyone down. They will die...because of me."

"That is where you're wrong, Solyana. You will not let anyone down. I am the Speaker of the Skies, and I have seen very clearly you are truly the chosen one." She made another trace across the crescent shape on her cheek. "Be brave now."

"Yes, Priestess Avi."

"Sweet girl." She leaned forward and kissed the top of her head. Her white hair, so long and hanging free, tickled the tops of Solyana's hands. "Your eyes be upward."

"And be filled with light."

Gamaliel and Lone found their places on either side of Solyana. The priestess turned to the people and lifted her metal staff.

"Oh, Mighty Beings of the Sky, may today mark the beginning of the end of this dark time. May we go free from here, released from guilt and doubt as we move forward, trusting in You to keep these precious chosen safe. Bring them swiftly, bring them whole, and let them find what they are looking for."

She paused and it felt like everyone held their breath.

"Your eyes be upward!" Priestess Avi finished with infectious exuberance.

"And be filled with light!" the people roared in return, coursing their energy into Solyana as she, Gamaliel, and Lone made their way down the steps, the people parting just enough to make a path to their sleds. Vinur was harnessed next to a dog twice his size just in front of Solyana's sled, his tongue flopping, his tail wagging with excitement.

The people cheered and clapped, children ran to touch their parkas and give them final gifts. A scrap of leather here, a jar of lard there, a small loaf of bread or block of hard cheese.

Lone and Gamaliel each stepped onto the runners of their sleds. Lone's parents were giving her one last hug, and Gamaliel was still searching the crowd, his eyebrows furrowed deeply, hoping to spot his young charge. Solyana rushed to her family one last time and the three of them embraced her in one massive hug.

"Be safe," Papa rumbled, and she felt it deep into her chest.

"I will"—she broke away from them—"I love you!" she shouted but was unsure if they heard her over the roar of the people. They were singing now, an ancient Mothmari song. Solyana clambered into the bed of the sled, feeling awkward and silly. She tried to sit as tall as possible.

"Hike!" Gamaliel called, and the dogs dug their claws into the snow as they brought the sleds up to speed. Solyana turned to watch her family's faces blur in the tears that struck her, whether from wind or sorrow, she didn't know. Solyana sang the last line, which she could hardly hear over the wind. The song lauded each Gift but had no line for Rána. It seemed ominous proof enough it wasn't normal, wasn't natural. So much resting on her frail shoulders, all from a change in the weather and a few words scrawled on a page.

They sped north, the Vatino churned by wind, the ice only just beginning to creep in from the shore. They took the same path as Solyana and Gamaliel had, just over a week ago, when they'd walked back together with a falcon carried between them. It would take a third of the time on sleds.

Her back was already sore as she leaned on the things packed tight beneath her. She hadn't thought about how uncomfortable the journey would be, shifting as the sled jumped and slid over uneven terrain. It made her feel grossly unprepared and vulnerable to the harsh indifference of the elements.

They were able to get around the Vatino in two hours and soon were pulling up to the base of Eldfall, the cave Gamaliel called home.

"Easy!" Gamaliel called, and Lone came to a stop beside them. Why didn't he just tell them with his mind? She had never actually seen him use his Tala. They had spent ample time together, yet she had never seen him so much as nudge Vinur in the right direction, or disperse a group of animals. The only proof she had was Gamaliel's story about his past. And her father, being his mentor, corroborating it. He hopped down and headed over the small hill to the cave.

"What's happening?" Lone demanded.

"We haven't found Jonas since he left the Temple last night." It was the first direct sentence Solyana had said to the girl since discovering she and Gamaliel used to be together.

"Ah."

Solyana looked over her shoulder at the girl and decided they wouldn't be alone long. If she wanted to pry about their relationship, she should ask now. "So, how long were you two together?"

Lone blinked slowly, her blonde-lashed lids rested low on her blue eyes. "Long enough to know I didn't want to live the life of a hermit." She gave a slight shrug, "But he's not such a hermit these days, is he?"

Solyana, feeling worse than before she asked, turned back, her ears burning red.

Gamaliel came back over the hill at a jog. "He's not in there."

"He's got to be back in town. Did you check every room at the Temple? I don't see—"

"His stuff, Solyana." Gamaliel's dark eyes connected with hers, and she saw the deepening distress that lay there. "It's gone."

"What?" Hopping out of the sled, she began jogging toward the cave. He grabbed her arm to stop her.

"This was laying where I usually keep my bed roll." He held up a small piece of parchment. She grabbed it, and her eyes grew wide.

"One of his paintings," she whispered. She pulled off her glove and touched the paint gently. It stained the tips of her fingers. "It's fresh."

"So *häfan* stupid! I should've just talked to him beforehand. Now we have no idea where he is. I can't leave. *We* can't leave!" He paced, his voice rising.

"It's not your fault, Gam," Lone jumped in and Solyana shot her a look.

"Where could he have gone? Let's think about this," Solyana said, trying to give Gamaliel something solid to think on.

He paced, his hands pulling at his hair, and jogged closer to the mountain once more. He crouched low over the packed snow. "He came this way," he announced, his breath condensing in a white cloud before disappearing with the wind. "There are runner tracks here, but they're disappearing." He pointed just by his feet, then extended his hand up toward Eldfall.

Lone's long legs brought her to Gamaliel in three strides and she examined the area. "Looks like he got himself a small sled and made his way up the mountain. Maybe we can catch him before he gets too far."

"Let's go," Gamaliel said, action a balm for his worry. He jumped back on his runners, and they were off again, even faster than before.

It didn't escape Solyana, the enormity of what they were doing. She'd heard stories growing up of brave men and women who'd sought to explore beyond their valley, but they always ended in unknowns or death. Sleds would return on their own, weary dogs and smatterings of blood revealing only partial truths. Sometimes a search party would be permitted to leave, only to find bodies frozen to trees or chunks of flesh torn by wild beasts. Even when timed correctly with the monthly blizzard, even in the best conditions with the best equipment, the voyagers failed or never returned at all. She knew her chances of succeeding were close to none, and the reality of it was hitting her as they sped along the perimeter of Eldfall in search of the small boy named Jonas.

Solyana pulled the small, painted parchment from her lap to take a second look. Jonas had painted a mountain, beautiful, majestic, and covered in green grass. Solyana had never seen such grass and wondered how accurate it was. How could he know? Lush trees dotted the hillsides, unlike the ones they passed now, bare trunks stretching skyward for what seemed like miles before they finally held a cluster of needles at the top. He had painted patches of multi-colored flowers: yellow, purple, and blue. She shook her head. The boy's imagination was astounding.

From their extensive study of maps in the last week, Solyana knew the plan was to take the lower route from Eldfall into the Hasta Pass. They would climb the mountain to the halfway point before following the curve into switchbacks between the Hasta Mountains. This would take them on a safer route, though it added a few hours to the trip, at most, a day. Time was important—the Norlos was at peak brightness for a single moon cycle—but surviving was just as essential to their success. Taking the Hasta Pass from the peak was far more dangerous, with its steep cliffs and possibility of avalanches.

After about a half-hour of mushing, Lone shouted across the wind, "Do you still see his tracks? I lost them a while back."

"No," Gamaliel yelled back to her. "We keep going. He's got to be up here somewhere."

Jonas's painting was dry now. Solyana had kept it clutched in her fingers, something about it kept her from tucking it away. Studying it again, she noticed a cave at the base of the mountain. Not just any cave, it looked exactly like the mouth to Gamaliel's home. She turned the page to look at it from another angle. Was it supposed to be Eldfall? Then she noticed it, a faint red dotted line that wound its way up the mountain and into a cliff face on the east side; she had mistaken it for a row of flowers.

"Gamaliel!" Solyana turned awkwardly on her stomach, desperate for him to see it. "Look! Jonas drew Eldfall."

"So?"

"It's a map! He drew where he was going! Look at the red dots."

Gamaliel snatched the painting from her hands. He studied it quickly, his eyes darting up and down, trusting the dogs knew their way. "It's flowers."

"It's not flowers." Solyana's hair loosened from the braid and whipped around.

Gamaliel studied it a moment longer. "If this is accurate, he's headed to the peak. Why would he go all the way up there? There's no way he would make it that far on his own. The kid barely knows how to walk in snowshoes." He passed the parchment back to her. "We keep heading toward the lower pass. He knew the direction we would go; if he's trying to come with us, he would stay on the same path."

"I don't think so Gam," Solyana said, trying to tread around Gamaliel's ego, wishing he would just listen. "How much time would we lose going up to the peak and back?"

Gamaliel rubbed his face with his hands. "Almost a full day. But he wouldn't go up there. He made our maps, he knows what direction we're—"

"I don't think he's trying to come with us, Gam!" Solyana didn't mean to shout but fear was beginning to choke her.

He blinked at her, his jaw flexing, his eyes riddled with guilt. "He wouldn't run away, he's too smart for that. It's illogical."

"He's a kid, Gam. A kid. There won't be a logical reason."

"What's going on?" Lone called from behind them. They had slowed exponentially.

"You're right." Gamaliel's eyes grew wide as they remained on Solyana, his panic becoming palpable. "*Häfa*, he went to the peak, didn't he?"

"Why in the *stars* would he do that?" Lone sounded ornery. Was she already regretting her decision to join them?

"He's a kid, he's scared," Solyana said, not wanting to reveal Jonas's Gift to Lone.

"We can't go all the way up to the peak, we would lose too much time." Lone folded her arms.

"I don't care about the time." Simmering now, Solyana thrust the map into Lone's face. "He literally left us a map, he's at the peak!" She jabbed her finger at the line of red dots. "There is a path. Right here."

Lone rolled her eyes, and Solyana ground her teeth as she said, "Look, he could be in danger! We go for the peak, final decision."

"Who made you the leader?" Lone asked as she took off her gloves to scratch her shoulder.

"The Celestials." Solyana shook her head.

Gamaliel, who had been pacing, stopped and sniffed the air. Looking passed Lone, his eyes grew wide. "Smoke!" Solyana followed his gaze and looked through the trees. Still so far from the peak, she could only get a glimpse, but sure enough, a thin line of smoke rose from the top of the mountain, too much for it to be a simple cook fire, ominous and dark.

Solyana and Gamaliel locked eyes. Jonas. He must be using his Heitt.

"Hike!" Gamaliel shouted and the dogs took off at a run.

Hours later, the dogs still pushing hard, Solyana found herself thinking about how she had never been without Priestess Avi's presence. She warmed the valley on the coldest of nights. When would they cross that invisible barrier when her Gift no longer touched them? Her fingers had grown numb beneath her seal skin gloves hours ago. She stared at them in the dim light of Gamaliel's lantern, swinging from a pole on his sled, careening dangerously back and forth. Papa had crafted the gloves for her years ago on a trip to Kana Ocean. She stretched her fingers inside, opening and closing her hand repeatedly until her nerves burned and shot fire up her arm, not quite painful enough for frostbite.

The smoke had thickened. Gamaliel and Lone mushed with their heads down, scarves pulled up to just below their eyes, as they passed into denser trees near the peak. When Solyana looked behind her, Gamaliel's watering eyes held terror of the unknown. She, too, imagined the worst.

The sleds finally broke through the last line of trees, and they stopped in front of an inferno. Almost every tree was aflame, the fire making a perimeter around the charred area. Smoke was thick and mixing with the steam of melting snow. Trees were burning to a crisp, and in the middle of it all was a small figure, kneeling on the ground.

"Jonas!" Solyana screamed over the roar of the flames and stumbled off the sled before Gamaliel could come to a halt. The dogs were panicking at the fire, stepping wildly, trying to break free of their harnesses.

"*Häfa*, no, NO! Jonas!" Gamaliel screamed, running frantically along the edge of the flame, trying to find a break, his face tight with fear.

The smoke and flame were too thick to see Jonas clearly, Solyana couldn't make out if he was aware of what was happening. Dropping to her knees, the smoke clinging to her lungs, she looked over to see Gamaliel charging toward the wall of fire circling the boy.

"Gamaliel!" She lunged for him, grabbing his parka. "You will die if you go in there!" The chaos drowned her voice and she was terrified he wouldn't hear, let alone listen.

"He will die if I don't!" he screamed.

Lone was somewhere behind them, shouting. They both turned to find her desperately trying to take control of the dogs that had begun to panic and whine. Each line of dogs tied to the last, one animal careening down the mountain would take all their supplies and Lone with them.

Solyana got as close to Gamaliel's face as she could and grabbed both sides of his head so he would focus. "You need to control those animals! I will go for Jonas!"

"I can't, you can't...I haven't—"

Solyana pressed her forehead against his own. "You can. You will. Use the Gift you were given. Save them, Gamaliel, and I'll save Jonas." How? She didn't know. But if she was chosen for this purpose, the Celestials would give her the strength to complete it. She peered past Gamaliel at the circle of fire growing larger around the boy. She wasn't able to save Rhuth, not yet, but she could do something about Jonas.

Solyana squeezed his hand, and he stood, stretching his hands out toward the group of dogs who were quickly entangling themselves in their own leads.

"There's too many!" he yelled to her, panic flashing across his face.

Lone realized what he was trying to do and motioned to him. "I will try to get a connection on their bones!" Solyana shuddered at the thought, but they had to do what was necessary to keep their animals from plunging off the side of the mountain. Lone and Gamaliel stood, hands outstretched to the dogs. The dogs slowed, they stopped barking and whining. It was working.

Solyana said a quick prayer of thanks and turned back to Jonas. How was she going to get to him? She wasn't immune to flame, as Jonas seemed to be.

She circled the ring, pulling her scarf over her mouth and nose. The smoke was thick, but thankfully a strong wind kept it from completely choking her. However, that same wind was feeding the blaze, high and pulsing.

She found a break in the living wall, just wide enough for her body to fit through. Before she could caution herself, she dove through, the flames licking at her, scorching her exposed skin. "Jonas!" she screamed, her clothes both protecting her from and trapping the heat that threatened to consume her.

Jonas's small frame kneeled in the dirt, the snow long since melted around him, the trees, spiraling columns of flame. She was able to make her way close enough to him to see his shoulders shaking. Was he crying? Was he aware of what was happening?

"Jonas!" she called out again, and this time she thought there was a flicker of hesitation in the fire from his hands. "Jonas! It's Solyana!" The flames stuttered. "Please, Jonas, please! Gamaliel is here! Vinur is here! You are putting us all in danger!"

The boy on the ground began emitting a guttural moan. It turned into speech, barely distinguishable, "HELLLLP MEEEE!"

Solyana needed him to look at her, to snap out of whatever state he was in. She crawled beneath his arm, his hands shooting the flame in a steady stream. She tucked herself in front of him, removed her gloves, and cupped his face in her hands. Her whole body felt like it would catch aflame at any moment, her lungs burning from the inside out.

"Jonas!" She coughed and sputtered. "Look at me, Jonas." She forced herself to calm and his eyes locked on hers.

"Take it from me, Solyana. Please, take it," he said between choking sobs, his nose running into his mouth.

"Take it? What are you—"

"TAKE IT FROM ME!" he screamed, and the flames erupted even stronger. Solyana closed her eyes, breathing deep.

The words came back to her.

"*Blood from the Gift must come to the one without, for the Gift is found in the blood. Establishing the connection together...and then apart. Utilizing it together, combining it, spiritual and physical, with all trust.*" But then she remembered the legends of the loss of Gifts, the resulting deaths.

"No! You could die! We don't know the effects of—"

"Do it! Please!" Jonas's innocent face was so contorted, it made Solyana sob. "I can't stop!"

Suddenly, Solyana's scar pulsed, urging her to act. She pressed a hand to it. It was cool to the touch. A plan formed, and watching Jonas writhe before her, she knew she had to try something, anything, or this Gift would kill him.

Solyana reached back to her waist where she had strapped the hatchet Avi had given her. She drew it out of its leather sheath and groped for Jonas's hand. Still shooting flame, Solyana prayed to the Father of the Day, asking him to stop his power and to guide her hand. The flame stuttered more starkly but refused to disappear.

Solyana lifted the hatchet to his hand and slid the metal head into the flame, pressing with care into his palm and slicing with quick efficiency. Immediately, the flame stopped and his bare, bleeding skin lay exposed. She caught his eyes. They were still on hers, his nose dripping, his breaths coming in gasps, his eyes accepting. Releasing the hatchet, she brought his hand up to the side of her face that had her crescent scar. Her hand over his own, she pressed his bloody palm to her cheek, blood cascading down her face and soaking into her scarf. She hoped she hadn't cut too deep. Bringing her other hand around the nape of his neck, she pressed their foreheads together.

"Please," Jonas whispered once more to Solyana, his body growing limp.

"Please," Solyana whispered once more to the Celestials.

The trees, so black and brittle, began to break. Solyana vaguely felt the resounding thuds as branches fell to the ground. Gamaliel's frantic voice registered in the back of her mind. The howling of dogs picked up again. Were they okay? Were they dying?

Then everything in her mind quieted as she focused solely on the Father of the Day. The sun, the mystery that it was, hidden from their valley, the cloud cover constant. But in her mind, she pictured it, bright and true, the essence of Heitt, the purest form of warmth and healing. The base of her skull began to thrum. Jonas was using his Heitt, and in turn, she knew she was using it too.

She saw her hand, glowing at the base of Jonas's neck and closed her eyes, feeling warmth come over her. Exhausted but serene, she didn't know how long they sat there, she and the boy. Finally, the flames died down, the howling quelled to whimpers, and she heard nothing but her own breath.

Solyana opened her eyes to find Jonas in her arms, too still, too quiet. She cradled him to her chest, his small frame always reminding her so much of Rhuth, too much like Rhuth.

Solyana's tears dripped silently as she prayed to the Celestials he was only sleeping. She could not bear if she was the reason for his death. Heavens, no. Please, no.

Gamaliel was beside her then, pulling Jonas from her arms, checking for a pulse, lifting his eyes. Solyana had never seen him so haggard.

"What happened?" he asked with rising panic.

"He…" Solyana stared at her palms before looking up, the sky filled with blue, green, and purple streams of light, bright and stretching beyond the Mothmar she knew. The view from the valley had always been too low to see it before, the overcast of clouds too thick.

The Norlos.

It filled the space above them with an ethereal glow. Solyana looked back down at her hands to find small flames flickering in each palm.

THE SLEEPING GIRL

T HE MENIAL TASKS KEPT her sane, the routine an anchor and guard against him, the one who still spoke to her, demanding, demanding. He could not break through as easily now, not with her barriers in place, and especially not when she kept her emotions in check, like a cloak, keeping her hidden.

Pallah rolled the pestle, crushing herbs to a fine powder. The crunch of it relaxed her, reminding her of a different time. When had she allowed herself to grow so comfortable? At least she finally did something about it. At least the time was finally here. She was getting tired of these bones, so old, so useless.

The robe she chose today was simple but elegant, something on which she never compromised. If she must be stuck in this body, she would look regal. Pallah dumped the herbs unceremoniously into a chalice and poured steaming water over top. It smelled wretched. She would feel bad, but the girl was useful still, and quiet; at this point, she knew too much. The *häfan* child figured things out much faster than she had, when it had been done to her, so long ago.

Pallah thought back as she walked the cluttered hallway back to the girl's room. How long had Pallah been trapped again? Too long. But she had turned out fine. She chuckled to herself.

She pushed the door open, revealing the dark-haired beauty that lay there, taking up residence in Pallah's home, taking up space, using her air. Something about the girl reminded her of Vámae when she was young. Maybe that's why it was easier to see her as deserving.

Pallah sat the chalice down on the bedside table and stroked the girl's hair. She felt the girl stand up in the Maze, defiant. Pallah chuckled to herself. How long had it taken her, to not cower in the corner every time her captor reached in, every time he showed her glimpses of what she was missing?

The girl was saying something, but it was inconsequential. She was more agitated these days, her sister gone and headed for the mountain. Pallah didn't like feeling annoyed, and this one was *annoying*. She tugged the tether hard and the girl dropped, crying out. Pallah smiled.

"Hush, girl. You've been aware for weeks I only listen when I choose to. Now, your sister will return with the answer to all our little problems. You know if you had just given me what I wanted, so much of this could have been avoided?" The girl was insolent, so Pallah tightened her tether. It had its intended effect. The girl dropped again. "You have a strength of Tala I have only seen when using the Taka Reu...yet you still follow the Celestials. You know, it intrigues me. Finding new beasts is getting quite inconvenient.

I'd really like to know how you manage to keep them alive when you do it."

The girl went quiet.

"Of course."

Pallah tipped the chalice down the girl's throat, using several of her accrued Dark Gifts together. How did she ever survive with only one? She chuckled again. "Goodnight, Little Fyug." She grinned wickedly, using the silly nickname her sister bestowed on the girl in the bed.

"Priestess Avi?" A head poked around the door and Pallah cursed them in her mind.

"Yes?" She turned with austere grace. "Chief Marus, what can I do for you?"

"I'd like to sit with Rhuth." The chief's lumbering form stumbled into the room, his grief clear at the turn of events for his family. Pallah had nothing against him. It was just how things turned out.

"But of course." Pallah extended a hand, welcoming him in. He walked past her, and Pallah thought she sensed animosity toward her. Understandable. She had completely disrupted his family, though he wasn't even fully aware to what extent.

Chief Marus sat by Rhuth's bedside, oblivious to the cries she was making inside. Pallah disconnected her tether from the girl. Too irritating. The concoction she gave her every day would keep her still when she wasn't connected. She backed out of the room and closed the door. As she entered her own quarters, she found herself staring in the mirror, as she often did. She stretched the skin of her face taut, willing it to return from its deflated state, as it had been so many years ago.

No matter, she would have a new one soon.

CHAPTER ONE

PATH OF PERIL

RISING FROM THE PEAK, blackened trunks pointed toward an evening sky that churned with color. These trees, burned to husks, surrounded a group of four, hemming them in, shielding them in a circle of melted snow and dirt, safe from the world beyond.

Solyana stared down at her home in the valley below, cookfires flickering to life. Her people, the Mothmarians, would be boiling snow and bones, enough to keep their families from hunger and thirst. Did they know the mountain above had almost broken upon them?

The raging fire consuming the peak must surely have been visible from the three villages of Vestur, Sodur, and Austur. Only by some miracle had the fire not produced an avalanche, as snow had melted and buried the trails, boulders, and wildlife in its wake.

The soft glow of the lantern by her feet extended to Gamaliel's back, his arms wrapped around the boy who broke the mountain.

Or had she broken it?

Lone thought so. She blamed Solyana for the wreckage, for the loss.

Solyana could still hear Lone's angry screams as realization struck; most of their supplies had disappeared and half their sled dogs had been swept away by the storm. Their chances of survival—already slim—were now next to nothing. A wall of tension barricaded the space between Solyana and the older girl, but she set it aside, more concerned with the man on the ground. Gamaliel hadn't uttered a single word since Jonas had collapsed, having given his Gift to Solyana.

The Norlos, the ribbon of color above, began to fade as the sun warmed the heavens. The group would need to continue on. They only had one moon cycle to reach the mountain where a boy waited; the boy who tethered light and angered the Celestials to the point of causing their valley's unending cold.

Solyana turned at the sound of crunching snow. Lone stood in a patch of white somehow untouched by the flames from the previous night. Her hood shadowed her face, her hardened gaze fixed on the valley below.

"We can go back," Solyana whispered, feeling small in the shadow of the mountain. "Jonas should be with Priestess Avi."

Lone stepped beside her, the tip of her pink nose peeking out from the fur of her hood. "Even if we wanted to, we couldn't."

Solyana tucked her braid into her parka and pulled up her hood, shivering against the cold. Heavy in her chest, her labored breathing caught in the frost. They needed to descend. "It would add two—maybe three—days, at most."

"You don't understand." Lone still refused to look at Solyana, even as she spoke to her. "It's impossible." Her arm extended, black parka dusted and smeared with ash, directing Solyana's eyes to the destruction. "Eldfall is impassable behind us. Boulders and trees felled by the storm will have created caverns buried beneath the snow—tombs in waiting. We continue onward, as planned."

"Then I'll try tethering to Jonas with my Heitt. I've been practicing on Vinur. It's not so much a tether but...like I'm cocooning him. Does it feel that way when you tether to bone?"

"You what?" Gamaliel's low rumble came from the ground and the two girls turned as the hunter staggered to his feet. Jonas was wrapped in a blanket, clutched in his arms. "You tethered to Vinur?"

Lone scoffed and shook her head as she walked away, leaving them at the edge.

"What? What's wrong with—"

"You don't tether to another person's beast, Sol." Gamaliel's face held lines and shadows. He looked like he hadn't slept at all. Maybe he hadn't. "It's...violating."

"I'm sorry, Gam. I didn't know." Solyana reached out to him, but he jerked away, so fast she thought she'd burned him. She turned her hands over, but they were empty of flame or light. "*Stars*, I'm sorry. Did I—"

"No." Gamaliel shook his head, holding Jonas close to his chest. "It's fine. Just don't—don't do it again."

Don't touch him again? Don't tether to Vinur again? A sliver of cold wound its way into Solyana's belly and coiled there, waiting.

"I'm not comfortable with you tethering to Jonas, either." Gamaliel laid the boy down by the embers of the fire.

"Why not?" She folded her arms. Her new power sat with burning tension at the back of her skull.

"It's too new." He turned and mirrored her stance. "You don't know how to wield it. And you saw what happens when it's unpracticed. Until we reach a time when the need outweighs the risks, please don't."

Her skin prickled with discomfort at his words, but she was just as unsure.

"And Lone is right," Gamaliel said. "We continue on."

Feeling more enemy than friend, Solyana's throat grew tight. She knew little of Heitt theory, but something had awoken inside of her when she received the power from Jonas. When they had used it together, she had accessed some kind of ancient knowledge, an instinctual understanding which had long lain dormant. Whatever comprehension Jonas had of his Gift had fused to her soul.

"I have *some* understanding. I'm not useless."

Gamaliel eyed her warily.

"Have I lost your trust so quickly? In only a night?"

"He's all I have, Solyana." He walked away from her and Solyana's heart dropped. All he had? What, then, was she?

With a sigh, Solyana stepped close to Jonas; his placid face would have seemed peaceful, if it weren't for the unknown of when he would wake...*if* he would wake.

Just like Rhuth. Too much like her. Solyana's eyes burned at the thought of her sister, and she swallowed the emotion rising in her throat, focusing instead on the boy in front of her.

The unknown dangers of his condition tugged at her. Gamaliel wouldn't have to know if she attempted a latch. She pressed two fingers to the hollow of his neck beneath his jaw, feeling a strong pulse. The steady beat calmed her as she stroked his sandy hair away from his forehead. The brightening light of morning revealed the freckles dusting his pale cheeks.

"What are you doing?" Gamaliel's voice came out urgent and strained, his shadow falling over her as the sun made its presence known over the Hasta Mountains.

"I'm not tethering to him," Solyana assured. "His pulse is strong."

Gamaliel nodded with a grunt before turning back to his work. Solyana wished more than anything he would offer her reassurances, a hug—anything other than wary looks and cold shoulders.

They finished loading the last few items between the two surviving sleds. Jonas's sled had been consumed by flame, and only sixteen dogs remained between them, including Vinur. Solyana scratched him behind the ears before climbing onto Gamaliel's sled. The wolf's tongue lolled out the side of his grinning mouth. At least someone still enjoyed her company.

Their original plan to take the lower pass was out of the question now. After last night's catastrophe, the mountain had become far too dangerous to scale back down. They had to continue from the peak. Eldfall was the first of many mountains in the Hasta Range that rose east into greater Mothmar.

They stood at the precipice of the pass. To continue across the mountain range, they would need to carefully weave their way down through the narrow path that was hardly visible between the peaks on either side. Solyana studied a sketch on a piece of parchment held in her hand. Before gently securing Jonas in Lone's sled, Solyana had checked his pockets for more clues as to why he had erupted into a human torch. She had found several scrolls and pieces of parchment untouched by flame. Many of them seemed to be recent sketches of surrounding terrain. Lone and Gamaliel dismissed them as more of his artwork.

Solyana had other theories.

The wind whipped ice into Solyana's face, and she pulled her scarf up a bit higher. Her parka kept her warm, thanks to her mother's expert craftsmanship. She snuggled deeper into it as Gamaliel surveyed the land beneath.

The sun crept ever higher, drawing the breath from her lungs. Of all the things that had happened, it was this that was most foreign to her. The skies of Mothmar bore a constant blanket of cloud that she, until now, hadn't realized was so debilitating.

Now that she was Heitt, she could feel the rays of the Father of the Day imbue her with energy, as if there were a direct link between them. She glanced at the boy bundled at the base of Lone's sled. How had Jonas gained energy to use his Heitt before? Without a visible sun, she couldn't imagine how he would even have been able to produce flame or even warm a cup of tea.

"I wonder how Avi maintains her power," she said out loud, turning in her seat to face Gamaliel on the skis behind her.

He pulled his hair into a knot on his head, taking a breath. "I've been trying to tell you. There's something off about that woman."

"I'm not saying she's doing anything wrong." Solyana's lips twisted in thought. "I'm just thinking about Heitt. The power itself is directly linked to the sun. I mean...it's in all our history. I never paid enough attention, or had reason to. But it doesn't explain how Priestess Avi is so powerful. She warms all three villages on the coldest nights. She is keeping my sister alive in darlöh. How can she do all of that without a daily connection to the sun?"

"Maybe it has to do with her..." He glanced at Lone, who was still packing a few things into her sled, and lowered his voice. "Taka Reu."

The argument on her tongue died as Solyana turned it over. The priestess had revealed she had been using the Taka Reu as a method of wielding multiple Gifts, to keep everything running smoothly. It wasn't entirely unbelievable.

"I don't trust her," Gamaliel said with a sniff.

Solyana turned away from him. "You've made that clear."

With a shift of the sled, Gamaliel hopped off and joined Lone. He gripped her elbow, drawing her close, and spoke in her ear. Unease wormed its way into Solyana's heart as she watched them. He was probably explaining the plan, but why did he feel the need to leave her out?

She was the least experienced in tracking, hiking, and sledding. But she still couldn't help the pit in her stomach that opened at the sight of them being so close. She remembered what Lone had said to her just before they left: *he's not so much of a hermit now, though, is he?*

Gamaliel and Lone turned, a ghost of a grin on Lone's lips as they approached Solyana.

"You ready for this?" Lone asked, pulling her black hood down to reveal her cropped, near-white hair. She eyed Solyana. "You're not going to combust into flame?"

Solyana ignored her and turned to Gamaliel. "Where exactly are we going?"

Gamaliel crouched beside her, pointing to the mountain peaks. "It gets really steep here. See how it stretches up both sides, leaving only a deep crevice to pass through? The problem is, the path only touches one mountainside, so the other drops into the abyss at the base of these mountains. And let's just say, even with Lone's Bein Fera, after a fall like that, your bones wouldn't have enough substance left for her to fix them up."

"I could try melting a bit of the path, decrease our chances of sliding off the edge," Solyana suggested.

"That would cause slippage in the snow. These mountains will already be prone to avalanches after the fire." Gamaliel crossed to the other sled and laid a hand on Jonas's forehead. "Hang in there, buddy."

"I understand, but perhaps it would make the way a little bit easier?" She wasn't an item packed in a sled; she had power now and wanted to use it. "I could practice on the snow on the way down to the pass and—"

"He said no," Lone interrupted. "It's too dangerous."

Solyana turned away from the girl, not wanting to give her the satisfaction of the hurt she knew was playing across her face. Was Lone the one chosen by the Celestials? What authority did she have to overrule Solyana?

"We've got to make it through this while we still have light." Gamaliel mounted his skis. "Then we'll trace the Norlos tonight, camp, and follow through in the morning. Everyone in agreement?"

Solyana nodded, avoiding both of their gazes, and continued staring down at the pass below.

"Lead the way, Gam," Lone spoke over her shoulder as she sauntered back to her own sled.

Gamaliel clicked his tongue, and they were off, each breath taking them farther away from the valley they called home.

They began at a brisk pace but slowed to a crawl within the hour. Solyana's stomach pitched and rolled as they reached the shallow ledge leading into the pass. The skis of the sled barely fit on the path, and occasionally the edge of one ski would slip over the drop before snow-packed ground climbed up to meet it again, sending her heart into her throat each time.

An eerie silence trailed after them, broken only by the scrape of skis and the pant of dogs. Solyana felt herself holding her breath, leaning toward the mountain in silent panic.

Gamaliel and Lone stood like twin stones, determination etched on their faces, a sheen of sweat on their foreheads.

Solyana peered around Gamaliel to see Jonas's mop of hair bouncing in time with Lone's sled. He would be fine, she assured herself. He had to be fine.

Did worry prickle at the backs of their minds as it did hers? Were they as keenly aware of how much was stacked against them? Pushing it from her mind over and over only layered her worries atop one another, forming a pile teetering on collapse. But she would hold steady, in spite of it all. Between starvation and cold, at least she could combat the latter.

"No! Gamaliel! Help!"

Lone's shrill cry pierced Solyana's thoughts, shocking her after sitting so long in quiet. The noise bounced off both peaks, echoing until it was smothered by snow. Lone's lead dog had stumbled off the cliff's edge, pulling the rest of the dogs and the attached sled behind it.

Gamaliel's hand flew out to the side, latching to the animals with his tether. He mumbled something between blue lips. Solyana watched as the dogs who remained on the cliffside dug in their claws and scrambled back to the side of the cliff's face.

"He's weighing them down!" Lone screeched, uselessly gripping the reins. The dog that dangled off the edge twisted and whined as he was buffeted. The rest of the team were sliding precariously close to the edge, unable to handle the hanging dog's weight.

Gamaliel pulled his sled to a halt, jumped off, and seized the line that held the dog off the edge. Gripping the animal by the scruff of its neck, he hauled it up and over the ledge, tossing it desperately behind him. On his back, Gamaliel panted harder than the dogs surrounding him.

The snow groaned and Solyana's eyes grew wide as the ground shifted around Gamaliel, the entire section of the ledge he was lying on dropping marginally. Reaching out her hand, Solyana gripped Gamaliel's forearm as the ledge beneath him crumbled and fell. Solyana wrapped her free hand around the other side of the sled, bracing her legs against the wooden sides as her team of dogs took off on what was surely Gamaliel's command, pulling their master from a drop to his death. Lone's sled rushed behind them, barely making it over the gap in the ledge, her blue eyes round with panic.

The dogs at a full run, Gamaliel pulled himself up Solyana's arm. She gritted her teeth with pain as he finally got to the skis of his sled. He released her and she flopped back, rubbing at her shoulder.

With a guttural groan, Gamaliel threw his hands out, connecting to the animals with his tether.

The dogs, heeding his call, came to a skittering halt. Solyana grabbed the sides of the sled to keep herself from being flung out headfirst.

Shocked silence clung to them like the frost on Solyana's eyelashes.

Then she heard a rumble.

Turning her head slowly, she and Gamaliel locked eyes.

"We need to move. *Now!*" Lone shouted.

"*Hike!*" Gamaliel commanded, and their sled sprang forward.

The thunderous roar of mountains shifting filled the atmosphere around them, a cadence of their flight through the pass.

Solyana peered out from her sled, catching a glimpse of Lone and Jonas. Behind them, the mountain snow careened down like a waterfall to swallow them up in its mighty wake. She had to do something.

Solyana got to her feet and crouched, one hand gripping the wooden side, the other reaching toward the mountains above. She drew as much energy from the sun as she could without producing flame and directed the heat into the mountain itself.

The avalanche picked up speed.

"What are you doing?" Lone shrieked, snow beginning to interfere with her skis and fishtailing her sled. The dogs ran faster, breaking formation in blind terror.

Solyana released her tether, scanning the scene behind them. The avalanche was barreling straight through the pass. If she could close the pass off, block it from—

Something clicked into place. She stood tall, ignoring Gamaliel's cries that she sit down, his voice fading beneath the roar of mountain.

Shoving her palms before her, she felt the fierce power of the Father of the Day rush through her as she directed all the heat she could muster to the far end of the pass.

High on the right side, there was a shift. Snow began to cascade down the side, subverting the avalanche, redirecting it to fall between one side of the pass and the chasm on the other.

The onslaught of snow slowed behind Lone's sled, and she turned to look. When she turned back to Solyana, she grinned. "Did you do that?"

Solyana nodded and Gamaliel gave her a weak smile. "We're not out of this yet."

Turning around, Solyana spotted his source of worry. The end of the pass didn't quite meet the ground they so desperately needed to reach. Only a steep drop from mountain to snowy earth awaited their arrival.

The dogs came to a halt and Solyana turned back to Gamaliel. "If I push heat beneath us, it may drop us slowly, create a more gradual slide to get us down to the ground."

"You just redirected that avalanche," Gamaliel said softly. "I think you can handle this, if you think you can."

Solyana nodded and turned back, heart in her throat. "Steady on, then." She heated the earth beneath them.

The path began to shift and turn, their sled careening this way and that through uneven snow. The dogs tripped and stumbled, a yelp ringing out into the biting air.

"Stop!" Gamaliel shouted and Solyana closed her palms, but it didn't abate.

Eyes wide, Solyana looked back at Gamaliel. "I can't!"

The snow began to crumble beneath them, attempting to pull them into the bowels of the pass. The dogs scrambled, looking for purchase and safety.

"I can't keep them going! The snow is pulling them down!" Gamaliel's voice held a note of resignation, and Solyana couldn't bear to hear it. "We're too heavy for them. They can't pull us through this." Eyes flicking from the dogs, to the pass, to Lone behind them; her thoughts couldn't keep up with the scale of the catastrophe.

"Let them go!" The words came from Solyana's mouth, but even she couldn't believe them.

"What?"

"If we release them, they can get out of here! And maybe—" She bit her lip, eyes still searching for a way out as the ledge began to crumble away and pull them faster downhill. "Maybe we can slide down without fear of running them over."

Vinur began to whine, and Gamaliel nodded quickly. "Grab Vinur and do it!" He turned back, shouting to Lone. "Release your dogs!"

The pass descended further, crumbling and falling away, the dogs barely keeping the lead.

Solyana reached for the hatchet in its holster. Priestess Avi had entrusted her with this gift for the boy on the mountain, but she could use it in the meantime. She swung it hard, severing the slackened leads. Grabbing Vinur's harness, she pulled him into the sled.

And the dogs, free of their lines, bolted down the disappearing ledge.

Their sled plummeted, escaping the mountain's appetite, only to be consumed by the rumble of the pass below.

A Letter to the Reader

How can I begin to thank you, Reader, for taking a chance on an indie author's debut novel. I began this story back in 2017, completed the first draft by 2020, and finally published in 2022. I can testify that writing and publishing a book is an arduous process—worth it though. You, taking the time to read it, is the final step. I am so thankful for your commitment to the characters of Mothmar and hope you stick around for the rest of the story. Now, if I could request one thing from you. As I don't have a marketing team behind me—*you* are my best chance at getting the word out about Daughter of the Sun. Would you do me the kindness of reviewing my book on Amazon and/or Goodreads? Reviews, shares on social media, and word of mouth are the three best ways of getting this book in the hands of those who will cherish it.

Your eyes be upward,

Amanda A.

Review
Here!

ACKNOWLEDGMENTS

When I was twenty-one, I made a goal to be published by thirty. My book will be released on my 29th birthday. I couldn't have done this without the help of so many amazing people. So, without further ado...

First, to my parents, to my mom Lisa, who encouraged that six-year-old with a pencil to keep writing. You always told me I would be an author one day—you were right. And to my dad, Tim, you always knew your Middle One would be an entrepreneur.

My sister Emma, who sat on a wooden stool next to the computer every night before dinner to hear the next installment of my unpublished (thank heavens) first novel, Horse Chicks. You've always been willing to let me read to you, however bad it might be.

To my husband who is my biggest fan, and my children who craft better stories than I do. I think there's too much to thank you all here on this page, I will tell you with hugs and kisses.

To the first two people outside of my family to be as excited about the world of Mothmar as I was. Thank you, Kevin and Nick, for listening, asking questions, helping me brainstorm, and staying up hours after game night was over. Your exuberance was life-giving in that season, and I am forever grateful for it.

Thank you to Abby, Christie, Nate, Ryan and Tyler, Beta-Reader Extraordinaires. You dove right into that 150,000-word mammoth of a draft without complaint and came out with questions, critiques and encouragement. That Mothmar themed dinner was, and still is, one of my greatest memories. And to Stacey, who was an unofficial beta-reader and put up with too many first-drafts, you inspired me to keep going.

When I switched from trying to find an agent to self-publishing, I started a Kickstarter to try to raise the funds to do it. We didn't make it and were only $2,000 away from our goal. But, after the end so many of you asked how you could still help, if you could still give. This is every name that helped me monetarily, each donation got me where I am today. Chris S., Sarah D., Rebecca B., Katie K., Colleen N., Laura T., Kate F., Matt G., Lauren M., Karen A., Sarah A., Judy J., Marissa M., Greg L., Kelly S., Alaina T., Courtney E., Emma S., Tim S., Mickey S., Erin S., Anna C., Helen H., Ryan D., Christie M., Oma, Eric B., Claire A., Caleb F., Elizabeth J., Laura E., & Jim from the coffee shop. You paid, almost entirely, for my publishing journey. Thank you for trusting me.

Oh, and speaking of coffee, I wrote and edited most of my book at my favorite coffee shops. Special thanks to Bold Coffee and Aromatic Roasters—without you I wouldn't be able to stay focused for those hours and hours of work. And when the caffeine became too much and made me jittery, I set up shop in my public library. Thank you, Chatham Community Library, but please, would you open earlier than 9am?

Thank you to all the lovely people I have had the pleasure of connecting with on Instagram. I didn't know what I was missing until I found the "bookstagram" community, and although it tends to be a source of distraction, it's also been one of the best sources of accountability.

Jessie of BBM, who knew writing blurbs and bios were so difficult? Thank you for coming along side of me and putting up with constant need to adjust things. Can I come visit you in Australia?

To Eva, word wizard and unexpected friend, who saved me from a poor editing job and helped transform my manuscript into the book it was always supposed to be. You've taught me more than all of my High School English classes combined; although I don't think I'll ever be able to use a semi-colon properly. (*wink, wink*) I can't wait to dive into book two with you.

ARC readers — I never imagined over sixty of you would sign up to read my book before release, I am humbled, I am grateful. Thank you for taking the time and effort.

Finally, and always, to my God and Savior. Who planted this desire in my heart to write over two decades ago—well, before time began really. You, the Master Storyteller, me the apprentice. May the stories you've gifted to me forever mirror the Greatest Story of all time. This be to your glory, forever and always, Amen.

ABOUT THE AUTHOR

Amanda Auler lives in Sanford, North Carolina with her husband and four growing boys. Though Amanda writes for every audience, her roots in Christianity shine through her work as she explores themes of redemption, forgiveness, and grace. When she's not writing you can find her baking cookies, drinking too much coffee, and staying up past her bedtime to watch anime with her husband.

Amanda's Links

www.ingramcontent.com/pod-product-compliance
Lightning Source LLC
Chambersburg PA
CBHW020052310726
48970CB00007B/2524